YORK

ALSO BY LAURA RUBY

The York Saga:
York: The Shadow Cipher
York: The Clockwork Ghost

Bone Gap
Thirteen Doorways, Wolves Behind Them All

YORK

—BOOK THREE—
THE MAP OF STARS

LAURA RUBY

WALDEN POND PRESS
An Imprint of HarperCollinsPublishers

Walden Pond Press is an imprint of HarperCollins Publishers.
Walden Pond Press and the skipping stone logo are trademarks and registered
trademarks of Walden Media, LLC.

York: The Map of Stars

ISBN 978-0-06-230700-2
Typography by Aurora Parlagreco
21 22 23 24 25   PC/BRR   10 9 8 7 6 5 4 3 2 1
❖
First paperback edition, 2021

To the ladies of the LSG, superheroes all

Liberty Statue

Station One

Starr
Hotel

Odd Fellows
Hall

Embassy of
500 Nations

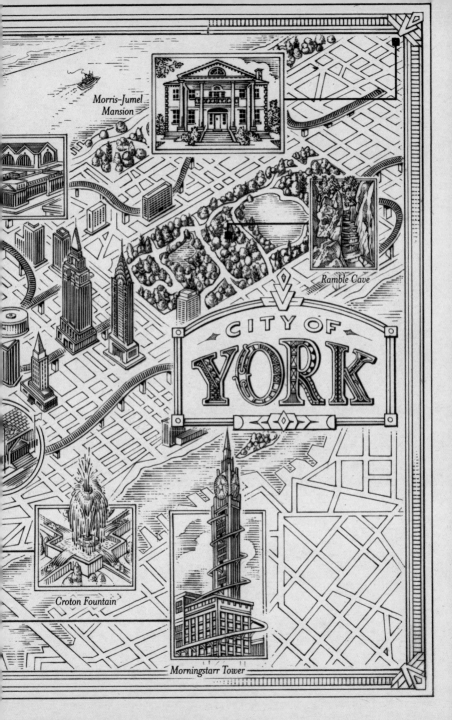

Morris-Jumel Mansion

Ramble Cave

CITY OF YORK

Croton Fountain

Morningstarr Tower

In my end is my beginning.

—MARY, QUEEN OF SCOTS

Peck's Slip, Manhattan
Winter Solstice, 1798

E ven hundreds of years ago, New York City was the stuff of legend. People came from all around the world to escape their lots, to find their peace, to seek their fortunes. *The streets are paved with gold,* some whispered as they huddled in the bellies of ships, shivering from the cold and damp. *There is honest work for honest folk,* said others, their stomachs rumbling, their mouths dry with thirst, praying over meager meals of moldy bread crusts. *There are treasures ripe for the taking,* still others said, tongues thick with too much beer, rubbing their dirty hands together in their eagerness to rob anyone with anything worth stealing.

Every day, ships from all over the world crammed the East River docks, disgorging their thin and weary passengers into the hum and buzz of the city beyond. From the cargo holds, deckhands unloaded bales of cotton and wool; barrels of rice, flour, and salt; chests of tea; puncheons of rum; and pipes of wine. From the counting houses, brandy-gulping merchants came to inspect the goods and ordered the hands to bring the boxes, barrels, and chests through the teeming crowds of people so that the bounty could be properly totaled and celebrated with ever more drink.

On this December night, darkness fell early—it was the solstice, after all. That did not mean the work ended early, however. Myles White toiled along with the rest of the hands on the deck of the *Aurora*, unloading the sugar, molasses, and coffee they had hauled all the way up from the West Indies, goods that would go for a pretty price in this city. But it had not been a pretty trip, not for Myles White. He had seen things on those faraway islands he wished to forget, to scrub from his mind, things that had haunted his dreams and whittled him nearly as thin as some of the hungry and homeless newcomers milling around the docks. Myles would not speak of what he'd seen in the Indies, or what he'd done. First because there was no one for him to tell, and second because he did not trust himself not to reveal his other secrets.

Like many who traveled the ships that clogged the

East River, Myles White had plenty of secrets.

Once the goods had been hauled away by the merchants, Myles got to work on the deck, sweeping and swabbing. No one had to order him to do it. He had learned long ago that the best way to prevent questions on such a ship was to work harder and faster than anyone else, to do the job before you were asked, and to do it so well that no one could find fault. He might be only a swabbie, but he was determined to be the best swabbie the *Aurora* ever had.

Even so, he could feel the eyes of Mr. Jasper, the boatswain, before the man spoke, could smell the drink and sweat wafting downwind.

"You there," said Mr. Jasper. "Swabbie!"

Myles turned. "Yes, sir?"

"When you're done with that deck, double-check that all the goods are out of the holds."

"Yes, sir," Myles said. "Of course, sir."

Mr. Jasper scowled, and took a long pull from a brown bottle. "You're that boy," he said.

Fear prickled Myles's skin like spray from an icy, roiling sea. "Sir?" he said, trying to keep his voice even.

"That boy who . . ." He swayed and had to grip the rigging to keep from falling over. "The one who . . ."

"Yes, sir?" Myles said again.

Mr. Jasper squinted hard at Myles, then made a noise at the back of his throat like one of the dock cats hacking up something disagreeable. "Ach, I don't care who you are. Swab that deck and then check the holds are clear before you take your leave. And be back by dawn or we sail without you. Any boy could take your place, mark my words."

No boy could take his place. Myles almost laughed, but coughed instead. "Yes, sir."

Mr. Jasper stumbled away, tripping and falling onto the dock before crawling off to one of the pubs.

Myles continued to work, the exercise keeping him warm in the chill darkness, and keeping his thoughts from more unpleasant things.

That is, until he heard the *thump*.

He stopped swabbing, tipping his head toward the noise. And there it was again: *thump, thump*. From somewhere below.

As far as Myles knew, Mr. Jasper had been the last of the sailors to leave the ship. So who, or what, could be making that noise?

He leaned his mop against the rigging, lit a lantern, and proceeded to check the whole of the quarter deck, the gun deck, the middle deck, and the lower deck. All were clear. By the time he reached the hold, in the deepest part of the ship, his lantern barely cut through the blackness. The *Aurora* rolled gently with the movement of the sea, but down here, the undulation felt more ominous, the boards creaking all around him. Myles fumbled in his back pocket for his knife, small but deadly sharp, a knife that had kept many a bored and drunken sailor from beating Myles for sport. With the knife in one hand and the lantern in the other, he crept through the freezing dark and soon came to the cabin of the carpenter. The carpenter lived down here because of the easy access to the hold, but also because he was a mean old man who hated everyone except for the rats, some of which he gave jolly names like Daniel Defoe and Jonathan Swift. Maybe the carpenter hadn't left for the evening?

Myles pressed his ear against the cabin door. He heard faint scratching, then mumbling and whispering. As far as he knew, Daniel Defoe and Jonathan Swift could not speak, no matter how much the carpenter wished they would. Myles took a deep breath and then threw open the door, thrusting the knife out in front of him.

Inside the tiny cabin, a dark-haired woman sat down abruptly on the bed, her hand trembling over her mouth. She was white, and not old, but not nearly as young as Myles. In the yellow light of Myles's lantern, her eyes were as black as the ocean at night, wide and dark and terrified, but also defiant, as if she were scared of the knife but also willing to meet it, whatever that meant for her.

"Who are you?" Myles said.

The woman licked her lips but said nothing. It was then that Myles noticed that there was someone in the bed behind her. Someone trying to stifle a cough.

"Who is that? Were you passengers on the last voyage?" Myles repeated. "You need to get off the ship or—"

"Or what?" the woman snapped. "Or you'll stab me?"

Myles had only stabbed one person in his whole life, and he'd been sure that person had deserved it. But he didn't know if this woman did.

He made a decision and tucked the knife away. "No. But if the carpenter or the boatswain or anyone else finds you, they'll throw you into the sea. Or worse."

The woman swallowed hard, gestured to the man in the bed. "My brother is sick. We only wanted to rest a bit."

Indeed, the man did look sick, sweaty and pale. And the resemblance between the man and the woman was unmistakable. Maybe she was telling the truth.

She said, "I thought everyone would be away for at least a few days."

"A few days?" Myles said. "We get a few hours. And

the captain will be back before then to make sure no one damages his ship."

"Oh," the woman said. "Right." She wrung her hands, frowning. In addition to the man in the bed behind her, there was a trunk at her feet. Myles had no idea how she'd been able to sneak the man and the trunk onto the ship without anyone else seeing her. But he had to get her off the ship before they did.

"Is someone meeting you on the docks?" Myles said.

She shook her head.

"Do you have family in the city?"

She shook her head again.

"Where were you going to go?" he said.

Her hands twisted and fluttered against her long skirt. "We thought we'd figure that out once we got to the city."

This was going nowhere. "Where do you hail from?"

"Too many places to count," she said.

Her accent was strange. German? Myles spoke a bit of the language, because it was the quartermaster's original tongue. *"Wo in Deutschland?"*

"Austria, really," said the woman. "Where are you from?"

"Me?" said Myles.

"Yes, you," she said.

"It's not important," he said, too quickly.

She lifted her chin. "Where we're from isn't important, either."

At that, he nodded. A lot of people didn't like to talk about where they were from. "Fine. You still have to go."

"Yes," she said, but she didn't move.

"Has your brother got the fever?"

"Which fever?"

"Yellow fever," said Myles. Was she daft?

"No! It's just a cold or something. And he's tired. We're both tired."

"Hmmm," Myles said. If they weren't passengers, if they were stowaways and he was caught helping them, it was he who would be thrown into the water. But the sick man reminded him of the islands, and of the sick woman there, and of the thing that Myles had done that he could not tell anyone, not ever, for fear they'd look too closely at him.

This woman was looking closely, though. She pressed one of her fluttery hands to her own cheek, as though feeling the lack of whiskers on Myles's.

Though he willed himself not to, he found himself mimicking her gesture, putting his hand to a cheek that he had disguised with soot just that morning. "I'm only fifteen," he said.

She wasn't fooled. "How has no one discovered you?"

"I'm careful," said Myles bitterly. He had been careful, but this lady had seen through him in a few minutes.

At this, she merely nodded. But he exploded as if she'd asked him a question, *the* question: Why?

"You should know why I had to!" Myles said, his voice loud, too loud. He cleared his throat and lowered his voice. "Who would want the lot of a *woman*?"

Her laugh was one of recognition, not amusement. "Who indeed?"

"They wanted to marry me off to some poor fool like I was no more than a fattened pig. They said I didn't have a choice. So I gave myself a chance."

"Right," she murmured. "You ran away?"

Myles nodded. He had no idea why he was telling this stranger his deepest secret, except for the strain of keeping it to himself for so long. "I stole some clothes and came to the docks. There are always jobs if you're willing to do them. I was willing."

She nodded again, thoughtfully. "I'm not sure you could say I—we—were willing, but we were desperate."

"Well, miss," Myles said, "I guess it's the same thing. Why don't we get your brother off the ship? Maybe we could find a suitable inn where you could stay."

"Thank you," she said. "You're very kind."

"I'm not," Myles insisted. "I'm *not* kind. If we're caught, I'll say I found stowaways, which is the God's honest truth. I won't lose my position here. I can't."

"All right," she said. "What's your name?"

He drew himself up stiffly. "Myles." He half expected her to ask for his other name, the name that he had buried when he'd put on these boy's clothes and come to this ship, but she didn't.

"I'm glad to meet you, Myles. Will you help me get my brother out of bed?"

Myles set the lantern down on the floor and took one of the man's arms while the lady took the other. Together, they hauled the man upright.

"Okay, okay," the man mumbled. "I'm up, I'm up. You could have just asked."

"Ignore him," said the woman. "He's peevish when he first wakes up."

"Who's peevish?" said the man.

"*What's* peevish?" said Myles.

"My brother," the woman said. "If you can take him, I'll carry the trunk."

Myles shook his head. "A lady shouldn't have to carry her own trunk."

"There are no ladies here," she said. But Myles took

the trunk, which was a lot heavier than it looked, and the woman draped her brother's arm around her neck. They hobbled out of the carpenter's cabin, and then across the length of the hold. It was slow going, but they managed to get both the man and the trunk off the ship and onto the dock without anyone paying attention.

Once on the dock, the woman covered her nose. "What is that smell?"

"What smell?" Myles asked. The docks and the streets beyond were littered in the usual effluvia—horse manure, soil from the chamber pots, rotting vegetables, and coffee—but it would be so much worse in the summer. He barely noticed it now that winter had gotten a stranglehold.

"You don't smell it?" The woman looked green in the lantern light. "I don't know if I can do this," she said, almost to herself.

Her brother lifted his head from her shoulder. "You can do it. We can. We have to."

"Are you really from Austria?" Myles said. "What I mean is, can you speak German?"

"Yes. A little. And . . ." She hesitated. "A bit of Yiddish, too."

"There's an inn a few blocks that way where you

might find a room. I've heard they don't ask too many questions. And you shouldn't say much in any case. Your accent is too strange."

They hobbled down the street. Once, a drunken man tried to take the trunk from Myles, but the woman hissed like an angry street cat, scaring the man off. Nobody else bothered them. Finally, they reached the inn, the Morning Star. When the woman saw the name on the sign, she laughed.

"What?"

"The Morning Star. I like it."

"Good," said Myles, though he had no idea what she was talking about. As Myles had heard, the mountainous ruddy man at the desk didn't ask questions of the woman except how many rooms she needed, and if she wanted food or a bath prepared.

"Both, please," she said.

The innkeeper named a price for the room and board. The woman fished in her coat and brought out a gleaming gold coin. The innkeeper's eyes went shifty. When the big man dropped the coin into the box below the desk without a word, Myles whispered, "That's too much."

"Is it?" said the woman. "I don't think so."

After the innkeeper left the desk to order a servant

girl to prepare a room, the woman pressed another few coins into Myles's palm, more money than he had ever seen at once, enough money to change his life right there and then.

"Miss," he said, stunned. "I can't . . . I can't . . ."

"Yes, you can," she said.

Myles whispered, "I stabbed a man. In the West Indies. There was a girl—she was sick and couldn't work and he kept beating her. I stabbed him and I helped her escape. I don't know where she is now. Where she went. If she's safe."

Again, he had no idea why he was telling her these things. The words felt as if they were being torn from him, ragged and bloody.

She said, "I was right. You are kind."

"But the man . . ."

"Was beating a girl. And you saved her. Wherever she is, I'm sure she is grateful. I'm grateful." The woman closed his fingers over the money. "Take this. And perhaps if you get sick of working on a ship, you can find me. I might have a job for you, too, someday. If you're willing."

"But I don't know your name."

She touched his too-smooth cheek. "You will."

NEW YORK CITY

Present Day

CHAPTER ONE
Tess

There are people who are human whirlwinds. They move fast, they talk faster, they think even faster still. Their fingers jitter against their legs, their knees dance when they sit, their lungs heave as if they've been running a race. At night, when they try to sleep, their thoughts spin and jive. Sometimes happily, but mostly the thoughts knit themselves into nightmares that could make a person twist and kick, maybe even scream themselves awake.

Tess Biedermann was such a person. A whirlwind, a worrier, a jitterer, a heaver, and a kicker. Her knees danced, her thoughts spun and knitted themselves into nightmares even when she was awake. Because of this, she never really understood the phrase "Time stood still," because Tess herself was rarely still, always leaping to the next thing, literally and figuratively.

But she was still now.

She sat on her bed in her room at Aunt Esther's house, a photograph in her hand. She had been trying to make sense of this photograph for hours, for days, for ages, and yet she couldn't wrap her mind around it.

"It's not us," said Theo, from the bed on the other side of the room. He'd been saying this for hours, for days, for ages, but that didn't make sense to Tess, either. This photograph was proof that there was magic in the world, and Theo didn't believe in magic.

"It's not magic, either," Theo said.

"You just read my mind," said Tess. "That's magic."

"I didn't read your mind—you've been mumbling the word 'magic' since we came back from the cemetery."

"I don't mumble."

"You mumble all the time. You talk to yourself and don't realize it. You have entire arguments while walking down the street."

"How do you explain this?" she said.

"Photoshop," he said.

"Doesn't look Photoshopped."

"Photoshop photos aren't supposed to look Photoshopped," he said.

Tess held out the photo to him anyway, but he didn't get up to take it. He didn't need to. He'd spent enough time staring at it himself.

In the photograph, a dark-haired man and woman sit at the foot of a tree, both them laughing. Someone had written *The Morningstarr Twins, 1807* along the bottom edge of the photo. On the back of the picture were the words *Now you know.*

Tess didn't know anything. She didn't know how these two people, grown people, looked so much like her and Theo. Okay, *exactly* like her and Theo. They had the same pointy noses, the same frizzy hair. Weren't people supposed to look different when they got older?

And if this was actually a picture of her and Theo, if they were the Morningstarrs, that meant that she and Theo had somehow found a way to travel back into the past. That she and Theo had built New York City and all its gleaming machinery. That she and Theo had held fancy parties for dignitaries and pirates and musicians. That she and Theo had laid into the streets and buildings the Cipher that had fascinated and confounded the world for a century and a half and then . . . disappeared.

Tess put her hand to her head, dizzy.

"They have to be relatives," she said. "Our great-great-great-uncle and -aunt or something like that."

"Our great-grandfather on Mom's side came to this country in the middle of the nineteenth century. We've seen the papers at Castle Garden. And Dad's family didn't get here until 1922."

"Explain it, then!" Tess said.

"I can't," said Theo. The words dropped out of his mouth as if he were spitting out bones. He couldn't explain it—not for sure, anyway—and Tess could tell it was eating him alive.

Nine, black and shiny with the dye that had been applied to disguise her markings, nudged Theo's fist until it relaxed. Then the cat stalked over to Tess and rubbed her big face against Tess's knee.

"Jaime doesn't believe we didn't know about this," said Tess.

"Would you?" Theo said.

"But we didn't know!" Tess said. "How could we know? We still don't know!"

"What don't you know?" said their mother, standing in the doorway.

Without missing a beat, Tess said, "Where Nine has been. And who dyed her fur black."

Their mother, a detective whose job it was to find lost things, frowned. "I'm trying to get to the bottom of it, but we keep running into dead ends."

"Dead ends," said Theo, and chuckled like a character out of a horror picture.

Their mother's frown got even deeper. To Tess, she said, "What's with your brother?"

"He's weird," said Tess.

"I can see that. Why?"

"He's always been weird."

"Right," said their mother. She crossed her arms and leaned against the doorjamb. "Is Jaime coming over today?"

Tess shrugged. Another thing she didn't know.

"He hasn't been here in a while. Did you guys have a fight?"

"Not quite," said Theo.

It hadn't been a fight. Tess, Theo, and Jaime had teamed up with the Cipherist Society to figure out another clue in the Morningstarr Cipher. At Green-Wood Cemetery in Brooklyn, they'd dug up a trunk with all sorts of strange items inside, items that had seemed to come from some other city, a city that looked like New York but wasn't—at least not the city they knew, the city they loved. And also hidden in the trunk was this photograph. This ridiculous, impossible photograph.

The mysterious Ava Oneal had taken one look and stormed out of the archives, where they'd been staying the night. Jaime simply handed the photo back to Theo and said nothing more. He said nothing when the Cipherists woke them for breakfast, nothing during the meal, nothing when Tess begged him to talk to her. And he'd said nothing since. Their texts went unanswered, so Tess had decided to call. Jaime's grandmother answered the house phone, and every time Tess called, she said, "Yes, querida niña, I will tell him that you'd like to talk to him. Yes, I will tell him you're sorry, though I have no idea what you're so sorry about, or why he is so angry. No, dear, he still doesn't want to come to the phone. All he does is draw and talk to those hamster-hogs and that little robot he carries around everywhere. When he is like this, I leave him alone, let him work things out for himself. That's what you need to do, too. Keep reaching out, but don't expect anything."

Tess did keep calling, but it was harder and harder. She felt terrible, and sorry, but she didn't know the right way to apologize for something she didn't understand herself.

And she *didn't* understand. She didn't understand anything about anything. She would have loved to ask Ava about this, Ava who had somehow—magically?—been alive for almost two hundred years. But Tess had no way to contact Ava, and it seemed that Ava was furious, too, and would stay furious for as long as she needed to, which could be another two hundred years.

"Tess!" her mother said.

Tess jerked and almost fell off the bed. "What!"

"Are you having a spell?"

"No," Tess said, casually letting the photograph drop facedown on the blanket. "I'm just thinking about Jaime. He's upset about something but he won't talk about it."

"Maybe give him some time?" said her mom.

"That's what his grandmother says."

"I don't think she's wrong. Remember how mad you were at me when Nine went missing? You needed time, too."

Time. They all needed time. But time had already played so many tricks on them. Nine had gone missing only a few weeks before, but it felt like eons, and it also felt like five minutes ago.

"You kids want lunch?" said their mom. "I'm making split pea soup."

"Soup!" said Theo. "That's for winter."

"It's nearly fall," said their mom. "And there was a bite in the air this morning. Made me feel like having some hot soup. Want some? I'll make some grilled cheese, too."

In the kitchen, Tess and Theo ate their lunch. Well,

Theo did. Tess swirled the soup so that a dark little hole appeared in the middle of the bowl. Is that how they did it? Traveled through a black hole? A wormhole? Some kind of science-fiction-y elevator that jumped around in space-time? Or maybe they were living in the multiverse, where many timelines existed alongside one another, and they had somehow moved from one timeline to a different one. But then, how had they not met themselves and shattered all of reality or whatever? Then again, who knows where Tess and Theo were in another world, another timeline. Maybe they lived in Idaho, maybe they lived in Beijing, maybe they lived on a generation ship exploring the whole of the universe.

"How's the soup?" said Tess's mom.

"Delicious," Tess said, though she hadn't even tasted it.

Tess had lived with Theo long enough to understand a bit about relativity. Most people thought time was a constant, but Einstein had said time was as changeable as anything else. Time slows down or speeds up depending on how fast you move relative to something else. A person traveling at light speed in a spaceship would age more slowly than her twin on Earth, because gravity bends time. And just recently, a mathematician concluded that, scientifically, time travel was possible.

Space-time is curved, he said. If it weren't, stars and planets would have to move in straight lines. So theoretically they should be able to turn that curve into a loop, making time travel possible. In the future, people might even be able to travel to their own pasts.

Bananas.

But.

Einstein had said, "Time only exists so everything doesn't happen at once."

Theo had also said that other scientists thought the whole thing was ridiculous. That even if time travel were possible—through wormholes or black holes or machines—humans would probably not be able to survive it. And what about the paradoxes? If Tess and Theo had actually gone back to 1798 and built New York City, did that mean they would have to do it again? Over and over?

She swirled the soup faster and faster. The image in the photograph was burned into her brain. It was hard for Tess to tell the ages of adults. Some adults seemed old when they were young, some adults seemed young when they were old. But she guessed that she and Theo—or whoever was in the picture—were in their thirties. And the singularities? People in their thirties have lives—work and spouses and pets and maybe even children.

Who had they left behind? And why? What would make a person give up her future to travel to the past? Were they trying to fix something? Avert something? A war? A plague? An alien invasion?

"Tess, you're spilling your soup everywhere," her mother said, dropping a wet rag next to Tess's bowl. On the floor under her feet, Nine was lapping up the soup that had dripped from the edge of the table.

"Sorry," she said.

"You're not hungry?"

"I'm hungry," said Tess. She spooned up what remained in the bowl but barely tasted it. After she finished the soup, she ate the grilled cheese, chewing methodically, like a goat. She would need the energy. Because she knew that the only way to figure out who was really in that photograph, the only way to prove that Ava was *the* Ava Oneal, the only way to uncover the real secrets of the Morningstarrs, was to keep going. The Morningstarrs, whoever they were, were trying to tell them something, and whatever it was had potentially ruined her relationship with her best friend. To fix it, they would have to solve the Cipher, once and for all.

Tess got up from the table and brought her bowl and plate to the sink. She rinsed the dishes and stacked them in the dishwasher.

"So you *were* hungry," Tess's mom said.

"I was. I am," said Tess.

"Still? Do you want some cookies? Your aunt Esther has some Fig Newtons in the cabinet."

Tess found the cookies, took a whole sleeve. "Come back upstairs when you're done, Theo."

"Okay," he said. Then, "Why?"

"You know why," Tess said, putting as much meaning as she could into the sentence.

At her tone, Tess's mom raised a brow. "What's with your sister, Theo?"

"She's weird," Theo said.

"You're both weird."

"You raised us," Theo said, tipping his bowl to slurp the last of his soup.

When she got back upstairs, Tess pulled her own trunk out of the closet. THE MAGIX, the top read. Though she had written it herself, the words felt foreign to her now, a language she couldn't decipher.

On top of all her other items were the things from the trunk they'd found. She unpacked the postcards and papers, tiny objects and diagrams: a little copper figurine that read *The Statue of Liberty, 1886*. Currency with all the wrong people on the bills. A piece of solar glass so thick and wavy that you could barely see through it. An antique solar battery. Magazines and articles on extinct animals and "oil rigs" and all manner of things, none of which made any sense. Diagrams of strange machines that looked nothing like the Morningstarr Machines that populated the city. And that photograph! That impossible photograph!

She started gathering everything up, and a business card made of stiff, yellowing paper fell out from within it all and fluttered to the floor. *Trench & Snook*, it read, with a Manhattan address underneath.

Trench & Snook.

The names sounded like something out of comic book, a movie, a fairy tale.

It was as good a place to begin as any.

CHAPTER TWO
Theo

After the events at Green-Wood Cemetery, Theo had become obsessed with doppelgängers.

Doppelgänger: from the German words *doppel*, meaning "double," and *gänger*, meaning "goer." Someone who was a replica, a lookalike entirely unrelated to you, a stranger with your face. There was an internet site devoted to doppelgängers where you could upload a picture of yourself and find your double anywhere in the world. Double-goers, doubling and going all over the place, showing up in old pictures just to freak you out.

In his research, Theo had discovered that such doubles were considered ill omens in some cultures. And he felt ill enough, overwhelmed with the possibility the photograph had presented. He believed that the people in that old photograph really were him and Tess, and he also couldn't believe it at all. A picture of people born in the twenty-first century wearing nineteenth-century dress, taken with a camera invented in the twentieth century? What kind of nonsense was that? It could have been doctored. Or staged. Double-goers posing for a photographer, the date scrawled later, meant to throw them off the scent.

But that didn't make sense, either. All the clues *led* to this picture.

Theo's scalp ached; he'd been tugging his hair so hard that his fingers were laced with dark strands. He forced his hand to grip the banister instead as he walked upstairs to where Tess and Nine were crouched over all the contents of the Junk Trunk. Another doppelgänger, this time of Tess's own trunk, The Magix.

"Is this the kind of stuff you keep?"

Tess's head snapped up. "What?"

"In The Magix? Is it stuff like this? Postcards and statues and articles?"

"Yes," Tess said, but she didn't elaborate. Instead, she got up and went to their desk, opened up the laptop. She banged on the keys. Scrolled. Banged, scrolled. Banged some more.

"What are you looking for now?"

"Trench and Snook."

"Oh, them," said Theo.

Another snap of the head. "You know them?"

"No, I'm waiting for you to tell me what you're talking about," Theo said.

Tess turned her attention back to the screen. "I found a business card in the Junk Trunk, a calling card, I guess, with those names on it."

"Okay," said Theo. "So?"

"So, the names are funny."

"Yeah?"

"In the photograph, we—I mean, *they* are laughing."

"And?"

"Like I said, the names are funny. Don't you think they're funny?"

"I don't think anything is funny anymore," Theo said.

"Well, I think they're funny," she said, her expression deadly serious. "It turns out Trench and Snook was an architecture firm active in the middle of the nineteenth century. They built a lot of stuff in Manhattan, mostly in Soho. I think this is the next clue."

"Of all the stuff we found in the trunk, this is what you think is the next clue? Because the names are funny?"

"When you say it like that, it sounds silly," Tess said.

"That's because it is silly," Theo said. "Profoundly."

"Well," said Tess, "it's no sillier than any of the other clues. And you, yourself, have been arguing all along how strange it's been that we have managed to solve clues that have stumped some of the smartest people in the world for centuries, and that we've done it almost instantly. That our gut feelings have proven to be right a lot of the time, almost like we were *meant* to solve it. I don't know how to explain that photograph, but I think the only way we'll figure it all out is by solving this Cipher. We've been going with our guts all along, so I'm going with my gut now."

"Your gut isn't where your brain is," Theo said.

"My gut is where my *second* brain is. The gut has as many neurons as the brain in your head does. Dad told me that."

"Double brain," said Theo, wondering what the word *brain* was in German.

"So, let's go."

"Wait, go where?"

"To Trench and Snook! This address"—Tess waved the business card in Theo's face—"is near Tompkins Square Park. The clue might be in the building where their offices were."

"You want to go now?"

"No, in 2025. Of course now!" Tess was turning an alarming shade of pink.

"I think you need to take some yoga breaths," Theo told her.

"You sound like Jaime."

Theo didn't respond. He didn't know what to say about Jaime—he didn't know what to say *to* Jaime.

"Let's go get him," Tess said.

"Who?"

"Jaime!"

"He might not want to see us," Theo said.

"True, but we have to keep trying anyway," Tess said. "And it doesn't seem right to look for the next clue without him. As a matter of fact, I think . . ." She trailed off.

"You think?" Theo prodded.

"I don't think we can solve the Cipher without him. I think we're meant to work together."

"That's the second time you've said 'meant.' What do you mean by it?" Theo said.

Tess stared at him. "You're expecting it to make sense?"

"Yes. No. Never mind."

"Come on, Mr. YesNoNevermind," said Tess. "We've got places to go."

They headed downstairs. Their mother was standing in the middle of the living room, watching the TV. Her new partner, Detective Clarkson, was standing there, too. He grinned when he saw Nine padding behind Theo and Tess.

"Hello there, Kit Kat," he said, scratching Nine on the ears. "Glad to see you're safe and sound. Where in the hot chocolate did your stripes go?"

"Dye," said Theo's mom absently. "Are you watching this? They're reporting that Lora Yoshida stole something from her ex-husband."

"Which ex-husband?" said Clarkson.

"She only has the one," said Theo's mom. "Darnell Slant."

"She stole something from the same person who's been bent on destroying everything the Morningstarrs built?" Tess said. "Good for her."

"What did she steal?" Theo asked.

"We don't know that she stole anything, we only know that Slant is saying she did," said his mom.

On the screen, a beautiful Asian woman with long black hair and giant sunglasses ignored a bunch of reporters thrusting microphones in her face as she sauntered down the steps outside a police station and into a waiting limo.

"What does Slant say she stole?" Tess said.

"I'll find out when I get to work," said their mom. "I might have to handle the interview."

Tess jerked her head at the screen. "Are you going to arrest him, finally?"

"I don't have anything to arrest him for," said their mother.

As if on cue, the news cut to Darnell Slant himself, his hair slicked back, his knife slash of a mouth red in his white face. He waved away the reporters' questions about whatever Lora Yoshida had stolen. "I'll let New York's finest handle that. What I'd like to talk about is the future of this city. For too long we've been stuck in the past. Relying on outdated, outmoded technology, outdated and outmoded architecture. That's why I purchased the last remaining Morningstarr buildings. The Morningstarr tech was marvelous for its time, but its time is up. It's *our* time now."

"Arrest him for being a jerk," Tess said.

"If I could do that, I would arrest half the people New York City," said her mother.

Darnell Slant went on: "We can honor those who helped shape the history of the city by creating our own tech, new and better tech. And by building new and better buildings with modern conveniences for modern people. Nobody wants to live in a museum. And who knows what those machines are up to. Doesn't anyone wonder?"

A reporter stuck a microphone under Slant's nose. "So, does that mean you'll be knocking down all the Morningstarr buildings?"

A slight smile tugged at the corner of Slant's slanty mouth. "Let's just say that in a few short weeks, you'll be amazed."

"Amazed," said Tess. "That's one word for it." She made a noise not unlike a growl.

"Are you growling?" said their mom.

"No," said Tess. "That was Theo."

"I do not growl," Theo growled.

"See?" said Tess.

"All right, you two," said their mom. "Don't you have somewhere to go? Something to do?"

"Now that you mention it," said Tess, "we were thinking about seeing a movie."

"Sounds fun," said their mom. As they were getting ready to leave, their mom called at their backs: "Don't eat too much popcorn!"

"We will!" said Tess, and shut the door behind them. She marched from the house so quickly that Theo had to run to keep up. He did not enjoy running unnecessarily.

"Slow down," he said.

"Speed up!" said Tess. "You heard what Slant said. We only have 'a few short weeks' before he does whatever the heck he's planning to do, which will be awful no matter what it is!"

"I don't know how a week can be any shorter. A week is a week," Theo said.

"Faster, Theo!"

But no one was speeding anywhere. It took a few trains and a whole hour to get to Hoboken.

"I'm not sure about this," said Theo, once they had emerged from Hoboken Terminal.

"I am," Tess said.

"He doesn't want to talk to us."

"That's only because he doesn't understand that picture."

"Yes, but *we* don't understand that picture."

"Right. That's my point."

"What?" said Theo.

"He's angry because he thinks we know what the picture means, that we kept something from him. Except we didn't. We're as confused as he is."

"I don't think that argument is convincing," said

Theo. "It wouldn't convince me."

Tess stopped marching and snapped, "Well, Jaime isn't you."

"I . . . ," Theo began. But what could he say? It was true. Jaime wasn't him and he wasn't Jaime. That had never seemed like a bad thing before, but now it felt like a bad thing. Like, if Tess had a choice, she'd pick her friend over her brother.

"Can I walk Nine?" Theo said.

Tess's brows bunched in puzzlement, but she handed over Nine's leash.

That many people on the street seemed to think Nine was some kind of panther and shrank away from them made him feel a little better. A little. But it was a good thing that the black dye that hid Nine's spots still hadn't faded. The viral video that seemed to show Nine biting a woman bloody was still making the rounds on social media, despite the fact that the "injured" woman couldn't be found and the charges had been dropped. For the gazillionth time, Theo wondered what had happened to that blond woman, where she had disappeared to, and whether she posed more danger to Tess and Theo and Jaime than Darnell Slant did. And then he wondered why he was thinking in nonsense words like *gazillionth*. Which was totally not a number.

"Mrrow?" said Nine, glancing back at him.

"I'm okay," he told the cat. He wasn't, but there didn't seem to be anything he could do about it. He couldn't do anything about the blond woman who had followed them around, he couldn't do anything about the trunk they had found in the cemetery, he couldn't do anything to explain the things they had found in it or the picture that implied that he and Tess were anything more than just a couple of almost—eighth graders.

But that was all they were.

As much as he hated to admit it.

They reached Jaime's building. In the bright sunshine, it looked impossibly new, impossibly clean, the river behind it blue enough to hurt. Tess put her hand on the door, then hesitated.

"What?" said Theo.

"He doesn't want to see us," Tess said.

"That's what I . . . ," Theo began. Then he said, "I know."

"The security guard won't let us upstairs unless he checks with Jaime or his grandmother first."

"Maybe you should have thought of that before you dragged us all the way out here," said Theo.

"Maybe you should have thought of it," Tess said, without much heat. Her face got that sad puppy expression that Theo hated. He'd rather shave his head and spend the rest of his life trying to spin gold from his hair than see his sister make that face.

"I have an idea," said Theo. He opened the door and walked up to the security guard, and after a moment, Tess followed. Today's guard was a white woman with a moon face and large biceps that bulged in the sleeves of her uniform.

"Hello," Theo said. "We're here to see Ms. Cricket Moran."

But the guard wasn't listening, or even looking at him. She said, "Is that a mountain lion?"

"No," said Theo.

"A jaguar?"

"No, this is a—"

The guard snapped her fingers. "A puma!"

"No," said Theo. "She's a—"

"A puma-jaguar!"

Theo said, "I don't think they made puma-jaguars."

"They made all kinds of hybrids," the guard said. "Ferrets and otters, ferrets and rabbits, hedgehogs and hamsters, mice and foxes."

"Mice and foxes?" said Theo. "No, that's not—"

"Yes!" the guard said. "Teeny-tiny little fox-mice. But I heard they were way too smart and escaped all the time. Anyway, they were working on some doozies before the larger hybrids were outlawed."

"Doozies," said Theo, remembering the giraffe-owary—giraffe plus cassowary—that had menaced them on North Brother Island. "Yep."

"Can we see Cricket, please?" Tess said. "It's kind of an emergency."

"Everything with Cricket is an emergency," said the guard.

"You know her?"

"Everyone in this building knows her. She's 'investigated' every tenant on every floor, looking for her raccoon," the guard said, putting air-quotes around the word *investigated*. "We've had to talk to her parents three times. But that hasn't stopped her."

"Someone stole her pet," Tess said. "Can you blame her?"

"She has a new pet," said the guard.

"She does *not*," said Tess.

"Have it your way," said the guard. "What are your names?"

Theo said, "Theo and Tess Biedermann."

The guard scooped up the phone and pressed a few digits. She asked for Mrs. Moran and told her who was downstairs. She put the phone back into the cradle and said, "You can go on up. You know where?"

"Yes, thanks," said Tess.

"Bye, puma!" the guard said.

"She's a cat," Theo said.

"Mrrow," said Nine.

The guard held up her hands in surrender.

The twins got on the elevator and watched the guard disappear as the doors closed.

"Do you think Cricket really got another pet?" said Tess.

"Possible."

"But how could she? What if Karl is still . . . out there?"

"She's just a little kid," said Theo. "Besides, Mom hasn't given up searching for him. And animal control is on the case."

Tess went silent the way Tess went silent; that is, she didn't say anything, but the very air around her was filled with questions, all flapping around like bats with wonky sonar.

They got off the elevator at the eleventh floor—Cricket's floor, and Jaime's. They headed first to the Morans' door and knocked.

The door flew open. "HALT! WHO GOES THERE?"

"Hi, Otto," said Theo. "Remember us?"

"Maybe," Cricket's brother said. He was wearing not one, not two, but three of his father's neckties. One was knotted around his head like a headband, another was belted around his waist, and the third was tied around his wrist.

He pointed at the tie on his wrist. "This is where I keep my throwing knife."

"Great," said Theo.

"Otto!" called a voice from inside the apartment. "Why don't you let Theo and Tess inside?"

"But they haven't told me who goes there yet!" said Otto.

"You know who they are," said the voice.

"Yes, but do they GO THERE?"

"Otto!"

"Okay," said Otto. He backed up and let the twins inside.

Theo didn't know much about decorating, but he thought the interior of the apartment was beautiful. Comfortable low couches in a light fabric, throw pillows in bright purples and oranges, the kind of art that was hard to identify but nice to look at anyway—lots of dabs and swirls.

Mrs. Moran was also beautiful, with her brown skin

and her big, relaxed smile. Theo didn't believe that anyone with Cricket and Otto for children could be relaxed, but maybe Mrs. Moran had given up coffee. There was an easel set up in the big window that faced the river, and a new canvas was sitting on it, just waiting for ink or chalk or paint.

Mrs. Moran hugged Tess, then Theo. She petted Nine, told the cat what a pretty kitty she was, how good she looked in black, that she should wear it more often.

"Cricket," said Mrs. Moran, "don't you want to say hi to our guests?"

Cricket's pigtails peeked up over the back of a chair. "Hi," she said, glum.

"Why don't you come over here and give them a hug?"

"I'm not a hugger," Cricket said.

"It's okay," said Theo. "I'm not a hugger, either."

Cricket's eyes peered over the top of the chair. "I'll hug Nine, though."

"Sure," said Tess.

Cricket climbed down from the armchair and walked over to Nine. Normally, Cricket was dressed in something outrageous or strange: scuba gear and a tutu, an army helmet with tap shoes, her father's pajama pants pulled all the way up to her neck. Today she was wearing exactly what she'd been wearing the last time they saw her: a brown shirt and pants with a little black mask on her face, like Karl, her pet raccoon who had been taken from her. Theo didn't know that such an outfit could feel so tragic, but here they were.

Cricket dropped to her knees and gave the cat a hug. Nine purred and licked Cricket's forehead.

Otto said, "We have a new pet!"

"No, you don't," said Tess.

"We do!" Otto insisted. "Right there!" He pointed at a low table that sat below the window. On the table was a bowl with one lone goldfish swimming around inside. "His name is Roger."

"Oh," said Theo. "Well. He seems . . . nice."

Cricket, muttering into Nine's fur, said, "He's not even a piranha."

There was a knock on the door. Otto yelled, "WHO GOES THERE?"

"Otto," said Mrs. Moran. But before she should say anything else, Otto threw open the door.

Jaime stood there, one hand raised as if to knock again. The smile on his face died when he saw who was in the Morans' apartment.

Mrs. Moran didn't seem to notice. "Otto, what did I say about opening the door before you know who it is?" she said.

"It's Jaime!" said Otto.

Mrs. Moran sighed and waved Jaime in. "Don't stand there in the hallway."

Jaime hesitated, then took a step into the apartment. He didn't meet Theo's eyes. "Hi, Mrs. Moran. Mima wanted you to have some tamales. She just made them." He held out a small container.

Mrs. Moran took the container. "Thank you! You know how much I love these!"

"Jaime's grandmother's food is the best!" said Tess, but if she was hoping that would soften Jaime's wooden expression, his stiff body, it didn't. He simply nodded in her general direction.

"Where are your glasses?" Tess asked.

Jaime pushed at his nose as if the glasses were still there. "I got contacts."

"Contacts?" Tess said. "We've been calling."

"I've been busy," Jaime said. His face seemed shuttered somehow, like a store that had closed up for the night. Or the year.

"School will start soon enough, right?" said Mrs. Moran. "I'm sure you all have been doing your summer reading."

"We've been doing a lot of reading," said Theo, which wasn't a lie, at least. He was so uncomfortable he didn't know what to do with himself. Fling himself out the window? Run screaming from the apartment?

Tess, still gazing at Jaime, said, "We're going out today. To . . . to . . ." She couldn't say "look for clues," so she settled on, "to a movie, maybe. Or a museum. Something like that. You want to come?" She swept her braid to her back, then pulled it forward again, saying, "We don't have much time."

Jaime didn't scowl, not quite. But there was none of his usual good humor, his normal chill. And whether he'd understood what Tess meant by "we don't have much time," Theo couldn't tell. "Sorry," Jaime said, sounding the furthest thing from sorry. "I have some *friends* coming over."

"Oh," said Tess, taking a step back as if Jaime had shoved her. "Oh."

From Jaime's front pocket, the head of a tiny robot appeared. "Oh no," it said.

Jaime used his index finger to tuck the robot back into his pocket. "Well. I should be going."

"OH NO," insisted the robot.

Another one of Jaime's pockets buzzed. He plucked out a phone, read the screen. His eyes widened. "I really have to go."

"OH NO OH NO OH NO," said Ono, muffled.

"Your robot is stuck," Otto said.

"My robot is fine," Jaime said, before turning and walking out the door, not even bothering to close it behind him.

After Jaime was gone, Cricket spoke for them all when she said, "Nobody and nothing is fine anymore."

CHAPTER THREE

Jaime

If you were to ask Jaime how he was, he would have said he was fine. Perfectly fine, even. Sure, he wasn't sleeping well, but that was no big deal. And maybe he'd lost his appetite, but sometimes a person just wasn't that hungry. And yes, he was a little distracted these days, but he was almost a teenager. (Teenagers! So distractible!) And yeah, it had been weeks since he'd seen the two friends he'd spent almost all summer with. But hey, people got busy. People *changed*.

Jaime Cruz, soon-to-be teenager, was very, very busy. And possibly a little bit, or a lot, changed.

"But what are you so busy *doing*?" his grandmother Mima had asked just that morning.

"Things," he'd said, pushing eggs around on his plate.

"Things," she repeated. "Like what kind of things?"

"Just . . . things."

"Uh-huh," said Mima. "Are you sure you don't want to call Tess and Theo today? I'm running out of things to say to them when they call."

"Don't answer the phone, then," he said.

Mima raised a brow. "Excuse me?"

"Sorry, Mima," he mumbled. "I'm just . . ."

"Busy," she finished. "Yes, I heard you the first four hundred times you told me." She sighed and took his plate. "I don't know what happened with you kids, but I think it would be better if you talked about it."

At this, Jaime merely shook his head. He didn't want to talk to Tess and Theo. And as much as he loved Mima, he didn't want to talk to her, either. The only person he really wanted to talk to, the only person who could possibly answer his questions, had disappeared, like the world's most frustrating magic act. All he was left with were endless drawings in a sketchbook and one funny little robot.

Until now.

Now Jaime ran out of the Morans' apartment to get back to his. Mima's text message said that his dad was—

"Here!" Jaime said as he burst through the door.

Jaime's father stood up from the couch. "My assignment ended a few weeks early and I thought I'd surprise—"

Jaime didn't let his father finish talking before tackling him with a hug, practically knocking him over. It didn't matter that he'd been mad that his dad had left in the first place three months before, that he was super mad that his dad *kept* leaving every time he got a new work assignment. It didn't matter that he was almost a teenager and should be communicating entirely in grunts and eye rolls.

Jaime said, "I missed you."

His dad laughed, patted his back. "I missed you, too, hijo." Jaime's dad let go of him and held him at arm's length. His warm brown eyes scoured Jaime's face. "You okay?"

"Fine," Jaime said, as he'd been saying every day for weeks, but tears pricked at his eyes. He blinked them away, hoping his dad didn't see.

If his dad saw the tears, he didn't say. What he did say was "Well. I love what you and Mima have done with the place."

Jaime snorted. He and Mima had barely touched anything in the apartment since moving in. The walls

were still toothpaste white, the photographs and paintings that had decorated their old place were still in
boxes. Mima hadn't bothered to unroll rugs or display
any of her favorite plates. You would have thought they
were getting ready to move out of the place rather than
trying to settle in.

Mima said, "We're taking our time decorating, aren't
we, Jaime?"

"You can say that again," said Jaime's father. He
looked as lean and strong as always. But maybe the
creases around his eyes were a little deeper, his skin a
little tanner from his time in Sudan. "And I know how
hard you've been working."

"I have," said Mima. "You like my shirt?" She pulled
on the hem of her T-shirt, which read THE HANDY
WOMAN.

"It's a great shirt. I'm going to want one of those for
myself." Jaime's dad put his hands on his hips and sur-
veyed the room. "This place could use some color. What
do you two think about yellow? Or blue? We could all go
to the paint store together and pick out shades for each
room. And maybe we should invest in a few more chairs.
Get this place looking like someone actually lives here."

Jaime was almost afraid to ask. "How long will you be

home? I mean, how long till you get your next assignment?"

"I already got my next assignment," his dad said.

Jaime tried to swallow his disappointment, but it practically choked him. "Where is it? And when do you leave?"

His dad grinned. "I don't have to leave."

"What?"

"My assignment is here, in Jersey. Just a half-hour drive away. I might have to take a few trips now and then, but I'm going to be home with you. How does that sound?"

A mix of feelings washed over Jaime. Happiness. Relief. Gratitude. And something unnameable, what he'd felt when he was little when he would wake up in the middle of a nightmare and wander to his dad's room and just the sound of his dad breathing made him feel better, made him feel safe.

Ono's head popped up from Jaime's pocket. "Land of Kings!"

His dad's eyes widened. "What's that?"

"This is Ono," said Jaime. "He only says two things. One is 'To the Land of Kings.' The other is—"

"Oh no," said Ono.

"O . . . kay," said Jaime's dad. "Is it broken?"

"OH NO."

"That's just how it talks," Jaime said.

Jaime's dad shook his head in wonder. "Is that the new thing now? Robots?"

Jaime tucked Ono back into his pocket. "Robots are the *old* thing."

"Where did you get it?" Jaime's dad said.

"I found it."

"Just lying around?"

Jaime shrugged helplessly. Technically, he and the twins had stolen Ono. Not that they'd known Ono was Ono at the time. At the time, Ono looked like nothing more than an ancient puzzle sitting on a shelf in a quirky little Brooklyn museum. Just one more piece of the riddle that was the Old York Cipher, just another clue, something they could "borrow" and return later. But then Ono became Ono, and Jaime didn't know how to give him back. He didn't *want* to give him back, and it seemed unfair that he should have to, and what kind of person did that make him?

Jaime ached to spill the whole story to his dad, from the very beginning, from the very first clue. He wanted to tell someone he could trust. But he couldn't say a word. He couldn't tell his dad what he had become. That he was a liar and a thief, friends with liars and thieves. That he'd thought he and the twins were all keeping the same secrets for the same reasons, but that the twins had even more to hide. That they hadn't trusted him with the truth—because surely they knew the truth—and now he couldn't trust them, either. That every good thing he'd tried to do had gotten all mixed up and he'd lost any sense of what he was doing and why he was doing it, of who, exactly, he was saving. That he'd sat in his room and drawn sketches of their old home at 354 W. 73rd Street imploding, caving in on itself, and had felt himself caving in as he drew. That he was just one big pile of rubble.

"Are you sure you're okay?" his dad asked. "You look . . ."

"What? I'm fine." Fine. FINE. FIIIIIINE.

"You seem distracted."

"I'm almost a teenager, Pop."

"What's your point?"

"Teenagers are distractible."

"Good to know," said his dad, his expression a combination of confusion and amusement. Comusement. Then, to Jaime's grandmother, "He *is* distractible."

Mima said, "You think?"

"Maybe he's hungry?" said Jaime's dad, as if Jaime

weren't standing right there. "I'm hungry. I could use a snack."

"I might be able to whip something up for you," said Mima.

Mima's idea of a snack: the tamales she'd just made that morning, plus beans and rice, Cuban sandwiches, and extra pickles. Normally, Jaime would have devoured everything in sight, but he only managed half a sandwich and a couple of forkfuls of rice.

"So where are the twins you've been spending so much time with?" said Jaime's dad, pointing with a pickle.

Jaime put down his fork. "They're . . . around."

"Around?"

Jaime shrugged. Again. (Teenagers! Always shrugging!)

"Did you guys have a fight?" his dad asked.

"Not exactly," Jaime said.

"But sort of?" said Jaime's dad.

"Well," Jaime said, "they lied to me."

"About what?"

Another shrug. This was what he had become. A big shrugging shrugger.

"Okay, did you ask them why they lied to you?"

"Not exactly," Jaime said.

"Ah," said Jaime's dad. "Okay, then."

"What do you mean?"

"I don't mean anything."

"You always mean something," said Jaime.

"Do I?"

"Yes!" said Jaime. "Yes, you do!"

Jaime's dad tossed the end of the pickle into his mouth, chewed, swallowed. "I mean, the heck with them, am I right? You don't need liars in your life."

"I don't," said Jaime.

"Right," said Jaime's dad.

"I really don't!"

"That's what I said."

Jaime opened his mouth to argue some more, but it was hard to argue with someone who was agreeing with you. But then why did he still feel like fighting?

Jaime ate some more of his sandwich in the hopes that he really was just hungry and the sandwich would fix him. And he went to the paint store with Mima and his dad and tried to pay attention when they picked out colors for the apartment—soothing blues and greens, mellow yellows and sunset oranges. He helped push all the living room furniture into the center of the room and cover everything with sheets. And, after a while, he forgot that he was a liar and a thief, he forgot about the Cipher, he forgot about the churning city across the river, chugging along without him. Jaime had the steadiest hand, his dad said, and Mima agreed. High on a stepladder, armed with a small bucket of paint and a thin, slanted brush, Jaime edged the wall where it met the ceiling, then all around the window frames. Mima and his dad chattered away in Spanish, and their words fell on him like a gentle rain, calming and cleansing. *Pues, le dije yo al hombre, ¿Qué haces? Eso no forma parte del plano. Y me dijo: ¿Cuál plano? Me pidieron que me quedara tres meses más, pero les dije que no. ¡Tengo que regresar a mi familia! Y con eso, me pidieron que fuera a Singapur. A ella le hubiese gustado este apartamento, ¿no te parece? Le hubiese gustado cualquier lugar donde estaban Jaime y tu, mi'jo.*

Pop is home, Pop is *staying*, Jaime told himself. And that fact was bigger and more important than some stupid puzzle, bigger and more important than the Morningstarr twins and the Biedermann twins and all the other twins with their secret languages and their secret secrets. Bigger than a mysterious woman named Ava who might or might not be a superhero, might or might not be a ghost.

Two whole days passed like this. Jaime and his dad and grandmother painting the apartment to life—yellow in the kitchen, orange in the dining room, green in the bathroom. As soon as the paint was dry to the touch,

Jaime helped his dad unpack the boxes of photos and hang them. Here was Jaime's dad as a boy, perched on a white horse; here was Jaime's mom as a girl, standing next to her prize-winning science fair exhibit; here were both of them on their wedding day, beaming bright enough to shame the sun.

"She was brilliant, your mother," said Jaime's dad as he checked to make sure the wedding photo was level.

"I know," said Jaime.

"I was so proud when she became my wife, prouder when she became Dr. Renée Cruz. One of the first black women to get a doctorate in physics. She would have changed the world with her work. Was actually changing the world when she . . ." He didn't finish the sentence, but Jaime did, in his head. *She was actually changing the world when there was an accident in her lab. She was actually changing the world when there was an explosion. She was actually changing the world when she died. She was actually changing the world when she died, and left the world a sadder place than it had been before, and still was now, because there was no one like her anywhere, in any world, and would never be again.*

Jaime's father stepped back from the wall of photos. "She loved you, hijo. Never forget that."

Jaime tried to speak but found himself unable to do anything but nod. He busied himself with another box, and found an origami woman made out of bronze paper. The figure had been given to him by a scientist-turned-artist his father had taken him to see when Jaime was six. The artist had told him that origami was a lot like math, a lot like science, and even more like magic. Ever since, when his fingers got tired of holding a pen or pencil, Jaime sometimes liked to fold paper into crickets, into hearts, into stars. But nothing he made was as beautiful as this bronze woman made of bronze paper, a woman who reminded him of his mother. Gently, gently, he tucked the figure onto a shelf, right next to a photo of his mother holding a toothless, grinning baby.

They finished hanging photos in the kitchen and dining room. Despite the lingering sadness over his mother, Jaime was happier than he'd been in a while, making this sterile apartment into a home. They had just started the second coat of robin's-egg blue in the living room, Jaime edging and his pop and Mima keeping up a steady stream of chatter, when Jaime heard a name that cut through his pleasant daydreams.

"Slant knows the Old York Cipher is just a story," his pop was saying. "He's playing a game with people."

Mima said, "He's not playing. He already bought up all the Morningstarr buildings. He's gotten so many tax breaks that the city is going to owe *him* money. He's running for mayor, and there's chatter about him running for governor after that."

"He's having too much fun doing interviews and movie cameos," said Jaime's dad. "He doesn't want to be mayor."

"No," said Mima. "He wants to be *king*. And if the Old York Cipher is real, and the treasure is real, and he finds it, maybe he'll get his way."

"Oh no," whispered Ono from Jaime's pocket.

Jaime's dad filled his sprayer with more blue paint. "People like him always get their way, Cipher or no Cipher. I'm not sure it will change anything for us."

"If it changes New York City, it will change things for us. It will change things for everyone." Mima wiped her forehead, leaving a blue streak in her hair that looked so good, she should probably keep it. "He's always talking about the future, but he wants us all to forget about the past. And he wants us to ignore what he's doing right under our noses. You can't trust a man like that."

"I don't," said Jaime's dad. "But then, I don't trust anyone."

"Except me," said Mima.

"Except you," Jaime's dad said. "And mi hijo. Even though he's too busy daydreaming to talk to his pop. Are you with us, Jaime?"

"Sure, Pop," he said. And he *was* with his dad, and with Mima. Always. But he was also with the city he'd grown up in, the city that had helped to raise him, the city in his imagination, the city he loved. And he would still do anything to save it.

Even if it meant working with liars and thieves.

Jaime put down his paintbrush and pulled out his phone.

CHAPTER FOUR
Merry

Miles away from Hoboken, in an elegant if oversized building overlooking Central Park, Merriweather "Merry" Roberts made the rounds one last time before her party was to begin. The marble steps leading to the front door? Swept and washed. The double door with its lion's head brass knocker? Cleaned and polished. The butler, Simmons, tall and lean in his black suit, standing at attention in the foyer? Combed and freshly shaven. All seven bathrooms had been scrubbed and scrubbed again, and brand-new Egyptian cotton towels thick as blankets were draped over the brass towel rods. In the dining room, the fifteen-foot-long table, dating back to the eighteenth century, was set with the finest bone-white china, handed down to Merry from her great-grandmother Merriweather. The elaborate chandelier that hung over the table, winking with soft light, was Tiffany, and worth more than most people made in a year. The silverware wasn't silver at all, it was platinum, and it had been given to Merry as a wedding gift by her father (and kept after Merry's necessary but embarrassing divorce, which had, unfortunately, required a small bit of blackmail and one attempted murder). And the napkins folded into gorgeous gold crescents on the plates were the softest blend of linen and silk, with a nubby texture not unlike skin.

Merry, white cheeks rouged, auburn hair coiled into an updo, wearing a green bias-cut silk gown, ambled around the table, admiring the shine of the platinum serving spoons, the tight folds of the napkins. Then she stopped abruptly in front of one place setting. She yanked the napkin off the plate and dropped it on the shoes of the nearest maid, who shivered before Merry even began speaking.

"I asked for crescents, not donuts," Merry said, her voice like sleet falling on a gray November day. "I want every napkin refolded. And they better be perfect—do I make myself clear?"

"Y-yes, miss," said the maid. One never referred to Merry as "ma'am." "Ma'am," claimed Merry, was a title for old women. Merry was far too young and vital a person to be called "ma'am" by anyone. But one never referred to Merry as "Ms.," either, because "Ms." was a name for feminists, and Miss Merry didn't approve of feminists. Everyone knew that women were more capable than men. It was obvious! But it was also gauche to crow about it. And Miss Merriweather Roberts was anything but gauche. Imagine marching in parades, wearing T-shirts with slogans on them? Girl power! You go, girl! Ridiculous.

While Merry's cowering maid hurried to gather up all the unacceptable crescents, an army of cooks and servers lined up in the kitchen. Merry sampled each dish, suggesting salt for this one, pepper for that one, and the immediate firing of one prep cook who had the gall to tell her that the whipped cream that was to be served with the tarts was *supposed* to be more savory than sweet. Desserts, she informed him, were, by definition, *not savory*. She then informed him that he would not be receiving his last check and had the man escorted out by her security guards, Bruno and Bruno. (The Brunos enjoyed nothing more than escorting people out of Merry's penthouse. She'd heard that when the Brunos got someone in the elevator, they hung the person upside down and shook all the valuables and bravado out of them before kicking them out of the building. Merry found this behavior a bit crass, but also a bit amusing. And Merry was terribly fond of . . . merriment. Joy was so hard to come by in this world.)

Merry left the kitchen and went to check the great room. As always, the floor-to-ceiling windows were spotless, giving the impression that the enormous room was open to the city around it. Cut-glass decanters sparkled with wine and spirits on the long walnut bar. Two rubber-gloved bartenders arranged slices of lemon and lime and orange in floral patterns. And groups of armchairs were loosely arranged around wooden gaming tables inlaid with ivory that Merry had acquired from an English estate.

Merry was ready for the game.

It was her favorite, this game, a game of her own invention. And she dearly loved to play.

"Merry!" a low voice called.

Merry sighed. As much as she adored these parties, her father hated them. He much preferred spending his time in his office with his pets. That was what he called them: pets.

Father, she thought, was getting a bit eccentric in his old age.

But he was still brilliant. And if she was being honest

with herself, he had helped her develop the game that her friends would be playing later that evening. He was a self-made man, her father. With only a modest investment of a million dollars from his own parents, Hunter Roberts had started a computer company from his prep school dorm room. Just when it became the biggest social media company in the world, and the very richest, he sold it to focus on philanthropy. He established collections in museums, wings of hospitals, laboratories and research centers around the globe. The Roberts name was on more buildings than Darnell Slant's, of which Merry reminded Slant every chance she got.

If more people in this world were like her father, Merry thought, they wouldn't whine so much. They'd pull themselves up by their own bootstraps, work hard, and save up for the things they wanted. How difficult was living within your means? If you could afford a yacht, you bought a yacht. If you could afford rice and beans, you ate rice and beans. It was dollars and cents! Or rather, *sense*.

People were so illogical, so self-defeating.

But then, that's what made the game so much fun.

Merry walked from the living room up the grand staircase to her father's suite. She knocked on the door.

"Come in!"

She put her hand on the handle, but before she could turn it, the door opened. A Morningstarr Lancelot stood staring at her. If a full suit of armor with no discernible eyes could be said to be staring.

"Father, please," Merry said. "Call off your soldier, will you?"

"His name is Bertrand."

"I am not calling an empty suit of armor 'Bertrand,'" said Merry.

"That's his name. And you're going to hurt his feelings."

"Father, Bertrand has no feelings."

"Thank you for using his name."

Merry rolled her eyes, but tried to hide the gesture by smoothing her already smooth brows. Her father's study was painted a rich teal. Bookcases lined three walls, and on the fourth was a marble fireplace. Hanging overhead was a Morningstarr dragonfly, wings gently flapping, creating a soft breeze. An ancient Roller stood on its hind legs in the corner, looming like a small bear. Mechanical spiders giggled in the bank of plants underneath the windows. Her father sat in a chair by the fireplace, a blanket over his lap. On top of the blanket sat a robot in the shape of a small dog, if a dog were shaped more like a pillow than an animal. Wonderful, thought Merry, a new metal monstrosity to clomp and clank around her house. Its "breathing" was loud enough to shame entire hives of bees.

Her father lifted the doggy bot. "Say hello to Winnifred."

"I do not want to say hello to Winnifred," said Merry, unable to keep the irritation out of her voice. It was fine that her father wanted to collect Morningstarr Machines. They were still worth some money on the collector's market, and they certainly made for compelling conversation pieces at Merry's lavish parties and events. But her father tended to get attached to the things, as if the things were alive. And then he started tinkering with robotics himself. He took apart some of the Morningstarr Machines, recombined them, added his own particular flair. (If you could call it flair.) He'd designed half the robots lurching and lurking around his rooms like . . . well. She didn't know what. Ghosts. Monsters. Toasters with legs.

"Woof," cried Winnifred the doggy bot, segmented tail wagging. "Wo-OOOF."

Merry winced.

"Say hello!" commanded Merry's father.

"Hello, Winnifred," she said.

"Woooooof," said Winnifred, settling back down on

Merry's father's lap. How had her father programmed the thing? Never mind, Merry really didn't want to know.

"Are you ready for the party, Father?"

"Party?"

"Yes, Father, the party. You've known about it for months."

"I don't like parties," he said. "I'd rather stay here with my pets."

Pets.

"Father, we're playing the game, remember? Don't you want to play the game?"

"I'm having a guest over for tea."

"What guest?"

"No one you know."

"Father, please."

"Eh," said her father. Merry wondered at what age one started believing noises like "Eh" or "Meh" or "Whaaaa?" were good substitutes for actual speech. She resisted the urge to bark, "Use your words!"

"Father, my guests will expect you to be there. Promise me that you will at least make an appearance."

Father grumbled. The doggy buzzed.

"Father!"

"Yes, yes," he said, waving her off. "I'll make an

appearance. Just for you, my dear Merry."

"Thank you, Father." She stood there, watching him pet his new . . . pet, and then turned, stalked from the room, closed the door behind her.

Briefly, Merry rested her forehead against the door. Good thing she had power of attorney. Otherwise, she might really be concerned.

Downstairs, the first knock sounded. The butler's mellow voice said, "Welcome. Allow me to show you to the great room."

Merry hurried to arrange herself in the center of said great room, a cocktail in one slim hand. "Hello, darling," she said as her first guest, a hedge fund manager, entered. Merry air-kissed Mr. Hedge Fund on the cheek so she didn't mess up her lipstick and then pointed him toward the bar. After Mr. Hedge Fund came Mr. Internet Billionaire—not nearly as rich and successful as Merry's father, but successful enough. Then the owner of a pharmaceutical company, the owner of a baseball team, the owner of a corporation that made rocket ships so that eventually people would be able to vacation on the moon, the owner of a media conglomerate, several more hedge fund managers—they tended to move in herds—some venture capitalists, a few skulking political operatives with questionable hygiene, a smattering of supermodels, a couple of TV commentators, a boating magnate, and one actual duke.

The guests mingled, sampling appetizers offered by tuxedo-wearing servers. They clinked glasses, tossed back amber liquid. Their laughter grew louder. After a long and sumptuous dinner under the Tiffany chandelier, Merry led her guests back to the great room. By then, the sky was streaked pink and purple, and the lights from the buildings shone in the distance. The guests took their places around each gaming table.

Merry stood in the middle of the room, in the middle of the city. She said, "Now it's time for this evening's entertainment. A game I invented with my dear father, Hunter Roberts."

At the mention of his name, her father appeared in the wide doorway, blinking as if he hadn't seen this many people in ages. Which he hadn't. Hunter Roberts didn't say a word. He nodded at the assembled guests and then fidgeted like a small, distracted boy. Then he turned and walked back to his office.

The hedge fund managers and venture capitalists and billionaires murmured and eyed one another over the tops of their cocktails. But they wouldn't dare say anything untoward about Merry or her father. Hunter Roberts still had more money and more power than all these people put together.

Which meant that Merry did, too.

"As most of you already know," she said, "the game is called Megalopolis. Last month's theme was 'War.' This month's theme is 'Power.'"

Merry took a stack of leather dossiers from a nearby servant and walked around the room, from hedge fund manager to hedge fund manager, tycoon to tycoon, passing them out. "Each of you will receive a new identity to play, and a certain amount of cash and some other incentives to advance the personal and political interests of your character. Everything is listed in the dossier. Game boards and dice are on the tables. We'll play three twenty-minute rounds with breaks in between."

One of the hedge fund managers opened his dossier and said, "Waitress? No way." He tried hand back the dossier.

Merry snapped, "You know the rules. No trading! And no complaining! Just like in the real world, you must accept the hand you're dealt. Next!"

The magnates and tycoons and CEOs alternately grumbled and celebrated as they were assigned characters like "truck driver," "doctor," "army captain," "city councilmember," "hairdresser," "entrepreneur," "college student," and "homeless teenager."

"I don't see why I have to play a homeless teenager," a tycoon whined.

"Luck of the draw," Merry said cheerfully.

"My goals are finding food! And a house! But I don't have any money!" said the tycoon. "How is this fair?"

"I'm the CEO of a corporation," said the CEO of a corporation. "My goals are increasing value for my shareholders and finding more tax loopholes. This is too easy. I'm going to clean up, Merry."

"We'll see," said Merry.

"You need to give me a job," said the tycoon to the CEO.

"You're homeless. You don't even own a suit," the CEO said. "Why would I give you a job?"

"I'm playing . . . Hunter Roberts," said one of political operatives, scratching at his greasy scalp. "I have five hundred million dollars to push my policy interests, which are mass deportation, freedom of discrimination in hiring and health care, and the institution of a national religion."

"Oh," said a supermodel. "That sounds super fun! But I think my identity is better. I'm Theo Morningstarr!"

"How is that better?" said a nearby magnate. "He had nothing when he came here."

"I pulled myself up by my bootstraps!" said the super-model, indignant.

Every New Year's Eve, Merry threw a costume party. Last year's theme had been "Heroes and Villains." Quite a few people dressed up as Tess and Theo Morningstarr but had different opinions about whether they were heroes or villains. In Merry's view, they were neither. They were simply fools who gave their mysterious, powerful tech away for free.

Behind Merry, the butler announced, "Mr. Darnell Slant."

Everyone turned as a tall, well-dressed man appeared, surveying his surroundings like a king surveying his subjects. Slant then stalked into the room the way he stalked into every room: as if he owned it. He wore a summer-weight suit, a crisp white shirt, no tie. His dark hair was slicked back from his forehead and Merry was fairly sure his cheeks were rouged, as if for a photo shoot.

"Merry, darling," Slant said. "Lovely to see you. Sorry I'm late." He bussed her cheek and then found an empty seat. "Please don't let me interrupt."

She smiled without showing her teeth and handed him a dossier. He opened it. He turned the dossier around and showed her the picture inside.

"It seems I'm playing myself."

Merry said, "The dossier doesn't say 'Darnell Slant,' it says 'Mayor of New York City.'"

"One and the same," said Slant.

"You're not the mayor."

"Yet."

"Hmmm," said Merry. She'd heard rumors that he was planning a wider political run after winning his bid for mayor, but she'd thought it was just boasting. Seeing the gleam in his eye now, perhaps she'd been wrong. He was arrogant, impossible, imperious, and occasionally ridiculous, which made him the perfect candidate for national office. Merry wouldn't tell anyone, but the character she was playing in tonight's game was herself. And she had five hundred million real dollars to advance *her* interests. She could use a good front man.

She said, "I hope you're playing to win."

"If there's one thing I know how to do," said Darnell Slant, "it's win."

This time, Merry did flash her teeth. Then she sat down at the table nearest the bar and said, "Let the game begin."

Darnell Slant laughed. "It already has."

CHAPTER FIVE

Tess

After Jaime ran out of the Morans' apartment, Tess nearly burst into tears. (The only reason she didn't was because Nine started frantically licking her knees, and it tickled.) Tess and Theo said good-bye to the Morans and then went to track down the next clue without Jaime. The yellowing business card read:

TRENCH & SNOOK

ARCHITECTS

293 E. 10TH STREET

NEW YORK, NEW YORK

GRAND DESIGN FOR THE UNEXPECTED

The address led them to a deli on the corner of 10th Street and Avenue A, but no one in the deli knew anything about the building's previous tenants.

"Trench? Snook?" said the man behind the deli counter. "Aren't those mobsters?"

"Nah," said the woman at the cash register. "Trench and Snook are characters in that movie. You know that movie."

"Which movie?" said the man.

"You know!" said the woman.

"If I knew which movie, would I ask you which movie?" said the man.

"You always ask me which movie," the woman said.

The man slammed a block of cheese onto his cutting board. "Because I don't know which movie!"

The woman made a *tsk*ing sound and then asked Tess and Theo if they wanted sandwiches. The pastrami was very nice, very lean.

So, since the day seemed to be a bust, they ordered pastrami sandwiches. The woman gave them extra pickles and coleslaw. Everything was delicious, but Tess couldn't eat much. It felt wrong to be investigating the Cipher when Jaime wasn't there with them, wrong to be sitting there eating sandwiches without Jaime making jokes about Trench and Snook, without Jaime drawing mobsters and movie stars in his sketchbook.

Theo finished his sandwich and Tess wrapped hers
for later, and after wandering despondently around
Tompkins Square Park, they went back to Queens, tired
and defeated. They'd been tired and defeated before.
They'd been forced to go home at the end of the day
without getting any closer to solving a clue. But this was
different. Because they didn't wake up the next morning ready to try again, despite what Darnell Slant had
said in his interview, that they only had a few short
weeks before they would be amazed. Or appalled. They
sat in their room, sifting listlessly through the contents
of the trunk they'd discovered in Green-Wood Cemetery, arguing even more listlessly about which piece of
paper, which figurine or article, was the next clue, if the
Trench & Snook card wasn't.

For the first time in months, Tess wondered what she
would do with herself if she *wasn't* searching for the solution to the Cipher. It had felt to her like the Cipher had
been encouraging them since the moment they set out
to solve it, responding to their every move as if it wanted
them to get to the end, but maybe it was merely toying
with them, sending them on wild-goose chases, only to
disappoint and thwart them, only to break their hearts
at every turn. Maybe the photograph—that impossible

photograph that implied that Tess and Theo Biedermann were Theresa and Theodore Morningstarr—was
just a joke the Cipher was playing on them. Maybe there
had been other people just like Tess and Theo, whole
crowds of people who had followed strange clues that
seemed to lead somewhere but never did, and those
people gave up or went mad or moved to Europe or Aus-
tralia or Idaho, somewhere without mysterious twins or
even more mysterious Ciphers designed to drive a person to distraction.

Their mom appeared in the doorway wearing her
work suit, badge clipped to her hip, hands behind her
back. "What are you two doing up here?"

Tess and Theo, sitting in piles of paper and junk,
said, "Cleaning."

"Cleaning? Are you two feeling all right?"

Tess and Theo: "No."

"Right," said Mrs. Biedermann. "Maybe I have something that might cheer you up?"

"A kitten?" said Tess.

"A robot?" said Theo.

Tess and Theo: "A robot kitten?"

"Nine is worth nine cats," said Mrs. Biedermann.
"And this whole city is crawling with robots. No, your
dad and I were talking, and we decided that it was about

time that you had these." From behind her back she pulled two clear glass phones, the latest models, each with thin solar panels framing the screen. One had a picture of Nine on the back, and the other had a picture of the Tower of London built out of Legos. She handed the Nine phone to Tess and the Lego one to Theo.

Tess brushed a finger over the photo of Nine. It was an older photo that showed all of Nine's spots and stripes. "Thanks, Mom." She tried to put as much enthusiasm as she could into the words, but as she was saying them, it hit her: she really didn't have anyone to call but Theo.

Theo said, "Thank you. These will be very useful. And convenient."

"Useful and convenient," said their mother. "I was hoping for a little bit more excitement, but I suppose I'll have to take what I can get."

"It's great, Mom, really," Tess said.

"There are some ground rules. We have limited data, so no streaming music videos or whatever you kids do."

"No music videos. Darn," said Theo.

"Funny. And I need you to call or text me when you're wandering around on one of your excursions, okay? I want to know where you are."

"Sure," said Tess. It seemed that the only places she was going were a random deli with very nice, very lean pastrami, and Aunt Esther's house in Queens, far away from the best friend she'd ever had.

Mrs. Biedermann left for work, leaving Tess and Theo with their new phones and the mess from the Junk Trunk all over the floor. Tess tried to focus, tried to at least *pretend* she was focusing. But, as usual, the what-ifs crowded her mind, piling up on one another, all of them shouting to be heard. What if they weren't solving the Cipher at all? What if it was all just a dream that she and Theo had cooked up because they had been so scared of losing 354 W. 73rd Street, and so devastated when they'd lost it anyway? What if Darnell Slant was going to keep buying up historical buildings and turning them into giant cracker boxes because there was nobody powerful enough to stop him? What if the lesson of history was that rich and powerful people got to do whatever they wanted to do and everyone else had to learn to live with that? What if the most important thing the Cipher wanted to teach them was that trying to save the world was a losing proposition and would only drive you apart from the people you cared about most?

Tess got so upset at the train of her own thoughts that she crawled into bed with Nine and stayed there for twenty-four hours. Her mother and father were convinced she had some sort of stomach bug.

"It's not a stomach bug. It's emotional malaise. It's ennui," Tess said from beneath the covers.

"Ennui?" said her mother.

"More like an existential crisis," Theo said helpfully.

"That sounds serious," said their father. "I brought you a mug of chicken soup. Chicken soup is excellent for treating existential crises."

"Oh, and Jaime called," said her mother. "I told him you were sick, but—"

Before her mom could finish, Tess threw off the sheets and ran downstairs, her mother's voice following her. "Tess! You have your own—"

In the kitchen, Tess scooped up the receiver of Aunt Esther's ancient wall phone and punched in Jaime's number.

"Hi," he said.

"Hi."

Silence.

Tess said, "My mom bought me a phone. But I forgot. So I ran all the way downstairs to use this one. The house one. My aunt's. It's on the wall. Isn't that weird?" She was babbling, but she couldn't help it.

Silence.

"Jaime?"

Jaime said, "I'm still mad at you. You should have told me. You should have trusted me."

"We do trust you!" said Tess. "We didn't have anything to tell."

Jaime went on as if Tess hadn't spoken. "But I think we should solve the Cipher. Once and for all."

"Okay," said Tess.

Silence from Jaime. And then: "Is that the only thing you can say?"

"No."

"Good."

Tess waited for him to say something more, but he didn't. And she didn't. Each of them listened to the other breathing.

Theo came into the kitchen, Nine at his heels, and the two of them stared at her, their eyes asking, *What? What's happening? What's he saying?* Tess held up a finger. To Jaime, she said, "Do you want to come over? Maybe look through the stuff we have from the trunk?" She gripped the phone, waiting for his answer.

"Okay," said Jaime.

Tess let out a breath, nodded at Theo. Theo said, "Woot!"

"Did Theo just say 'woot'?" said Jaime.

"No," said Tess.

"Somebody said 'woot.'"

"Maybe it was the mechanical spiders," said Tess. "You know spiders. They like to celebrate."

"Okay," said Jaime.

"Maybe you can come over at lunchtime?"

"Okay."

"Is that the only thing you can say?" Tess joked.

"No," said Jaime.

She thought she detected a smile in his voice, but she couldn't be sure. "Uh, see you soon."

"Right," he said.

"Right."

She hung up the phone. A sense of relief washed over her like a wave. No, things weren't perfect, and yes, Jaime was still mad.

But he was coming over to see her, to see *them*, and that was not nothing.

"Woot," she said.

A few hours later, Jaime arrived. When Tess opened the door and saw him standing there, she blurted, "You look taller."

"I saw you at the Morans' two days ago. I'm not taller," said Jaime.

"Yes, but you look it."

From behind Tess, Theo said, "He looks the same to me."

Jaime smiled half a smile. "You haven't changed, either, Theo."

"I actually *am* taller," Theo said.

"Your hair is taller," said Jaime.

"Ha-ha," said Theo. "Like I haven't heard that before."

"So, are you going to let me in?"

"Yes!" said Tess, and stepped aside to let him enter. Nine charged at Jaime, mrrowing wildly, nudging his knees until he crouched to hug her and scratch her ears. Her purr was so loud, the spiders tending to Aunt Esther's houseplants started to giggle.

Ono popped up from Jaime's pocket.

"Hi, Ono," said Tess.

"To the Land of Kings," Ono said.

"Nice to see you, too."

Jaime seemed to remember himself, remember that he was still angry. His half smile fell. He stood, suddenly all business. "We should go look through that stuff you have."

"Wait just one minute, young man!" Aunt Esther came into the front room with a plate of Fig Newtons.

"First, you must sit and have a cookie."

"Hello, Ms. Esther," Jaime said, his voice warm again.

"Hello, dear Jaime. And it's *Aunt* Esther. Now sit, and take a cookie. I'm going to bring you some iced tea."

They sat and ate cookies and drank iced tea as Aunt Esther told them about the time she'd spent as a snake researcher in Florida. "People buy baby boa constrictors and then are surprised when the cute little snakes grow into big snakes. So! They release the snakes into their backyards or along the side of the highway or wherever. And then the giant boa constrictors slither around and constrict everything there is to constrict. Quite a problem, as you might imagine. There was one time we found an eighteen-footer curled up in a golf bag. That golfer did get quite the shock."

"When was this, Aunt Esther?" Jaime asked.

"Oh, some time ago," said Aunt Esther. "There was a lovely young woman who came on one of our expeditions. A writer. Her name was Kate, I believe. Kate Messner? She was very interested in all the snakes. And insects! Wrote a book called *Chirp*. Anyway, this was all before I was in Sudan."

"Wait," said Tess. "When were you in Sudan?"

"After I was in Florida," Aunt Esther said, as if the question was silly. "A beautiful country."

"My dad was in Sudan," Jaime said.

"Was?" said Theo.

"He's back now," Jaime said. "For good. He got a job in New Jersey, so . . ."

Tess remembered all the pictures of Jaime's dad around Jaime's old apartment, remembered the drawings that his dad had sent Jaime from Sudan. "Jaime! That's so great!"

"It is," Jaime said, smiling. But his happiness seemed to war with his hurt as his smile crumpled and his brows caved over his nose. Tess wanted to fix it, but she didn't know how. One more "sorry" wasn't going to do it.

Aunt Esther took the now-empty plate and stood. "I've chattered at you long enough. I'll let you get back to doing whatever it is you need to do."

She started to walk into the kitchen, stopped, turned. "Jaime, dear. Don't stay away so long. We missed you."

Jaime's mouth worked, but all he could get out was "Okay."

CHAPTER SIX
Theo

T heo felt odd.

Well, odd*er*.

But he wasn't the only one.

Tess was looking at Jaime as if he'd figured out how to fly, Jaime was looking everywhere but at Tess, and Nine couldn't figure out whose knees needed licking, whose fingers needed nibbling the most, so she sat down on the floor and groomed herself.

Usually, Tess would be charging around, directing everyone, but she seemed to have lost all sense of purpose. Jaime would have made some suggestions in his amiable Jaime way, but he seemed to have lost all his amiability.

"So," Theo ventured, "let's maybe look for some clues?"

Neither Tess nor Jaime answered the question, but they followed him upstairs.

In the twins' room, Jaime took in the mess of artifacts and papers on the floor. "It looks like you've been working hard."

"Not really," said Theo. "Tess has been having an existential crisis."

"Theo!"

"Well, you have!"

"It was malaise!" Tess said. "It was ennui."

"What's the difference?" said Theo.

Jaime sat down on the floor. "I guess I might have an existential crisis, too, if I'd just found out I was a Morningstarr."

Found out. Tess said, "So . . . you believe us? That we don't know any more about that photo than you do?"

Theo continued, "That it's not what it looks like? That it's *impossible*?"

Jaime ran his hand through his 'locs. "I don't know what I believe. But it doesn't matter now. Let's figure out where we need to go next."

"But—" Tess began. Theo shook his head at her—*Don't push it.*

So she didn't, for once. Instead, they explained that they'd gone to the address on the Trench & Snook business card and found only a deli.

Jaime examined the card, turning it over in his hands. "Why do you think this is the next clue?"

Theo stuck his fingers in his hair. Tess put on a sweatshirt and then took it off. Nine mrrowed. None of them said anything about living puzzles that operate on faith.

"Well, did you look up Trench and Snook to see if they're a real business?"

"We did!" said Tess, as enthusiastically as she did when they were in school and she knew the answer to the teacher's questions. "Trench and Snook was an architecture firm active in the mid-nineteenth century."

"And you looked up all the buildings they designed in the city?"

"Uh . . . ," said Tess.

"Funny!" Theo said. "We completely forgot to do that!" He was proud of himself for not going to the nearest wall and banging his head against it.

Jaime said, "So maybe we should do that first?"

"Okay," said Tess.

Tess waited. Theo did, too.

Jaime said, "I thought your mom got you phones.

Don't you want to try them?"

"Oh!" said Tess. "Well. I guess I could. But you're so good at, um . . ."

"Looking things up on phones?" Jaime finished for her, brow raised. "Yes, that's my superpower. Phone research."

Tess suddenly found the end of her braid fascinating. Theo felt even odder. Jaime was here and he was talking to them, but the Morningstarr twins and hundreds of years of history were sitting between them.

Still, Jaime did pull his phone from his pocket and looked up Trench & Snook. "Okay, so these guys built *a lot* of stuff, especially in SoHo, around where their office was, I guess."

"SoHo? But the address on the business card isn't in SoHo," Theo said.

"This website seems to think they had offices in SoHo," said Jaime. "But it's not like people on the internet haven't been wrong before." He thumbed through the search results, silently reading.

Tess dared to sit on the floor next to him the way she would have before that impossible photograph ruined everything. She looked over his shoulder as he read, and he didn't move his arm, or inch away from her, or glare, or make gagging noises, or any one of a million other things he could have done, maybe things that Theo would have done, if Theo were Jaime.

Which was why Theo groaned when Tess *did* push it, blurted, "Have you seen Ava?"

"Oh no," said Ono.

Jaime stiffened, stopped thumbing. "Where would I have seen her?"

"I don't know. I just thought—"

"That she's my friend now? That she wants to hang out with some kid who draws comics?"

"You drew *her*, though," Tess said. "Before you ever saw her."

Jaime shook his head and plowed on as if Tess hadn't said anything goofy. "Here's a list of the buildings that Trench and Snook worked on. A lot of them have been torn down, but there are some still standing."

"What?" Tess said. It seemed she'd already forgotten what they'd been looking for in the first place. "Which buildings?"

"There's 280 Broadway, sometimes called the Sun Building or the Marble Palace. Built in 1846."

"The Marble Palace. That seems like a possibility," Tess said.

"Why?" said Theo.

"I don't know. Because it's a palace?" said Tess.

Jaime said, "And then there's Odd Fellows Hall."

Something in Theo's brain itched. "What's that one?"

"It's 165–171 Grand Street. Built in 1848. A New York City landmark."

"Look at the card!" said Tess. "The last line. 'Grand Design for the Unexpected.' Maybe that's a clue? Grand Street? And 'unexpected' meaning 'odd'?"

Jaime went back to thumbing through his phone. "You tell me. You're Tess Morningstarr."

She shook her head. "I'm Tess Biedermann. I'm the same person I was a few weeks ago."

"None of us are the same," said Theo.

For the first time since coming through the door, Jaime looked straight at him.

Theo said, "I think we should try Odd Fellows Hall."

Jaime stood. "Odd Fellows for odd fellows. Sounds about right."

They walked to the Underway station and took the N train, then caught the 6. It took only a few minutes from Canal Street to make it to 165 Grand.

None of them said a word the whole trip.

Odd.

But even with the silence, traveling together, the three

of them and Nine, felt familiar, felt right, not odd.

So Theo was more optimistic than he'd been in a while when they stood in front of Odd Fellows Hall, a blocky brown building with just enough architectural flourishes to make it interesting but not enough to make it busy. And he happily used his brand-new phone to look up the Order of the Odd Fellows.

He read aloud, "The mission of the Order of Odd Fellows is 'Visit the Sick, Relieve the Distressed, Bury the Dead, and Educate the Orphan.'"

"Huh," said Jaime. "That sounds altruistic and creepy at the same time."

"That's our jam, though," said Tess. "Altruistic and creepy."

Jaime made a sound that was almost a laugh. Almost.

"Funny," said Theo.

"Their acronym is OOF," Jaime said. "That's funny."

Theo consulted his phone again. It really was quite useful and convenient. "According to this article, the building has a library and reading rooms, space for natural history, science, and art exhibits, and lots of meeting areas. The laying of the cornerstone in 1847 was this big party, but also contentious, because of what was—and wasn't—deposited in the stone."

Tess, who apparently found her own phone equally

convenient, read, "The name of the architect was hidden in the stone, but instead of Joseph Trench, they put the name Joseph *French*. And Snook wasn't mentioned at all."

"Poor Snook," Jaime said.

"He was snookered," said Theo. At Tess's wince, he said, "Oh, come on! That's hilarious!"

"If you say so," said Jaime. "But that sort of fits with the other clues. Snook being forgotten and all."

Tess pointed at the cornerstone, which was marked with a plaque. "I think we need to find out what's in there."

Jaime said, "I don't know how we're going to do that."

"Maybe Ono can punch his way in," said Theo.

"Oh no!" said Ono.

"Ono can't punch his way in," Jaime said. "We'll have to do something else."

"Hammer and chisel?" said Tess. But that wasn't going to work, either. Even if they could hammer their way into a huge block of stone, it was broad daylight, and the streets were crowded with people.

"Wait, show me the card again," Theo said.

Tess slipped her phone back into her pocket and handed him the business card. Stiff, yellowing vellum. Very stiff. Almost like plastic.

Theo said, "If Trench and Snook had offices in SoHo, why does this card have an address in the East Village?"

"Maybe that's not an address," said Jaime.

"Maybe," said Theo, "this isn't a business card."

"Hmmm," said Tess.

Without consulting one another, they walked to the cornerstone of the building. There was a modest metal plaque affixed to the stone that read *Dedicated on the seventh of June, in the year 1847, for the Order of Odd Fellows.*

Jaime said, "They named themselves the Odd Fellows because so many people thought it was odd to do good for others."

"People still think that's odd," Tess said.

"This is also odd," Jaime said as he ran his fingers around the frame of the plaque. "There's a small slit here."

"Let me guess," Theo said. "It's about the size of a business card."

"Or a *key* card."

Aware that they were feeling up a building in the middle of the day, in the middle of the crowds that were passing by, Theo, Tess, and Jaime each took out their phones and stared at the screens, as if the excitement of finding another clue hadn't hit them. Because it *had* hit them. Theo's hair felt as if it was practically standing on end (even more than usual). Tess was nearly tap-dancing. As cool as Jaime was acting, as closed up as he was trying to be, he couldn't help his jangling knees and the fingers typing against the leg of his jeans.

And when Ono whispered, "To the Land of Kings?" Jaime patted the little robot and murmured, "Kings, dude, kings."

"Everybody look casual," Theo said.

Tess muttered, "As if you ever looked casual in your whole life."

But Jaime stepped in front of Theo, hiding everything but Theo's hair from the people walking by. And Tess stood next to him, pointing out something on her phone, shielding Theo further. Quickly, Theo shoved the card into the slot Jaime had found.

Click!

The plaque wasn't a plaque—it was a door. Theo opened it just enough to reach inside, remembering only as he felt around the small chamber that it could be booby-trapped with anything—mechanical snakes, mechanical scorpions, mechanical fire ants, mechanical snapping turtles.

A small voice at the back of his mind said, *If you are Theodore Morningstarr, would you set a trap for yourself?*

I might, he told it.

No, you wouldn't.

"Shut up," Theo muttered.

"We didn't say anything," said Jaime.

"I wasn't talking to you," Theo said, his hand falling on something metal—a gear or something—and some papers. He scooped them out of the chamber, checked to make sure there was nothing else left inside, and shut the door. He shoved the items into his front pocket and turned around. He fully expected to be met with a phalanx of camera phone–wielding blond women in red dresses, all of them accusing him of theft, but New Yorkers, being New Yorkers, ignored the kids hanging around the corner of this historic city building, too intent on getting coffee or getting to work or getting ahead to care what Theo, Tess, and Jaime were doing. Only Nine got any attention at all, a quick "Hello, kitty" or "Nice cat" before the speaker disappeared around the corner.

It seemed as if they were going to get away with the contents of the chamber without anyone noticing, when Theo noticed the man standing on the other side of the street.

More specifically, a man the size of a small dump truck, in a too-tight business suit, with brown hair slick with goop, skim milk–blue skin, and eyes so dark they were almost all pupil, black and glittering.

Staring right at them.

"Uh, guys?" said Theo.

"Yeah," Jaime said. "I see him, too."

Nine lowered her head and growled softly.

"What's he doing?" said Tess.

"Besides staring?" Theo said.

"He's not moving. Why isn't he moving?" Tess said.

"Maybe he's not looking at us?" said Theo.

"He's looking at us," said Jaime.

"What's he waiting for?" Tess said. "Backup?"

Theo said, "I think he's waiting for the walk sign."

"You can't be serious," Jaime said, and looked up to see the sign blinking red, counting down the seconds. "You're serious."

Nine's growl got louder. A passerby made a wide berth around her.

"We need to run," Tess said.

"If we run, we'll just call attention to ourselves," Jaime said.

So, they moved as briskly but as casually as they could down Centre Street. Theo glanced back over his shoulder only to see the man in the suit advancing on them, lumbering like a rhino on its hind legs.

"Oh no," bleated Ono. And the three of them started jogging, then running, forgetting about not making a spectacle of themselves.

"We need somewhere to hide," Tess huffed.

They ran past a school, but schools were closed. The Buddhist Temple? Too quiet.

"Up there, around the corner," Jaime said. "Duck into the first place that looks open."

They rounded the corner onto Hester. Nine dragged them into an Asian market crowded with people.

"Excuse me, pardon me, excuse me," Tess said, as they maneuvered their way to the back of the store. They hunkered down next to a display of packages of dried tofu and vegan "prawns."

A sales clerk staffing a nearby table of samples said, "Would you like to try some dairy-free, gluten-free, soy-free ice cream? Ten percent off until four p.m.!"

"Uh, right after we tie our shoes," said Jaime, keeping low.

The sales clerk leaned over the table. "You're all tying your shoes?"

"We wouldn't want to trip over our laces," said Tess.

"Safety first!" Theo said.

The sales clerk leaned out even farther and lowered

her voice to a whisper. "Are you guys running from the cops?"

"What?" said Theo. "No!"

"Are you running from the mob?"

"The mob?" said Jaime.

"Are you running from your parents?"

"We're not running from anyone!" Tess said.

"Sure," said the clerk, straightening up. "There's a weird guy looking in the window. His suit is like, two sizes too small."

Jaime said, "Would you tell us when he goes away, please?"

"Is that who you're running from?"

"Yes," Jaime said.

"I don't blame you. I would not give that man any of my samples. But he just walked away. Coast is clear."

Jaime put his hands on his knees and hung his head in relief. Theo tried to catch his breath. Tess closed her eyes and covered her mouth with the back of her hand. Nine sniffed at some packages of ramen on which the orange store cat was sleeping. The orange cat's name tag read "Pebble."

Jaime said, "I don't know about you, but I could use a snack."

The clerk happily gave them each a cup of ice cream,

even Nine. They sat on the floor enjoying their dairy-free, gluten-free, soy-free, and possibly food-free treats, silently thinking about the man who had almost caught them, and about the treasures burning a hole in Theo's pocket.

CHAPTER SEVEN

Jaime

As Jaime polished off his third ice cream sample, hungrier than he'd been in weeks, he thought this entirely abnormal situation felt way too normal.

Instead of doing normal, every-soon-to-be-teenager things—sleeping late, chasing basketballs or dates, bingeing way too much TV, arguing with his dad—he was sitting on the floor of an Asian grocery store, plowing through a tray full of samples with the Morningstarr twins, who were also the Biedermann twins, all of them liars and thieves, all of them evading capture by yet another creep.

He didn't want it to feel normal. But it did.

He didn't want to feel excited about finding another clue. But he did.

(Teenagers! So excitable! And fickle, apparently.)

To distract himself, he asked if he could buy a whole dairy-free, gluten-free, soy-free ice cream. It wasn't half bad for something with no food in it.

The sales clerk actually clapped. "Yay!" she said, and ran to a nearby freezer case. She brought back four treats—one for Nine—and Jaime and the twins pooled their money to pay for them. They gathered at the cash register behind a tall man with two long dark braids and a linen suit, also buying the same treat. He held up his treat and saluted them.

"Good choice," he said. "Dairy isn't good for kitties."

"Mrrow," agreed Nine, licking her chops.

The three of them, plus Nine, followed the man out the door. He continued walking down Centre Street, but Jaime and the twins hesitated, scanning the sidewalks, searching for any sign of the milk-pale man and anyone else who might be chasing them.

The man with the braids turned. "I couldn't help but overhear that you kids were having a bit of trouble? I'm headed to the Croton Fountain, if you want to walk with me for a while."

Jaime glanced at the twins, and the twins glanced at Jaime, all of them suspicious. But Nine hauled on her leash so hard that Tess lurched forward.

The man's eyes sparkled. "Smart cat."

Another abnormal thing that felt entirely too normal: letting a giant cat make your decisions for you.

"Thank you," said Tess as they started to walk again. "There are a lot of creeps running around the city."

"Any reason that particular creep was bothering you?" the man asked.

Tess opened her mouth, then closed it.

"Random creep, then. I hate those. I'm Sam, by the way."

Before Jaime or Theo could caution her, Tess said, "I'm Tess. And this is Nine. That's my brother, Theo, and that's Jaime."

The man nodded, took another lick of his ice cream. He didn't seem to be in any real hurry, but he wasn't exactly moving slowly, either. And for some reason, Jaime imagined that very little got past this man. His brown eyes were too sharp.

Jaime said, "Why are you going to the Croton Fountain?"

"It's peaceful there. And I work at the embassy nearby."

"The Embassy of the 500 Nations?" Theo asked.

"That's the one."

"What do you do there?"

"Lawyer," said Sam. "Basically, I do treaty enforcement work for the Seneca Nation and several other Nations." His dark eyes went sparkly with amusement when he added, "So I have a lot of experience with random creeps."

"What do you have to enforce?" asked Theo. "I mean, aren't treaties . . . treaties?"

"There's always someone who decides that they can never have enough stuff. So they're happy to take yours, and everyone else's."

"We've met people like that," said Jaime.

"Don't doubt it," Sam said.

"Some people have holes in them," Jaime said, surprised by the vehemence in his own voice. "Black holes, like the ones in space. They suck in everything."

"I'd say that's about right," Sam said mildly.

They strolled along in companionable silence for a few more minutes, until they heard the waters of the fountain, then saw them: four "rivers" running in all directions, linked to a spring below. Crowds of people took pictures in front of it. At least three wedding parties were posed around the perimeter.

"I always forget how beautiful it is," Jaime said.

"Makes you wonder about what the water looked like before all these buildings were here," Tess said.

"That it does," said Sam.

"Seneca," said Theo. "Your people were always here."

"You know your history."

"Everyone keeps saying that," said Theo, glancing at Jaime. "But I'm not so sure."

At this, Sam merely raised a brow. Then he said, "Well, if you three are okay, I should get back to my office."

"Thanks for walking with us," Jaime said.

"No problem," said Sam. He pulled a card from the inner pocket of his linen jacket. "If you meet any more random creeps, give me a call."

Jaime took the card, not sure if he should be flattered or insulted that this man thought that they—that *he*—might need a lawyer one day. But then, considering how many things they could be arrested for already, Sam wasn't wrong.

Jaime looked up to thank Sam again, but the man was already loping away, shiny braids swinging. Jaime's fingers itched to draw him, but he'd left his sketchbook at home.

"I need to get a linen suit," Jaime said.

"You'd look good in a linen suit," Tess said. Then bit her lip hard enough to draw blood.

"Where are you going to wear a linen suit?" said Theo irritably.

"I don't know," Jaime said. "My birthday's coming up."

"You're going to wear a suit on your birthday?"

"Why not?"

Tess swallowed. "Are you . . . going to have a party? Or something?"

Her question reminded him that he was supposed to be mad at her. Mad at Theo. Mad at the world. He stuffed Sam's card into his back pocket. "Let's sit by the fountain and take a look at what we found at Odd Fellows."

Tess's face crumpled, but Jaime wouldn't let himself feel guilty about that. She was the one who should feel guilty. She and her brother were the reason that they were running around the city being chased by goons in the first place. She and her brother were the reason that 354 W. 73rd Street had come crashing down. She and her brother were the reason why Jaime had to live in Broboken, of all places.

But he sat with them on the edge of the Croton Fountain, the *shhhh-shhhh* of the water telling him they still had work to do. Slant—and the rest of the black holes—weren't going to stop sucking up everything in their paths, so Jaime and the twins couldn't stop looking for answers, no matter where those answers led.

"What do we have?" Jaime said.

Theo glanced around to see if anyone was looking—rogue Guildmen, rogue robots, rogue rogues—but everyone was too busy enjoying the sun and the fountain. He pulled a folded sheet of paper from his pocket along with a medallion or gear of some sort. Tess took the metal disc and examined it. Theo unfolded the paper and frowned.

"What?" said Jaime.

"It's a flyer for Coney Island." He handed it to Jaime so Jaime could see it. On the flyer was a picture of a robot, an automaton. The automaton was a dark-skinned, mustachioed man dressed in a turban and a coat with a fur collar. On a large desk in front of the automaton was a chessboard with pieces set up for a game. "Best the Turk!" screamed the flyer. "And win a prize!" The edge of the flyer was decorated with chess notations: e4 e5, Nf3 Nc6, d4 exd4. Pawn to e4, pawn to e5, knight to f3, etc.

Jaime quickly punched in "The Turk" on his phone. "Guess what's still at Coney Island at a place called Poseidon's Pavilion, beating everyone at chess?"

"A flyer for Coney Island hidden in a vault in a

building erected in the 1840s?" said Tess. "Was Coney Island even a thing then?"

"Doesn't matter," said Jaime. "You—I mean, the Morningstarrs—already knew what would happen. They knew Coney Island would be a thing. So they planted it."

"But what if you can't time travel with anything?" Theo said.

"Why not?" said Jaime. "How do you know what you can and can't travel with? Unless there's something you haven't told me."

"There's nothing we haven't told you," Tess said. "We don't know anything about time travel."

"I—"

"We don't know anything about time travel," Tess repeated, loud enough that a couple holding hands nearby gave them quizzical looks.

Jaime hooked a thumb at Theo and said to the couple, "He watches a lot of sci-fi. They're always arguing about it."

"Oh," said one of the men, a redhead with freckled brown skin. "He should read Einstein, then."

"I've read Einstein," Theo muttered. "Hasn't everyone?"

"Focus, Theo," Tess said, leaning in so the couple couldn't overhear. "What do you think this thing is?"

She held the circle of metal in her palm. It was silver or platinum, with notches cut out of its edge like a gear. But it also had weird symbols on it that might mean something but could also mean nothing.

"No idea," said Theo.

"Jaime? What do you think?"

Jaime said, "I think I know how to play chess."

But Coney Island would have to wait. It would take at least an hour to get there, and who knew how long to wait in line to play the Turk—if that's what they were supposed to do.

"Tomorrow?" said Tess. The hope in her voice clawed at Jaime.

"Yeah," he said. "Text me tomorrow and we'll figure out a place to meet." He turned and walked away before Tess had a chance to say anything else or, worse, try to hug him.

"Oh no," said Ono mournfully.

"Cut it out," Jaime said.

Instead of taking the Underway, Jaime walked all the way downtown to catch the ferry back to Hoboken. Jaime loved the ferry, loved the wind in his hair, the sun silvering the water. But now, when he looked down into the depths, he also imagined all the things besides fish lurking beneath the surface. Machines shaped like sharks, machines shaped like squid. He imagined tentacles rising up out of the water to curl around the boat, squeezing it like a piece of fruit. And he imagined Ava Oneal appearing out of nowhere in front of him, ready to take on every monster.

But Ava wasn't here. He hadn't seen her since the day they had raided the cemetery and found the photograph that proved who the twins really were.

Except . . . except . . .

. . . photos could be doctored.

The twins said they had never seen the photo before, they said that they didn't know how it came to be and couldn't explain it.

What if they were telling the truth?

What if this wasn't a game the Morningstarrs played, but someone else's game?

It used to be that possibilities excited him. New things, new people, inspired characters and comics, stories of all kinds, that filled his sketchbooks and his imagination. But now Jaime's head ached with all the possibilities. The possibility that Tess and Theo were lying, and the possibility that they weren't. The possibility that he would see Ava again, and the possibility that he wouldn't. The possibility that they would never solve the Morningstarr Cipher, and the possibility that they would. The possibility that all they'd done for the last couple of months was chase ghosts and that nothing they did would make any difference to anyone, and the possibility that they had the power to change everything—the city, the world.

He rubbed his forehead to ease away the growing pain, the growing dread. Because he'd always imagined that all the possibilities, all the choices he made, would bring him somewhere good, would make him into a person he'd recognize even now, someone worth knowing, someone worth *being*. But what if he grew up to be someone he didn't like? What if he grew up to be someone he despised?

"Are you all right?" asked a white woman about Mima's age, with the type of crinkles around her eyes and mouth that said she'd spent most of her life smiling. She had a shock of fabulous silver hair. Superhero hair. "I have some ginger candy in my purse if you're feeling seasick."

"I'm fine, ma'am, thank you," Jaime said.

"Maybe you should sit down, just in case," she said.

He was about to refuse, but then he said, "Yes. Good idea." He sat down next to her.

"My name is Mary," she said, and handed him a piece of candy.

"Thank you, Mary. I'm Jaime."

"Hello, Jaime." Mary looked out on the water. "It's beautiful, isn't it? I love the view of the city from the water, the way it rises up out of the mist."

That was what Jaime liked about it, too. "I have a lot of drawings of the skyline from the ferry."

"Drawings?" she said. "How nice. Are you an artist?"

"No," he said, feeling the emptiness of the pocket where he'd always tucked his sketchbook. "I just like to draw."

"Isn't an artist a person who likes to draw?" said the woman.

"I'm not sure it's that simple," Jaime said.

"Oh, I think it is," said the woman, smiling sagely. "Do you have any drawings with you?"

"I left them at home," he said.

"That's too bad. I would have liked to see some. I bet you're very talented."

"Thank you, ma'am," he said, politely, though there was no way she would be able to tell if he was talented just by looking at him. And she *was* looking at him. He felt the weight of her appraisal—frank, but warm and kind. Being seen this way made him as twitchy as Tess, so he tucked his hands beneath his legs and watched a woman in a big hat that obscured her face try to get through the crowd without spilling the two hot drinks she was carrying.

"You don't believe me," Mary said, "but I have a sense about these things. You're going to go places." She nodded at her own statement as if nothing could be clearer or more evident. "You will go places. Magical places other people only dream of."

Jaime stood up and went to stand at the railing, so terrified and yet so hopeful that this stranger was right, that he would go places, magical places, that he couldn't bear to sit with her any longer.

Which was when someone shouted, "Watch out!" and shoved him right over the side.

CHAPTER EIGHT
Cricket

Back in her beautiful apartment in Hoboken, Zelda "Cricket" Moran was in mourning.

Wearing the same outfit she'd worn every day for weeks—brown shirt, brown pants, and a little black mask—she lay on the floor on her mother's favorite kilim carpet and whispered, "Karl. Karl. Kaaarrrl."

Her brother, Otto, said, "Mom! Zelda is doing it again!"

"Don't call me Zelda," said Cricket.

"Please, honey," said their mother from the kitchen. "Get up off the floor."

Otto poked at Cricket's feet. "Yeah, get up off the floor, weirdo-girl."

Cricket opened her eyes. Her brother had one of their father's ties wrapped around his head like a headband. The tie was printed with little happy-faces. "Who are you calling 'weirdo-girl'? Have you seen yourself lately? You're positively WACKADOO."

"I don't think the word 'wackadoo' is in the dictionary, dear," said their mother. "Actually, I'm not sure it's a word."

"I'm not bound to the dictionary any longer, Mother. I'm not bound to anything. I am BOUNDLESS."

Otto said, "I don't think so. I think you're full of bounds. You have bounds all over the place."

"I do not!" said Cricket. "Mom, Otto is being PRE-POSTEROUS."

Otto assumed his "martial arts" pose. "Say that again and I will carrot-chop you."

"No one is carrot-chopping anyone," said their mother. "Otto, leave your sister alone. She's sad."

"I'M BOUNDLESS," Cricket insisted, though she didn't get up from the floor.

"And sad," said their mother, who came to sit on the couch "It's okay to be sad."

But it wasn't. Not for Cricket. Cricket was the kind of girl who feared nothing and no one. Cricket was the kind of girl who never let the world get her down. Cricket was unstoppable.

At least, Cricket had been unstoppable with Karl around.

But Karl was gone.

Now she felt like everyone else, or what she assumed everyone else felt like. Tired and boring and bored and angry and sleepy and sad, all at the same time.

Stoppable.

Cricket rolled over and spoke into the rug. "Did you call Detective Biedermann to see if she found any more clues about Karl?"

"I checked with her the other day, remember?" said her mother gently.

"Maybe you should call her again."

"Let's wait a few more days. In the meantime, how about you and Otto and me go out for a while? We could go up to the pool on the roof."

"I don't want to get my hair wet," Cricket said.

"I bought you that new swim cap. The one you said looks like an anemone."

"Swimming is for fish."

"Roger isn't so good at it," said Otto. Roger, their goldfish, liked to swim backward.

"Roger is an excellent swimmer, and so are you, Cricket. But we don't have to go swimming. We can go to the park. Or to a museum. We can do anything you want."

Cricket sat up. "Can we spy on NEFARIOUS types?"

"We can do anything but spy on people."

"I didn't say spy on *people*, I said spy on NEFARIOUS types."

"Cricket."

"Fine." Cricket lay back down. "You're no fun."

"Well, if you don't want to go out," said her mother, standing, "I'm going to get some work done for a kitchen design. She's a real bear, this one."

Otto ceased carrot-chopping. "Your client is a real bear?"

"Bears are very picky about their kitchens," said Cricket. "Everybody knows that."

"Roger doesn't know that," Otto said.

"Even Roger. Why do you think he swims backward?"

"Now who's being preposterous?" their mother said. "Maybe you two can find a movie to watch or a book to read together." She reached down and patted Cricket on the shoulder before heading for her office.

Otto turned on the TV and found a cartoon.

Cartoons were for babies. Cricket got up and went to the bookshelf. She'd already read all the books here. At least, all the ones on true crime. But she wasn't interested in true crime right now. She'd had enough true crime to last her forever. Or at least till next week.

Speaking of picky, Cricket's mom was picky about her books, which were always arranged in alphabetical order (and not by color, which she claimed was a thing other designers did, and which she thought was NON-SENSICAL). A few of the books looked interesting—*Two Naomis*, *Orphan Island*, *A Crooked Kind of Perfect*, *Iron-Hearted Violet*—but it was the books on the middle shelf that caught Cricket's eye, not because they were brightly colored or books Cricket had read, but because they were neither. These were the books her mom said were special, ones passed down through her family. They were very old, with worn-out spines, some with the leather peeling off. They looked like Cricket felt. She tilted her head to read the titles. *All the Stars in the Sky*, *Hurricane Hall*, *Penelope*, *The Lost Ones*, *Empire of the Moon*.

Cricket pulled the first book off the shelf. On the cover, it read *All the Stars in the Sky: Poems by A Lady*. Cricket had never heard of a lady named A Lady, but she supposed it could happen.

Inside was written:

Butterbean,

I loved these poems when I was a girl, so I'm giving them to you. I hope they help you find your way, just as they helped me.

Love,

Mama

Cricket knew that name. "Butterbean" was Grammy Jo's special name for Cricket's mom. Butterbean would be a silly name for anyone, but when Grammy Jo said it, it sounded special, like Grammy Jo was saying, "I love you, and also you are a princess and a queen and a warrior and a superhero all in one, like a kick-butt sundae."

Cricket wanted to be a kick-butt sundae.

Cricket sat down with the book of poems and turned to the last page. Her mother said it was a terrible habit, but Cricket always read the ends of books first, because she didn't like surprises. She began to read:

The Map of Stars

Don't speak to me of azure skies
or lazy bees and butterflies.

Stay your lips from talk of spring, the
cleansing rains the clouds will bring.

No more blossoms, no more Mays,
no more trees in wind's ballets.

Enough of maidens seizing days,
under Apollo's blazing gaze.

Birdsong, lamb's bleats, puppies, dawns,
pellucid pools aswirl with swans.

I am sick to death of sunny things,
of beating hearts and beating wings.

I yearn for stillness darkness brings,
the truth of love, its potent stings.

All of nighttime's lonely hours,
are brighter than what sun devours.

I trace the stars that shine anew,
the map that leads me back to you.

Yes, the poem was about hearts and stars and mushy stuff, and she wasn't sure she understood it, but Cricket read it under her breath three times anyway. She had a funny feeling, a feeling that wasn't just one feeling, but a combination of too many feelings all at once. She felt like yelling just to get them all out.

A buzzing sound startled her. Her mother's phone on the counter. Cricket set the book aside and went to answer it.

"State your business," she said.

"Hello?" said a voice on the other end. "Mrs. Moran?"

"*Ms.* Moran," Cricket corrected. "Your business, please!"

"This is Dhruv at the security desk. We've had a report that you might be interested in."

"What kind of report?"

"Well," said Dhruv, "it seems that there's a raccoon stuck in the elevator?"

CHAPTER NINE
Tess

Tess, Theo, their dad, and their aunt were sitting around the kitchen table, the remnants of dinner still littering its surface, when Mrs. Biedermann walked in, face pale and drawn. Detective Clarkson, right behind her, was even paler.

Mr. Biedermann stood up to kiss Mrs. Biedermann. "You two look exhausted."

"You'd be exhausted if you'd had to question Lora Yoshida for three hours."

Tess kicked Theo. Theo said, "OW!"

Their parents said, "What?"

The twins said, "Nothing."

"Funny," said their mom. "That's exactly what Lora Yoshida said she stole from Darnell Slant. Nothing!"

"Maybe that's true," Tess said.

"Maybe it is," her mom agreed. "Still, it's our job to investigate the claims, and her story doesn't quite add up."

"It's a heck of a story, though," said Clarkson.

"What story?" said Tess.

"It's too long to get into. Besides, we really can't discuss it."

Tess couldn't help but press. "What did Slant say she stole?"

Her mother kissed the top of Tess's head. "Slant who?" she said. "Stole what?"

Aunt Esther stood up. "Have a seat, Miriam. You, too, Detective. I'll fix you some plates."

Detective Clarkson slumped in a chair. "Thank you. That woman—Lora—knocked the cheese fries out of me." He glanced at Tess and Theo. "Not literally."

"I will fill you up with grilled chicken and vegetables," said Aunt Esther. "Better for you than cheese fries."

"Fig Newtons for dessert?" said Clarkson.

Aunt Esther beamed. "If you like. We also have ice cream. And pie."

"Hot dog!" Clarkson said, clapping his hands together.

"I cannot condone hot dog pie," said Aunt Esther.

Tess and Theo left the adults to not talk about talking to Lora Yoshida, and went to their room. If they were right about the next clue, they had a trip to Coney Island the next day—and a chess match to prepare for.

Of course, Theo didn't think he needed any preparation. Chess! he'd said. What could be more fun?

"What if we don't have to play the Turk to find the next clue?" Tess asked him.

Theo frowned. "Of course we have to play the Turk. Why wouldn't we have to play the Turk?"

"Maybe the clue has nothing to do with chess."

"That makes no sense," Theo said emphatically, as if the Cipher made sense, as if the Morningstarrs made sense, as if Tess and Theo could make sense of the Morningstarrs if they *had* made sense, as if Tess and Theo could make sense of them even if they *were* them, which they decidedly were not.

"Okay," said Tess. "What if we lose?"

"We won't lose," said Theo, with the tiniest trace of his old swagger. But he pulled out his old chess manuals anyway and sat down on his bed to study. "You should look at these, too. You need to brush up."

"I was always a better player than you," she said.

"If by 'better,' you mean you lost more games in a more spectacular fashion."

"'Spectacular fashion.' You are such a dork."

"You would know." Theo kicked one of the manuals off his bed to the floor, where Tess sat with Nine. "That one is for beginners."

"Ha, ha," said Tess. But she opened the book and started reading. Just in case.

She was still reading a couple of hours later when her phone and Theo's phone started ringing at the same time, so loud that even Nine jumped (luckily, because Tess's phone was underneath the cat). Tess pressed the green button and a video of Jaime popped up. He was sitting in a brightly painted room with a blanket around him. Someone was talking in Spanish—Mima?—and someone else was . . . singing?

"What's going on?" said Tess. "Where are you?"

"We're at my apartment. And we're celebrating."

Tess tamped down the disappointment she felt. Jaime was having a party and hadn't invited her. But he'd called, and that was something. She took a deep breath and plastered a smile on her face.

"Great!" she said. "What are we celebrating?"

"The fact that I didn't drown," he said.

"Huh? What do you mean?"

There was a commotion on the screen and someone yelled, "WHO GOES THERE?"

"Is that Otto Moran?" Theo said. "Shouldn't he be in bed?"

Jaime said, "We're also celebrating the fact that we found—"

More commotion as someone grabbed the phone. Cricket Moran held the phone so close to her face that the screen was mostly pearly baby teeth. She rapped, *"I trace the stars that shine anew, the map that leads me back to you!"*

"Is it someone's birthday? What's happening?" said Theo.

"We didn't find Karl!" said Cricket's mouth.

"I'm so sorry, Cricket."

Cricket ripped off her black mask, one dark eye filling the screen. "You don't get it! Karl found *us*!"

"What?"

"IT'S SO METAL!"

It was too late to go to Jaime's apartment, so they had to wait until morning to get the whole story. Which meant that Tess got exactly zero hours of sleep. Despite the lack of rest, however, she dragged Theo out of bed early.

"Mom! Mom!" she said. "Guess what?"

Her mom was at the sink, rinsing out her coffee cup. "Jaime fell into the river, but he's okay. And they found Karl."

"Of course she knows everything already," said Theo, yawning, his big hair smashed on one side.

"Theo, you look like a listing ship," said their mother.

"Is that how you talk to your son?" Theo said.

"Theo, you look like the world's cutest listing ship. Better?"

Theo slumped in a kitchen chair. "Ships can't be cute."

"Speaking of ships," Tess said, "do you know what happened to Jaime? I mean, specifically?"

"I know he's okay. And I know the detectives who are on the case. I'll see what I can find out. And I'm going to follow up on Karl," said their mother. "Where are you two going today? Jaime's?"

Tess swallowed. She didn't want to admit that they hadn't been invited to Jaime's or to the Morans' to celebrate Karl's return.

"We're meeting Jaime downtown. We're thinking of going to Coney Island."

"That sounds fun," said their mom. "I haven't been there in ages. Don't eat too much junk and make yourself sick. And don't be home too late or I will text all your friends your embarrassing baby pictures."

An hour later, they found Jaime sitting on a park bench, sketchbook in hand. Tess dropped down on one side of him and Theo dropped on the other. Nine sat at Jaime's feet and mrrowed hello.

Jaime cracked a smile. "Meow to you, too, Nine." Nine rubbed against his knees until Jaime scratched her between the ears the way she liked. Tess tried not to stare at him, but her eyes roved over him anyway, looking for injuries.

"What?" said Jaime.

Tess tugged at her braid, embarrassed to be caught staring. "You were pushed into the river, you said."

"Yeah," he said. "And before you ask, no, I have no idea who did it, or why. By the time I came to the surface for air, the ferry was already chugging away from me. And then I had to spend ten minutes trying to dodge boats before the police boat got there to pull me out."

"That's so scary!" said Tess, thinking of sharks.

"You're not thinking of sharks, are you?" said Jaime.

Theo said, "She's totally thinking of sharks."

"I was not! But I'm glad there weren't any."

"Me too," said Jaime. "It was wild, though."

"So, you really are okay?" Tess said.

"I am now. I was worried about Ono. What the water would do to him. I shouldn't have worried, though. He turned into a very tiny submarine with very bright lights. The rescuers saw his lights in the water."

"Good robot!" said Tess.

"Land of Kings!" Ono said, not even bothering to pop his head out of Jaime's pocket.

"And what about Karl?" said Tess.

"That story's even wilder. Dhruv, the security guard on duty, told us that he was sitting at the desk reading a newspaper when a couple came running out of the elevator, shrieking about giant rodents and infestations and whatever. But when he went to investigate, the elevator doors had already closed. And then the elevator stopped between floors five and six and the alarms went off. When they finally got the elevator doors open, there was Karl—sleeping, or unconscious. He's really skinny, but he'll make it. He's at the vet's recovering from . . . whatever or wherever he was."

"And nobody saw anything?" Theo wanted to know.

"No," Jaime said. "Dhruv checked the video, but the cameras are aimed too high to catch things that small, I guess."

"So we'll never know where he was," said Tess.

"Mrs. Moran talked to your mom and the animal control people. They're going to question Dhruv and the couple who first saw Karl, but I don't know if they'll learn anything else." Jaime scratched Nine thoroughly under her chin. "I'm just glad that both Nine and Karl are back. One less thing to worry about. Uh, two less things." He seemed about to say something else but stood instead, tucking his sketchbook back into his pocket. "Let's get going."

"Are we sure we shouldn't take a taxi or something?" said Theo. "What if a Guildman gets twitchy?"

"We don't have the money for a taxi," Tess said.

"If we're going to solve the Cipher, we're going to have to risk it," Jaime said. "Unless your Old York Cipher Society friends want to fly us in their airship."

"I don't want anyone else to get hurt or kidnapped," said Tess.

"Just us," Theo said.

"What are you two worried about?" Jaime said, already starting to walk to the Underway station. "You wouldn't be here now if you got hurt or kidnapped later, right?"

Tess said, "Jaime—" but Theo touched her arm, shook his head. Theo was right. No use in arguing about it again. Jaime would believe them or he wouldn't. He would trust them again or he . . .

"Come on, Nine," Tess said, and followed Jaime. Theo reluctantly did, too. He reluctantly walked down the steps, reluctantly got on the B train, reluctantly sat down. He eyed the Guildman in his box with suspicion, though this particular Guildman wasn't paying any attention to them at all, not even to Nine, who got attention wherever she went.

"Is that Guildman . . . texting?" said Theo.

"I think he is," Jaime said.

Tess said, "Since when do Guildmen text? Since when did they get phones?"

Jaime sighed. "Since when do stone eagles fly?"

Not so long ago, the three of them had unwittingly freed twenty-two enormous Morningstarr Machines previously hidden in stone. But it might as well have happened in another century, with different people altogether. When the Guildmen were only concerned with litter on the trains and didn't spend their time threatening kids' lives or texting their friends.

And another thing that was different: "Where's the caterpillar? The one that cleans the Underway cars?"

Both Jaime and Theo looked right to left, up and down. "Maybe that's who the Guildman is texting," said Jaime. "Maybe the caterpillar is late."

"Maybe it was out partying last night," said Tess.

Jaime leaned back in his seat. "Nah. Caterpillar was up bingeing its favorite movies."

"*Spider-Man*? *Ant-Man and the Wasp*?" said Theo.

Jaime snorted. "That wasn't half bad."

Theo said, "What wasn't?"

"Never mind," said Jaime, who pulled out his sketch-book and quickly sketched the texting Guildman. Though the behavior of the Guildman was strange, and the missing caterpillar was strange, the familiar scratch of Jaime's pencil was soothing. Tess closed her eyes and didn't open them again until Nine nibbled her fingers.

She sat up straight. "What? What?"

"You fell asleep," Theo said.

"I did not!"

"But you did!" said Theo.

"People!" said Jaime, who was already standing, hanging on to a strap overhead. "We're almost there."

They got off the train to catch the Q headed for West 8th Street. The Guildman on this car wasn't texting anyone, and the caterpillar was making its methodical march through the cars, cleaning the floors and walls. This time, Tess kept her eyes open, in case the Guildman decided to jump out of the car and the caterpillar hatched into a moth or a monster or a shark. (Or the Guildman hatched into a shark. That would be really weird. Or maybe not.) But two uneventful stops later, they arrived with no one and nothing jumping or hatching. Outside, it was a bright, sunny day—warm, but with a cool breeze that swept off the water. Three Rollers, glinting in the sunlight, rolled a tidy sphere of trash into an open manhole and quickly disappeared after it. Soon, the roar of the coasters at Luna Park competed with joyful shrieks of their riders. They passed the swing ride and the Wonder Wheel and finally hit the boardwalk, which was packed with bathing suit—clad people sticky with sunscreen. And though it was still early, the rich aromas of funnel cakes and cotton candy and pizza danced in the air.

Jaime held up his phone. "So, the Turk is supposed to be at this place called Poseidon's Pavilion, about a quarter mile that way."

"Why wouldn't the Turk be at a museum? Isn't the salty air bad for machines?" Tess said.

"According to this article," Jaime said, "museums have been after the guy who owns the Turk, but he won't sell it to anyone. He says it brings in too many challengers and too much business. Apparently, the Turk's never lost."

"Wait, never?" said Theo.

"Never."

"I don't believe it. I would have heard about an unbeatable chess machine before now," Theo said. "Everyone would have. No one would stop talking about it."

"Maybe the losers are too embarrassed to talk about it," Tess said.

Jaime said, "The article says that no serious chess players will play the Turk because everyone's sure it's rigged somehow."

"How, though?" Theo said.

"Maybe it's just the Morningstarr version of a computer like Deep Blue," Tess said. "Lots of people don't want to play a machine programmed to make thousands of calculations a second. They want to play people."

"Whatever the Turk is," Jaime said, "plenty of amateurs want to play it."

"Let's hope there aren't that many challengers today," Tess said.

They made it to Poseidon's Pavilion, which turned out to be a rather run-down arcade that smelled of burned peanuts. A few people played a lazy game of Skee-ball, and a group of teenagers tried to impress one another by punching a bag as hard as they could while a meter measured their punching power. Antique arcade cabinets—*Pac-Man*, *Space Invaders*, *Donkey Kong*—lined the walls.

And overhead, a peeling sign that read "CHALLENGE THE TURK!" pointed toward the back of the pavilion.

Tess and Nine led the way, charging through the arcade, until they saw him. The Turk.

"Wow," said Tess. A dark-skinned robotic man, turbaned and mustachioed, sat behind a huge desk with a chessboard on top. "I didn't expect him to look so . . ."

"Beatable?"

A small boy, also dark-skinned, about eight years old, stood by the desk. That was when Tess noticed that a game was already in progress.

Tess smiled at the boy. "Are you a challenger?"

The boy rolled his eyes with Cricket energy. "The Turk isn't much of a challenge so far."

"No?" said Theo. "How's the game going?"

"I opened with the Dragon," said the boy.

"As you do," said Tess, though she only had a vague notion what the Dragon was.

"But he just fianchettoed his own king's bishop!" the boy said scornfully. "Can you believe it?"

"He just what?" Tess said.

"Hmmm," said the boy, raising his little-kid brow. "I hope *you're* not a challenger."

"Why?"

The boy bent at the waist and rested his chin on his folded hands. "Because you'll lose, that's why."

Tess struggled not to roll *her* eyes at the boy. "I could

just play him again."

"You can't," said the boy, not even glancing up at Tess. "Don't you know? The Turk only gives you one shot."

"A day?" asked Theo.

Now the boy glanced up. "No. One shot a *lifetime*. If you lose or draw, you can never play him again."

CHAPTER TEN
Theo

One shot.

In a lifetime.

Hahahahaha.

Ha.

HA.

He should have studied more.

He should have studied harder.

"We should have studied harder," he muttered. "We should have practiced. Why didn't we practice?"

"Well," Tess began.

"We should go home and practice," Theo said.

"We don't have time for that," said Tess.

Theo stuck his hand in his voluminous hair. "There's always time for study and practice."

Tess and Jaime both steered him away from the Turk and his current challenger.

"We don't even know if we have to play him to figure out the next clue," said Tess.

"Of course we have to play him!" Theo stuck his other hand in his hair. "Why hide a clue with a chess player if you're not going to play chess?"

Jaime patted his shoulder. "Okay, okay. Keep your voice down."

"Theo, put your *arms* down. You look like you're about to take off," Tess said.

"Besides, we got this," Jaime said.

Theo put his arms down. "Tell me you're a chess master."

"I'm pretty good," said Jaime.

"I'm pretty good, too. And so is Tess."

"Thank you," said Tess.

"Pretty good is not good enough." Theo stuffed his hands back into his hair. Nine swirled around his legs, rubbing her face against his knees.

"We'll be fine," Jaime said. "You know we'll be fine."

"How do I know that?"

Jaime's face did that shuttering thing that it had been doing the last couple of days. "You know that because you *knew* that."

Theo sighed so heavily, it sounded like he was blowing out birthday candles. Tess tugged on her braid and looked down at the floor. What would it take to convince Jaime that Tess and Theo were not who he thought they were? Theo had no idea. No idea how they would convince Jaime, and no idea how they were going to beat a machine—made by mysterious geniuses—that had never been beaten, ever.

That is, if they were even going to get a chance to play the machine. The small boy was taking his time figuring out his next move.

The boy said, "Stop hovering."

"I'm not hovering," said Theo.

"You're hovering. I won't be rushed."

"How do you know you can only play one time?" Tess said to the boy.

The boy pointed to the wall, where a sign read, "Take your BEST SHOT at beating THE TURK, because you only get ONE SHOT."

"Okay, but how does he . . . it . . . know?" said Tess.

The boy pointed to another sign: "WIN, LOSE, OR DRAW: THE TURK REMEMBERS. HE ALWAYS REMEMBERS."

"Now," said the boy, "will you be quiet, please? I'm trying to concentrate."

Jaime took off his glasses, wiped them on his T-shirt, put them back on. "Let's play that game over there."

Theo threw up his hands, not caring if he looked as if he was about to take off, but he followed Jaime anyway. "*BurgerTime*? Do you really want to play a game called *BurgerTime*?"

"No," said Jaime, over his shoulder. "But I think you could use a distraction. You're freaking out."

"I am not freaking out. And if I *were* freaking out, I would have very good reason for freaking out."

"Uh-huh," Jaime said. "Come on. Try it." He lowered his voice. "And we can keep an eye on the kid and his game from here without being creepy about it."

"Fine, fine," Theo said. He stepped up to the game, which seemed to be about building a burger while you're being chased by . . . food. He pushed some quarters into the machine and started up the game.

"I think you have to shoot Mr. Pickle with pepper," Jaime said.

"What?" said Theo, right before he died.

"Oops," said Tess. "You're dead."

Ono popped his head out from Jaime's pocket. "Oh no."

"My turn," said Jaime.

"You *did* want to play *BurgerTime*," Theo said.

"It's better than arguing with a little boy," Tess said. "Besides, we need to think this through. If we have to play the Turk, how are we going to approach the game? And if we don't have to play the Turk, if playing the Turk isn't the point, then how are we going to get a closer look at the automaton and the desk and the chessboard without people getting suspicious?"

"Hopefully, we won't have to 'borrow' it," said Jaime. He deftly maneuvered Peter Pepper, the main character of *BurgerTime*, around the game, piling up ingredients.

"Have you played this before?" Theo asked.

"Nope," said Jaime.

"Yes, you have," said Theo.

"When would I have played *BurgerTime*? Oh, got you, Mr. Egg!"

"I'm going to want a bugburger after this," Tess said.

"That's the last thing I'll want." Theo watched as the little boy playing the Turk made a move. The Turk turned his head from left to right and then right to left, considering his options.

Theo lowered his voice and said, "What if the little boy wins?"

"He won't," said Jaime, toggling the joystick. "Come on!"

"Jaime," Tess said, biting her lip.

As if Jaime understood that Tess was about to explain once again that they weren't the Morningstarrs, couldn't possibly be, and therefore had no idea what would happen, Jaime said, "I just meant that the odds are against him winning, that's all." He let go of the joystick. "Welp. I'm dead, too."

Tess put another coin in the machine. "Let me try."

Theo didn't bother to watch Tess try to outrun Mr. Pickle and Mr. Egg. Behind her, at the desk, the Turk's hand shot out, moved a piece across the board. The little boy gasped. "No!" he said, stomping his foot. "No, no, no!"

The chessboard slowly tipped, dumping the chess pieces into a compartment underneath it before flipping over completely. Then the Turk leaned back in his seat, rested his arms on the desk, and went still.

"Come on!" said the boy.

The Turk didn't move.

The little boy kicked the side of the desk and marched past Theo, Tess, and Jaime, muttering words he shouldn't know under his breath.

"Told you he wouldn't win," said Jaime, after the kid was gone.

"Aaaaand I'm not going to win this game, either," Tess said.

"Let's get back there before someone else comes to play," Theo said. At the gaming table, the automaton seemed to be waiting for them. "He's staring at us. Don't you think he's staring at us?"

"Let him stare," said Tess. "We need to examine this whole setup in case the clue isn't about chess."

While Jaime and Tess crawled around, peeked under the desk to check out the inner workings, scrutinized the Turk's robe and turban, and inspected the chessboard and pieces, Theo thought about chess, and all the famous matches he'd read about the night before. Morphy vs. Allies. Emanuel Lasker vs. José Raúl Capablanca. Though there was some debate, many experts agreed that the greatest game of all time was Garry Kasparov vs. Veselin Topalov, known as "Kasparov's Immortal Game." Kasparov sacrificed two rooks and still chased Topalov's king all over the board.

Openings and defenses whipped through Theo's brain: the King's Gambit, the Closed Ruy Lopez, the Philidor Defense, the Poisoned Pawn. Where to start? Which to use? As if he or his sister or his friend could play like Kasparov. Even Kasparov lost to Deep Blue. Even if they knew the perfect moves to—

Oh.

OH.

"Tess," Theo said. "Where's that flyer that we found in the cornerstone?"

Tess pulled the folded paper from her back pocket and handed it to Theo. All around the edge of the flyer were chess notations. He'd thought they were random decorations when he first saw them, but . . .

"Look at these. On the edge."

Jaime read, "D5, c6, ra4. You think these are moves in a game?"

"Maybe moves we have to play," Tess said.

They all looked at the Turk. The Turk stared back, as if daring them to try.

Theo squared his shoulders. "Come on."

"Which one of us?" Jaime asked.

"All of us," Tess said firmly. "Right, Nine?"

"Mrrow," mrrowed Nine.

"To the Land of Kings!" Ono added.

They decided that Theo would start the game, so he sat in the chair opposite the Turk. He fed three dollars' worth of quarters into the slot on the side of the desk. As soon as the last quarter fell, the Turk pulled his arms off the table. The chessboard tipped again, this time staying open so that the chess pieces could be seen in the well below. The Turk held out a hand over the pieces.

An invitation.

"You want us to set up?" said Theo.

The automaton didn't answer, simply moved his hand to the side so they could reach in and pull out the pieces. They set up the board, black on one side, white on the other.

Jaime said, "Who plays which?"

In answer to Jaime's question, the board rotated so that the white pieces were in front of the Turk and the black ones were in front of Tess, Theo, and Jaime.

The Turk stared at Theo.

Theo stared at the Turk.

Theo said, "What are you waiting for?"

The Turk's king started the game on square e1, as it always did. In algebraic notation, each square of the chessboard could be identified by a unique combination of a letter and a number. The vertical columns of squares—files—were labeled *a* through *h* from White's left to right. The horizontal rows of squares—ranks— were numbered *1* to *8* starting from White's side of the board.

"Rank and file," Theo muttered.

Was there a hint of a smirk on the automaton's face when his arm lurched over the neat rows and columns to pincer up a knight, dangling it over the board, teasing, before moving the piece to f3?

"Is there an f3 on the flyer?" Theo asked.

Jaime and Tess consulted the flyer.

"No," Jaime said, his eyes scanning all around the sheet. "If we're right about these being moves in a game, maybe these are the ones we have to make in response."

"Agreed," said Tess.

Theo considered the board. "I'm thinking knight to f6."

Tess and Jaime pored over the flyer. Then Tess pointed. "Yes! Right here!"

Okay, so nothing exciting or unpredictable. Theo moved their knight to f6.

The Turk responded with a pawn to c4.

Theo got up and let Tess sit in the seat.

Tess said, "Knight to c6. Okay?"

"Yes, that's what we have here," said Jaime. "Do it."

"Okay." Tess moved the knight.

The Turk then moved his pawn to d4.

Jaime sat in Tess's place. "On the flyer, after knight to c6, do you have g6?"

"Yes!" said Tess.

Jaime moved their pawn to g6.

And the game continued like this, slowly, with some unconventional game play from the Turk, but nothing shocking until . . .

The Turk moved his bishop to g5.

"That's weird," said Tess. "Isn't that weird?"

"That's weird," said Theo. "Even weirder, I think we're supposed to offer a knight sacrifice. Knight to a4."

"What do you think, Jaime?"

"We've come this far," Jaime said.

Tess made the move.

The Turk responded with his queen to a3. Jaime sat down. Their knight took a pawn on c3. Back and forth they went, move after move. Nine snuffled all around their feet, tickling them with her whiskers, calming them. Even though the moves were on the flyer, even though the game seemed as if it were predetermined, Theo's heart thwacked against his rib cage as if he were in a real match with a real opponent, trying to beat a real clock.

Pawns and rooks and knights shifted all over the board, move twelve, thirteen, fourteen, fifteen, sixteen. Then the Turk moved his king to f1.

"What now?" said Tess, who was sitting at the board. "We have to protect the queen, right?"

"Uh, no," said Jaime. "I think we have to sacrifice her."

"That can't be right. Are we trying to lose?"

"Maybe," said Theo.

Both Jaime's and Tess's heads whipped up. "What?" they said, in unison.

"Remember what Grandpa Ben always said? That the process is the thing? Not the end result? Maybe that's what we're dealing with here. We're trying to solve the Cipher, not win a chess game."

But on their forty-first move, rook to c2, the Turk's head turned left and right, surveying the board for what seemed like hours. And then he lifted his hands in a signal of surrender.

"Wait . . . that's it?" said Tess. "We . . . won?"

"I think we did," said Jaime.

A mechanical clunk issued from the tabletop. The chessboard, instead of rotating the way it had before, stayed level, rising up on a pair of scissoring hinges. Underneath the board was a deeper well than had been revealed before, this one lined in black velvet. In this well were more chess pieces, very different from the black and white pieces they had played with. These were made of some silvery metal that glinted like Rollers in morning sunshine.

The Turk reached into the well and pulled out an elaborately decorated queen. He held the piece out to Tess. She hesitated only a moment before taking it. The Turk reached in again and pulled out a king. He swiveled in his seat and held this piece out to Jaime, who took it. The Turk reached into the well one last time for a knight. He held the knight out to Theo. Theo took the piece, strangely warm and tingly in his hand.

They were expecting the Turk to pull something else from inside the well—another flyer, a business card, a map, a photograph, something that would guide them to the next clue—so it was a shock when the Turk spoke. His tinny voice was so startling that the three of them nearly fell backward onto the dirty floor.

"Find. The. Other. Eliza. Who. Still. Haunts. The. Heights."

And then the chessboard flipped over, the pieces crashed into the well, and the whole tabletop slammed shut.

CHAPTER ELEVEN

Jaime

When Jaime was pushed off the ferry into the river, it happened so fast that he was underwater before he knew what had happened, before he even knew to swim. He drifted, still and stunned, as the fish teemed all around him, the whole world hushed, the whole world blue and blue and blue.

Until Ono buzzed against his chest, prodding him to kick till he reached the surface. He gasped for air, scratching at the pocket that held Ono, hoping that the water wouldn't hurt it, hoping the water wouldn't kill it.

"Ono!" Jaime said. "Ono!"

Ono beeped and buzzed in his hand. "Land of Kings," it said, and shuddered. Its arms and legs collapsed and rearranged themselves until Ono was not a bot but a boat, a little metal boat with a blocky Ono head sticking up out of the middle, two eyes that shone red in the late-afternoon light. Ono chugged around Jaime in a circle, his own personal homing beacon.

"I guess you're okay," said Jaime. And he was okay, too—well, if you didn't count the whole being-shoved-into-the-river part.

"Look out!" someone yelled.

Jaime turned to see a sailboat banking sharply away from him.

A man in the boat screamed, "What are you doing in the water, kid?"

"That's a good question," Jaime said to no one. The sailboat didn't stop to help, however. It kept tacking away as if Jaime were nothing but a nuisance.

Jaime turned again to see the ferry in the distance. It had slowed some, and seemed to be trying to turn around, but that could take a while. He told himself to relax as best he could, to remember the swimming lessons he'd had as a kid, his dad teaching him how to tread water by gently cycling his legs and keeping his arms spread out on the surface, sweeping back and forth. But his clothes were sodden and heavy, and it wasn't as easy as it had been in a bathing suit. And there were other boats in the river, so many boats. Ono was doing his best, buzzing and blinking so that Jaime was easy to spot, but if help was coming, it was taking its sweet time, and Jaime didn't know how long he could last out here before he got hit. Someone on the ferry must have called—

Called! His phone!

Jaime dug around in his side pocket. The phone was still there.

"You better be waterproof like the salesman said you were," Jaime told it. He kicked his legs harder so he could punch in 911.

"What's your emergency?" said a staticky voice on the other end of the line.

"I was pushed off the ferry between Manhattan and Hoboken," Jaime said.

"Where are you now, sir?"

"I'm in the river!"

"Excuse me?"

"I'm in the river! Treading water! And if someone doesn't get here soon, I'm going to have to take off all my clothes before they drag me to the bottom!"

"Do you have a life jacket?"

"No!"

"Do you know who pushed you?"

"No!"

"Okay, I'm going to get some people out to you right now. Can you tell me about how long you were on the boat before you fell in?"

"I don't know . . . about halfway to Hoboken?"

"Stay on the line with me. Let me know when you see the police coming."

Jaime was getting more and more tired. "Can you tell them to hurry? I like swimming, but not this much." A thought came to him, something that Tess said all the time. "What if there are sharks?"

"There aren't sharks," said the voice on the phone.

"How do you know?"

"Don't worry about sharks."

"How can I not worry about sharks if there are sharks?" said Jaime.

"Even if there were sharks, sharks don't like the taste of people."

"Now I'm thinking about the taste of people," Jaime said.

"Keep an eye out for boats," said the voice.

"Land of Kings! Land of Kings!" Ono buzzed.

A rescue boat powered toward Jaime. "They're here!" Jaime shouted into the phone, and hung up.

When the boat got near, someone tossed an orange life jacket at Jaime. He tugged the jacket over his shoulders as the boat lurched and bobbed its way over to him. By the time a ladder was lowered over the side of the boat and hands were reaching down for him, Jaime was more tired than he'd ever been in his life. Still, he made sure to scoop Ono out of the water before allowing himself to be hauled over the side.

He lay gasping on the deck of the boat as rescue workers swarmed him. Did anything hurt? Did he think anything was broken? Was he having trouble breathing? What happened? Was he sure he had been pushed? Could he have simply slipped? Could it have been an accident? Did he have a history of fainting and falling off ferries?

Jaime answered their questions as well as he could, Ono resting on his chest. At some point, Ono had transformed back into its robot shape, but its little form still hummed with heat and energy, as if it were trying to keep Jaime warm all by itself.

And that was what holding this chess piece felt like, as if he weren't holding a king but a tiny thrumming engine. He half expected it to grow legs and arms or maybe wings; he half expected it to start talking. But the king's face was as inscrutable as the Turk's, keeping its secrets to itself.

Tess yanked him out of his reverie. "I don't know

about you guys, but I'm starving."

Theo said, "I could use some ice cream. And pizza. Not necessarily in that order."

"Yeah," said Jaime. He tucked the chess piece into his other front pocket while Ono chanted, "Kings, kings, kings," like a mantra.

Lunch was pizza and then ice cream, followed by freshly made funnel cake so hot it burned the roof of Jaime's mouth. But he didn't care. It was delicious.

"So," said Tess as they sat down on a bench to finish their funnel cakes. "What do you guys think of the riddle?"

The riddle! He'd almost forgotten what the Turk had said.

"'Find the other Eliza who still haunts the heights,'" said Theo.

"The other Eliza," Tess said thoughtfully, licking sugar from her fingers.

Jaime stuffed the last bit of funnel cake into his mouth and pulled out his sketchbook so that he could write down the clue. He chewed, swallowed, said, "Since Eliza Hamilton was already a clue, I'm guessing it's a different Eliza."

"And the heights," said Tess. "Which kind of heights? Like, high heights, or heights as in a neighborhood positioned on a hill?"

"Hmmm," said Theo. He consulted his phone. "If I search 'heights' and 'Eliza,' I still get Eliza Hamilton. She built a school in Washington Heights. And a library in Inwood."

"Has to be someone else. Maybe somewhere else," Tess said. She tore off a small piece of funnel cake. She was about to eat it when she saw Jaime watching. "Did you finish yours?"

He was embarrassed to say yes, though he couldn't imagine why. Plus, he was supposed to be mad at her. Mad at them both. But it was hard to be mad while sitting on the boardwalk in Coney Island, the taste of a funnel cake on your tongue.

"Here," said Tess, offering him a piece.

He should refuse out of principle, he thought. He should refuse so that she was reminded that she was a liar and a thief and he was Not Happy about that. But he took the piece of cake, because, well, cake. And because he was *not* Not Happy. He had the same satisfied feeling that he always had when they figured out a clue. Plus, the king thrumming in his pocket felt magical somehow. A whole different kind of clue.

"Aha!" said Theo, still scrolling through his phone. "I might have found it. Her, I mean. Listen to this: 'In 1921, at the oldest house in Manhattan, the Daughters of the American Revolution held an auction—an auction with a specific purpose in mind. They wanted to scrub the historic house of any evidence that Eliza Bowen Jumel had ever lived there, though she spent fifty-five years of her life within its walls. Bags full of Eliza's letters, allegedly about such people as Benedict Arnold, Thomas Jefferson, Aaron Burr, even Napoleon Bonaparte—were sold for a pittance.'"

"Eliza Bowen Jumel," said Tess. "I've never heard of her."

"Me neither," Theo said. "But she was married to Aaron Burr."

"Wait, *the* Aaron Burr? The shot—Alexander Hamilton Aaron Burr?" Jaime said.

"That's the one," Theo said. "When they got divorced, only three years after they were married, she hired Alexander Hamilton's son to be her lawyer."

Jaime laughed. "Petty. I like it."

"Her house is called the Morris-Jumel Mansion, so whatever the Daughters of the American Revolution did to make people forget Eliza Jumel didn't work. And it's still standing in Washington Heights," Theo said.

"I guess I know where we're going tomorrow," said Jaime.

Tess glanced at him sharply, then looked away.

"What?" Jaime said.

"Nothing," she said. "Morris-Jumel Mansion it is." Then she smiled. "So who wants to ride the roller coaster with me?"

A Cyclone, Electro Spin, Sling Shot, and two Underway trains later, they parted ways, promising to meet the next day at the bike rental kiosk in Central Park by Columbus Circle. Instead of walking to the ferry—Jaime wasn't going to risk the ferry again for a while—he took the Underway downtown. The Guildman in the box, a short, hard-faced man with close-cropped hair and brown skin, took no particular notice of him. And neither did the Guildman on the PATH train that took Jaime to New Jersey. Just the day before, he had been treading water in the river above him, and now he was traveling through a tunnel below it. He felt as if he'd lived on two entirely different planets in twenty-four hours.

He put his hand over the pocket with the chess piece inside it, resisting the urge to take it out and examine it in front of everyone. It had cooled somewhat, but Jaime still felt a kind of itch in his fingers as he touched it, the tiniest vibrations, like when a ladybug crawls over your skin and you feel the brush of its minuscule feet. The question rose unbidden: Why had the Turk given him the king? And the real question came after it: If the Biedermanns were the Morningstarrs, why had *they* given him the king? What was he supposed to make of this? Or was he not supposed to make anything of it? Was it entirely random? But nothing the twins did—either set of twins, Biedermanns or Morningstarrs—was random, not really. Even Tess, who Theo claimed was so erratic and chaotic and nervous, was logical about the things she did. It was just a Tess kind of logic.

And Tess said that she and Theo weren't the Morningstarrs.

He wanted to believe her. But his friends being the Morningstarrs explained so much—too much. Like the chess game they had just played, which was less a game and more like plugging a code into a machine. A code that Tess and Theo had left for themselves. But how? And why? And why was Jaime a part of it now, if he hadn't been a part of it two hundred years ago?

Unless he had.

He ran his hand over his hair, still a little fuzzy from his dunk in the river, though he'd washed and conditioned his 'locs and retwisted the roots. What if Tess and Theo were the Morningstarrs, but they didn't know it and couldn't believe it? That would mean they would have to find a way to travel back in time. And despite how many comic books he'd read, and how often time travel happened in those comic books, nobody could travel back in time.

A little voice in the back of his head said, *Not yet, anyway.*

He shifted in his seat. The woman next to him, mom aged and redheaded and white, glanced at him and then clutched her computer bag tighter.

Ono popped out of his pocket. "Oh no," it said disapprovingly.

The woman got up and grabbed one of the poles instead, her eyes cutting to Jaime every few seconds.

Warmth flooded his face as he tried to ignore this woman and the weird way she was looking at him, the weird way she was acting. Even if he had a time machine or a wormhole or a worm machine, what would make a person *want* to travel back in time? Jaime had had a good life, but there were still people, like this creepy carrot hanging on to the pole, who looked at him as if he were about to club them and steal their shoes. And that was *now*. Today. What would happen to him if he were to go back even twenty years? Fifty? One hundred? What would happen to him if he traveled all the way back to Civil War times? To the Revolutionary War era?

He knew what would happen. The same thing that had happened to so many people who looked like him back then.

Nothing could make him go back.

Nothing.

The train stopped and the redheaded woman shot out the door, running off to wherever creepy carrots lived. Ono made a buzzing noise that sounded as if it were blowing a raspberry.

Jaime patted Ono. "Thanks, dude."

"Land of Kings," Ono said.

Jaime took the steps two at a time and burst into the sunlight. Even though the bros of Broboken bobbed all around him, he had to admit that the place was growing on him. A little. The view of the river was pretty, at least. And his father was here. And he was staying. For good. That was something that Jaime had never dared hope for, and it had happened.

So Jaime was in a good mood when he opened the door to his apartment, a good mood when he stepped inside.

Which was when he saw Mima and his dad sitting at the kitchen table with two big white men he'd never seen before, men wearing suits.

"Jaime," said his dad. "These men are here to ask you about the ferry."

One of the men stood. "I'm Detective Cherry and that's Detective Murphy." He held out a meaty hand for Jaime to shake. "How are you feeling today?"

Even though Jaime hadn't done anything wrong—not today, anyway—a flutter of nerves erupted in his gut. "I'm feeling fine, thanks."

"Good, good," said Detective Cherry. "That's good."

Jaime's dad got up and motioned for Jaime to sit in his seat. Detective Cherry sat down next to him.

Detective Cherry said, "Listen, Jaime. I know you've been asked this before, but I need to ask you again. Do you remember what happened on the ferry?"

Jaime told the detectives what he'd told the rescue workers and the cops who had interviewed him right afterward: that he had been leaning against the rail, looking out onto the water, when someone behind him shouted, "Look out!" and shoved him over the side. He didn't see anyone, and he didn't know why anyone would push him.

"Hmmm," said Detective Murphy, scratching notes.

Jaime wanted to say, "Hmmm? What does 'hmmm' mean?" But he said nothing.

Detective Cherry said, "Listen, Jaime. We interviewed a bunch of people on the ferry, and we found some witnesses. One of the witnesses got photos of the person who pushed you. I'm going to show you some pictures, and I want you to tell me if any of these people look familiar, okay?"

The butterflies in his guts multiplied. "Okay."

The detective opened a manila folder and spread six pictures on the table in front of Jaime: six black women, all of them with fine features and medium-brown skin.

One glance at the pictures and he saw her among them. He would have known her anywhere, the way you would know a person if you'd drawn them over and over and over again, which he had.

"Do you recognize any of these women?" Detective Cherry asked.

"Take your time," said Detective Murphy.

His father's hands cupped his shoulders as they all waited for Jaime's answer. Jaime examined each picture slowly, carefully. Then he looked up, making his face as calm and inscrutable as the Turk's, as the face of the king in his pocket.

"I'm sorry," he said. "I've never seen any of these people before."

CHAPTER TWELVE
Karl

A few miles away from Jaime's apartment, in a cramped cage at a veterinary hospital, Karl stirred. He stretched one back leg, then the other. He scratched at his belly, which was strangely itchy, and was annoyed to find his back paws bandaged.

"Look! I think he's waking up!" a voice said.

Karl did not recognize the voice, though he was far too exhausted to be frightened of it. Other voices joined in a chorus, chattering about hydration levels and temperature and heart rate and so on, but he was also too exhausted to register such statistics, even his own.

"Karl! Hey, buddy! Hey, Mr. Floof!"

Buddy. Mr. Floof. No one called Karl such undignified things. "Buddy" and "Mr. Floof" were the kind of names moody teenagers gave to pet boa constrictors or mole rats when they believed themselves to be the agents of irony.

"Karl! You've got some people really worried!"

With both paws, Karl covered his masked eyes and rolled over. There were so many things he wanted to say, *Oh, do shut up!* being the most pressing, followed by, *Surely you must have other duties besides disturbing the rest of convalescing patients?* and then, *If you would like to make yourselves useful, you will bring me a bowl full of Cheez Doodles so that I may snack upon waking.*

But of course he could say none of this. Despite all the racket, Karl kept his eyes closed, not terribly interested in seeing the world outside the cage he was in, or the seriously rude people who kept interrupting his nap. Karl hadn't had such a long and restful sleep in weeks, and he deserved a small snatch of peace and quiet, did he not? He had been through an Ordeal, with a capital O, the likes of which would make the bestseller list, if only he were able to type.

Karl tried to relax, to ease himself back into the dream he'd been having, the lovely dream in which the little girl with pigtails like antennae—what was her name? Something adorable and sweet, but also snappy— was riding her tricycle with Karl in the basket. They traveled through the halls of an old building while the little girl pointed out all the areas of interest to him. "Look, Karl," she would say, pointing to a piece of molding or a bit of tile, "that is a SIGNIFICANT ARTIFACT. And that is also a SIGNIFICANT ARTIFACT." Sometimes, when they passed by one person or another, she would declare that person to be NEFARIOUS and worthy of serious inquiry. According to this adorable and sweet and snappy little girl, many people and many things were worthy of serious inquiry.

Well, she was correct about that.

Karl's mind searched for respite, but he couldn't bring his restless thoughts to heel. His brain kept flashing on sights and sounds and smells and sensations that made his limbs twitch all the more. The lab. The doctor who resembled nothing so much as a newt. The injections and the surgeries designed to do . . . what? Karl had no earthly idea.

When he was first captured and brought to the lab, though his situation had clearly been dire—his cage small and uncomfortable, his kibble dry and entirely unappetizing—he had been too frightened to make a peep of protest. Back then, the doctor wasn't as scary as Karl's animal companions. If you could call them companions, which Karl would not. He and the other animals were merely test subjects, playthings for the doctor with the exophthalmic eyes. Karl would never forget the large and fuzzy-legged thing that was some horrifying cross between a wolf and a . . . spider? He would be haunted forever by the way it laughed before it launched itself at the bars of its cage, mandibles gnashing: *Heh, heh, HEH!* And then there was the blue monkey with the voice box of a bird that would belt out a song called "Last Train to Clarksville" when it wasn't swearing so much that Karl couldn't help but be astonished by both its vehemence and its creativity. Mice with prehensile tails, all hanging from the tops of their cages like tiny, furry piñatas. Gators that weren't quite gators and rabbits that weren't quite rabbits, dogs and cats and foxes and even smiling quokkas, rendered into mismatched monsters with too many or two few of everything, so scared or enraged by what had happened to them that they could barely function.

Except Octavius. He was the only one besides Karl who had a name instead of a number, given to him by lab assistants who seemed to think it was hilarious. Instead of languishing in his tank the way so many of the others did, Octavius wouldn't stay still for injections, he wouldn't perform tricks, he wouldn't stop throwing anything that was put into his tank right out of it—food, coral, other fish. Octavius was a marvel of rebellion. While the rest of the animals cowered whenever the doctor came near, Octavius would reach up and smack that horrid man right across the face with a tentacle. A thing of beauty, it was—a rebuke, a refusal, and a challenge all at once. It was something they all wished they could do, stay strong in the face of such mistreatment and fear. But even the spider-wolf—or wolf-spider, or whatever it was—didn't have that kind of courage. Only Octavius stood, er, swam, strong. Karl liked to think that he and Octavius had a bond of sorts, a friendship. When the blue monkey sang his song too many times in a row, when one of the many-legged, many-toothed things wouldn't stop screeching, Karl would put his tiny hand up against the glass, and Octavius would press a tentacle likewise, as if to say, *Greetings, friend! I, too, find this terribly annoying and quite stressful. We both deserve better.*

And then one night, after a particularly awful procedure that Karl wished he could forget, he blearily woke to see Octavius's many tentacles working at the mesh that covered his cage. Karl didn't understand what Octavius was doing until a screw fell to the floor, and then another, and another. It took Octavius nearly thirty minutes to get the last three screws, but he managed to do it. (The doctor would regret giving Octavius three eyes and fourteen tentacles.)

After all the screws had fallen to the floor, Octavius lifted the mesh top of the tank and then climbed out. Flesh that had been mottled and gray against the pebbles at the bottom of his tank turned as beige as the tile when he hit the floor. His third eye was larger than his other two, and rose up on a short stalk from his mantle like a periscope. He slithered along the floor, keeping tight to the sides of the room, that periscope eye fixed on the camera mounted in the corner, which swept lazily from one direction to the other. As soon as the camera was pointed away from him, Octavius slithered forward. When the camera swept back, Octavius froze, his skin blending in with whatever was behind him.

So fixated was Octavius on that camera that he didn't see the wolf-spider/spider-wolf slide the tip of one leg—a leg with a curving scythe of a claw—through the bars of its cage, ready to slice Octavius into sushi. Without thinking, Karl grabbed his food bowl and banged it against the bars of his cage, chittering as loudly as he could, a warning. But he should have known it would warn others. An alarm blared. All the animals, all the monsters chattered and screeched. Octavius shrank away from the spider-wolf/wolf-spider, flattening himself against the floor. The door opened and a shaft of light cut through the darkness, guards silhouetted in the doorway.

"Who's there? What's going on?" one of them barked stupidly, ridiculously, if he wanted to hear an answer that made any sort of sense.

The animals replied by screeching louder, copying Karl and banging their food bowls against the bars of their cages. Karl banged the loudest to keep the guards' eyes off Octavius, who was working at the lock on the wolf-spider/spider-wolf's cage. Instead of trying to slice Octavius, the wolf-spider/spider-wolf burst from its prison, launching itself at the guards, who screamed and fell into a pile in the hallway. Octavius slithered around the room, using all fourteen tentacles to unlock cages and lift the mesh off the tops of tanks. The creatures lurched and shambled and flapped and flew around the room. Octavius finally reached Karl's cage and made quick work of the lock. A tentacle gently curled around Karl's middle, lifting him up and out of the cage and depositing him on the floor.

Thank you, dear Octavius, Karl chittered, *brave and noble friend.*

Octavius gave him one last squeeze and then nudged him, as if to tell him to get moving. Karl didn't need any more prodding. He waddled as fast as he could, pausing only to grab a key card off one of the dazed and mauled guards. With key card clenched firmly in his teeth, Karl ran for the door at the end of the hallway. He dragged himself up onto the chair next to the door and slapped the key card against the reader.

And the door swung open.

So shocked was Karl that he froze for a few seconds, before leaping into the waiting arms of the darkness.

Karl didn't know how many nights he'd traveled, only that he'd traveled far, so very far. He spent his days hiding in parks and in garbage cans, dodging determined Rollers and equally determined dogs, and his nights foraging for the scraps of food that would keep him going. *Hoboken, Hoboken, Hoboken* rang in his brain, the spell that would get him home to his family. He walked until the pads of his paws were raw and bloody, until the flesh began to melt off his poor starving bones. He was a mere ghost of himself when he stowed away on a container ship bound for New Jersey, curled in the darkest corner he could find, so ruined that even the city rats, those hardened criminals, left him alone.

He crawled out of the ship onto the docks, making his lonely way up Sinatra Drive. He passed places called Crash Fitness and Puzzle Up Escape Room and

Hungry Wolf Tavern, all of which made him shiver. But he kept going. He had only his ears and his nose to rely on now. To comfort himself, he hummed "Last Train to Clarksville." When he finally reached the building and smelled its familiar scent, new carpet and chlorine and sweat and something else, something that smelled like people he knew, people he loved and who loved him, he shadowed a couple as they lurched through the doorway, silly with wine or with each other. The guard at the desk barely looked in their direction as he buzzed them in, and the couple was far too silly to notice the dazed raccoon who joined them in the elevator, and collapsed there, unconscious to the world.

"Come on, come on, little fella," said a voice. "Wakey, wakey."

Karl woke again with a start. He was not in an elevator, he was at the vet's, and the people were murmuring at him as if he were a kit instead of a full-grown adult. It was extremely vexing. He rolled over and opened his eyes. Many pairs of human eyes gazed back.

Shhhh! he chittered at them.

"He's so cute!" said a mouth.

Stuff and nonsense!

"I think he's talking to us," said another mouth.

Bring me Cheez Doodles! Quick, man! For I am famished after my long journey!

"Excuse me, coming through, excuse me!" another voice piped up, a small voice, a kit's voice.

"Miss, you're not supposed to be back here."

"The doctor said it was okay. She needs to see him," a woman said.

The many pairs of eyes and mouths moved away and were replaced by the face of a small girl, brown eyed and bronze skinned, a small girl wearing a black mask. For him? For him!

The adorable girl, the sweet and snappy one. Oh, how his heart filled. But her name, what was her name?

"Karl!" she said, stripping off her mask. Her eyes were filled with tears. "Karl, I missed you!"

He wanted to tell her about his journey, he wanted to tell her how much he'd missed her as well, he wanted to tell her how grateful he was even to be in this cage, watched over by well-meaning buffoons, he wanted to tell her that he had just remembered her name, and it was the most perfect name for the most perfect little kit.

He stood on all fours and chittered at her, at them all.

"What's he doing?" said another voice, the mother of the little girl, almost as lovely as her daughter.

He chittered again.

"What is it, Karl? Do you want something?"

He wanted what was on the desk behind them. He grasped the bars of his cage and shook them.

"He wants to get out. We need to let him out," said the little girl.

"I don't think—" began one of the vet techs, but this little girl wouldn't wait for his permission—this little kit was unstoppable. She yanked open the cage, reached in, and gathered him up.

"You're so skinny!" she said, nose in his fur. "I'll fatten you up again. I promise. You will be my best chonky boy."

He reveled in this embrace for a few precious moments. Then he wriggled in her arms until she put him down on the floor. He waddled over to the desk and climbed onto its top.

"What the heck is he doing?" someone said.

Karl grabbed a pad and pen and started to write.

CHAPTER THIRTEEN

Tess

Tess got home from Coney Island still tasting funnel cake, still thinking about the chess pieces the Turk had given them.

Theo had gotten a knight, a piece that moves in a distinctive "L" shape—two squares horizontally and one square vertically, or vice versa—and can't be blocked. It simply jumps to new locations.

Jaime had gotten the king, a piece that moves exactly one square in any direction but has one special move it can make only once a game—castling.

And Tess's piece, the queen, can move any number of squares and in any direction.

What were they supposed to do with the pieces? Did it mean there was another chess game in their future? Was there some significance to the pieces they got?

"Tess, you've hardly touched your chick'n. Is there something wrong?" her father asked.

"Oh no! It's great, Dad, thanks." She forked up a big bite of grilled chick'n, popped it in her mouth, and chewed. "Ummm," she said. "It's good."

"I'm glad," her father said. "But please don't talk with food in your mouth."

"You're such a pig, Tess," Theo said.

"Aboabink aboabink," she said. She slipped a piece of chick'n to Nine, who gulped it back. "Where's Mom?"

"Where do you think?" her dad said.

"Work," said Tess.

"Wabork," said Theo.

"Wabork schmabork," said their father, who seemed to think this was hilarious. Dads were so proud of their dad jokes.

"Where's Aunt Esther?" Theo asked.

"That I do not know," said their father. "She does so many things that I can't keep up with her."

"Oh, she's probably racing in the Iditarod," Tess said.

"Kayaking down the Amazon," Theo said.

"Climbing Mount Everest."

"Rocketing into space."

"All of that sounds ridiculous and yet entirely

plausible when it comes to your aunt," said their dad, getting up to scrape the remains of his dinner into Nine's dish. "We'll have to ask her when she gets home."

"She won't tell us," said Theo. "She never explains."

Their father piled dishes in the sink and squirted everything with soap. "Some people like to be mysterious. Like you two."

"What?" Tess and Theo said at the same time. "Us?"

"Yes, you two. You've spent the whole summer either out all day with Jaime or holed up in your room doing who knows what. Care to share?"

Tess didn't look at Theo, Theo didn't look at Tess. They both studied their dinner plates with intense concentration. Their father laughed.

"See? Mysterious."

"We're not doing anything," Tess said.

"Sure, sure," said their dad.

"We're not!" Theo insisted.

"In that case," said their dad, "maybe you two want to sit with your dear old dad and watch a movie."

Tess was about to say no, but their dad looked so hopeful that she couldn't. So that's how they found themselves sitting in front of the TV after dinner instead of researching Eliza Jumel and the Morris-Jumel Mansion. Their dad found a movie on one of the streaming channels and they settled in to watch *The Lost Girl*, which was about another set of twins, girls, who were separated into different classrooms at school by their parents, who thought the girls would be better off developing their own interests instead of relying on each other, something Tess thought was ridiculous.

"I mean," she said, "they obviously have their own interests already. And what's wrong with working together and relying on each other? Why are adults so dopey?"

"Alas, another mystery," said her dad.

The story was just starting to heat up—a creepy teacher who might be an ogre! Things disappearing all over Minneapolis! Weird dolls! Weirder crows!—when their mother came through the door.

"Hey, hon," said their dad, pausing the movie. "Long day?"

"The longest," said their mom. "You wouldn't believe half the stuff that's going on. Or maybe you would."

"What's going on?" said Tess.

"I shouldn't talk about it," said their mom, raking a hand through overlong hair in need of a trim. "But one thing I can tell you is that I heard there's a witness in Jaime's case."

"Someone saw who pushed him?" Tess said. "Really?"

"Yeah, got a picture and everything," said their mom. "It's probably on the news right now."

The twins' dad switched over to a news app, and sure enough, the hosts were talking about a woman who had allegedly pushed a young boy off a ferry boat traveling from Manhattan to Hoboken.

"Anyone who knows the woman in this photo or has any information should contact the police immediately."

On the screen, a woman in a silvery-gray coat glanced at the camera. Tess gasped.

"What?" said their mom. "Do you recognize her?"

"Noooo," said Tess, her voice too high, too tight. "She's just . . . very pretty."

"Pretty people can be criminals, too," said their mother. "It has nothing to do with how you look."

"I know, it's just . . ." Tess had another thought. "Did Jaime identify her?"

"No. He says he never saw her. But we've got people out looking for her. And now that her picture is on the news, it will be hard for her to hide for long."

Theo started to laugh and then covered it with a cough.

"That sounds nasty, Theo. Do you have allergies again?" said their dad. "I'll get you a pill."

"No, Dad, I'm fine," Theo said, but their dad ran upstairs to the bathroom anyway.

"I'm surprised they haven't engineered allergies right out of us," their mom said absently, taking off her rumpled suit jacket.

"Isn't genetic engineering illegal?" Tess said.

"I was kidding, Tess."

"Besides, if they engineered allergies right out of us," Theo said, "the drug companies would go out of business. I bet that would upset some very powerful people."

"Wow, you two are fun," said their mom.

"What's more fun than discussing the ramifications of capitalism?" said Theo.

"Was that a joke?" said their mom.

"What?"

Their dad came down the stairs with a pill. "Here you go!"

As Theo took his allergy pill and their dad went to the kitchen to warm up their mom's dinner, Tess tried to figure out what she thought about the woman on the screen. There were several possibilities:

1) It was Ava herself, she was still angry, and she had decided to punish them all by pushing

them off boats. (Note to self: No more boat rides.)

2) It wasn't Ava at all—it was a person impersonating Ava. (Note: That would mean that someone else knew that Ava was still kicking—literally and figuratively—after more than a hundred fifty years.)

3) It was Ava, but she had another reason to push Jaime into the water, something not immediately obvious in the photograph. (Note: Further study of the photograph necessary.)

4) It was a complete coincidence and had no meaning whatsoever. (Note: Too adorable?)

Way, way too adorable, Tess thought. So either it was Ava or someone who looked like Ava. But why would Ava push Jaime off a boat . . . unless she was trying to save him from something worse? And what was worse than being tossed into the river? What if there were sharks in the river? What if there were things *worse* than sharks in the river?

Jaime was fine, though. And he had come with them to Coney Island. And he had brought his sketchbook again, the way he always had. Despite her concern and confusion over seeing Ava/Ava's impersonator on the news, Tess smiled to herself, happy that the three of them would be going uptown together, looking for another clue.

"What are you smiling about, Tess?" said her mom, who had come back into the living room with her dinner.

"Oh, just this awesome movie we were watching."

"Yeah? What's it about?"

Tess and Theo talked to their parents about the movie: about twins, about school, about nature, and about magic. And then they watched the end of the movie together. When Tess lay down to sleep, she realized that the few hours she'd spent with her parents that night were the longest time in months she'd gone without worrying about something or someone, about forces she couldn't control. She fell asleep with Nine curled up on the bed beside her, purring softly in her ear.

The next morning, Tess and Theo had the house to themselves. Their parents were both at work, and Aunt Esther was off Aunt Esthering. The twins talked about the woman on the TV, whether she was Ava Oneal (maybe?) or wasn't Ava Oneal (maybe?), whether they had to be more careful (probably?) and/or avoid boats (definitely). And then they researched the Morris-Jumel

Mansion and Eliza Jumel while Lance happily whipped up some pancakes for breakfast. They were talking about Eliza Jumel, about how she was born in poverty, lost her parents and brother, and then moved to New York City, changed her name, and became an actress. She married Stephen Jumel, a rich French Haitian businessman, and became an art collector.

"But New York society never quite accepted her," Tess read, "even though she managed the business affairs of her family with great skill. Well, that's not shocking."

"Because New York society was made up of snots?"

"Because New York society was made up of snots who were suspicious of smart and accomplished women."

"That seems counterproductive," said Theo.

Tess squinted at him to see if he was being sarcastic, but he seemed as serious as always. Huh. Theo wasn't the type of boy who made a lot of comments about girls being weak or dumb or useless the way some boys at school did, but that didn't mean he hadn't said ignorant things in the past. Maybe he'd grown up some. For a brother, he was okay.

Maybe she had grown up some, too.

Lance was sliding another stack of pancakes onto the platter in the middle of the kitchen table when the doorbell rang.

"Is Jaime meeting us here?" Tess asked.

"I don't think so," said Theo. "But if he is, we have plenty of pancakes."

"I'll go see," said Tess. She went to the door and looked through the peephole. A beefy middle-aged man with dusty, mushroomish skin and wig-stiff light brown hair stood at the door, smiling.

Tess opened the door. "Yes?"

"Oh hello there!" the man said. "How are you today?"

"Uh, fine," Tess said. "Can I help you?"

"I'm with Citizens for a Greater New York City. Would I be able to speak to your parents?"

"Sorry, they're not"—she remembered just in time never to tell strangers that they were home alone—"available right now."

"That's too bad," the man said. His smile was big and bright but didn't seem to reach his eyes, eyes that weren't focused on Tess but rather on the room behind Tess, as if he were trying to get a look into the house. She wanted to suggest that he stay outside, because clearly he needed the vitamin D.

He said, "Is there a good time for me to visit?"

"A good time?"

"Yes, a time when your parents will be home."

"I didn't say they weren't home," Tess said. "They're

home. They're just not—"

"—available," the man finished, still smiling. Tess didn't care for the finishing *or* the smiling.

Nine padded up behind Tess and stuck her big whiskered face between Tess and the screen door. She took one look at the man and growled. The man growled back.

"Okay!" said Tess. "Well, thanks for stopping by."

"Would you mind giving your parents this information sheet? We're having a meeting tomorrow night and we're hoping to get as many people in the community to come as we can." He held up a sheet of paper, on which the words *Citizens for a Better New York City* were emblazoned. "I'm sure they'll want to come."

Tess said, "How do you want to make it better?"

His posh diction slipped a bit. He said, "Huh?"

"You said you wanted to make New York City better. How do you want to do that?"

"That is an excellent question! We want to restore commonsense values and, at the same time, move the city forward."

Nine growled louder. Tess agreed. "What does that mean?"

"I'd be happy to discuss it with your parents," said the man. Again he peered behind Tess. Tess returned the favor by peering behind the man. Outside, leaning against a solar lamppost, was another man, holding the same sort of leaflets that this one was holding. He also had stiff, sprayed hair combed straight back, though his was dark. His mirrored sunglasses were aimed right at them.

It was the odd fellow who had followed them from Odd Fellows Hall.

"I hear my mom calling me," Tess said. "Leave your stuff in the mailbox." She began to shut the door.

The man said, "Your parents will want to come to our meeting. Our featured speaker is Darnell Slant. You might have heard of him."

It seemed to Tess that the man's smile and the man's eyes—his whole entire face—went glinty and hard with amused malice as he spoke. The man tucked the information sheet into the box next to the door.

"Mr. Slant is not someone you can ignore. He's going to be mayor, you know. And after that, senator. Or governor. Maybe even president. A man like that has all sorts of resources. All sorts of . . . friends. And if you make an enemy of him . . . well, I don't even want to say. Of course you would never do that, would you? A smart girl like you? Especially when you think what a man like that, a powerful man, the most powerful man in the country, could do to your whole family." He leaned in closer. "A man like that could make a phone call, one phone call, and everyone you love could just . . . disappear forever. A puzzle you would never be able to solve."

Tess slammed the door shut, locked it, breathing hard. She thought she heard the man laugh, a scratchy, creaky laugh, full of cobwebs and dirt, the kind of laugh that creepy dolls in scary movies make.

Through the door, the man's voice buzzed like a wasp. "I suggest you and your parents come to our meeting."

Tess backed away as if the man could explode the door with the power of his mind, and who was to say he couldn't?

"Who were you talking to?" Theo asked when Tess backed into the kitchen.

"A mushroom man with snap-on hair like a Lego."

"Wait, was he a mushroom man or a Lego?"

"Both? He wants us to come to a Citizens for a Better New York City meeting."

"Us? Why?

"I think Slant knows we're onto something."

"The Lego knows Slant?"

"And I think Slant will try to hurt us, all of us, if we don't stop."

CHAPTER FOURTEEN
Theo

Theo went quiet, trying to make sense of what Tess had just told him.

He gave up.

"Tess, what are you talking about?"

So Tess went over everything the man had said, from asking about their parents to the Citizens for a Better New York City meeting to the weird comments about Slant and about disappearing everyone they love. Theo stuck his hands in his hair. Then he pulled his hands from his hair and marched to the front window. He hooked a finger around the bottom edge of the curtain and peeked outside. Across the street, two large, blocky men stood leaning against the streetlights. And Tess wasn't wrong: Their hard and shiny hair did look as if they had snapped it on that morning. And she wasn't wrong that one of them was the same creep who had followed them just a few days ago.

"Are they still there?" Tess asked.

"Two Lego men. Yeah."

"Great. What do we do now?"

"We don't panic," said Theo.

"I'm not panicking," said Tess, though it was obvious that she was running catastrophic scenarios through her head.

"It's going to be fine," said Theo.

"I don't want to end up on a cactus farm," Tess said. Nine rubbed Tess's knees.

Theo said, "I'm not going to ask why you think we'd end up on a cactus farm."

Tess practiced her deep breathing, then said. "We should check the back window. See if there are more of them in the yard."

Together with Nine, they went to the back of the house and peered through the curtains.

"I don't see anyone," said Theo.

"They could be hiding in the bushes," Tess said.

"We're allowed to walk in our own backyard. And if there's anyone back there, Nine will warn us. And then we call Mom. Maybe we should call her anyway."

"And tell her what? That a Lego man gave us a flyer?"

"She'll believe us."

"She'll say I'm having a spell," said Tess, with only a hint of bitterness. Theo couldn't blame their mom for thinking that Tess was worrying too much over too little, but he also understood that sometimes a person needed someone to listen. And besides, there were real dudes hanging out in front of their house, watching them. She wasn't conjuring that up.

"Those guys are creepy," Theo said, "but they're no match for Nine, right, Nine?"

"Mrrow," Nine agreed.

Tess scratched Nine, and Nine rose up on her hind legs to press her nose against Tess's, her version of a kiss.

"Okay," said Tess. "I don't want to let these guys stop us. If we can't go out the front, we'll sneak out the back, even if we have to climb under the fence through the dirt."

"Uh . . . maybe we can climb *over* the fence and skip the dirt part."

"Remember Aunt Esther complaining that there was a board loose in the back fence and that the neighbors wouldn't repair it? And their fer-rabbit kept getting in and eating her begonias? I bet they haven't fixed it yet. Maybe we can get out that way."

They helped Lance clean up the breakfast dishes and then ventured out into the yard. It was a small city yard with an old wooden fence around it, but there were still plenty of places to hide if you wanted to. Aunt Esther was fond of plants, and the perimeter of the yard was riotous with flowers and vines and bushes—perfect for shielding mushroom Lego men. Nine lifted her nose in the air and sniffed. Her ears rotated like satellite dishes trying to pick up a signal.

When Nine yawned and sat down, Theo whispered, "I think that means there isn't anyone back here."

"We should be careful anyway," Tess said. "For all we know, they have the whole block surrounded."

They crept to the back of the yard and pushed aside various plants and bushes. Sure enough, there was a loose board that they could lift like a trapdoor. They ducked under it and ended up in the neighbors' backyard. A brown fer-rabbit watched them from its cage. It thumped its feet when Nine passed by.

"Sorry, bunny, we're just passing through," Tess said to it.

"It doesn't speak English," said Theo.

"Says you."

They sneaked alongside the house till they made it to the other side of the block. In the nearby yards and on the sidewalks, they saw the regular collection of people, no Lego men in sight. They didn't waste time. They practically ran to the Underway station and hopped on the train to Manhattan, preferring to spend time with possibly creepy Guildmen over absolutely creepy Lego men.

After an uneventful trip on the Underway, they arrived at Columbus Circle and walked to the bicycle rental place. Jaime was sitting by the rental booth, eating a pretzel.

At the same time, all three of them said, "You're not going to believe this." And then all three of them laughed.

"I don't even know why we say that anymore," said Theo, "considering."

"So what happened?" Jaime asked.

"We were accosted by two mushroom Lego men," Tess blurted.

"I . . . can't even picture that," Jaime said.

Tess explained about the blocky men who had threatened their whole family, about Slant and about what he could do to them, and about the weird meeting that the men wanted their parents to attend.

"Citizens for a Better New York City," said Jaime. "Sounds so innocent."

"I don't think it's so innocent. At least, I don't think

those Lego men are so innocent. They looked like gangsters. Gangsters who Darnell Slant has kept in a basement for a couple of years till they resemble nothing so much as fungus."

"So what you're saying is that these guys were extremely handsome," Jaime said.

"Ugh," said Tess. "I'm tired of Slant and his minions. Why do they always look like mushrooms or nutcrackers or comic book villains?"

"Yeah," said Jaime dryly. "You'd think they wouldn't want to be such clichés."

Tess punched him playfully and Jaime punched her back. Then they must have remembered that they weren't getting along as well as they used to and took a step away from each other.

Theo didn't have time for their weirdness. "And what were you going to say, Jaime?"

"Well, I wasn't visited by Lego men, but I *was* visited by some cops. They showed me some pictures of a *certain person*."

"Yeah," said Theo. "It's all over the news now."

"They said she pushed me into the water. Why would she do that?" Jaime said.

"Maybe she had a good reason," said Tess. "Maybe she was protecting you."

"Someone did shout, 'Look out!' before I went overboard. But the cops didn't say anything about me being in danger."

"Maybe they just don't know what to look for," said Tess. "Maybe they don't know where to look. Maybe they just don't know anything."

They were all silent a moment, and then Theo said, "So where are we going to look for this next clue?"

Both Jaime and Tess frowned at him. "At the Morris-Jumel Mansion," Tess said.

"Yes, I know that," Theo said, enunciating each word. "Where in the mansion? What are we looking for?"

Tess said, "Well, the Turk said, 'Find the other Eliza who still haunts the Heights.' So the clue has something to do with her specifically."

"Maybe there's a painting of her at the house," Jaime said. "Or maybe some of her letters or journals or something."

"In other words, we don't know what we're looking for," said Theo.

"What else is new?" Jaime said.

They walked to the Underway station and caught the C train, which tunneled under Central Park and Seneca Village before bursting out of the ground on tracks high in the air. Even if you rode this line every day, you'd be hard-pressed not to put down your phone or book or magazine and gaze down upon the Cathedral of Saint John the Divine, Morningstarr Park, the brownstones of Harlem. Theo was not one for form over function, but he could not deny how beautiful the city was from here, a bustling beehive of activity, all of it honeyed by the midmorning sun.

They passed the Sugar Hill Children's Museum and Coogan's Bluff and finally made it to 163rd Street. They took the stairs down three flights to get to ground level, and then, a block later, had to climb up a short set of stone steps to get to Sylvan Terrace. The solar glass cobbles here were worn, and the yellow clapboard houses were straight out of the nineteenth century. It was easy to imagine that time had stopped somehow.

The mansion sprouted up in front of them, a white house with four columns—a house big enough to be called grand, but plain enough to be called modest. Because it was a warm and sunny day, the line to enter the house was thin: a small group of Japanese tourists and their translator, a black family with three little girls in tight pigtails, and an older white couple wearing identical Bermuda shorts.

Theo, Tess, and Jaime got in line behind the Bermuda shorts people. Theo was sure that Nine would terrify them, but the woman looked down at Nine and said, "Oh look! An emotional support panther!"

The black dye covering Nine's stripes and spots hadn't yet faded, so "panther" was a reasonable guess, though panthers generally weighed about thirty to one hundred pounds more than Nine, which is what Theo told the couple.

"Don't listen to him," said Tess to the Bermuda shorts people. "He gets pedantic when he's hungry."

"We just had breakfast," Theo said.

"What's 'pedantic'?" asked one of the pigtailed little girls.

"It means acting like a know-it-all," Tess said.

"I hardly know it all, but I do know quite a bit," said Theo.

"I meant that he gets pedantic when he breathes."

The Bermuda shorts couple laughed, and Nine nudged their knees. The three pigtailed little girls watched Nine, intrigued.

Tess said to them, "Her name is Nine. She's friendly. You can pet her if you want."

The girls glanced up at their parents, who nodded

their approval. The girls soon surrounded Nine, giggling at the feel of Nine's whiskers against their skin.

One of the girls, the tallest one, said, "How does she help you?"

Tess said, "When I get nervous, she calms me down."

The little girl said, "Do you get nervous a lot?"

"Yeah," said Tess. "I do. Sometimes for good reason, but sometimes for not so good reasons."

"So do I," said Jaime.

"Yeah," said Theo.

The little girl gazed at them in wonder that they would admit such a thing. Then she curled an arm around Nine's neck and put her face in Nine's fur. "Me too," she said. "Me too."

The doors of the mansion opened, and a guide beckoned them inside. They all shuffled into an octagon-shaped parlor, where the guide, a thin, pale woman wearing period dress, gave them some background on the house. Since Theo had already read about the house, he knew everything she discussed: that the house was built as a summer home by a man named Colonel Roger Morris for his wife, Mary, that enslaved and indentured people worked on the surrounding grounds, and that when the Revolutionary War broke ut, the Morrises left town because they were loyal to the king.

"Oh no," said Ono, piping up from Jaime's pocket.

At the sight of the robot, the three little girls chirped in delight, but they quieted when their mother hushed them.

The guide went on about the history of the house, the fact that George Washington had used it as his temporary headquarters in 1776.

"When we go upstairs, you'll be able to see Washington's War Room, as well as the secret passageway that connects the room to the rest of the house!"

The little girls clapped with excitement and the Japanese tourists smiled at them. Theo smiled for an entirely different reason: A secret passageway might be the perfect place to hide a clue. Jaime must have had the same idea. He had his sketchbook out and on a picture of the mansion had scrawled SECRET PASSAGEWAY? He showed the drawing to Tess, who raised her brows.

They followed the small group through the lower floors of the mansion, as the guide described the architectural features and the furniture and the wallpaper. Finally, they made it upstairs to the second-floor War Room. The guide pointed to a panel on the green wall and then opened it for them. There was a funny cut-out drawing of George Washington peeking out from behind it.

The little girls gasped and all the tourists snapped pictures, including Theo, Tess, and Jaime.

"Can we go inside?" asked one of the little girls. "Please?"

"I'm sorry, the passageway isn't open to the public," said the guide. "We have to keep some of the mansion's secrets, don't we? Okay, everyone follow me! We're about to meet Mrs. Eliza Jumel, the woman who lived in this house for more than fifty-five years and eventually married Aaron Burr, the man who shot and killed Alexander Hamilton."

"Ooooh!" said the little girls, and raced to follow the guide.

Theo dropped to one knee to tie his sneaker v e r y s l o w l y. To Tess and Jaime, Theo mouthed, *Go ahead. I'll check!* and gestured to the secret panel that hid the passageway. Tess and Theo hurried after the group. They could stall for time, but Theo knew he had only a few moments before the guide would wonder what was taking him so long.

He stood and went to the door, pushing past the

cartoon replica of George Washington, and entered the passageway. No wonder they didn't let anyone back here; behind the door were piles of boxes and papers and stairs leading to wherever. Theo pulled out his phone and quickly took as many photos as he could, but there was no way he could empty the boxes or go through the papers or count the stair risers without getting caught, and what if the next clue was hidden there? He was just starting to despair when a sharp voice said, "What are you doing in here?"

He fumbled with his phone, almost dropping it down the dark staircase. A woman, in period dress like the other guide, glared at him.

"I'm sorry," Theo said. "I just wanted to see the passageway."

"Do you make a habit of trespassing?"

"No?" he said.

"You're not certain?" said the woman. Her dress was a rich green fabric with a black pattern. She looked like she was wearing the draperies you might find in a funeral home.

"I'm sorry."

"You said that!" she snapped. "Oh, off with you! Get to the kitchens!"

"The kitchens? But the tour isn't in the kitchens yet."

"That's where they will be, boy," said the woman. "At the hearth." She shooed him through the door and then shut it behind him. He took a chance and pressed on the door, but it was locked. Just as well. He was happy that this guide hadn't throw him out of the house entirely.

He left the War Room and was about to race downstairs, but he heard the voice of the original guide coming from one of the bedrooms, saying, "One of the most amazing women of the early nineteenth century was Eliza Jumel. She was born in America but traveled to France as a young woman, where she was celebrated as quite the beauty. She was a big supporter of Napoleon, and decorated this bedroom with French Imperial furniture, as you can see. She liked to tell people that this bed belonged to Napoleon and his wife Josephine, but that was likely a fib."

The room was a sea blue with a big satin-covered bed against one wall. When the guide wasn't looking, Tess ran her hands along the bed frame and even over the covers until one of the Japanese tourists frowned at her. She blushed and put her hands in her pockets.

The guide said, "The swans on the canopy are supposed to represent mates for life, but it wasn't that way for the Jumels. In 1832, Stephen Jumel fell out of a carriage onto a pitchfork."

"Ow!" said Jaime. "But . . . how do you fall onto a pitchfork?"

"Oh, that didn't kill him," said the guide. "He was bandaged up and brought back to the house. But Eliza dismissed the doctors for the evening, and the next day, Stephen was dead."

"So, are you saying that Eliza did something to him?" asked the dad of the trio of little girls.

"Some people have wondered if Eliza loosened the bandages so that her husband would bleed to death, but maybe the wound was more serious than the doctors thought. In any case, we'll never know." The guide smiled. "Let's go to the room where the cabinet met in 1790. If any of you have seen the musical *Hamilton*, you'll know about this meeting. It was the first rap battle in the show."

One of the Japanese tourists said, "'You coulda been anywhere in the world tonight, but you're here with us in New York City'!"

Another said, "'Jefferson, you have the floor, sir'!"

The whole tour group broke into song, while the tour guide clapped along. Theo took the opportunity to examine all the paintings in the room. When his eyes locked on the largest one, he almost fell over. His voice cut through the rap.

"Who is *that*?" he said, pointing at a portrait of a woman with two children.

A woman wearing a green dress that looked just like funeral home drapes.

The guide said, "That's Eliza Jumel, of course."

CHAPTER FIFTEEN
Jaime

Jaime worried that Theo was going to throw up all over Eliza Jumel's French bedroom.

"Are you okay?" Jaime whispered.

"Uh-huh," Theo said.

"You don't look okay."

"Uh-huh."

"Theo!"

"What?"

Jaime lowered his voice. "Do you see something in the painting? A clue?"

Theo shook his head. Nine rubbed her face on the legs of his jeans.

"Did you see something else?" Tess said.

"No," Theo said. "Yes. Maybe."

"That clears things up," said Jaime.

The guide, who had led the group out of the room, leaned back into it. "There's more to the house. Come on! You don't want to be left behind."

Reluctantly, Jaime, Tess, and Theo followed the group to the room where it happened—where the founding fathers had had their cabinet meeting. While the guide went on about Jefferson, Hamilton, Madison, and Washington, Tess and Jaime lurked about, clue hunting. But Theo didn't examine moldings or doors, paintings or décor. He just stood there in the middle of the room, shaking his head.

To Tess, Jaime whispered, "What's with your brother?"

"I don't know," Tess said. She pinched Theo's arm, but he barely seemed to notice.

Jaime said, "We should be looking for clues."

"Clue's not in here," said Theo.

"What? How do you know that?" Tess said.

At this, Theo laughed way more loudly and hysterically than normal, to the point where one of the little girls with pigtails put a finger to her lips to shush him.

Theo stopped laughing. He whispered, "I found Eliza who haunts the Heights."

"You mean in the painting?" Jaime said.

"Not there," Theo said. "The clue is in the kitchen."

"Okay," said Jaime, "but—"

"Don't ask me how I know," Theo said.

The guide said, "And now let's go to the kitchen. You'll notice, when we get there, that the kitchen is much larger and more comfortable than a lot of modern kitchens."

The guide led the group to the kitchen and showed them an enormous brick hearth. "In 1842, Eliza Jumel was in Saratoga Springs on vacation when she met a woman named Anne Northup. Anne was quite a talented cook, so Eliza brought her and her children back to the mansion."

"Northup," said Jaime to the guide. "The name's familiar."

"You might be thinking of Solomon Northup, a black man born free. He was a fiddler who accepted an offer to join a traveling show. But the men who made the offer tricked him. He was drugged and sold into slavery in the 1830s. His story is documented in the book and the movie *Twelve Years a Slave*. Solomon was Anne's husband."

So far, all the Morningstarrs' clues had to do with lost or forgotten history, lost or forgotten *people*. Like Anne Northup, who cooked for Eliza Jumel after her husband disappeared. Did she suspect he'd been sold into slavery? Did she believe he was dead? Did his children believe this? Did they have memories of him, or were they too young when he was taken? Just thinking about these things made Jaime's chest ache.

Next to him, Theo typed something into his phone. He showed it to Jaime.

We need to look in the hearth.

As the guide talked about how arduous making a meal was back in the nineteenth century, Jaime and Theo knelt to examine the hearth more closely—Jaime on one side, Theo on the other. The red bricks of the surround were blackened in sections. Metal cookware hung over a pile of ash-gray logs. When Jaime dared to duck his head inside the hearth, the bricks of the chimney laddered up like an endless series of smaller and smaller doors. But he saw nothing unusual. It was only when he ran his fingers against the brick that he found it: a circular seal of some kind, an imprint of a circle.

"Excuse me!" said the guide. "Please don't stick your head in the chimney!"

"Sorry," Jaime said.

"He has a thing for chimneys," Theo said. "He just loves them."

The guide blinked, gathered herself. She smoothed her long printed gown and said, "Next, we'll—"

Tess interrupted. "Excuse me. I was just thinking— What can you tell us about Eliza Jumel's marriage to Aaron Burr?"

"Well!" said the guide. "It wasn't a happy marriage. As a matter of fact . . ."

The guide went on about the unhappy marriage for a few minutes and then said again, "Next, we'll—"

"Why would the Daughters of the American Revolution want people to forget Eliza Jumel ever lived here?" Tess said.

"Excuse me?"

"The Daughters of the American Revolution? They auctioned off all her stuff? They wanted people to forget her? Why? Why would anyone want people to forget history?"

"I . . . I don't know," said the guide.

Jaime stopped listening while Tess distracted the guide and the rest of the group with her endless questions. He reached across the fireplace and snatched Theo's phone from his hand, typed: *I found some sort of seal inside the chimney. Shaped like a circle.*

Theo took the phone, read the screen, and typed back: *Did you try pressing on it? Is there a lever or a button or anything?*

Jaime waited until the guide was turned away before pressing on the seal.

Nope. No buttons or levers.

And then he remembered one of the first clues they'd found, early in the summer, back at the Tredwell house. He carefully ripped a piece of paper from his sketchbook so as not to make too much noise, then, quickly as he could, held the paper against the seal and rubbed his pencil against it. When he looked at what he had, his stomach sank in disappointment. There were no discernible letters or numbers, just some raised lines zigging and zagging all over it, mazelike. He handed the paper to Theo, who frowned, then typed:

Looks like the gear of a bicycle.

It did. Why the Morningstarrs—whoever they really were—would put the imprint of a bicycle gear inside a chimney was anyone's guess. But some other gears turned in Jaime's head. He grabbed Theo's phone and typed: *Where's that metal disc we found at Odd Fellows Hall?*

Theo read what Jaime had typed and pointed frantically at Tess. When the guide looked at him quizzically, Theo pretended to fluff his already fluffy hair.

Under his breath, Jaime called to Nine. "Here, kitty." Nine's ears rotated, and then she led Tess over to the hearth.

Jaime whispered, "Do you have that disc in your bag? The one we found at Odd Fellows Hall?"

Tess nodded. While the guide answered questions from the other tourists, Tess reached into her bag, found the disc, and slipped it to Jaime. And then they had to wait another five minutes until the guide said, "Okay, let's go outside to tour the grounds!"

The tourist group including the family with the little girls followed the guide out the door, but Jaime reached into the chimney and slapped the disc onto the seal. A force that felt like a magnet pulled the disc into place with a snap. The center of the disc popped, creating a knob or a button.

"There's a button now," Jaime whispered. "Should I push it?"

Both Tess and Theo said, "Yes!"

Jaime pushed it.

Nothing.

He turned the knob to the left.

Nothing.

He turned the knob to the right.

Nothing.

He spun the knob until there was a cracking sound and dust showered his head. He tugged on the knob again, thinking that he might have opened a hidden door, but the disc pulled away along with one of the bricks. He managed to catch the brick before it fell into the cooking pot hanging over the fire. But it took him only a few seconds to realize that this brick was too light to be a brick.

"Are you guys coming?" said one of the little girls from the tour group, the middle girl, from where she stood in the doorway.

Jaime hid the "brick" behind his back. "Yes! We were just taking some pictures."

"Okay," said the girl. "My mom said to get you because you probably wouldn't want to miss anything. The lady is talking about a soldier who died when he fell down the stairs. And now he's a ghost!" She said this with the utmost delight, as if this was the best thing she'd ever heard and she would gladly live in a whole house full of ghosts, which meant she was a very cute but very strange little person, in Jaime's opinion.

"We'll be right behind you," said Tess.

The girl flashed a grin and then ran off, pigtails bobbing. Jaime checked the space where the brick had been, in case there was anything behind it, but there was nothing but a hole and a patch of mortar. Tess opened her bag and Jaime put the brick inside. Just another artifact they were "borrowing." Then they went to catch up with the group.

They found them on the grounds outside. The guide

was still talking about ghosts.

"In the 1960s, a group of schoolkids claimed that a woman standing on the balcony right up there yelled at them because they were making too much noise. When the kids saw the portrait of Eliza Jumel in the upstairs bedroom, they said they were sure that Eliza was the woman who yelled at them. We've had many a ghost hunter here at the Morris-Jumel Mansion."

"That's great," said Theo. "Really fabulous. Yup." He nodded and then kept nodding, as if he were a bobble-head on a dashboard.

"Are you okay?" said Jaime.

"Ha!" said Theo. "Totally fine! Why?"

"Because you're acting like a weirdo?" said Tess.

"That's nothing new," Jaime said.

"Ha-ha!" Theo said. "Ha-ha-ha!"

The mom of the little girls said, "Maybe he needs to sit down?"

The dad of the little girls said, "He probably needs some lunch."

"I could use some lunch," said Jaime.

To the guide, the littlest girl said, "You should have lunch here so people don't act like weirdos."

Her sister said, "It should be a ghost lunch. With ghosts."

The oldest girl rolled her eyes. "Ghosts don't eat lunch."

The middle sister said, "What do you know about ghosts, Livvy? You're scared of your own dolls."

"Only when they stare at me!" said Livvy.

"We're going to get my brother some food," Tess said, hauling on both Theo's and Jaime's arms. "Thanks for the very informative tour!"

"You're welcome!" said the guide. "Come back and visit us soon!"

As they walked away from the house, Theo turned, looked up at the balcony, and, for some reason, shuddered.

They hopped the Underway back downtown. For lunch, they picked up burgers and fries to go at a nearby Bug's Burgers and brought the food to Central Park. They found a secluded spot to eat. When they were finished, they passed around the brick/block/box to examine it more closely. Instead of a solid brick, there were seams at the corners.

"Tiles?" said Tess.

"Looks like it," Theo said.

"And there's definitely something inside," said Jaime, who shook the box so they could hear whatever it was rattling around in it. Jaime thought they might have to find a tool or a rock to pry or smash off the brick tiles, but they popped off easily, leaving a metal box of some sort, the disc still attached to its front.

Jaime turned the box over. "Maybe it's a tiny safe."

"Then we'd need some way to unlock it," Theo said.

"The disc is still on the front," Tess said. "Maybe we have to turn it."

"Yes, but how far? Which direction? How many times?" Theo said.

"Details, details," Jaime said. He spun the disc the way he had at the Morris-Jumel Mansion. Left, right, all the way around one way, all the way around the other. But nothing happened.

"Maybe it's a puzzle box?" Tess said. "Does anything slide around?"

"No," said Jaime. "It feels almost solid. Here." He handed it to Tess, who tried all the things Jaime had tried. Then Theo did the same.

"Has to be a combination, then," said Tess. "Something to do with that disc."

"But there aren't any numbers on the disc. No letters, either," Jaime said.

Theo pointed to one of the notches on the edge of the disc. "This notch is a little deeper than all the rest.

And there's a notch on the top of the box. So, if we line these up . . ." Theo spun the disc until the notches lined up and then pulled on the knob. And pulled again. And pulled.

"Welp," said Tess, "that's not it."

"Ugh," said Theo, splaying himself on the grass.

"Giving up so soon?" said Tess.

"I'm not giving up, I'm resting up," Theo said.

"By the way," Jaime said, "what happened back there?"

"What do you mean?"

"How did you know this was hidden in the hearth? And what was the whole laughing-like-a-hyena thing about?" Jaime said.

"Hyenas don't laugh," Theo said.

"You know what I mean," said Jaime.

Theo covered his eyes with both hands. "Promise you won't make fun of me."

"Nope," said Tess. "But tell us anyway."

"Fine," Theo said. "The ghost of Eliza Jumel told me that the clue was in the hearth. Happy?"

"I am definitely not happy about that," said Jaime. "I am the complete opposite of happy."

"What do you mean, 'ghost'?" Tess said.

"Is there another meaning of 'ghost' that I'm not aware of?" Theo said. "A woman who looked exactly like that portrait of Eliza Jumel was in the secret passage. She told me to go down to the hearth."

Jaime thought about this. "The Turk did tell us to find the Eliza who *haunts* the Heights. Haunts as in ghost?"

"Or someone wants us to think so," Tess said.

"Who would want us to think so?" demanded Theo. "And if that person wasn't a ghost, then what was she?"

"I don't know," said Tess. "Some kind of projection?"

"Projection from where? And how?"

"A hidden camera? Maybe triggered by your face or voice or something?"

"She looked as real as you. As real as Jaime," Theo insisted.

Tess lifted her hands in surrender. Watching all the emotions tick across her face—confusion, frustration, determination—and Theo flopping around in the grass, Jaime now knew one thing was completely clear: the twins didn't know anything more about the Cipher than Jaime did. They hadn't kept anything from him, not on purpose. And even photographs and videos could be altered to tell any sort of story.

Jaime scooped up the box and gave it back to Tess. "Put this away."

"But we haven't solved it yet!"

"It's hot, and I think we need a break," said Jaime. "Let's go to a movie or something."

Tess looked at the block in her hands, glinting in the sun, then tucked it into her bag. "A movie sounds like a great idea."

Jaime stood. "Come on, Theo. We'll find a theater with no ghosts in it."

"Very funny," said Theo.

Later, while they sat in a second-run theater watching *Spider-Man: Into the Spider-Verse 2*, Jaime thought about ghosts, about echoes of people in the things they left behind, and all the ways in which those things and the people they belonged to got forgotten, or erased. Like the Daughters of the American Revolution trying to erase Eliza Jumel from the house she had lived in for fifty-five years. And how, in trying to erase Eliza, they erased Anne Northup and her children from the house, too.

He tried to focus on the movie. He loved the world of the Spider-Verse, a world of many timelines existing at once. But his mind kept drifting. He imagined a timeline in which Solomon Northup was never kidnapped by slavers, a timeline where he and Anne owned their own grand home, and Anne cooked for no one but her own family and her own friends, the people she invited in. And though it was unlike him, Jaime fell asleep in the dark of the theater, dreaming of a place where Anne and Solomon's children grew strong on their mother's food and their father's presence, a place where everyone was loved.

CHAPTER SIXTEEN

Imogen Sparks

*T*wo a.m. Imogen Sparks crossed her arms to ward off the bite in the air as she walked, her long tulle skirt flouncing, her combat boots quiet as ballet slippers on the sidewalk. The nights were growing colder. Soon the haze and heat of the summer would dissipate, and the chill would sink its teeth in, not letting go of the city until spring. She welcomed it. Fewer people on the streets at night. So much easier to spot anyone on her tail. Like the men she'd lost a few blocks back. Not very good at their jobs, those men, lumbering and clumsy, wearing identical ill-fitting black suits.

Still, it was a bad sign.

Imogen willed herself to walk briskly yet casually past the kids loitering around the Croton Fountain and paused at the door of an old warehouse, where a modest plaque marked it as the home of the Old York Puzzler and Cipherist Society. Not for the first time, Imogen thought it might be better to cover up the plaque, or chisel it off. Not for the first time, Imogen thought it might be better to hire some real guards for the place, instead of the Cipherists taking turns sleeping there at night. But who could they trust with all their treasures—and their secrets—except themselves?

Imogen fished around in her handbag and found her compact. She pretended to check her lipstick while aiming the mirror behind her. No men in ill-fitting suits, no women, either. It wasn't too long ago that she and the other Cipherists had been accosted at Green-Wood Cemetery by a vicious band of blond lady fighters/news hostesses with the same silly hair and the same talent for kickboxing. And though the Cipherists had gotten the better of those women in that battle, Imogen wasn't exactly looking for a rematch.

Satisfied that she hadn't been followed, she slipped her compact back into her purse.

"Ms. Sparks?"

Imogen gasped, whirled around. "Where did you come from?"

A few feet away stood a disheveled man with longish

gray hair and a face so ruddy that it was red even in the dark. Broken capillaries mapped his nose and cheeks. His shirt had a ketchup stain on the shoulder. Or maybe it was blood. He held a large envelope.

"Ms. Imogen Sparks?"

"Yes. What? Who are you?"

He handed her the envelope and then smiled with tiny corn teeth that needed a good cleaning. "You've been served."

"What?"

The man whistled and sauntered away.

Imogen tore open the envelope and scanned the papers. A wave of rage flooded her when she read what was on them. She stuffed them back into the envelope and jammed the whole thing into her purse. She jabbed the buzzer next to the door to the Cipherist Society.

"Ray? Omar?" she said. "It's me."

No response.

She buzzed once more. "Ray. Come on, wake up!"

Still no response.

"Omar! Hello? Are you guys playing Scrabble again? Without me?"

Again, no response.

Now annoyed as well as enraged, Imogen dug around in her purse for her keys. Of course, they'd fallen all the

way to the bottom. She yanked out an enormous jumble
of interconnected keychains and searched for her Captain America fob, the one with the shiny brand-new key
to the shiny brand-new lock they'd just had installed for
extra security. She was about to insert the key into the
lock when she saw the scratches on the trim plate. Not
scratches, *gouges*. Tool marks? Had someone tried to pick
the lock? A dread far colder than the night chill sank
into her bones. This time, she didn't bother with her
mirror. Quickly, she looked behind her, to the left and
to the right. The street was empty. She dug around in
her purse for the compact "umbrella" she kept for circumstances like this one. Then she slowly opened the
heavy wooden door, which squeaked like something out
of a horror film.

Inside the small lobby of the building, the air was
heavy and still, warmer than it had been outside, with
a strange musty smell she couldn't place. Her heart
thumped as she slapped the light switch, and it thumped
again when the lights refused to come on.

Someone had left tool marks on the door lock.

And someone had cut the power.

Imogen swore under her breath. She clicked the button on the umbrella that wasn't exactly an umbrella and
a blue glow emanated from its tip. She aimed the blue

light all around the lobby, but there was no one lying in wait for her.

"Woman up, Immy," she muttered to herself. She marched across the lobby to another wooden door and opened it. Behind the wooden door was a shiny steel wall with a keypad in the middle. She touched the keypad and its cover fell away, dangling by its wires. Someone, it seemed, had tampered with this lock, too.

Imogen swore again. She pushed the keypad back into place and punched in the code, hoping the mechanism was still operational. The steel wall opened and Imogen stepped inside. Once the wall closed behind her, she advanced to the next keypad, damaged like the first. She coded in, then stepped back, ready to swing at whoever came at her.

A hole opened up in the steel, dialing wide like the pupils of a cat. The archives beyond were nearly pitch-black.

"Ray?" she whispered, walking slowly out onto the platform. "Omar?"

She almost screamed when another voice, thin and squeaky, said, *"Ray? Omar?"*

But she could just make out the shape of a large bird perched on the railing.

"Auguste?"

The bird said, feverishly, frantically, *"For the moon never beams, without bringing me dreams of the beautiful Annabel Lee."*

"You scared me to death! What are you doing up here?"

"And the stars never rise, but I feel the bright eyes of the beautiful Annabel Lee."

"It's all right, Auguste," she murmured, though it clearly was not. The chill in her bones got even chillier as she took several sluggish steps toward the railing and willed herself to look down three floors into the heart of the archives. The endless walls of shelves that housed their books and manuscripts were still neat and tidy. The glass cases that housed priceless artifacts seemed undisturbed. But where were Ray and Omar?

There was a *thump* and a crash from somewhere below. A dark shape sprinted across the enormous room, heavy feet thudding.

Adrenaline pumped through Imogen's veins. She ran down the filigree spiral staircase so fast that she made herself dizzy, so fast she nearly fell onto the rug at the foot of the stairs. Jamming herself against a wall of books, she panned the not-umbrella's blue light around the large room. As it had in the lobby, the air smelled musty and vaguely animal.

Heavy feet thudded again, this time heading for the kitchen. Imogen whipped the light in that direction but saw nothing. A minute later, there were thudding sounds going the other way. Keeping her back against the wall, she slowly sidestepped to her right, panning the light back and forth.

Until she almost stumbled over a body.

Someone was collapsed on the floor behind one of the chairs

"Omar!" she said. She knelt beside him and pressed her ear to his chest. She almost cried when she heard the strong, steady beat of his heart.

At her touch, Omar stirred. He blinked slowly at her, a swelling over his eye, his nose broken and bloody, and then said, "My nose!"

"You're going to be all right," she whispered.

"I liked my nose," Omar said. "It was a good nose."

"Shhh!" she said. "Someone's still in the archives."

"Oh dear," said Omar.

"Don't move. I'm going to find Ray." Imogen stood, and Omar gripped her leg.

"Be careful."

She nodded and kept moving, listening intently for the footsteps. She eased herself around the glass display cases that housed encrypted letters from Benedict Arnold, belts etched with strange symbols, stones tooled by Guildmen. She made it to the other side of the room, to the bookcase that doubled as a door to the kitchen. She was just about to pull the red volume that opened the door when something slammed into her back. Her forehead hit the bookcase with such force that she staggered, almost falling to her knees. But she did not fall. She swung around and jabbed with the umbrella that was not an umbrella. There was a buzzing sound as her weapon erupted, followed by a bellow of pain.

"Got you," Imogen said, before she was shoved to the floor so hard that she slid some feet before coming to a stop. There was a ferocious crash and then the shattering of glass, the thunder of heavy feet up the staircase. Auguste squawked and launched himself from the railing above, spiraling down to land at Imogen's side.

"I'm all right, Auguste," she breathed. "Are you all right?"

"THE BEAUTIFUL ANNABEL LEE!" Auguste said.

"Does Annabel know kung fu? Because that would be useful right about now," Imogen said, pulling herself off the floor. She cocked her head, listening for more footsteps, but all she heard was the filigree staircase vibrating like a tuning fork.

Behind her, the bookcase swung open, and Imogen shrieked.

Ray Turnage stood there. "Ugh," he said, holding his

head. "I don't know what hit me."

"Same guy who hit me, I think."

"Could have been a giant sentient anvil, for all I know," Ray said. "Got me from behind. Never saw a thing. Knocked me clean out."

Imogen helped Ray to the nearest chair. Then she got Omar seated next to him. She explored the rest of the archives but found no one. Eventually, she went to the kitchen and got Ray and Omar some ice wrapped in towels.

"Omar, what happened to you?" Imogen said.

Omar's good eye dialed like the door to the archives, as if he'd just remembered how his nose had gotten broken. He said, "I went to the kitchen to get some coffee. When I came back out, someone was in the archives, waiting. A big guy, but that's all I registered before he hit me. And not just once. And he smelled like he hadn't had a shower in years."

"I saw a weird disheveled guy outside. But he wasn't that big," said Imogen.

"What guy?"

"Whoever he was, he works for you-know-who," Imogen said.

"Voldemort?" said Omar. "Really, Imogen. You can say his name."

"*Slant,*" said Imogen, with such venom that the name sounded like a swear. "I'm not afraid of saying his name, I just want to spit every time I say it. Anyway, he's suing us for the building."

"He can't do that," said Ray. "The Society owns this place."

"Yeah, well, tell that to the Biedermann kids. They lost their home to that greedy jerk. He's not going to stop until he owns the whole city."

Omar groaned again. "Now my head hurts as much as my poor beautiful nose."

"You still have your nose," said Imogen. "It will have more character now."

"Are you saying it didn't have character before?"

"You two need a doctor," she said. "And the society will need a lawyer."

"I don't know about the lawyer part, but Delancey can check us out later," Ray replied. "Was anything stolen?"

"I heard a crash, but I don't know," she said. "I have to get the lights working first."

"No one's ever broken into the archives before," Ray said. "I didn't think anyone could."

"I programmed this security system myself," said Omar. "No one should have been able to."

"Somebody figured it out," said Ray.

"Obviously," said Omar, annoyed, then said, "Ow," and pressed the ice pack back against his nose.

Imogen went to the electrical supply closet and turned on the generator. The archives were bathed in bright light. Imogen pressed the button on her not-umbrella and the blue glow went dark again. She set the umbrella aside and examined each of the intact display cases before making it to a bank of cases that had been smashed, dancing carefully around piles of shimmering glass. Here was an encoded letter from World War II, here were some photographs of the original Navajo Code Talkers. She nudged a toe through the glass. Where was . . . ?

"Oh no," she said.

"Did you find something?" said Omar.

"I didn't find something," said Imogen.

Ray said, "What does that mean?"

"It means that the letter from Mary, Queen of Scots, is gone."

From far above, up on the platform, a voice said, "We have bigger problems than that."

The three Cipherists looked up. At the top of the filigree staircase stood a small black woman dressed in a long silvery-gray coat.

"Hey!" said Imogen. "Who are you? What are you

doing here? How did you get in?"

The woman walked down the staircase. "The same way you did, I expect."

"Will someone please tell me what's going on?" Omar honked.

The woman's gait was so smooth that it almost seemed as if she were gliding instead of walking. Her gray coat billowed behind her like a cape.

"You're Jaime Cruz's friend. Or aunt. Or whoever," said Imogen.

"Whoever," said the woman, with a ghost of a smile. "It left this sticking in the steel wall."

"'*It*'?" said Imogen. "Left what?"

The woman held out something large and brown and wickedly sharp, as thick as her own wrist.

A claw.

CHAPTER SEVENTEEN
Tess

When Tess and Theo were little, Grandpa Ben had taken up woodworking. He loved making puzzles, particularly puzzle boxes. As the twins got older, Grandpa made more and more intricate puzzles for them to solve. The boxes always had tiny gifts in them—two pieces of candy, two stickers, two finger puppets.

So they could handle the puzzle box they'd found at the Morris-Jumel Mansion, Tess told Jaime. No problem at all. They'd have it open by the next morning.

They did not have it open by the next morning.

"Maybe it's not a puzzle box," said Theo after Tess dropped it to the floor and fell back on her bed, groaning.

"It's a frustration machine, that's what it is," Tess said.

"The last time we had a puzzle to solve, the spiders helped us solve it, remember?"

Tess sat up. "You're right!" She scooped up the box and brought it to the living room, where the spiders were pruning the houseplants.

But the spiders had no interest in this new puzzle box, not when she set it on the coffee table, not even when she nestled it in the dirt below the ficus tree. The spiders gathered in a ball and, in an imitation of the Rollers outside and every cat who had ever lived, dumped the puzzle box out of the pot and onto the floor.

"Some help you ladies are," said Tess.

The spiders giggled.

The spiders were no help, and Ono wasn't, either. When Jaime arrived later that morning, he set Ono next to the puzzle box and said, "Can you open it?"

Ono banged a little fist on the top of the box. Spun the disc on the front. Kicked it. Kicked it harder. Hopped around while holding one foot, bleating, "Oh no, oh no, oh no."

"It's okay, Ono," Jaime said.

"Now what?" Theo said.

They shouldn't have gone to that movie last night,

Tess thought. They didn't have time to act like regular kids—going on roller coasters, eating funnel cake and pizza and burgers, going to picture shows. They had a cipher to solve.

She scooped up the box and shook it just to hear it rattle.

"Don't break it!" said Theo.

"It doesn't sound breakable. It sounds really small, actually." Tess held the box near her ear and tilted it. Whatever was in the box slid from one side to the other. Next to her, Nine's ears rotated in kind.

"Sounds like a ball rolling around in there," she said.

"Let me see," said Jaime. He took the box and tilted it the way Tess had. "It does. Like it's a tiny pinball machine."

A pinball machine? A pinball machine! Tess said, "What's a pinball machine?"

Jaime said, "You don't know what a pinball machine is?"

"No! I mean, what is a pinball machine *essentially*?"

Theo said, "Are you asking us or telling us?"

"If you're telling us, you should probably tell us," Jaime added.

"A maze!" Tess shouted.

"No need to get excited," said Jaime, but Tess could

tell that Jaime had gotten excited, and so had Theo.

"This gear on the front has all these zigzags. Maybe it represents the maze inside the box?" said Jaime.

"And if we solve the maze," said Theo.

Tess said, "We open the box!"

"We'll have this solved in no time!" Theo said.

They did not have it solved in no time.

The maze imprinted on the metal disc was amazingly complex, with sharp turns and dead ends all over the place. And since they couldn't see the ball moving through the channels, they couldn't be sure they were on the right track, or on the wrong one. They would lean the box carefully, carefully, for minutes at a time, thinking they were making progress, only to tilt it and feel no movement when there should have been a channel for the ball to roll down. Their only choice then was to roll the box around until the ball sounded like it was back in the center, and try all over again.

By lunch, they were all as rattled as pinballs. Nine had fallen fast asleep on her back with her paws in the air, Ono nestled beside her, but leaped to her feet when the door flew open and Aunt Esther stomped inside with some paper bags full of groceries.

"Hello, children!" she said. "Why so glum?"

"We're not glum," said Theo, sounding completely glum.

"Low blood sugar," Aunt Esther announced. "I can spot it a mile away. Don't even need to test your blood, though I am an excellent phlebotomist."

"Of course you are," said Tess.

"Help me with these bags and then I'll make you some of my famous paninis," said Aunt Esther.

"Did you own a sandwich shop?" said Jaime.

"No," said Aunt Esther. "Why do you ask?"

"Never mind," Jaime said, standing. "I'll help you with the bags."

All three of them helped with the groceries and then sat at the kitchen table while Aunt Esther grilled up some cheesy sandwiches.

"Delicious!" said Jaime.

Aunt Esther bowed, twirling her spatula. "Of course. Would you like another?"

"Yes, ma'am, thank you!" Jaime said.

Aunt Esther piled up meats and cheeses on thick slices of bread. "I'm glad to see you looking so well, Jaime. Anything more on that woman who pushed you into the river?"

All three of them stopped eating. Jaime said, "Not that I know of."

"Hmmm," said Aunt Esther, not turning around. "I have to say, she looked a bit familiar to me. Did she look familiar to you?"

"No?" said Jaime, his voice climbing up at the end. It was hard to lie to Aunt Esther.

But Aunt Esther didn't seem to notice. "Maybe she has one of those faces. Anyway, I'm sure lots of people are looking for her."

To save himself from responding again, Jaime tossed some crusts into his mouth and simply nodded.

Aunt Esther said, "Are you kids getting excited for school?"

Again, all three of them stopped eating. Tess said, "We've got a long time before school starts, Aunt Esther."

Aunt Esther plopped Jaime's second sandwich into the grill pan, where it sizzled. "A long time? It starts in a couple of weeks. I should take you shopping for supplies. We just got the list in the mail. A very detailed list, I might add. Notebooks and pens and pencils, as you might expect, but also paper towels and a remarkable amount of glitter. What are you going to do with all that glitter, is what I want to know."

Tess stared down at the quarter of a sandwich left on her plate. They *really* didn't have time for movies and fun and sandwiches. Tess grabbed her plate and dumped the rest of the sandwich into the trash. "Thanks for lunch, Aunt Esther."

"Jaime isn't finished yet," said Aunt Esther. "Don't be rude."

"But—"

"Tess," said Aunt Esther, her tone a warning. Tess sat, her knee jiggling. Nine, who had been sprawled at Jaime's feet, walked over to Tess and licked her shins.

Aunt Esther flipped Jaime's sandwich and then laid a heavy pan on top of it to press it.

Jaime said, "So what have you been up to, Ms. Esther?"

"*Aunt* Esther," said Aunt Esther. "This and that, as is my wont. I'm thinking of taking up weaving again. I have my looms around here somewhere."

"I didn't know you—" Theo began, and then said, "Weaving sounds cool."

"It is very cool," said Aunt Esther. "I made the rug in the living room."

"You did?" said Tess. "When was that? Before you were a phlebotomist?"

"Oh, I was never a professional phlebotomist. That was just a hobby." She pulled the pan off Jaime's sandwich and then put the sandwich on Jaime's plate.

Jaime ate his sandwich in four quick bites, as if he

was afraid Aunt Esther was going to take up phlebotomy again and would be seeking volunteers.

"We'll help with the dishes," said Tess.

Aunt Esther piled up the plates. "I'll take care of them. You go back to your game. Summer's almost over, so you should get in as much fun as you can. I'll bring you some cookies."

Fortified by the paninis, and alarmed by the prospect of having only a couple more weeks before they would be spending their days in classrooms covered in remarkable amounts of glitter, they tackled the box again. This time, Jaime made another rubbing of the disc on the front of the box, and they used a magnifying glass to study the puzzle. They mapped out all the right moves ahead of time. Since Jaime had the steadiest hands, he held the puzzle while Tess and Theo called out the directions—"Right! A little farther, a little farther! NOW DOWN! RIGHT AGAIN! OH NOOO!"

It took a whole sleeve of Fig Newtons and another dozen tries, but finally, finally, there was a *click* and a *pop*.

Two joins appeared on the top of the box, joins that hadn't been there before. Jaime used his thumb to slide the narrow panel to the side, and the top of the box came away.

Nestled inside the box, in a bed of velvet, was a small

silver dagger-like thing. Jaime took it out of the box and held it up.

"What is that? A knife?"

"Not sure," said Jaime. "But there's something written on the bottom. 'Cleopatra's Needle.'"

"Great, we have to go to Egypt," Theo said.

"Not necessarily," said Tess.

"I was making a joke. Why doesn't anyone understand my jokes?"

"Jokes, funny, et cetera," said Tess.

"Besides, Cleopatra's Needle was in Egypt but now is in Central Park. Everyone knows that," Theo said. When he saw Tess and Jaime glaring at him, he added, "Everyone *else* knows that."

"Show-off," said Jaime.

Theo punched in "Cleopatra's Needle" on his phone. "Okay, so the Needle is a 3,500-year-old obelisk that was once in an ancient Egyptian city known as On in the Bible and called Heliopolis by the Greeks. It now stands in Central Park, right behind the Met, off Fifth Avenue. There's a twin obelisk in London on the Thames that's also called Cleopatra's Needle."

"I guess we're going to London," said Jaime.

Tess laughed.

Theo ignored them both and kept reading: "The

obelisk was offered to New York City by the Egyptian Khedive in exchange for cash. So they bought it."

"Better than stealing it," said Jaime. "When was that?"

Theo hesitated. Then said, "Eighteen eighty-one."

"But," Jaime began but didn't finish. He didn't need to. They all knew that the Morningstarrs had disappeared in 1855.

Theo continued, "Under the obelisk are a bunch of time capsules with different things in them: the works of Shakespeare, some machinery, military medals from something or other, coins, a copy of the Declaration of Independence."

"Any one of those things could be the next clue," said Tess.

"Get this," Theo said. "'A parade of nine thousand Guildman marched up Fifth Avenue for the cornerstone ceremony. There are rumors that the Guildmen buried something in the base, but nobody knows what, and the Guildmen would never tell.'"

"That's got to be it," said Tess. "The Guildmen are machines, right? Morningstarr Machines? Maybe the Morningstarrs trusted them with this clue. Told them what to do with it."

"If they told them what to do with it, they had to know

what would happen twenty-five years *after* they were gone," said Jaime.

They sat with this information for a few minutes before Jaime pushed on. "If the next clue is in the base of the obelisk, how do we get into those boxes?"

"Maybe we get in the way we got into the plaque at Odd Fellows Hall? With a key."

"And maybe this," said Tess, pointing at the miniature obelisk, "is the key."

It was not the key.

Though Theo wanted to take more time, study the box and the key, Tess dragged him and Jaime to Central Park that afternoon hoping to solve this clue, and quickly. They did, however, take the time to question the Guildman on the Underway trains, a Guildman who looked up from his cell phone balefully and then went back to texting as if they were nothing but empty bug-burger wrappers blowing around on the train car floor, something to be swept up by the caterpillar, whenever the caterpillar showed up for work.

But no matter how quickly they'd solved the clues, it was never quick enough. Again, Grandpa Ben's words echoed in Tess's head: The process was the thing, the goal in and of itself. But now her head and her heart were not convinced. She wanted to get to the real end of this, whatever that end was. She wanted answers—about the world, about herself.

She didn't say any of this. She was pretty sure Theo and Jaime felt the same way, as all three of them stood at the foot of Cleopatra's Needle, sighing under a graying sky.

"Looks like rain," said Theo.

"Feels like rain," said Jaime.

The humid air left a tacky film on Tess's skin, making her more irritable, more impatient. The messenger bag she wore was heavy with various items: the miniature obelisk, the puzzle box, the chess pieces, various items from the trunk they'd dug up in Green-Wood Cemetery—everything and anything that could be a key. But there was nowhere they could find to put a key, no sign a key was even needed.

"Okay, maybe this isn't that kind of puzzle. Maybe we need to decipher something from the obelisk itself," Theo suggested.

The obelisk did have hieroglyphs etched into its surface, but the ones at the bottom were faded, barely visible. Also, they were more than three thousand years old. Also, also, the obelisk was about seventy feet tall.

"Great," said Jaime. "I don't read hieroglyphics. Do

either of you read hieroglyphics?"

"No," said the twins together.

It started to rain, further setting the mood. Tess sat down in the grass anyway.

"It's raining," said Theo.

"I'm thinking," said Tess. She pulled the miniature obelisk out of the box and examined it. Maybe it was also a puzzle box, meant to be opened. She shook it but heard nothing. She ran her fingertips over the tiny markings on the surface of the statuette.

Hmmm.

"Theo, do you have that magnifying glass?"

Theo handed her the glass. Tess examined the markings on the statuette and then the ones on the obelisk. "The markings on this statuette are different from the ones on the real thing."

"Different how?" said Theo.

Tess blinked. "They're in English."

CHAPTER EIGHTEEN
Theo

Don't say I told you so don't say I told you so don't say I—

"I told you we should have studied the statuette!" said Theo.

"You did not tell me there were English words on it," said Tess primly. "And they're not English words, precisely. They're Turkish-Irish. Interspersed with the hieroglyphs."

"Turkish-Irish?" said Jaime. "Isn't that what you call the language you two speak to each other?"

Tess didn't respond. Neither did Theo. What was there to say? Theo thought about his Grandma Annie and her fondness for Alice in Wonderland:

". . . one can't believe impossible things."

"I daresay you haven't had much practice," said the Queen.
"When I was your age, I always did it for half an hour a day.
Why, sometimes I've believed as many as six impossible things
before breakfast."

How many impossible things could Theo believe
before September? How many impossible things could
Theo believe before *dinner*?

"Theo, you're doing that thing with your lip," said
Tess.

Theo let go of his lip. "What does the statuette say?"

The three of them gathered around. Jaime took out
his sketchbook to write down the words:

tabo gabet abin

gabo abup

tabo gabo abup

gabo abundaber

tabo gabo abundaber

gabo thraboabugh

abamblabe dabown

thabe Rabamblabe

habit thabe swabitch wabith

yaboabur beabst pabitch

> *to get in*
>
> *go up*
>
> *to go up*
>
> *go under*
>
> *to go under*
>
> *go through*
>
> *amble down*
>
> *the Ramble*
>
> *hit the switch*
>
> *with your best pitch*

"'Get in go up go under'? That makes no sense," Tess said.

Jaime went to push his glasses up the bridge of his nose before he remembered he had contacts now. He said, "The R is capitalized. The Ramble could be a specific place."

Tess already had her phone out. "It's a thirty-eight-acre woodland area within the park."

"We don't have time to search thirty-eight acres of anything," said Theo. "Remember Slant said something amazing would happen in 'a few short weeks'?"

"And by 'amazing,' you mean horrible, right?" Jaime said.

"Hold on," Tess said. "There's also something called the Ramble *Cave*. Apparently, it's been closed to visitors for decades."

"It does say 'amble *down* the Ramble,'" said Theo.

"Hmmm," Jaime said. "First it says, go in, up, under, through, but it's backward. Through, under, up, in. So maybe the only way to get into those time capsules is from underneath?"

"And the Ramble gets us there," Tess said.

"Where's the cave?" said Jaime.

Tess said, "On the north end of the lake, north of Gill Bridge and south of Oak Bridge."

"That's across 79th," Jaime said.

"We should get moving, then," said Tess.

"We need to prepare!" Theo said. "I didn't plan on spelunking today."

Tess held up the bag. "I have tools and some rope in here."

"Since when did you start carrying rope around with you?"

"I always carry rope with me," said Tess.

"To tie up the sharks?" Jaime said.

Tess lifted her chin. "To tie up the criminals."

Jaime said, "What if we're the criminals?"

Neither Tess nor Theo had an answer for that.

Theo said, "Let's go."

They moved as fast as they could, taking turns with Tess's heavy bag clanking at their hips. They stopped only to grab some snow cones at one of the many carts tooling around the park and then kept walking. A fine mist fell from the gray sky, jeweling their hair and clearing the fields and paths of people. Only a determined band of bubble-soccer players stayed to bounce along in the wet grass and mud, laughing as they did.

They crossed 79th Street and found the Ramble, the wooded area by the lake. Tess called up a picture of the cave on her phone. "We're looking for an arch. The steps to the cave should be on the right side."

In the Ramble, the trees and vegetation grew greener, denser, a wild space within the sculpted park. Here the canopy was so thick that the rain didn't reach them. The soft drops plunked on the leaves and the tunes of the birds were muted and mournful; squirrels scuttled unseen in the brush. Theo could almost imagine they weren't in Central Park anymore, that they weren't in New York City anymore. And then he told himself he was being ridiculous and reminded himself how much he hated to be ridiculous.

"It's . . . quiet in here," said Tess.

"Uh-huh," Jaime said. "I can't say I like it. Reminds me too much of the island." He shuddered.

Some weeks before, they'd gone looking for another clue on North Brother Island—a supposedly abandoned, unhabited island that was now a bird sanctuary. But they'd found creatures far more dangerous than the robins that hopped around these woods. They'd discovered a hidden compound, plus attack dogs and attack *men* and one ferocious giraffe-owary that had tried to eat Tess, and then were saved from them all by a woman in gray. A woman who was hundreds of years old, who was supposed to be dead but somehow wasn't.

Yeah. Shuddering was the appropriate reaction.

They passed under a stone arch that looked like something out of the Middle Ages. The trees suddenly thinned, and the light here was weak and the color of algae. Faint sloshing sounds emanated from the brush.

"We're close," said Tess. "We need to look for some steps cut into the stone."

"Why do I feel like you should have more than some chess pieces and a rope in this bag?" said Jaime.

"Oh no," piped Ono from Jaime's pocket. Nine mrrowed long and low.

"We'll be fine," said Theo, reassuring them, but also himself.

The skin of the lake was pocked by the rain. Happy ducks quacked in the water, diving and surfacing, too used to humans and their animals to care about three kids, a cat, and a tiny robot.

Theo kept his eyes on the vegetation on their left, the way the map directed, and he saw them behind a metal fence.

"There they are! The stairs!"

Tess didn't hesitate. She climbed right over the fence. "Throw me the bag."

Jaime tossed her the bag, and she caught it. He climbed over. Nine cleared it with one leap. Theo managed it without breaking his arms or getting his hair caught, so he considered the endeavor a success.

Beyond the fence, the narrow stone staircase was furred with moss and dark with rain. It led straight into a cave so dark that it might as well have been a hole in the universe.

"That looks welcoming," said Jaime.

"Come on," Tess said, shouldering the heavy bag. She took the steps way too fast, almost slipping before Jaime caught her, righted her.

"Thanks," Tess said, breathing hard. "I got a little excited."

Of course Tess was more excited than scared. That was Tess for you. Worried about absolutely everything but willing to fling herself into almost anything. Even a hole in the universe.

(Stop thinking about holes in the universe, stop thinking about holes in the universe, stop thinking about holes in the universe, STOP.)

More carefully now, they picked their way down the slick staircase until they got to the opening of the cave. The mouth of the cave wasn't as dark here, wasn't as black or as mysterious or as big. Still, Tess rummaged in her bag and pulled out some glow sticks. They each snapped one and shook it. The green glow from the lights illuminated the mouth of the cave. Theo held his glow stick against the wall of the cave but didn't see any writing. No graffiti or carving. Which was odd.

Jaime seemed to know what he was thinking. "Maybe they clean this?"

"They clean the cave?" said Theo.

"Stranger things," said Jaime, not even bothering to finish the saying. They pushed forward, moving slowly in the dark. Theo turned once to look behind them.

Now it was the green of the park that looked like a hole in the universe.

(Stop it stop it stop it.)

They trudged along for another ten minutes, long enough that the green park became nothing but a pinprick in the dark. Then Tess stopped and held up her glow stick.

A wall of rocks blocked off the rest of the tunnel.

"Welp," said Theo, "I guess we need to find another way."

"No!" said Tess, "I feel a breeze."

"Yeah," Jaime said, holding his hands near the pile. "It's coming through the rocks. These are loose."

"Why would they leave a pile of loose rocks instead of just walling it off?" Tess asked.

"Air flow? Or water flow, maybe?" Theo said.

"Water flow?"

"In case of flash floods," Theo said.

"Thanks for putting *that* in my head," said Jaime.

"Happy to help," said Theo.

"Through," said Tess. "The clue said we have to go through. I think we have to dig through this wall."

"Just what I wanted to do today," Jaime said. He pointed up. "We should start up there. That way, the rocks are less likely to crush us."

"They won't crush us," Theo said, just a tad hysterically. Though the pile wasn't that high, it was higher than the fence that had blocked off the mouth of the cave. It was higher than Theo wanted to climb.

Again, it was Jaime who seemed to know what he was thinking. "At least it's not as high as the Underway tracks."

"And there aren't any rogue Guildmen around," Theo said.

"As far as we know," said Jaime.

"Thanks for that," said Theo.

"What was that you said? Oh! Happy to help!"

"Ha-ha."

Nine scaled the rocks easily, as if she were born to do it, which, considering the fact that she was descended from wildcats, she was. Or maybe she was part goat. She balanced at the top of the pile, mrrowing at them.

"We don't have four feet, Nine," said Tess, hauling herself onto the first boulder.

"Or paws," Theo said.

"Or extra lives," added Jaime.

They ascended the rock pile, freezing when some loose stones tumbled down and hit the dirt floor of the cave with a *thud*.

"Careful!" said Theo.

"No duh," Tess said, sending another avalanche of pebbles Theo's way, uncarefully.

(*Uncarefully* is not a word. What's the matter with you?)

Tess was soon at the top of the pile. "There's a stone wedged in here. I'm going to try to pry it loose." Tess gripped the stone, pushing and pulling at it. Under Theo's feet, the other rocks rocked.

"Tess," said Jaime, a warning in his voice.

"I know," Tess said. "I almost got it."

The rocks continued to tremble.

"Hurry!" said Theo.

Tess pulled the stone away. "There!" She held up her glow stick to see to the other side of the pile. "We can get through! It's a bit of a drop, but not too far."

"If you're going to go, you need to go now," Jaime said as a rock bounced past him.

Tess turned her body so that her feet entered the hole first, and then she disappeared.

"Are you okay?!" Theo yelled.

"Yeah," came Tess's voice, muffled by the wall of rocks.

Nine leaped through the hole next. Jaime scrambled up the pile. Before he jumped, he looked back at Theo.

"Go!" said Theo. "I'm fine."

He wasn't fine. Once Jaime had wriggled through the hole, the pile of rocks convulsed. Theo launched himself up to the opening at the top of the pile and, with no time to turn around, went through the hole hair first. He landed in a heap on top of his sister and Jaime, all of them falling to the dirt. They scrambled backward to get away from the shuddering, trembling, rumbling rocks, and held their collective breath. But the rocks didn't give way. After a few minutes, the rocks settled, the wall still intact.

For now.

"I hate to be a downer," said Jaime, "but I'd say that getting out of this tunnel is going to be a lot harder than getting in."

"Maybe we don't come back this way. Maybe we get out of here at the other end of the tunnel," said Tess.

"I hope so," said Theo, checking his whole body for hematomas.

They picked themselves off the ground and kept walking. Thankfully, the cave was large enough to stand up in, and there were no signs of monsters or machines. Theo ran his hands over the rock walls.

"This feels natural, like it's been here a million years," he said.

"The article I read said that the cave was here before the park was built."

"When was that?" Jaime asked.

Tess didn't respond.

Jaime said, "Let me guess. It was after the Morning-starrs disappeared."

Again, Tess didn't say anything. What was there to say? That the Biedermanns weren't the Morningstarrs, but the Morningstarrs were clairvoyant? Just the other night, his dad had shown Theo an article about some scientists who were working on a system that could infer a person's moods using Wi-Fi. Every person gave off radio frequency signals that could be picked up and fed through an algorithm, which meant that if the tech worked, scientists would be able to tell if anyone in the world was happy or sad or angry. Would it be so bonkers to imagine that the Morningstarrs possessed some kind of tech that could predict the future?

(Yes, it was completely bonkers.)

And yet.

They kept walking, falling into an uneasy silence. It was so still and so quiet down here. The Underway train tunnels must have been close by, but who knew how many feet of rock were between this tunnel and those? They could get lost down in the Ramble, *under* the Ramble, and no one would ever find them.

(Shut up.)

Nine left Tess's side and came to snuffle at Theo's fingers. He hated to admit that he needed her, but he needed her. He kept one hand on the top of her warm head as they walked, and his muscles relaxed.

Then Tess stopped short and Jaime slammed into her back.

"Sorry," Jaime said, but Tess was pointing at the ceiling of the cave.

"Look! A lever!"

And there was. A round metal hatch jutted from the rock overhead, and on that hatch was a long metal arm. Theo was so relieved to see it that he picked up the nearest rock, aimed, and smacked the metal arm with a *clang*. The arm shifted and the hatch dropped open. A skinny ladder slammed into the ground.

"That was impressive," said Jaime. "You should play baseball."

"That's the first time he's ever thrown anything that went in the right direction," said Tess.

"Pitch, you mean?" said Theo.

"Maybe you want to climb the ladder, Mr. Accurate?" said Tess.

"You know what happened the last time I climbed a ladder," Theo said.

"Giant stone eagles came to life and almost murdered us to death," Jaime said.

"Exactly."

"There are no stone eagles here," Tess said. "And we'll take turns."

The ladder wasn't as high as the one that he'd last climbed, the ladder at Station One, where they'd unleashed a battalion of formerly hidden Morningstarr Machines on an unsuspecting city. But though there had been eagle sightings around New York City, no one had reported any damage. And no one knew where the eagles were roosting, now that they weren't roosting on the roof of Station One.

"Oh, I'll go first," said Tess.

Before Theo could move, Tess grabbed the bag with all the various items in it, stuck her glow stick between her teeth, and started climbing. She took the rungs two at a time.

"You don't have to go so fast!" said Theo.

"Yes, I do," Tess said. The upper half of her body vanished through the hatch.

"What do you see?" said Jaime.

"A blank wall, blocking whatever is beyond the hatch. But with one hole in it." Her hands rummaged in her bag and freed the miniature obelisk.

"Wait!" said Theo. "If that's the key, and you unlock it, you could—"

Too late. An avalanche of who knows what fell from the hatch, sending Tess down along with it.

CHAPTER NINETEEN
Jaime

For one scary second, it looked like Tess was going to fall right on top of them. She somehow managed to catch hold of one rung on the ladder, but that didn't stop the barrage that rained down on Jaime and Theo. They crouched and covered their heads while they were pummeled with jingling velvet bags, weird bits of machinery, books, papers.

When the storm was over, Jaime stood, coughing, in a cloud of dust. Theo stayed in a crouch. "I disapprove of ladders," he said.

Tess let herself fall back to the ground. "What's all this?"

They knelt to look through the treasure. True to the articles they'd read about the time capsules, they found bags of coins, illustrations of such machines as "the self-acting spinning mule" and a mechanical hand, the complete works of Shakespeare, a box that contained an ancient camera, sets of gears and other bits, an article about a sea monster sighting, and what looked like a clockwork machine with a doll's head.

Tess picked up the doll and read the tag attached to it. "'A model for a crawling doll.'"

"That is the scariest thing I've seen . . . well, today," said Jaime. "It's the scariest thing I've seen today."

"Not something you want to cuddle with."

"I think we should give it a proper burial," said Jaime.

"It had a proper burial and we just opened the casket," said Theo.

"Ach, Theo," said Tess.

"Ach, yourself. It's true," Theo said. "What else do we have?"

Jaime picked up a yellowing piece of paper. "It seems we have the Declaration of Independence."

"Oh wow," said Tess. "Do you think there's a clue on the back?"

"I think we're going to get arrested," said Jaime.

"We're not going to get arrested, we're just—"

"Borrowing this stuff. Yeah, I know. It doesn't feel like that," Jaime said. Absently, he patted Ono.

Ono whispered, "Kings."

"Kings," said Jaime. "Anyway, this declaration looks like a declaration. There's nothing on the back."

"Maybe there's something hidden. Something written in invisible ink?"

"If there is, we'll have to wait until we get out of here to figure it out," Jaime said. He opened a nearby velvet bag. "More old coins in here. Just these coins alone are probably worth a fortune."

"Jaime," Tess said.

Borrowing, borrowing, borrowing. "I know." Still, he couldn't help but think about the two cops who had come to see him about Ava. How they'd taken down every word he said. The pictures of the other women they'd shown him. Who were those women? What had they done? What did the cops *think* they had done?

What did they think Jaime had done?

He shook these thoughts away and focused on the pile of "treasure" in front of them. Some pictures, some postcards, more articles. Nothing looked particularly clue-like—or maybe everything looked particularly clue-like—until he came upon a scroll tied with a dusty ribbon. Attached to the ribbon was a message: *Who can find justice in the Halls of Justice?*

"Guys?" he said.

"What?" said the twins together.

He held up the scroll and showed them the message.

"The Halls of Justice?" said Theo.

Jaime plucked the ribbon loose and unrolled the paper, unveiling a drawing of a low flat building about the size of a city block. The label on the drawing read "THE TOMBS."

"Oh," said Tess.

"Great," said Theo.

"We have to break into the headquarters of the New York City Police Department," Jaime said. "No problem. No problem at all."

As they trudged back through the Ramble, Jaime's mind yammered: *We're going to get arrested, we're going to get arrested, WE'RE GOING TO GET ARRESTED.*

How in the world were they supposed to do this? How *could* they?

The twins were probably thinking the same things. Or maybe Theo was. Tess, well. Who knew what Tess was thinking? She'd shouldered the now much, much heavier bag filled with all the junk from the time capsule—even the awful doll that was probably haunted and/or a murder machine—and marched like a soldier back to the entrance of the cave, not looking back to see if they were following. When they reached the pile of rocks, Nine leaped through the opening. Tess crouched as if she was going to try to do the same, whether she would wreck herself on the rocks or not. Ono went bonkers in Jaime's pocket, bleating and buzzing.

"Wait!" said Jaime. He set Ono on the ground. Ono's arms and legs grew and grew until Ono was less a robot and more a ladder, with its little face in the center.

"Why didn't you do that before?" said Theo. "When we were trying to get *into* the cave?"

"Oh no," said Ono.

"Everyone's a puzzle," said Tess. She climbed the ladder, wriggled through the opening, and tumbled down the other side.

"Are you okay?" Theo yelled.

"Fine!" said Tess. "It's a bit bumpy on reentry, though."

Theo and Jaime picked up Tess's bag full of "treasures." Theo climbed the ladder with the bag on his back and stuffed it through the opening.

Jaime gestured for Theo to go next. Theo did as Tess had, though the tumbling and crashing noises on the other side of the wall were worse.

"Still alive?" Jaime said.

"Yes," said the twins. "Barely."

Jaime climbed up the ladder. He managed to jam his legs through the opening, one after the other, so that he could reach back and grab Ono. Ono retracted his elongated limbs until he was Ono-sized again. Jaime tucked the robot into his pocket before easing the rest of his body through the hole. The rocks shivered under his weight, but held as he slid down the pile to the ground.

"That went better than I thought it would," said Theo.

"Yeah," Jaime said, picking himself up and dusting himself off.

Theo shouldered Tess's bag. "Ready?"

"I—" Tess began, when the rocks shivered again. The pile spat out a few stones that came rolling down.

Theo said, "We should probably—"

The pile coughed up a few more stones. A rock the size of a human head almost smashed Tess's feet. Nine mrrowed. Ono beeped.

"Go!" said Jaime.

They hurried back through the cave, first walking fast, then breaking into a run. Behind them, the shivering turned into rumbling, and the rumbling turned into thundering. They were gasping for air when they broke out of the cave and into the woods. They ran into a nearby copse of trees and turned to watch as a wall of stones filled the entrance of the Ramble Cave, sealing it off. A cloud of dust was quickly washed away by the rain.

"Think the Morningstarrs planned it like this?" said Jaime, hands on his knees, still breathing hard.

"Come on," said Tess, not bothering to answer Jaime's question, which wasn't really a question anyway. "Let's get out of the park before someone else comes."

But they needn't have worried about people coming after them. Once they burst from the Ramble and into the open fields of the park, they found the place nearly deserted. The dark sky above them cracked. Rain lashed the grass, the flowers, the trees, the statues. Already soaked to the skin, they ran for the nearest Underway station. All three of them knew that finding the next clue at the Tombs was going to be the most challenging thing they'd faced so far, so they agreed to go their separate ways and tackle the problem in the morning.

Jaime volunteered to bring their "borrowed" treasure home and sift through it, and Tess and Theo didn't seem that sad about letting it go. (Or maybe they were just glad to be rid of the creepy mechanical doll buried at the bottom of the bag.) On the Underway platform, Jaime clutched the damp messenger bag tightly and tried not to drip on anyone. But his fellow passengers were just as soaked. And they weren't paying attention to him. They were stamping and fidgeting as they waited for the next train, which was uncharacteristically late by eight minutes. And then, when they finally piled into the crowded car, they were nudging bits of trash with their feet, frowning. The train car was . . . dirty? The Guildman was in his booth, not texting, not doing anything. He wasn't scanning the passengers for people not following the rules, he wasn't looking for suspicious activity, he was just gazing listlessly at nothing in particular. Why was the train car so messy? What was wrong with the Guildman? Where was the caterpillar?

"Something's wrong with the machines," said a white man with a whiter mustache sitting across from Jaime. "Something's always been wrong with them."

No one responded, but no one disagreed, either.

"We ought to get rid of them," said the man. "It's never been natural anyway. A bunch of metal bugs running around doing who knows what."

Jaime couldn't help himself. He said, "We know what they do. They clean up the city."

"Not cleaning anything now," said the man. "And it's not just the caterpillar here. The Rollers by my building haven't been cleaning the last few days, either. And what *else* are they doing?"

"What do you mean?"

"It's all right, though," the man said, sniffing. "Slant will get rid of them."

"Get rid of them? Why?"

"It's about time we upgrade! Centralize! Get someone to run things!"

"The trains already run," Jaime pointed out.

"This train was twenty minutes late!"

"It was only—"

"*You* might have an extra twenty minutes, but I don't! Somebody needs to be in charge!" the man said.

The Underway train stopped and the man stomped off, red-faced and angry, though Jaime wasn't quite sure why. The rest of the way home, Jaime held the messenger bag tighter, as if faceless thieves were about to rip it from his hands.

It was a damp, wrinkled, and exhausted Jaime who let himself into his apartment that evening. Mima had left a note on the counter letting him know that there was a plate in the fridge for dinner, that his dad was working late, and that she was bowling with her team of ladies. While his food warmed in the microwave, Jaime jumped into the shower. Once he was clean, he pulled on fresh clothes and sat down at the kitchen table to eat the barbecued chicken, green beans, and mashed potatoes Mima had left him. At the mere smell of the food, his stomach rumbled, and he realized how hungry he was. He devoured the entire meal in minutes. He was just licking the spicy-sweet barbecue sauce off his fingertips when the doorbell rang. He put his plate in the sink and went to answer it. He opened the door to find a very short astronaut standing in the hall.

"Hey, Cricket," he said.

Cricket Moran took off her helmet, which was a painted football helmet with some foil for a faceplate. "How did you know it was me?"

"Just a guess," Jaime said.

"I smell barbecue," she said.

"Do you want some?"

"No, thank you." She nudged him out of the way and entered the apartment, pulling a wagon, also covered in foil, behind her. Something was curled up in a pile of blankets in the wagon.

"Is that who I think it is?" Jaime asked.

"I don't know. Who do you think it is?" Cricket said.

"Hold on," said Jaime. He ran to the kitchen and threw open the snack cabinet. He grabbed a bag, closed the cabinet, and ran back. He opened the bag. A fuzzy brown face with a black mask peeked out from under the blankets.

"Hi there, Karl! Good to see your face again! Would you like a snack?"

A tiny hand reached for the bag, and Jaime gave it to him. Crunching sounds came from under the blanket.

"I'm glad he's finally home and safe," said Jaime.

Cricket switched her helmet from one arm to the other. "Thank you."

"No problem. Do you want to sit down?"

"No," she said, switching the helmet back to the other arm. In decidedly un-Cricket-like behavior, she wouldn't meet his eyes.

"Is everything okay? Do you need something?"

"I have a secret," she said.

"Okay."

"It's a SECRET secret."

"Okay."

"I would tell my mom, but she might worry."

"Yeah. Moms do that sometimes."

Now she met his eyes. "You are not NEFARIOUS."

He almost winced but didn't. He said, "I hope not."

"So I think I can tell you."

"Only if you want to."

"It's Karl."

"What about him? I thought he was going to be okay."

"He's my best boy! But he's . . . different."

"Different in what way?"

As if to demonstrate, Karl threw aside the blankets. He was lolling on his back, casually eating Cheez Doodles.

"You know him better than I do, Cricket," said Jaime, "but he looks the same to me. Maybe a little too skinny, though. Needs more snacks."

"Do you have a pencil and paper?" said Cricket.

"Uh, yeah." Jaime pulled out his sketchbook and his pencil. He flipped the book to a clean page and handed it and the pencil to Cricket. He thought she might take some notes or write a SECRET message or whatever, but instead she offered the sketchbook and pencil to Karl. Karl put down the bag of cheese snacks and took the items in his tiny hands. He held the pencil in the air . . . thinking? Then he scribbled something on the page. He turned the sketchbook so Jaime could see what he'd scribbled.

My dear Mr. Cruz, I have quite the story to tell. You might want to sit down.

And Jaime did. He really, really did.

CHAPTER TWENTY
Darnell

Darnell Slant sat in the green room of the Queens Community Center and flicked through the latest tweets popping up on his feed. Cat video, cat video, cat picture, cat video, llama video, cat video. One of those videos was currently the number one trending topic.

"What's with all these cats?" he said irritably. And by this he meant, *Why am I not the trending topic? I should always be the trending topic.*

"Did you need something?"

Darnell looked up. Candi stood before him, eyes cool, red dress cutting her off at the knees, shoulder-length blond hair perfectly curled and fluffed. Maybe overfluffed. If she kept styling it that way, he'd have to talk to her about it. He couldn't have his official spokeswoman walking around looking like some sort of poodle-sheep in heels.

"Where are the reporters?" he asked her.

"They're outside waiting for your announcement."

"Right," he said. "Is Merry here yet?"

"Miss Roberts prefers to operate behind the scenes," said Candi.

"What does that mean?"

"It means she isn't coming. Remember? We discussed this the other day."

"I don't remember discussing it," said Slant. He did remember, but he'd hoped that Merry would change her mind. It wouldn't hurt to have one of the richest women in the city—in the country!—standing behind him at the podium while he announced his candidacy.

But then, he didn't *need* to have Merry, or anyone else, standing at the podium with him. He could win this election for mayor of New York with one hand tied behind his back. Both hands. Hands *and* legs. The current mayor was a dweeby little nerd with a nasal voice. Nobody wanted to listen to some pipsqueak yammer on about education or community building or whatever. The mayor had a doctorate in history, for Pete's sake! He wrote a whole book on the Morningstarrs! As if the Morningstarrs were still alive, still relevant somehow, not dead and buried long ago. As if anyone wanted to read an entire book on them when they could just listen to a podcast.

No, the people of New York City didn't need a history nerd. They needed someone to take charge. Someone smart enough to know that innovative and important technological developments couldn't be left in the hands of ordinary citizens. What did ordinary citizens know about running trains or producing energy? Nothing! And ordinary citizens didn't care, either, as long as the trains ran on time and the lights turned on, and they could take the kids out for a bugburger and fries every once in a while.

What they needed was someone who would push this arthritic city into the twenty-first century. Someone who had the know-how to buy up all the Morningstarr buildings and remaining Morningstarr tech and privatize it, *monetize* it. Someone who would get rid of lurching Rollers and caterpillars and spiders and every other antiquated machine and replace them with sleek machines of the future. Put the tech to work—not just on the streets, but in investment portfolios. Harness all that power and make it drive profits for the business leaders—the visionaries! the risk takers!—of the city.

Visionaries and risk takers like Darnell Slant himself.

His phone twittered. Again, he scrolled through his feed. Again, he didn't see his name. This time, he saw *her* name.

"Blast it," he said.

"Sir?" said Candi.

"I thought you said you had the Lora situation taken care of."

"I do," Candi said, fluttering outrageously long false lashes. "The nondisclosure agreement she signed is ironclad. She can't say a word about you."

"No, she's busy not saying anything," Darnell said. "And that says everything."

"I don't think so," said Candi.

"I don't pay you to think," said Darnell. "I pay you to *do*. And what I'd like you to *do* is to get my mother's locket back."

If Candi was thinking about who actually signed her checks, she didn't mention it. And if she doubted that the locket was really his mother's, she didn't mention that, either. She said, "I'm working on it."

"Work faster."

"I've had her place tossed on three separate occasions. My contacts at the bank have searched her safe-deposit boxes. Even the police have questioned her repeatedly. She denies taking it."

"She took it when she left," said Slant. "I *know* she did. And I know she still has it. Offer her money."

"I have."

"Offer her more."

"She doesn't want your money," said Candi.

"That's not what her divorce attorney said." Slant tossed his phone onto the couch. "What a snake that guy was."

Candi laid an exquisitely manicured hand on his shoulder. "Mr. Slant," she said, "be patient. I have my best people on the job. If she has your mother's locket, we'll find it." Her eyes twinkled. "Who knows? Maybe Detective Biedermann will find it for us. I hear she is the best."

"You invited her to come tonight?"

"Of course," Candi said. "I invited the whole family."

"We should take some pictures with them, send the pictures to the papers." He had a lot of support in the city, but he'd heard some grumbling. Some pictures with a lady detective could be useful.

"Is she pretty?"

"Who?" said Candi.

"The detective."

"Darnell."

"I'm just asking."

"She's married. Plus you knocked down her house."

"It wasn't her house. It was my house."

"Precisely the issue."

Darnell grunted, stood. He peered in the mirror and fixed his bangs. "Are you keeping an eye on those kids?"

"They're still running around the city. But they haven't met with the society members in the past few weeks. If they found something important, we're certain they would go to the society with it."

Darnell peered at her. "'*We're* certain'?"

"Me. I'm certain."

He stared at her a moment longer, but her expression didn't change. He turned back to the mirror. "They aren't going to find anything. If there was something worth finding, someone would have found it already."

"Hmmm," said Candi.

"But if they do find something, I want to be the first to know." He straightened the knot in his red tie. "What about that . . . animal?"

"Dr. Munsterberg has other concerns now."

"I hope that one of those concerns is beefing up his security," said Darnell. The doctor was another dweeby little weirdo in a world full of dweeby little weirdos, but

Candi had convinced Darnell that he should invest in the man's lab, that the man was at the forefront of . . . something. And what had happened? Some creatures had escaped. Darnell didn't need anything else to manage. He was going to have the biggest and most prosperous city in the world to run. And after that, he would have the world itself.

But Candi wasn't finished talking about the weirdos. "He's worried about the woman."

"What? Who is? Which woman?"

"Dr. Munsterberg," said Candi patiently. "He's worried about the woman who was working with the children and the society."

"The one that got the better of you and Goodson?"

At this, Candi's red lips twitched. "I escaped."

"Goodson didn't, though. Who knew he was such a lightweight?"

"I did, sir," said Candi. "Dr. Munsterberg says—"

"Dr. Munsterberg is a little dweeb," Darnell said.

"Miss Roberts thinks he's an important dweeb," Candi said.

"An important dweeb is still a dweeb," Darnell said. "Where's my speech?"

"It's loaded in the teleprompter. And I'll put a copy on the podium for you."

"Good," he said. "You kept the part about Station One?"

Candi sighed. "I did, but I still wonder if it's too soon to announce specific plans on that."

"What are you talking about? The people are going to love it. That station is old and crowded and filled with strange machines. We'll knock it down and build something new and fabulous, without all that ancient technology. We'll make a deal with a train company to manage all the transportation, generate some real money for this city."

"What about the Guildmen?"

"What about them?"

"They filed a motion in court."

"What? What kind of motion? They can't file a motion. We haven't done anything yet."

"They're not happy."

"Progress is always going to be uncomfortable for somebody. Once we make a deal and they see how great it is, they'll adjust," said Darnell, smoothing his brows. "Everyone always does."

"Whatever you say." Candi checked her phone. "You're on in ten minutes. I'll be back in five to get you."

"Thanks."

Candi walked away, high heels snapping on the floor tiles. An ice princess, that one. She thought he didn't know how ambitious she was, how much she was kissing up to Merry Roberts. But of course he knew. That was what he would have done, if he were her.

Still. He would watch his back.

You could never trust a woman.

Darnell stood in front of the mirror and rehearsed his speech out loud, enunciating each line. He'd taken elocution lessons to get rid of his chewy Queens accent, but sometimes it came out and people commented on it. *Laughed* at it. Like the people at Merry Roberts's gatherings. Bunch of snotty jerks, they were. He went to the same fancy schools they did, and they still treated him like trash.

When he was mayor, he'd make them all pay. He'd make them all *grovel*.

He was humming to himself when Candi returned. He followed her out of the green room and into the conference space. As he stepped up to the podium, the cameras flashed. Darnell Slant raised both arms, as if he'd already won.

CHAPTER TWENTY-ONE

Tess

Tess's mind was always buzzing with what-if questions.

Except when it wasn't.

Sometimes, the sheer number of what-if questions got to be too much and threatened to drown her. So she shut them out. Her brain conveniently erased what it found too overwhelming to think about.

Like the mushroom Lego man who had come to the door yesterday.

Tess had been sitting with her family at the dinner table, brain uncharacteristically *not* buzzing with endless questions, instead humming with pleasure at the pasta she was eating, when her mother said, "I got a strange call today."

"Ummm," said Tess.

"It was a woman who represented Darnell Slant. She said that there were seats for the whole family at an event? That we were special guests? Do you know anything about this?"

Tess coughed up little darts of spaghetti as Theo helpfully smacked her back.

"I'd take that as a yes," said Tess's dad, stabbing into a meatball.

"A man came to the door and gave Tess a flyer," Theo explained. "We didn't think he was serious, though."

"Why would they have special seats for us?" said their mother. "Did the man say?"

Tess took a gulp of water. To tell or not to tell, that was the question.

As it had many times before, Tess's mouth decided for her. She put the water glass back on the table and said, "He threatened us. He said that we would want to go if we know what's good for us. He said that Slant would hurt us."

Tess's mom sat very, very still. Her eyes got hard. "He said . . . what?"

"He didn't threaten us directly. It was more like, 'You wouldn't want anything to happen to you,' or whatever. He looked like a mushroom."

"Like a mushroom," her mother repeated. Tess's parents shared a meaningful glance.

"A really big one," Theo added. "Also a Lego."

"A mushroom Lego," Tess said.

"Did this mushroom Lego say why he wanted us at this event?"

"He said he was going around the neighborhood. But he seemed to be looking for you, specifically. Or maybe Dad. Or both of you. He kept trying to look behind me into the house."

Tess's dad said, "I'm having flashbacks to 354 West 73rd."

Her mother checked her watch. She pushed back her chair, wiped her mouth with her napkin, and threw the napkin on the table. "Well, if Slant wants me there, he's going to get me. Because I want to know why he sent mushroom Legos to my house to scare my children. The event is probably still going on."

"Mom," Tess began. "Don't. What if—"

"He can't hurt me, Tess. And he won't hurt you. Any of you. If I have to arrest him for being a jerk, I will."

"You said you couldn't do that," said Theo.

"Maybe I changed my mind." She stood and took her plate to the sink, dumped it in the basin. She snatched her jacket from the back of the chair and swung it around her shoulders like a cape. She checked her pocket for her badge.

Their dad stood, too. "I'm coming with you."

"Honey, you don't have to."

Their dad's voice was steely. "Miriam, I am coming. Call for backup if you want, but I am coming with you."

"Should we—" Tess and Theo began.

"No!" shouted their parents.

"You stay here," their mom said. "Lock the door. Don't answer it for anyone. And if anyone rings the bell or knocks or calls or even breathes near the house, you call me, okay?"

Tess and Theo nodded. Their parents marched out of the kitchen and then out of the house. Tess and Theo both flinched when the front door slammed.

"Think I should have told her?" said Tess.

"We probably should have told her when it happened," said Theo.

"We had other things on our minds." Tess picked up her fork and then put it back on the plate. "I'm not hungry anymore, are you?"

"No," said Theo. "Let's clean up."

They cleared the table and washed the dishes, put the leftover food away in the fridge. Then they went upstairs to their room. Nine watched them from her perch on Tess's bed. Normally, they would be taking this time to go through the things they'd found in the cave, but they'd given the bag of discoveries to Jaime. Now they sat on the floor, picking at the rug. Tess tried to imagine what her mom would do when she arrived at the meeting where Slant was speaking. She envisioned her mom slapping cuffs on him, dragging him off to the Tombs.

The Tombs.

If the Tombs really were the site of the next clue, how were they going to explore them?

Theo knew her well. "How are we going to get into the Tombs?" he said.

"I don't know," said Tess.

"I'm not even talking about the thousands of cops all over that building, I'm talking about Mom."

"I know."

"I feel bad enough that we've been keeping things from her."

"She doesn't want to hear about the Cipher. If she knew we were still looking for it, she'd be mad. You remember how she used to get with Grandpa Ben. She thought it was a bunch of nonsense. His whole life's work. A bunch of nonsense."

Theo nodded.

"So we can only tell her when we solve it."

Theo nodded again, pulled on his lip. After a long silence, he said, "I've been thinking about doppelgängers."

"Okay."

"You know, doubles?"

"I know what a doppelgänger is." Tess hesitated, then she just spat it out, the thing that had been itching at the back of her mind. "I don't think the people in that photograph, the Morningstarrs, are doppelgängers."

Theo rested his head against the side of his bed. "Me neither."

"And I don't think the photo was doctored."

Theo closed his eyes, then opened them. "Me neither."

"I think . . . I think . . ."

Theo's hands disappeared into his bushy hair. "Say it. Just say it."

"I think they might be us."

Theo twitched as if she'd poked him with a pin, a knife, a sword. "It's impossible."

"Yes. But what if it's true?"

"I don't know. I don't know what to do if it's true. I don't know how to . . . I don't know how . . ."

Tess wasn't sure what he meant: He didn't know how

they were going to keep on living? He didn't know how they were going to keep on *being*? She didn't, either. The enormity of what she'd just said weighed her to the floor; for a minute, she couldn't move. Then she said, "We're going to keep doing what we're doing. We're going to keep looking. Even if we don't like what we find."

Theo opened his eyes. "Why?"

"Because if we are the Morningstarrs, then we set this all up. We set this in motion. Maybe we even set these clues for ourselves. For a reason. We wouldn't do this without a reason. And if we're not the Morningstarrs—"

"I vote for that one."

"If we're not the Morningstarrs, we need to know the truth anyway. Don't you need to know the truth?"

"I thought I did," said Theo.

"You do. You always have and you always will want to know the truth."

Theo's mouth quirked up on one side. "But you can't know that."

"I know you," said Tess.

"If you tell me that you know me better than I know myself, I'll vomit so hard I'll turn myself inside out."

"I know you better than I know *myself*," said Tess. "At least sometimes that's how it feels."

Theo scrubbed at his cheeks with both hands. "Yeah."

Another thought itched at the back of Tess's brain. "And maybe I know—we know—Mom, too."

"What do you mean?"

"Well, if someone threatened us, what would Mom do?"

"According to you, someone *did* threaten us. And she's now going to freak out at some community meeting. Probably on camera."

"She doesn't freak out. She goes by the book. But she'll do anything to protect us, right? Keep us close."

"Keep us close?"

"Yeah, like maybe take us to work with her?"

Theo leaned forward. "Take us . . ."

"To the Tombs," Tess said. "Where we'll be safe."

Tess did know their mother. When their parents came home, their mom was in a fury, a particular kind of fury—quiet, white-hot. She charged into the kitchen. Banging sounds echoed all the way into the living room. Lance came clomping out of the kitchen, looking about as concerned as an empty suit of armor can look.

"Is Mom okay?" Theo asked their dad.

"Slant wanted to take a picture with your mother."

"A picture? Why?"

"Because he assumed we were supporting him," said

their dad, making the sort of face toddlers make when someone spoons mashed green beans into their mouths. "He thought we were there because we wanted to be a part of his 'movement.'"

"What did Mom say?" Tess wanted to know.

"Well," said their dad, "she informed him that if he ever threatened her family again, or sent anyone to our house to speak with our children without parental permission, she would make his life a living hell. That is not a direct quote, by the way."

"What did Slant say?"

"He smiled as the cameras flashed. I'm not even sure he heard what she said."

"Or maybe he just didn't care as long as he got the picture he wanted."

More crashing sounds from the kitchen. *SLAM! BOOM! SMASH!*

"In any case, your mom's on a tear," their dad continued. "And I'm afraid that she might want to put you two in custom-made giant hamster balls to keep you safe. Maybe with an army of attack dogs."

"Mrrow," said Nine, indignant.

"Attack cats," their dad corrected. "It might be best if you two stayed close to home, at least for the next day or two. I know you've been spending your days wandering, but I don't think that's the best idea right now."

Tess knew her father, too. "We have a project we need to do for school," she said. "For our civics class."

"A summer project?" said her father. "When is this due?"

Tess did her best to look embarrassed. "Right when we get back."

"And you haven't started it?"

"Well . . . ," said Tess.

"Tess! Theo! School is important! You have to keep up with your assignments!"

"Sorry, Dad," Theo said.

"We lost track of time," said Tess.

Their father sighed one of his long-suffering sighs. "Okay, what's the project about?"

"Social justice," said Tess. "We're supposed to write a paper about justice and what it means."

"And who gets justice and who doesn't?" said their father.

"Yes," said Tess. "And we were thinking that maybe Mom would be able to take us to work with her. To see how she does her job. Maybe we could interview some of the other officers and detectives."

"And that way, we'll be safe," Theo added. "I mean, what could be safer than being with Mom?"

"Being with Mom at the headquarters of the New York City Police Department," Tess said.

Their dad stroked his chin, thinking. Then he said, "Okay. Let's ask her."

It didn't take much convincing for their mother to agree to take Tess and Theo to work with her. And it didn't take much more convincing to get her to agree to take Jaime, too.

Tess texted Jaime. **Can u come with us tomorrow?**

Think so.

Did you find anything?

???

On the scroll.

Will look later.

Can't you look now?

Cricket is here.

And???

Long story. Too long for text. Tell you tomorrow.

OK. Meet you at the Tombs. 9 am.

Which is how all three of them ended up standing in front of the headquarters of the New York City Police Department—aka the Tombs—with the twins' mom—aka Detective Miriam Biedermann. The building looked more like an Egyptian temple than a tomb, with four huge columns marking the entryway.

Theo read from his phone: "'Designed by John Havi-land, the building's Egyptian facade was inspired by the temple at Dendera, a temple dedicated to the goddess Hathor. The building is connected to the courthouses across the street by an enclosed pedestrian bridge called the Bridge of Sighs.'"

"Why is it called the Bridge of Sighs?" Tess asked.

Her mother said, "It's named after a bridge in Venice. Back in the day, people passed over this bridge on their way to prison. It's said that they could take one last look at the city and sigh."

"The goddess Hathor helped souls transition from one world to the next," said Theo.

"You mean transition from living to dead?" Tess said. "That's cheerful."

"I don't think it's meant to be," said Jaime.

"I don't think so, either," said Tess's mom.

The building was both old and enormous, so enormous that Tess couldn't take all of it in without turning almost all the way around. Early that morning, Tess had gotten some more texts from Jaime telling her that he'd examined the scroll they'd found in the Ramble Cave, as well as the message on the scroll: *Who can find justice in the Halls of Justice?* But he hadn't found anything else that indicated *where* in the "halls of justice" they needed to look.

So, Tess asked herself, if you were Theresa Morning-starr—and what if you are . . . were . . . are . . . were . . . whatever? Where, exactly, would you hide the next clue? In a pillar? In a cornerstone? In an interview room? In a closet? On a bridge? In a cell? Since her mother said that Nine had to stay home, Tess shoved her hands into her pockets to keep them from shaking. Of all the things they'd done, all the places they'd been, and all the places they'd searched for clues, this task seemed the most impossible.

Tess's mom led them up the stairs and into the building. Though Tess did her best to study the space, she was distracted by the people flooding by, all of them nodding at her mom or greeting her with a "Good morning, Detective," delivered with solemn respect. Her mother pointed out this or that feature of the building: up is where the cops and detectives work, up and over is how you get to the Bridge of Sighs and then the courthouse, head left if you're looking for the best vending machines in the building.

"Where do you keep, I mean, where are the . . . prisoners?" Jaime asked.

"Lockup is downstairs," said Tess's mom. "And before

you ask, no, I'm not going to take you there."

Her mother flashed her badge and ID at the guards in front of the elevators, and then they were rattling up to the third floor. They exited and walked down the hallway into a bustling office crowded with desks. Nearly everyone at these desks was talking on their phones, though they, too, nodded or waved at Tess's mom as she passed by.

Tess's mom herded them to the back corner of the large room, where a desk was pushed up against a dirty window. "Here we are," she said. "Have a seat."

Tess, Theo, and Jaime sat in the chairs opposite Tess's mom. Detective Clarkson, her mom's partner, ambled over carrying two cups of coffee. He set one cup in front of Tess's mom.

"Hey, kids!" he said. "Detective Biedermann told me that you're here to observe us for a school project?"

"Yep!" said Tess. "We're writing about justice."

"Cool beans," he said. "You came to the right place."

"I hope so," said Tess.

"Speaking of justice," said Detective Clarkson, "did you hear any more about that woman who pushed you off the ferry, Jaime?"

Jaime pulled off the strap of Tess's messenger bag and put the bag on the floor between them. "Some people came to show me pictures, but I didn't recognize any of them."

"Huh," said Detective Clarkson. "That's too bad. I'm sure the guys on the case won't stop looking, though. Did you want to check in with them today?"

"Maybe later," said Jaime. "I'm more interested in learning about what you do every day."

"You're one tough cookie, aren't you?" Detective Clarkson said, sipping his coffee. "If someone pushed me off a boat, I wouldn't be thinking about anything else."

"I'm not so tough," Jaime said. "I mean, I don't want to tell my grandmother that I waited until the last minute to do this project."

Tess's mom and Detective Clarkson laughed. To Clarkson, Tess's mom said, "Okay, so if nothing new has come up overnight, I'm going to take the kids on a tour."

"About that," Detective Clarkson began.

At that moment, the once-noisy room hushed. A gorgeous Asian woman dressed in black—black dress, black heels, black sunglasses, black scarf streaming behind her like a trail of smoke—tacked through the sea of desks, followed by four men in black suits. The woman and her entourage stopped in front of Tess's mom's corner desk.

"Hello, Detectives," she said in a warm voice. "It seems that you can't get enough of me. This is the second time you've requested my company?"

"I thought we agreed on tomorrow," said Tess's mom.

"I like to be spontaneous," said the woman.

Once more, Tess's mouth was faster than her brain. "Is that . . . are you . . . ?"

The woman removed her sunglasses, revealing beautiful dark eyes. "It is, and I am."

"Kids," said Tess's mother, "meet Lora Yoshida."

CHAPTER TWENTY-TWO
Theo

Theo willed his sister not to blurt anything that might hint at the real reason they were at the Tombs.

And she didn't. Instead, she blurted, "You were married to Darnell Slant! Mom, I thought you said you were going to arrest—"

Theo elbowed her, hard.

Tess rubbed her arm and mumbled, "How could a person marry a man like that?"

Lora Yoshida's smile didn't waver. "Some of us make mistakes when we're young."

"Terrible mistakes!" Tess said.

"Yes," said Lora Yoshida. "Terrible mistakes that one must spend years, perhaps even a lifetime, atoning for.

I certainly hope you don't make those kinds of mistakes, Ms. . . . ?"

Tess rubbed her shoulder as if she'd been stung. "Biedermann. My name is Tess Biedermann."

Lora Yoshida shook Tess's hand. "Pleased to meet you, Ms. Biedermann." She looked at Theo's mom. "This is your daughter? What a lovely girl." She seemed to mean it. Then she turned to Theo. "And you are a Biedermann as well?"

"Theo," croaked Theo, his tongue fumbling over his own name.

"Theo," Lora Yoshida repeated. "You have truly spectacular hair."

"Uh," said Theo, "huh." Lora Yoshida was very beautiful and smelled like something perfumey and sweet. When she shook his hand, her fingers were long and slim. He wondered if she played the piano.

"Do you play the piano?" he asked.

"I think my brother means 'thank you,'" said Tess. "And maybe 'nice to meet you.'"

"Of course he does," said Lora Yoshida.

"Jaime Cruz," said Jaime when Lora Yoshida offered her hand to him.

"Lovely to meet you as well, Mr. Cruz," said Lora Yoshida.

"We're doing a project on justice," Theo offered, for no particular reason he could understand.

"Well, that's wonderful," said Lora Yoshida. "And you've come to the police station to see justice in action, I take it?" Her expression was filled with amusement. She tucked her glasses into her large handbag. "Perhaps you would like to sit in on my latest interview?"

"Yes!" Theo practically shouted.

"No!" said the army of suited men with Lora Yoshida.

Lora Yoshida waved her hand at the men. "Oh, what could it hurt? You'll all be watching. And maybe the children will learn something. What do you say, Detective Biedermann? Care to make it a party?"

Theo's mom considered Lora Yoshida for a long while and then said. "If you don't mind, then I don't mind. I'll take you to the interview room."

Lora Yoshida flipped her scarf over her shoulder. "Oh, allow me. I know the way."

As the group of them filed into the interview room, led by the twins' mom, Detective Clarkson muttered, "I don't know what the cream sauce is going on, but I don't like this."

"What's not to like?" said Lora Yoshida. She and her people—lawyers, Theo supposed—sat on one side of a long table, and Theo's mom and Detective Clarkson sat on the other. Theo, Tess, and Jaime took chairs at one end of the table and tried to make themselves invisible. It didn't work. Lora Yoshida beamed at them.

"It does feel like a party. Except there are no hors d'oeuvres. One does enjoy a snack in the morning. Perhaps some caviar on toast."

"Sorry," said Theo's mom. "No caviar here, though I could get you some potato chips and a soda from the vending machines."

"No, thank you, Detective," said Lora Yoshida. "Well, shall we get started? What would you like to ask me about today?"

Theo's mom opened a file folder and leafed through it. "As you already know, your ex-husband—"

"Ugh. Please don't call him that." Lora Yoshida shuddered.

"No problem," said Theo's mom. "Mr. Darnell Slant has claimed that you stole a certain necklace belonging to his mother."

"Mr. Slant doesn't have a mother. Mr. Slant crawled out from under a rock," said Lora Yoshida.

"Lora," said one of the suited men.

"Oh, I forgot. *Allegedly.* Allegedly, Mr. Slant crawled out from under a rock. In my humble opinion."

"Ms. Yoshida," said Detective Clarkson, "it would help if you took this seriously."

"I am deadly serious," said Lora Yoshida.

"As I was saying," Theo's mom cut in, "Mr. Slant claimed you stole a necklace belonging to him."

"However could I do that?" Lora Yoshida said. "Mr. Slant owns properties all over the city and probably has vaults in all of them. I don't know how to break into vaults, Detective."

Theo's mom removed a photo from the file. "This photo is a still taken from a surveillance camera at the Starr Hotel."

"You mean the Slant Hotel?" said Lora Yoshida, the smile falling from her face. "Or has he not yet renamed the latest priceless antique building he purchased?"

His mom's expression didn't change. "Is this you, Ms. Yoshida?" She slid the photo across the table.

Lora Yoshida studied the photo. "I can't say it is."

"You can't say, or you won't say?"

"Same difference," said Lora Yoshida. "This person, whoever it is, needs a stylist. No one wears a unitard these days. It's ridiculous. You might as well scream, 'I'm a cat burglar!' No subtlety at all." She nudged the photo with a fingertip, as if the bad styling might catch.

Theo's mom pulled another photo from the file. "Do you recognize this?"

Lora Yoshida took the second picture. "This appears to be a necklace."

"Do you recognize it?"

Lora Yoshida slid the picture back to Theo's mom. "It looks cheap."

"Apparently, it has a lot of sentimental value to Mr. Slant," said his mom.

"One would have to have a heart in order for something to have sentimental value," Lora Yoshida said. "Darnell Slant doesn't have a heart. Allegedly."

"He doesn't have a necklace, either," said Detective Clarkson.

"The poor dear," said Lora Yoshida. "He can buy a new one."

"Have you seen this necklace before?" said Theo's mom.

"I can't say," said Lora Yoshida.

Theo's mom sighed and put both pictures back into her file. "I need another cup of coffee. Would you like anything, Ms. Yoshida?"

"No, thank you, Detective Biedermann," said Ms. Yoshida. "I'll just wait here for you."

"Be right back," said Theo's mom.

"Take your time," said Lora Yoshida. When Theo's mom stepped out of the room, with Detective Clarkson right behind her, Lora Yoshida turned her gaze on Theo, Tess, and Jaime. "So, children, what do you think of the interview so far?"

"I think you don't want to answer any questions," Theo said.

"Hey!" said one of the suited men.

But Lora Yoshida laughed. "I think your mother doesn't really want to ask me any questions."

Theo pressed the issue. "Did you take the necklace?"

"What necklace?" said Lora Yoshida, and laughed again. She seemed to be having a great time for a person sitting in a police station.

"Why did you marry him?" Tess asked.

"Kid, that's none of your business," said one of the suited men.

"It's all right, Bert," said Lora Yoshida.

"My name's Bart."

"Yes, whatever," said Lora Yoshida. She put her elbows on the table and leaned toward Tess. "How old are you?"

"Thirteen," said Tess.

"So I can assume you've never been in love?"

Tess flushed a furious shade of summer tomato. "No."

Lora Yoshida said, "Sometimes, we fall for a person. But it's not like it is in the movies—we don't fall in love because that person is a good person or a kind person. We fall for a person because that person *isn't* good or kind, and because we were treated unkindly when we were young. We fall for that person's wounds because we, ourselves, are wounded. And the unkindness of this not-good, not-kind person feels familiar, and we imagine this familiarity is love. And we tell ourselves that if we are good and kind enough ourselves, we can fix that not-good, not-kind person, heal that person and make that person love us back. And in so doing, we can also heal ourselves, rewrite the story of our lives." Lora Yoshida paused, laying her hands flat on the table. "Of course, it's a mistake. A heartbreaking mistake. You can't fix someone else. They can only fix themselves. It took me a long time to learn this lesson. I hope you never have to learn it. Not the way I did."

"I . . . ," said Tess. She fingered the surface of the table where someone had scratched a sad face. "I'm sorry."

"So am I," said Lora Yoshida, flipping her glossy hair over one shoulder. "I could be working on another art piece instead of being one of your mother's guests, as much as I enjoy her company."

"If you didn't take the necklace, you must be angry that Darnell Slant keeps saying you did," said Theo.

"I don't waste much time on anger these days," said Lora Yoshida. "I'd rather pour my frustrations into my work. Besides, it amuses me to be a thorn in Darnell Slant's side. It's the least I can do."

"Jaime's an artist," said Tess.

"Really? What kind?" said Lora Yoshida.

"I draw a little," said Jaime.

"He's really good," Tess said. "Jaime, show her some of your drawings."

"That's okay," Jaime said. "You don't have to look at them."

Ono poked his head out from Jaime's pocket. "Oh no."

Lora Yoshida's face filled with delight. "Who is that?"

Jaime took Ono from his pocket and put the robot on the table. "This is Ono."

Lora Yoshida beamed at Ono. "Pleased to meet you, Ono. My name is Lora Yoshida." She used her thumb and forefinger to shake Ono's tiny hand.

"Land of Kings," said Ono.

"I would love to see your drawings, Mr. Cruz," said Lora Yoshida, still beaming. "If you'd care to show me."

Jaime reluctantly pulled out his sketchbook. "I'm just

playing around a little. They're nothing special."

"Oh no," said Ono.

"Your friends think you're being too modest, so you probably are." Lora Yoshida opened the sketchbook to the first page. She took her time with each drawing, examining them. "These are lovely," she said. "You are quite talented. And versatile, too. Landscapes *and* figures. So much energy and movement." She stopped at a drawing of Ava Oneal, glanced up at Jaime. "Who is this?"

Jaime shook his head. "Just a character I made up."

"A character," said Lora Yoshida. "Not a real person?"

"I can't say," said Jaime.

"Why?" Theo said. "Does she look familiar?"

"Perhaps she has one of those faces." Lora Yoshida closed the sketchbook and gave it back to Jaime. Then she turned to her lawyers.

"Bert, can you and the boys go out there and find out what's keeping Detective Biedermann? I would like to leave here sometime today."

"Bart," said Bart.

"Thank you, Bert," said Lora Yoshida as the men filed out of the room. Once they were gone, she stood and unwound the scarf from around her neck. She yawned and stretched, draping the scarf over the camera in the corner of the room as she did. She put a finger to her lips: *Shhhh.*

None of them said a word. She reached under the collar of her dress and pulled out a silver chain on which hung a locket. She draped it around Tess's neck. Tess shivered when the chain touched her neck, but she allowed Lora Yoshida to fasten the clasp. Lora Yoshida leaned down, her lustrous black hair forming a curtain.

"This locket isn't mine," she whispered. "But it's not Darnell's, either. And it's definitely not his mother's. A friend found it in a place you'd never find Darnell Slant."

"Where?" Jaime asked.

"The library," said Lora Yoshida. "It was hidden in a first edition of a book called *The Lost Ones.* Someone had hollowed out the pages and tucked it inside. My friend was worried that the wrong people would get ahold of it, so she asked me to find the right people. Darnell stole it from *me.* He only wants it because I have it. And now you do."

"But why—" Tess began.

Again, Lora Yoshida put her finger to her lips. Then she pulled the scarf away from the camera and sat back in her seat.

Tess had just tucked the locket into her T-shirt when Detective Clarkson burst into the room. "What in the sloppy joe is going on in here?"

"Detective," said Lora Yoshida. "We were waiting for you."

"Did you do something to the camera?"

"Me? Whatever could I do to the camera?" said Lora Yoshida. "I'm not a photographer."

"Ms. Yoshida," Theo's mom said from behind Detective Clarkson, "I'm sorry we were gone so long. I brought you a soda." She put a red can on the table. "We have a few more questions and then we're finished."

"No champagne?" Lora Yoshida shook her head and opened her purse, rifling through it. "I think we're finished now."

Theo's mom took a deep breath. "Ms. Yoshida. I'm sorry about this. We have to follow up on complaints."

"I understand the pressure you're under better than you think," said Lora Yoshida. "I know you have a job to do. But so do I. And it doesn't include coming to the Tombs for any more visits, as pleasant as these visits have been." She got up from her chair. "Tell Mr. Slant that if he makes any more complaints against me, I'll have to sue him."

"We'll sue the whole city," said Bert/Bart from the

doorway, and the suited men with him all nodded vigorously. "That might put a damper on his mayoral campaign."

"Or it might *help* his campaign," grumbled Detective Clarkson.

Lora Yoshida smiled, but it wasn't a happy smile. "Perhaps that's what he wants. Did you ever think about that? That you believe that you're doing exactly what *you* want to do when you're really doing what someone has manipulated you into doing?"

Now Theo's mom smiled the same sort of grim smile Lora Yoshida had. She scraped the photos together and slipped them back into the file folder. "Thank you for your time, Ms. Yoshida. You're free to go."

"Is anyone really and truly free? That's what your children should be writing about for their school projects." Lora Yoshida put on her sunglasses and walked to the door. She paused and looked back. "Who can find justice in the Halls of Justice?" Then she swept out of the room, the scarf trailing behind her.

CHAPTER TWENTY-THREE
Jaime

Jaime's dad liked old cartoons. Ever since he'd gotten back from Sudan, one of his favorite things to do was to watch Looney Tunes cartoons, with Bugs Bunny and the Road Runner and the rest, some of the episodes as old as Mima. He would laugh at Bugs and Tweety and Sylvester the cat and Elmer Fudd. He even laughed at Pepé Le Pew, a skunk who falls in love with a cat and won't stop grabbing her and kissing her no matter how much she tries to get away.

"This is creepy, Dad," Jaime had told his father. "That skunk is a criminal."

His dad didn't put Pepé Le Pew on anymore.

Now, touring the Tombs with the twins and Detective Biedermann, Jaime felt like Pepé Le Pew's cat, itching to get away, except his arms weren't flailing and his feet weren't running. Instead, he listened as Detective Biedermann talked to them about crime and punishment, investigations and evidence, justice and injustice. She told them about how people filed complaints and reports, how she went about gathering clues. She couldn't talk about cases in progress without the permission of the people involved, but she did talk about cases she had been able to close and how she'd done it. By working the phone, she said, or pounding the pavement. Asking questions, sometimes the same ones, over and over again. Just like you did when you were trying to solve a Cipher, Jaime thought.

So he nodded and took photos when Detective Biedermann led them on a tour of the building, said hello when she introduced them to this officer or that detective. And yet the whole morning, his whole body screamed, *LET ME OUT OF HERE.* Not just because the old, musty building with its creepy crypt vibe gave him the jitters—though it did—but because he wanted to be alone with Tess and Theo. He wanted to get a closer look at the locket around Tess's neck; he wanted to ask them what they thought of Lora Yoshida, if they thought she had recognized Ava Oneal from Jaime's drawings. He was almost certain she had. And he was even more certain that she'd given them the locket because she had recognized Ava. But did that mean she knew where Ava was? Were they friends? Could a seemingly immortal superhero woman have friends?

And what about what Lora had said before she left: *Who can find justice in the Halls of Justice?* Those were the same words that were on the scroll they'd found. Did that mean that Lora Yoshida herself was the next clue in the Cipher? Or that the locket was? And if either of these things were clues, then wasn't that proof that the Morningstarrs had known what would happen in the future? That they had known that Tess and Theo would be at this place at this time, that they had known *Jaime* would be at this place at this time, that Jaime would show Lora Yoshida his sketches and she, in turn, would offer up the locket? And if the Morningstarrs knew the future— how? Because they'd built a machine to predict it?

Or—because the Biedermann twins really *were* the Morningstarrs.

The Tombs, the twins, Lora Yoshida, Ava Oneal, the locket, the feel of Ono in his pocket, Detective Biedermann's careful explanations of her job, the sheer weight of history made his legs slow, his feet heavy, as if he were wading through a sea of something dense and suffocating. He had once read about a wave of molasses that had swept from a collapsed tank in Boston in the early twentieth century. The wave reached twenty-five feet high, moved at thirty-five miles an hour, and killed twenty-one people. Jaime imagined drowning in molasses, the thick sugary scent of it, the sticky fluid sucking at your limbs and filling your nose and mouth and swallowing you down down down down . . .

"Look down and you'll get a nice view of the city," Detective Biedermann was saying.

They were standing on the Bridge of Sighs. Jaime looked out the window, looked down. The street cut a wide path below them; the blue sky above wore a silvery lace of clouds. How many people had stood right where he was standing and sighed, wanting more than anything to go home?

"What do you three want for lunch?" Detective Biedermann asked them.

"I don't care," said Tess. Her hand was at her throat, and Jaime knew she was thinking about the locket, maybe even feeling its shape under her fingers.

"Theo? Jaime? Opinions?"

Jaime spoke for them both: "Whatever you'd like, Mrs. Biedermann."

"Since when do you guys not have an opinion about lunch?"

"Since today, I guess," said Theo.

"Today has been a lot," said Detective Biedermann. "The whole summer has been a lot, I know. For all of you. And maybe I shouldn't have let you sit in on that interview."

"Oh no," said Tess. "We're glad you did. It was really interesting."

It was Detective Biedermann's turn to sigh. She tugged thoughtfully on her lower lip; Jaime now understood where Theo might have picked up that gesture. She let go of her lip and said, "I don't always like everything I have to do."

"Nobody does," said Detective Clarkson. "Right?"

They all stood there, thinking about not liking what you have to do, and doing it anyway.

Detective Clarkson said, "I vote for falafel. Who's with me?"

They didn't get back to the twins' house until dinnertime, and didn't get a chance to talk about Lora Yoshida, the locket, or anything else until after they'd eaten Aunt Esther's homemade corn chowder, salad, and crab cakes, plus Fig Newtons for dessert. They helped clean up the dishes and then ran to the twins' room with Nine on their heels. Once the door was closed, they all fell on the nearest surface: the beds, the floor.

"I feel like I've been hit with a wave of molasses," Jaime said, spread-eagled on the rug.

"Me too," said Theo.

"Oh no," said Ono. Nine sniffed at Jaime's pocket. Jaime set Ono in front of the cat. The cat mrrowed and Ono burbled back. Ono waddled away and Nine bounded after it, both of them making happy buzzing noises.

Tess, however, had already sat up and taken off the necklace given to her by Lora Yoshida. Even though it was still light outside, she turned on a lamp and held the locket under it.

"Anything on it?" said Jaime. He was going to get up and look for himself, but he was too comfortable on the floor. Or too flattened to move.

"No," said Tess. "It's plain on both sides."

"Open it," Theo said. "Maybe there are pictures inside it."

"Pictures of a baby Darnell Slant, all pink and jolly?" said Jaime.

"Ugh," said Tess. "Darnell was never a baby."

"Everyone was a baby once," Jaime said. "Even Darnell."

"You're feeling sorry for him?" said Theo.

"No," Jaime said. "I'm feeling sorry for myself. I'm tired and I think my brain is broken."

"Yeah?" Tess said, trying to pry open the locket. "Who broke it? Lora? My mom?"

"You. You two broke it."

Tess stopped struggling with the locket. "What do you mean?"

Jaime, still too comfortable to get off the floor, rolled over to look at her. "I mean that I think there are two possibilities here. One, the Morningstarrs could tell the future. They knew exactly when our old apartment building would be destroyed, knew precisely when and where we would have to be in order to follow the clues. Some of the objects involved in steps of the Cipher didn't even *exist* until after they were dead. Maybe they built a machine that could let them see the future. Maybe a supercomputer or something, something that could predict things."

"What's the other possibility?" Theo said.

"You know what the other possibility is," Jaime said. "You're them. Or they're you. Both." He struggled to sit up. "Which means—"

Theo clapped his hands to his face. "Don't say it."

"Which means they—you—had some way to travel through time."

"Or maybe this is all a dream," said Theo.

"We're not going to know until we know," Tess said.

Theo said, "My sister, the human fortune cookie."

"But you have to admit it's true," said Tess. "Ugh, I can't get this open." She put the locket on the side table and flung herself back on her bed.

Jaime lay down, too, looking at the ceiling. The twins had pasted fluorescent stars up there, and in the lamplight, they looked slightly greenish. Tiny alien stars. Next to him, Nine and Ono chased one another around the room. When Nine cornered Ono, a tiny propeller erupted from the robot's head, and it hovered in the air like a helicopter.

"Did you know Ono could do that?" said Theo.

"Ono can do a lot of things," Jaime said. Then he sat straight up. "I forgot to tell you! What I was going to tell you when you called earlier!"

"What?" said the twins.

"You have to promise to keep it a secret, though. Because I promised Cricket."

"Who are we going to tell?" Theo said. "We only talk to you."

"Y'all need more friends," said Jaime as lightly as he could, though secretly he was pleased. "It's about Karl."

"Karl? Is he okay?" Tess said.

"Uh, I think so," said Jaime. "He's little different now, though."

Theo asked the same question Jaime had asked when Cricket came to see him: "Different how?"

"Well, he learned how to write, for one thing."

Now Tess and Theo both sat up. "Write? What do you mean, write?"

"I mean he knows how to write. With a pen and paper. English. Words and sentences and paragraphs."

Theo said, "That's not—"

"Possible?" said Jaime.

But Tess would not hold on. "Well, what did he say—I mean, write?"

"He said he was kidnapped by a man of ill intent. Those were his words."

"'A man of ill intent'?"

"Some kind of scientist who was experimenting on animals. Mixing and matching characteristics, it seems. Blending them. Making hybrids."

"Hybrids?" Tess said. They all looked at Nine, who was leaping to catch Ono, her open mouth a smile.

"Yeah," Jaime said. "And not like the friendly pet ones everyone has. Spider-wolves and other kinds of things."

"Spider-wolves?" said Theo. "Who would want to make a spider-wolf?"

"*Why* would you want to make a spider-wolf?" Tess said.

Jaime said, "Remember that hand monster thing those creeps Stoop and Pinscher had at 354 West 73rd? What if that hand thing came from the same place? And what if it's the same person who had that lab at North Brother Island?"

"With the giraffe-owary," Theo said.

"Was Karl kept on the island?" Tess asked.

"No, he said it was somewhere in Manhattan, I think. He couldn't say where, exactly. Except that it was very far, and that he walked day and night, even traveled on a boat, to get back to Hoboken and his family."

"Poor Karl," said Tess.

"He said his only friend at the lab was a 'dear fellow' named Octavius. An octopus with fourteen legs."

"Stop it," said Theo.

"That's what he said. He said that this scientist did experiments on all of the animals, maybe animals that were already hybrids. He's not sure what the scientist did to him, or he didn't want to say. He wrote that whatever it was, it was 'deeply unpleasant.'"

Theo made a gargling sort of noise.

"You broke *his* brain," Tess said. "Do you think that they had a chance to experiment on Karl? Is that why he could write in complete sentences?"

"I think the doctor might be making weapons," said Jaime. "Living weapons."

"What *for*?" said Tess.

That was what Jaime kept asking himself: Why would you need an octopus with fourteen legs, or a raccoon who wrote like a nineteenth-century novelist?

"I don't know," Jaime said. "Here. Cricket let me take a picture of one of the pages."

In the photo, a sheet of paper was covered with tidy, tiny script:

I know not what motivates this villainous man, only that he is relentless in his efforts, and quite connected. Numerous people visited the lab, people the doctor referred to as "investors" in their presence, and "necessary evils" after they departed. It seems that these visitors were funding the doctor's experiments, so he was obliged to tolerate their visits and even demonstrate some of his accomplishments. One man in particular seemed to be fascinated by all the poor creatures trapped in this gulag of nightmares and suffering. He visited again and again, asking all manner of questions, offering more and more funding. The doctor gifted him with two rats, Lev and Igor, that he had taught to drive tiny, rat-sized cars. (Do not feel too sorry for Lev and Igor, however. They bite.)

"An investor. Do you think Karl is talking about Slant?" Tess asked.

"Could be," Jaime said. "Karl didn't know his name."

"Maybe they're building some kind of animal army?" Theo said.

Jaime said, "Maybe they're expecting some kind of . . . war."

He hadn't known what he was going to say before he said it, and his own words hung in the air like a fog, obscuring everything.

War.

War.

War.

WAR.

"Oh no," said Ono, touching down on the night table where Tess had tossed the locket. It snatched up the necklace.

"Hey!" said Tess, then jumped.

"What?" said Jaime.

"Ono got it open! How did you do that?" Tess said.

"Land of Kings," said Ono, offering her the locket.

"Well, what's inside it?" Theo said.

Tess looked down at the locket, up at Jaime, down at the locket again. Then she held it up, the platinum face of the locket winking. "There's a picture in here."

"What kind of picture?"

"Maybe it was torn from a newspaper? It sort of looks like Ava," Tess said.

"Let me see," Jaime said. He got up and took the necklace from her. Inside the locket was a fuzzy black-and-white picture of an elegant black woman, hair pulled back tight, a proud tilt to her head. At first glance, he thought he was seeing a picture of Ava Oneal, too, but no, the brows had a slightly different shape, and so did the angle of the nose and the jaw.

It could have been Ava's sister, but it wasn't.

He knew who it was.

He knew.

When Jaime exhaled, it sounded like the sighs of every man and woman who had ever crossed a bridge from before to after, every person who had wondered if what they had lost would ever be found again.

"It's my mother," Jaime said. "This is a picture of my mother."

CHAPTER TWENTY-FOUR
Ava

Ava Oneal sat on the roof of the Old York Puzzler and Cipherist Society building, legs dangling over the side. She knew that they were looking for her—the police, Slant's people, their minions, the minions of those minions—but she didn't care. Let them look. Let them catch a glimpse of her booted feet as they turned their heads to the sky above. People like that had been looking for her for more than a hundred fifty years, and would look for a hundred fifty more. If she didn't want to be caught, they would never catch her.

Never again, that is.

She lifted her legs and pulled her knees in tight, enjoying the chill of the night air on her skin. This was the only time she dared go outside without her gray coat, and she reveled in the darkness, inhaling the barely perceptible touch of dew that would jewel the grasses of the parks in the morning. Here in the heart of the city, the stars were barely visible, but the bright face of the moon smiled down at her. As much as she loved the sun, she loved the moon more. Its energy was serene, calming, like a doting mother's. Not that she remembered her mother. Not that she remembered herself, her own name, her true one. As with so many others before her, her past had burned away till there was nothing but ashes in the wind.

"Ashes in the wind," she muttered out loud. "That's a good name for a book." And then she said, "My dear, you're becoming quite melodramatic in your dotage."

Melodramatic or not, it was true, however, that her past *had* burned away. But it had drowned first. At least, that was the story she'd been told when she was just a small child in Baltimore, when she had screwed up the courage to ask the cook where her mother was.

"Fell into the river and didn't come back up," the cook had said. "A long time ago."

"Where's my daddy?"

"What do I look like, your family Bible? Now hurry up and fetch that pail of water I asked you for."

Ava could still feel the weight of that pail of water,

the dampness seeping into her clothes and her shoes because she couldn't keep the liquid from sloshing no matter how hard she tried, no matter how hard the cook would slap her for bringing a half-empty pail. She didn't ask about her parents again for years, until the lady of the house took a liking to her, pulled her out of the kitchen, and had her educated alongside her own daughters, little white girls with butter-blond hair and blue eyes. The lady liked to tell her guests that she didn't have slaves or servants, she had family. And then she would ask Ava to read a Bible verse or recite her letters for the entertainment of the lady's company. When Ava began to compose poetry, the lady sent it to the local paper, where it was published. The lady held salons for other ladies, who would sip tea and nibble sweets while Ava performed her poems and recited psalms: "The Lord is my shepherd," and "I know all the birds of the mountains and Zīz is mine." These same ladies would compliment her speech and her manners, her poetic talent and her pretty brown face. They complimented one another on their open minds and open hearts.

Until she turned fifteen, and the lady who didn't have slaves or servants declared that she had made a match for Ava, a perfect match.

Ava was confused. "A match?"

The butter-haired girls clucked like a brood of chickens. "You're getting engaged, silly!"

The lady of the house explained that the match in question was a coachman at a nearby estate, and that they had made arrangements to buy him.

"Buy?" said Ava. "But . . ." She didn't finish the sentence. Her match was enslaved just as she was, and they would be expected to marry and have babies, who would also be enslaved, who would grow up and learn their letters, perform for guests, and never be allowed to leave—unless the lady wanted them to, unless the lady made other "arrangements."

"But, madam, I'm too young to get engaged," she said.

"Nonsense! We'll wait a respectable amount of time for the wedding, to be sure, but you are quite old enough."

"Your daughters aren't yet engaged," Ava said. "And they are two and three years older than I am."

"Yes, but my daughters are a different matter entirely. They are far more delicate than you are. They are ladies. Their father will not allow them to get engaged before they are twenty."

Delicate. The word tripped off the lady's tongue, *tap, tap, tap.* Ava had never wanted to be delicate before. That was when she had asked, "What if my father returns, and doesn't want me to get married? What if he thinks I'm too delicate?"

The delicate girls clucked again. The lady simply looked confused. "Stop talking such nonsense. And you're strong as an ox."

An ox.

Ava didn't take much with her when she ran away. Just two spare gowns and some underclothes, a sheaf of poems she couldn't bear to part with. She lost the poems almost immediately, when she had to splash through a swamp to avoid some blackbirders hired to find her. And she tossed the dresses soon after. She stole some shirts and pants from a clothesline, hacked off her hair, and rubbed dirt on her face, then made her way into the seething stew of New York City. People hiring at the pubs and docks couldn't tell if she was black or white, boy or girl, and maybe they didn't care as long as she was strong enough to do the work she was hired to do— rough work like shoveling out stables or unloading fish when the boats came in. But she didn't mind the work, not the sore muscles or the blisters or the smell of horse and dirt and fish on her skin. The city was a place a person could disappear, even a small and wiry black girl with curiously formal speech. And when a ship heading out to sea needed a new swabbie, she took the job and left her old life on the shore.

As desperate as she was to get away, she wasn't sure she'd take to the water. After all, water was what had taken her mother, if the cook could be believed. But she loved the ocean, the smell of it, the sharp cold spray that needled her cheeks, the slap of the waves against the hull, the roar of the surf. No one on the boat asked the boy called Myles White to recite verse while they drank tea, no one wanted to marry or marry off the skinny, scruffy boy who was as silent as a ghost. And though she endured the punches and kicks of drunken sailors, she got better at evading them, better with the small knife she carried for protection, too good, perhaps.

There were entire years of Ava's long life that were a blur, and there were mere moments that were etched indelibly in her memory. The moment she'd climbed from the window and run for her life. The moment her first book was published. The moment she laid eyes on Samuel. The moment she gave her heart freely.

There were other moments, too. The moment she found the two strangers stowed away on the *Aurora*, a twin brother and sister who claimed they were from Austria but couldn't speak German. The moment the woman had put more money in Ava's palm than she had ever held in her entire life. The moment she laid eyes on the woman again: in the halls of Eliza Hamilton's New York City orphanage, when Myles was calling herself Ava, and the woman was calling herself Theresa Morningstarr. The moment when she'd grabbed Theresa's wrist with a ruined hand and said, "Help me," after she'd been pulled, wrecked and dying, from a fire.

Theresa Morningstarr had helped in the only way she could. And now there was no one left to blame.

Ava inhaled the darkness again, drew it inside her and held it. The darkness had been her only constant companion through the decades, while the people she'd dared to care for had died or disappeared or drifted away, frightened by her unlined face, the dark hair untouched by silver. She had her poems and her stories for company, the worlds she'd held in her head and spilled onto the page, but it wasn't enough, even for a ghost. There was a time when she'd hated the darkness for its loyalty to her, for its relentless attention, when all she'd wanted to do was hide from the world, curl up and sleep forever. Which was when Samuel had found her, and she had found Samuel. For a time, she was happy. But it was not to be.

So many things were not to be.

She exhaled. No use dwelling on what did not, could

ıot happen. Better to turn her attention to what could. Now, when she prowled through the streets, snuck between the buildings that were being bought and sold and made and unmade, some for the first time since the Morningstarrs had built them, the entire city felt tense, the people full of bemused anxiety, as if everyone was waiting without knowing what they were waiting for, or what was waiting for them. She had felt this anxiety before. It was the kind of anxiety that sent people searching for answers anywhere and everywhere, the kind of anxiety that made people look for someone who had an explanation and a plan, no matter how ludicrous the explanation or how horrifying the plan.

And she—the one woman who should be least afraid—was afraid. Not for the first time, she wished for the Zīz, a bird so big its wings blocked out the sun.

"*It was many and many a year ago, in a kingdom by the sea,*" a voice said. Next to her, Auguste Dupin, the mynah bird, flapped his wings.

"You've been so quiet that I almost forget you were here," said Ava. She stroked the bird's glossy black feathers.

"*I was a child and she was a child,*" said Auguste.

"I know about your Annabel Lee," Ava said. "It's a sad story."

"We loved with a love that was more than love."

"Both of us are filled with sad stories, aren't we?"

Auguste said, *"A wind blew out of a cloud."*

"As winds do."

Auguste pressed his head in her palm and so Ava petted him some more. She'd brought him up to the top of this building for a bit of privacy. She liked the members of the society, and was grateful for their company and their help, but she couldn't afford to get too close to any of them, no matter how kind they were, how committed to justice, how committed to the boy called Jaime Cruz and the twins.

The twins.

That those children, those earnest children, could be the same people she'd known so long ago! She had loved the Morningstarrs, but she had hated them, too. She didn't know what to do with these children, didn't know how to feel about them. Even if they would grow up to be the Morningstarrs, they weren't the Morningstarrs yet. Tess was Benjamin Adler's Gindele, his little deer; so was Theo. And Jaime Cruz, already big and strong but also so gentle, his hands the hands of artists, hands that had drawn her likeness before he'd ever gotten a glimpse of her face. And so much like fawns they all were, big eyes and long limbs and curiosity. So how

336 • LAURA RUBY

could she hate them? How could she even be angry?

And yet here she was, sitting on top of a building like Jaime's drawings, like that character from the books and picture shows—Batman? Catman?—still angry. The last time she'd visited Benjamin, and she'd been visiting often, he'd suggested that her rage was what had kept her going all these years.

"'For it is not light that is needed, but fire,'" she'd said. "'It is not the gentle shower, but thunder. We need the storm, the whirlwind, and the earthquake.'"

"Meshugaas," Benjamin said. "Craziness."

She laughed. "Wendell Phillips and Frederick Douglass might agree that craziness is exactly what we need. So, what has kept you going? What has made you search for the origins of the Old York Cipher for so long?"

He'd shrugged and said, "I had an itch in the brain."

An itch in the brain. A question. Ava had a question, too. This one for Auguste. Another reason she'd brought him to the top of this building in the middle of the night. Because Benjamin had hinted in his roundabout way that he had once, long ago, whispered something to Auguste, an answer, a discovery, a secret he hadn't trusted anyone else to keep, especially not his own guttering mind. And Auguste would reveal this answer, if only you asked the right thing.

"Auguste," she said. "If *I* were the singer, what would be my song?"

Auguste ruffled his feathers, flapped his wings. For a moment Ava thought he might try to fly away—and she would have understood if he had—but he didn't.

Instead, he threw back his head and started to sing.

CHAPTER TWENTY-FIVE
Tess

Tess and Theo did not say a word as Jaime examined the picture of his mother.

They did not suggest that it was impossible. They did not suggest that it was doctored somehow, a fake. They did not ask who or why or how he came to be holding it, the intricate sequence of events that had to have transpired to get this locket into his hands. They just waited. Even Nine and Ono stopped playing, sensing that something was happening that might need their attention.

Jaime swiped at his eyes. "Stupid contacts," he said. Nine rubbed her face against his arm, purring.

After a while, Tess ventured, "Are you sure it's your mom? For a minute I thought it was Ava."

"Black women don't all look the same," Jaime snapped. "It's my mother."

"I'm sorry. I didn't mean . . . Never mind," Tess said.

Jaime sighed. "I know what you meant. And she sort of does look like Ava. Could be her sister." Then he said, "I should check to see if there's anything behind this picture. Or maybe some clue about where it came from, or something about the next clue. But I don't want to rip it."

Tess slid off her bed and knelt next to Jaime. Theo did the same, kneeling next to Tess.

"Maybe if we use a letter opener or a knife, we can pry it out without tearing it," Tess suggested.

Ono said, "Oh no," and waddled over to where they were crouched. It held out its robot hands. Jaime placed the locket in them. Slowly, gently, Ono tucked a tiny metal finger underneath the picture and ran the finger all the way around the perimeter of the locket. The picture—a small oval of newsprint, they could now see—popped up. All three of them exhaled in relief.

"Thanks, Ono," Jaime said, taking the locket and the picture from the little robot. He handled the picture they way one would handle a baby bird, cradling it. He flipped it over in his palm. "It's folded. Do you guys have tweezers?"

Again, Ono came to the rescue. One of his hands flipped, whirred, and became a pair of pincers. Jaime laid the picture facedown on the carpet and Ono used the pincers to unfold it.

When it was done, a newspaper article dated May 21, 2000, lay before them. The article announced that Renée Cruz had just received her doctorate in astrophysics, one of only a few black women in the country to do so. At the time of her graduation, she had already done important research into mirror neutrons and was eager to do more experimentation, she told the paper. There were whole worlds to be discovered. The article went on to say that her state-of-the-art lab at T&T University would be funded in part by the Mega Foundation, as well as numerous other enterprises and business leaders around the city.

But that was not the most remarkable thing about the article. The most remarkable thing about the article was what was written in the margin in ink:

You have the tools, you need the plans. Find them in the belly of the beast. The first movable staircase on the left, first door on the right.

Play fair.

And then, in a completely different hand:

Hurry.

"'Play fair,'" said Jaime. "That's funny. Nobody has played fair."

"We have," said Tess.

"No, we haven't." Jaime pointed at Ono. "Explain that. Explain this locket. Explain the ledger we took from that house uptown. Explain the stuff we took from under the obelisk in Central Park. We haven't been borrowing. We've been *stealing.*"

"From who? From Slant?" said Tess. "Just because he was able to game the system and buy all these things that previously belonged to the city? I'm not going to feel bad about that."

"Are you saying that you plan to give all this stuff back? Who do we give it back to?"

"The city," said Tess, firmly. "When we figure this out, everything goes back to the city."

"Oh no," said Ono.

"Most everything," Tess said. "I think you get to decide where you want to go, Ono."

"Land of Kings," said Ono.

Jaime touched the article with the picture of his mom, his fingers trembling slightly. "I just want her to be proud of me."

"She is," said Tess. "She would be."

"You don't know that!" Jaime shouted.

Tess wanted to shrink away from Jaime's sudden anger, but she didn't. "Yes, I do."

Jaime shook his head. "I never even got to know her. Everything I know about her I learned from pictures and articles and videos. The world got her, but I didn't."

"I'm sorry," said Tess.

Jaime didn't say, "It's okay," the way people do, because it wasn't okay. He said, "I wonder who wrote this. Who thought we had the tools but need the plans?"

"Maybe Ava wrote it? Or Lora Yoshida?"

"And who wrote 'hurry'?" Jaime said. "And what does any of this have to do with my mom? Like, why write it on an article?"

"Maybe so that you would—*we* would—pay attention to it," said Theo.

"'You have the tools, you need the plans.' What does that mean?" said Tess. "We don't have any tools. We have lots of papers and coins and a weird doll."

Theo said, "We have Ono. He's unlocked this locket and done a bunch of other things."

"Okay," said Tess. "That's one tool."

"Oh no," said Ono.

"You're not *just* a tool," Jaime soothed.

"Kings," Ono said.

Jaime leaned forward. "What if some of the other stuff we've found is more than what it looks like?"

"What are you talking about?" Tess said.

"What if they're like Ono? They can do other things. Or they have a different purpose than the obvious."

"What purpose?" Tess asked.

"I don't know. Maybe we have to use them in a different way. Like, put them together or something."

"Huh," Theo said.

"I don't think we're looking for clues anymore," Jaime said. "I think we're looking for *parts*."

"So we have to build something," Theo said.

"But we need the plans to do that," said Tess.

"They're in the belly of the beast," said Theo. "What beast? Did the beast swallow the plans?"

"A beast with movable stairs," Tess said. "Escalators?"

Theo said, "Escalators in the belly of the beast. A building? Which city building could be the belly of the beast?"

"The 'belly' is the middle," said Tess.

"So, the Tower," said Jaime.

They nodded.

Morningstarr Tower. The former home of Theresa and Theodore.

Current home of one Darnell Slant.

It got too late for Jaime to make the long trip back to Hoboken, so he called his dad and asked if he could stay over.

"Sure," said his dad. "Make the most of your summer. You don't have much time left."

They set up sleeping bags in the living room and tried to distract themselves with popcorn and movies. But it was hard to focus. Even harder to sleep. Tess tossed and turned, her dreams filled with monsters both human and animal. When the first light of the morning streamed through the windows, Tess dragged herself from her sleeping bag and stumbled into the kitchen. Lance clomped in, too, so she asked him for pancakes. He was happy to oblige. The pancakes would have to make up for the lack of rest.

Soon after, Theo and Jaime were up and soaking their own stacks of pancakes in butter and syrup. Since the twins' parents were still in bed, the three of them talked in hushed voices about their next moves. Break into the Tower? But how? Darnell Slant was bound to have guards all over the place, and cameras, too.

"'Play fair,'" said Jaime. "That's what the clue said."

"Huh?" said Theo, his mouth full of pancake.

"We visit just like every other tourist," said Jaime. "That's fair enough."

"Slant isn't going to give us a tour," said Theo, his mouth still full.

"Slant isn't going to notice us. He might not even be there," said Tess.

"We can hope. Besides, if he is there, we can tell him what we told your mom," Jaime said. "That we're working on a school project. Doing research."

Theo swallowed. "Slant doesn't care about school. And he knows we've been researching the Cipher. He has to know. He'll be suspicious."

"Maybe we don't tell him it's a school project," Tess said. "What does he care about?"

"Money," said Theo.

"Power," said Jaime.

"Attention," Tess said. "Maybe we need to flatter him."

"We're just a bunch of kids," Theo said. "He's not going to care if a bunch of kids tell him he's handsome or whatever."

"That's not what I mean," said Tess. "He was desperate for our family to come to his announcement, right? He wanted that picture with Mom. So—what if we tell him that we disagree with Mom? That we support him? That we think he'll be a great mayor. The greatest mayor who ever lived, maybe."

"Appeal to his vanity," said Theo.

"I like it," said Jaime.

"Okay, but how do we do this?" Theo said. "What's *our* plan?"

Tess held out her plate for more pancakes. "I say we walk through the front door."

They finished their breakfast and left the house as early as they could, keeping an eye out for menacing mushroom men. But they arrived at Morningstarr Tower—Tess refused to think of it as Slant Tower, despite the new sign on the front of the building—without being bothered by anyone. So much of it looked the same—the beautiful gray stone, the same stripe of solar glass windows going all the way up the front of the facade, the same curl of the Underway tracks twisting around the building, the same whooshing sound as the trains glided around and around.

"Are you sure about this?" Theo said, looking up at the Tower. There were signs in the windows: "PLEASE PARDON OUR MESS. OPEN DURING RENOVATION!"

Tess remembered the last time she'd visited Morningstarr Tower. She and Theo had been with Grandpa Ben. Grandpa had talked about the history of the building, how it had taken the Morningstarrs fifteen years to complete, how there were twelve elevators that could move in any direction, rooms that could be combined and recombined, escalators that disappeared into the guts of the Tower and only the Morningstarrs themselves knew where they went. Grandpa Ben had called the Morningstarrs luftmenschen—dreamers—always with their heads in the clouds. What would Grandpa say if he thought that his grandkids were the same people who had invented the solar cell and the Lion battery? What would he say if he thought his grandkids were the luftmenschen who had dreamed this very tower into existence?

"Tess?" said Theo. "I'm not sure. Are you sure?"

"No," said Tess. Her heart was thwacking against her ribs. She imagined being swarmed by guards and blond news hostesses and mushroom Lego men, carried off and hidden somewhere where no one would find her. But she opened the door and marched through it anyway, Theo and Jaime behind her. She was happy to see that Slant hadn't redecorated yet. Walking into the lobby was like entering the body of some enormous slumbering creature. The floor was a warm, creamy marble. The koi pond still sat in the middle of the enormous space, and a waterfall still tumbled from natural-looking rocks into the pond. Beds of green plants and flowers flourished in the light shining in through solar glass windows and skylights dozens of stories up. The floors of the Tower overlooked the main lobby, curving around it like ribs. The only mark of Slant's takeover were the security cameras in every corner, and the "Out of Order" signs draped at the entrance of the escalators. Did that mean he had already discovered the secrets of the Morningstarrs? Did he know that plans for some kind of machine were hidden here? Did he have them already?

Were they too late?

Three carefully coiffed young women sat at the front desk taking calls. One of them, a white woman with lush brown hair that fell over one shoulder, smiled at them. "Welcome to Slant Tower," she said. "What can I do for you?"

"We're doing a project for school. Is it okay if we look around?"

"Of course!" she said. "Are you doing a report on Mr. Slant?"

"Uh, yes," said Tess. "We're writing about the future leaders of America."

Theo coughed and Jaime thwacked his back.

"Fantastic!" the young woman said. "I'm sure you'll all get an A!"

"Mm-hmm," Tess said, willing herself not to roll her eyes.

"Just be careful! We're under construction, so some areas might be off-limits."

"Thank you," said Tess. They walked past the desk and into the wider area behind the desk. There were a few tourists here and there, but mostly they had the place to themselves. The security guards patrolling the space gave them a cursory glance but nothing more.

All they had to do was get up the escalator without anyone noticing. Find whatever plans the message had been talking about. Get back down again. Get out of the building.

No problem.

Yikes.

Tess had been worried that Nine would call too much

attention to them, make them too recognizable, so she'd left Nine at home. But Nine could have made quite a distraction, enough for them to sneak upstairs unnoticed.

"We need a distraction," Tess said.

"I could fling myself into the koi pond," Theo offered.

"If any of us does anything too over the top, the guards might do more than just kick us out of the building. They could call the cops."

Of course, all of them remembered the bare interview room at the police station, the Bridge of Sighs. Tess and Theo's mom, with a file folder and photographs.

"What about Ono?" said Jaime. "Ono might be able to distract them."

Ono's head popped up from Jaime's pocket, eyes blinking on and off.

"Maybe he can use his propeller. Fly around the lobby. People might think it's a bird, or maybe a Morningstarr Machine," said Theo.

Jaime patted Ono. "I don't want him to get caught."

"He won't get caught if he flies high enough. What do you think, Ono?"

Ono's head turned all the way around, like an owl's. It said, "Land of Kings."

Jaime checked to make sure no one was looking, then

set the little robot on the edge of the koi pond. Ono's propeller popped up from his head and it took off, buzzing loudly.

Just as loudly, Jaime said, "What is that?"

"I don't know," said Theo, loudly as well. "A bird, maybe?"

"If that's a bird, it's going to poop all over everything!" Tess said, covering her head with her arms.

Ono took to its job with everything it had. It zoomed this way, zoomed that way. It punched through a nearby bush in a flurry of leaves, beheaded entire beds of flowers. It flew low, mussing the hair of the receptionists at the front desk, who started to squeal and wave their arms around. Ono banked off the wide chest of an oncoming guard and then whirled higher and higher till it was just a blur overhead.

Tess tugged Jaime's arm and then Theo's. While everyone in the building—guards and receptionists and tourists—was busy trying to figure out what, exactly, was intent on wrecking the place, the kids crouched low and hurried to the first escalator on the left. Tess lifted the "Out of Order" sign and ducked underneath. As quickly and as quietly as she could, she ran up the unmoving escalator stairs. Jaime and Theo followed. When they got to the top, they leaped off, dropping behind a wall, breathing hard. On this floor, the gardens were dried up and brown, the fountains empty. Two more sets of escalators sat idle, with the same "Out of Order" signs as below, but here, the escalators had been stripped, their gears and motors visible, blue and red wires like exposed veins and arteries. Tess was stricken with a strange sort of sadness at the sight of them.

Theo tapped her arm and tore her attention back to the problem at hand. He mouthed: *First door on the right.* On either side of the escalators, rows of doors to abandoned offices were arranged in two arcs that hugged the rounded interior of the building. She lifted her head slightly so she could follow the line of doors until she identified the first one on the right. They would have to crawl all the way around to the front of the building to get to that door, which was right next to the windows on the front of the building.

Jaime waved to Ono, who was still whirling high overhead, and then pointed down.

Ono made one more circle and then dove back into the lobby. The shrieks of the people told Tess, Theo, and Jaime that everyone below was occupied and probably wouldn't be looking for movement up here. They kept close to the wall, half scooting, half crawling toward the first door on the right, just as the message in the locket had said. Still crouching, Tess reached up and turned the knob, hoping that it wasn't locked.

It wasn't.

She pushed open the heavy wooden door and they crawled into . . .

A broom closet.

"Well," said Jaime. "Anyone need a mop?"

CHAPTER TWENTY-SIX
Theo

Theo eased the door closed behind them after they were all inside. Jaime turned on his phone to light up the darkness. "This can't be it."

"This was the first door on the right," Tess insisted.

"Next to the first movable staircase on the left," said Theo.

They got to their feet and searched the mostly bare shelves.

"There's one roll of toilet paper over here," said Theo.

"Is there anything written on it?" Jaime asked.

Theo unrolled the paper until he looked like he was standing in a pile of snow. "No. Nothing."

There was a rusty bucket with a mop handle poking

out of it, some old bottles of cleaner.

"Maybe whatever we're looking for is on the walls," Jaime suggested. "Let's move these shelves."

They shoved the shelves aside, used their phones for light. But there was nothing on the walls except for some rolls of old wallpaper.

They shone their lights on the ceiling and the floor. They searched under the shelves to see if there was anything stuffed underneath them. Sweat slid down Tess's back. She didn't know how long Ono could keep up the chase downstairs.

"What if we made a mistake?" Theo said. "Maybe the locket wasn't a clue at all."

"We didn't make a mistake," Jaime said, still feeling along the undersides of the shelves.

"I wonder if there's a panel or a secret door or something," said Tess.

They pushed and pressed on the walls and the floor. Theo and Jaime hoisted Tess up so she could press on the ceiling.

Nothing.

Tess didn't want to say it, but she said it. "We're running out of time. Ono can't keep everyone distracted forever."

Jaime stopped pushing and pressing, instead shining

his light again at the rolls of old wallpaper. He pulled at the edge of the closest one, revealing a pattern of musical notes and dancing people. "What about these musical notes?"

"What about them?" Theo held up his own phone to look more closely at the wallpaper. "C, G, G, A, G, B, C."

"Does it spell anything?" said Tess.

"How many words have three G's?" said Theo. "Baggage? Not enough A's."

"What if we're not supposed to spell anything, we're supposed to play the notes?" said Jaime.

"'Play fair,'" said Tess. "Play nicely?"

"Play well, maybe," said Jaime.

"There's a rest here," Theo pointed out.

"Wait, I know this one. We all know this one." He knocked on the wall to demonstrate. Da, da, da, DA da . . . DA! DA!

And with that, the walls of the closet collapsed, accordioned, and refolded themselves into a pyramid, with Tess, Theo, and Jaime trapped right in the middle of it.

"What in the world—?" Tess had time to say, just before the pyramid shot straight up, pasting the three of them to the floor.

Theo, Tess, and Jaime bounced and rolled and tumbled around the "closet" as it hurtled up and then sideways and then down and then up again.

"Why did they always make stuff like this?" Theo yelled in the darkness. "Why couldn't they just pick a direction and stick to iiiiiiiiiit—OW!"

And then, as quickly as it had started, the room stopped moving. The walls collapsed again, reconfiguring themselves into a much larger, more elaborate shape, sharp angles on all sides, made with bits and pieces from other rooms. There were random doors on the walls, walls on the floor, floor tiles on the ceiling. Tiny lights previously hidden burst into life, casting the strangely shaped room in a soft glow.

The three of them cautiously sat up.

"Anybody break anything?" Jaime said.

"I don't think so," said Tess. "Theo?"

"I'm okay," Theo said.

Jaime got to his feet and walked over to one of the angled walls. This new room was shaped like a circle in the center, with five pointed alcoves on all sides. "It's like being stuck inside of a star."

"I hope we're not stuck," said Tess.

"Look," said Theo. In the middle of the "star," there was an elegant but modestly sized desk.

They walked over to the desk. A green blotter covered the top, its surface dotted with spots of ink and random letters. In one corner of the desk, there was an inkwell with a pen. And in the other corner, there were schematics.

Theo looked over the plans. They were for some sort of machine, just as they had suspected. He was almost afraid to look too closely, afraid to learn exactly what sort of machine it was, exactly what they would have to build.

Afraid to think about whose desk this was.

"I guess we found the plans," said Tess. "That was easy." She grabbed them off the desk.

"Hey!" said Theo. "I wanted to examine those!"

"Examine them later," Tess said.

"Wait," said Jaime. "I have an idea."

"What?"

He took the plans and folded the paper in half, then in half again. He did this twice more, until the plans were barely the size of his palm, and then added a few more folds. He held it up.

"Are you doing origami?" said Theo.

"Badly, but yeah."

"My grandpa liked origami," Tess said.

"I do, too," said Jaime.

"This room folded up like origami," Tess added. She didn't have to say more. She didn't have to talk about what a coincidence it was that her grandfather liked paper folding and Jaime liked paper folding and wasn't it funny that they'd ended up in a room that had folded itself into a different shape?

When Jaime was done, he held up the plan, which now looked like a palm-sized heart. "Just in case we're caught and searched."

"I don't like the sound of that," said Theo.

"We can check when we get out of here," Jaime said, and stashed the heart away.

"*If* we can figure out how to get out of here, wherever in the Tower we are."

"Maybe we do the same thing we did before," Theo suggested.

So they did. They knocked on the walls and on the floor.

Nothing.

Theo went back to the desk. Lifted the blotter, checked underneath, and put it back down. Opened all the drawers.

"Anything?" said Jaime.

"Nope," Theo said, stuffing a hand in his hair. Think, Theo, Think.

Jaime tapped the letters on the green blotter. "You know, my dad keeps a Post-it on his laptop with his password on it."

"Why do adults *do* that?" said Tess.

Theo yanked his hand from his hair and slapped his own forehead with it. The three of them crowded around the desk. Written among the blots and crossed-out scribbles was this:

EMT OIB BQPS

"I bet that's a cipher," said Jaime.

"We just have to figure out which kind," Theo said. He pulled out his phone. "I don't have a signal. Do you?"

Jaime pulled out his phone. "No."

"So we can't use a program to see if we just need to rearrange the letters."

Tess paced around the desk. "We've been gone for almost twenty minutes already."

"Relax. No one knows we're here. No one's keeping track. And we're going as fast as we can."

Tess paced around the desk the other way.

"You're making me dizzy," said Jaime.

Tess stopped pacing. "The handwriting on the article said hurry!"

Theo said, "It also said to play fair, whatever that's supposed to— ARGH!"

"What?" said Jaime.

"The Playfair Cipher! Invented by a guy named Wheatstone."

"Why not the Wheatstone Cipher?" Jaime asked.

"What? I don't know. But you use diagraph substitution."

"Right," said Jaime. "I use diagraph substitution all the time."

"You do?"

Tess slapped the desk with both palms. "Theo!"

"Sorry. First you choose a key word. You write out the key without repeating any letters in a five-by-five square, followed by the rest of the letters in order. You combine I and J so twenty-six letters in the alphabet become twenty-five, and fit perfectly in the grid."

"Sounds so simple," said Jaime.

"Doesn't it?" Theo said.

"No," said Jaime.

"Do you have a pencil or a pen or something?"

Jaime handed him a pencil.

Theo leaned his elbows on the desk. "Say the key word was 'Jaime.' Your key would look like this."

A I M E B
C D F G H
K L N O P
Q R S T U
V W X Y Z

"If you wanted to encipher a word or a message, like—"

"'Hurry'?" said Tess.

"Hurry," Theo said, "you split the letters into groups of two. *Hu-rr-y*. Double letters need to be separated by an *x*. Like this:"

HU RX RY

"Then you consult your key to find your pair of letters. Every pair is in the same row, the same column, or neither of those things. You replace letters in the same row with the letter to their right. Letters in the same column are replaced by the letter below them. If the letters in your pair don't appear in the same row or column, then you replace the letter in the row with the letter that's in the same column as the second letter. So, if we use the key to encipher the diagraphs, we get PZ for HU, SW for RX, and TW for RY."

"Man, this cipher is bonkers," said Jaime. "Who would use it?"

"The British in World War One and the Australians in World War Two," said Theo.

"So how do we decipher the letters on the blotter?"

"Well, if our phones worked, we could just put them into a decoder," said Theo.

"Yeah, except our phones don't work."

"We probably need the key word."

"Great," said Tess.

"Maybe it's another word on the blotter?"

But there weren't any other words on the blotter, none that weren't crossed out. They ended up trying a few anyway, but they didn't work.

"We've been stuck a half hour," said Tess. "I don't want to spend the rest of my life in here."

"Try the word 'out' as the key," Jaime suggested.

Theo did. "Nope."

"'Leave'?"

Theo scribbled some more. "Nope."

"'Exit'?"

Theo made a square with *exit* as the key word, and then worked backward. "E would give you T, and then M would give you H," he muttered. "The red door? The red door!"

```
E X I T A
B C D F G
H K L M N
O P Q R S
U V W Y Z
```

"Great," said Jaime. "But I don't see any doors in here."

"Neither do I," Tess said.

"There has to be," said Theo.

"Look at the lights!" Jaime pointed at the rows of winking lights the size of pinpricks. "They're not all white. Some are different colors. Like that!" Jaime ran to a panel outlined in the faintest bluish light.

Tess and Theo scanned the oddly angled room. Tess found a panel vaguely lit green.

"Here!" said Theo. Tucked away in one of the arms

of the star, blue lights outlined a panel near the floor.

"That's a small door," Jaime said. "How are we going to fit?"

"Do you think we should knock, or . . . ?" Theo said.

Tess shouldered them both aside and opened the tiny door. As soon as she did, the walls collapsed around them once again, folding and refolding. The desk disappeared; the blue and green and red and all the other doors flipped out of sight.

"Oh, shhhhhhh—" Jaime said, before the room shrank in on them and they had to duck to keep the ceiling from knocking them out. They dropped straight down, their feet lifting off the floor with the speed of it. They hurtled diagonally, then up, then down, then spun around like a top, something that was entirely unnecessary, in Theo's opinion, not that he could say so, for fear of throwing up.

Then the room stopped its infernal spinning and hurtling and upping and downing and unfolding, and came to rest gently, gently, with a faint *hiss*.

They waited for another minute to make sure the Morningstarr Tower didn't have any more surprises, but it seemed they had tired it out. For the moment.

Theo raised his head, found his phone, turned it on.

"We're back in the broom closet."

"Finally," said Tess.

The door opened. In the doorway, a blond woman in a red dress stared down at them, two mushroom Lego men looming behind her.

CHAPTER TWENTY-SEVEN

Jaime

"You didn't think it would be that easy, did you?" said the woman.

"You call this easy?" said Theo.

Jaime knew her instantly. It was the woman who had accused Nine of biting her. The woman from Green-Wood Cemetery who had taunted and trapped them. The woman who had fought with Ava and then vanished. Candi, her name was Candi. If there was anyone in the world who didn't deserve that name, it was this woman. Sweet, she was not. Jaime said, "You finally got a haircut. Or a new wig. Looks good."

"Thank you, Mr. Cruz," said Candi. "You're also looking well. No injuries after your fall into the river?"

"Did you have something to do with that?"

"You know who did it. Your little friend in the long gray coat. The one who believes she's a superhero. She's a touchy thing. I was only intending to chat with you. I'd even bought you a hot chocolate."

"In other words, she beat you. Again," Jaime said.

Candi smiled. "She got lucky."

"I thought you worked for Duke Goodson," Tess said. "She beat him, too."

Candi leaned in close. She smelled like hair spray and breath mints. "I'll tell you a secret. I have always worked for myself." She leaned back again. "Bruno?"

Both big mushroom men pushed into the closet. Jaime and the twins backed up, but there was nowhere to go, and no time to try knocking again. The men hauled them out of the closet and dragged them to the escalators. As they were paraded down the frozen escalator stairs, Jaime looked around for Ono but didn't see the robot anywhere. He prayed the robot was hiding, or had escaped the building entirely.

The big men shoved them into the elevators and then stood in front of them, grinning like maniacs as Candi punched the button for the penthouse. The elevator went up and then drifted left and right. Jaime felt a sense of déjà vu, not for the movements of the broom closet they'd just been in so much as for the elevator back at 354 W. 73rd Street. Even though Jaime's heart was pounding, even though he was scared out of his mind, he missed that place, every single thing about it.

"I hate this elevator," said Candi, ruining the moment. "It has a mind of its own. It never goes the same route twice. And you never know when you're going to get anywhere. It's maddening!"

"I think it's kind of cool," said Theo, voice chilly.

"We're replacing them with ones that work properly," Candi said.

"But will you have this view?" said Jaime. The elevator car emerged from the inside of the building through a glass tunnel that now ran up the building's facade. Glass on the sides and the back of the elevator car made Jaime feel like he was flying. People in the Underway car that curled around the Tower waved at them, and Candi waved back.

"We'll lose the machinery that controls the cars but keep the view," said Candi. "That's what Mr. Slant wants, and what he wants, he gets."

"Not always," said Tess.

Candi said, "You'd be surprised."

The elevator dinged and the doors opened. A long hallway stretched out before them. Like in the lobby, the floor was creamy marble, and the blue walls were adorned with paintings. Not of the Morningstarrs, but of Darnell Slant. Here was Darnell Slant as a little boy on his father's lap. Here was Darnell Slant as a smooth-skinned young man in a hunting jacket, a sword—a sword!—resting on one shoulder. Here was a present-day Darnell Slant in some kind of metal chair that looked more like a throne.

"Interesting décor," said Jaime dryly.

"That's the newest painting," Candi said. "We've only had time to swap out the art. We'll tackle bigger renovations later."

"Where are the old paintings?" Tess asked.

"What old paintings?"

"The ones that the Morningstarrs had."

"Oh, those. Mr. Slant is going to make a deal with some museums for those."

"He's not going to donate them?" Theo said.

"They're worth a lot of money," said Candi. "You can't just give them away."

"Why not? Doesn't Slant have enough money?"

Candi laughed. "Nobody ever has enough money."

"Especially people with enough money," said Jaime.

They reached a set of double doors tall and wide enough to admit elephants. Candi opened the doors.

Behind them was yet another highly coiffed young woman sitting behind an antique desk. This room had a rose-colored Persian rug underfoot, and numerous bookcases lined the walls.

"This is a nice room," Tess said.

"It's going to be gutted at the end of the month," said Candi. "Britni, tell Mr. Slant we're here."

On Britni's desk were four monitors. The one monitor Jaime could see had its screen broken up into sixteen different views. Camera feeds, he guessed.

Britni picked up a phone, waited. "Sir? They're here." She listened, then gestured to another set of huge wooden doors. "Go on in."

Candi opened the doors and led Jaime, Theo, and Tess inside the office, the burly men bringing up the rear of their sad parade. Behind the doors was an office that appeared to have been shipped in from another place and time. Instead of worn marble, the floor was polished black granite so shiny it looked like a sea of ink. The walls were stark white, and decorated with black-and-white photographs of Slant, Slant, and more Slant. There were no bookshelves, but there was a long white leather bar along one side, complete with a set of crystal decanters set on top.

And at the end of the long room, behind a huge black

desk the size of a pool table, sat Slant. He was scrolling through his phone.

Jaime said, "I guess we know which room was first on the renovation list."

"Oh yes," said Candi over her shoulder. "Mr. Slant had owned this property not twelve hours before the contractors were in here tearing out all the old junk."

As they got closer to the desk, Jaime could see that Slant's desk chair was the metal one from the painting in the hallway, the black bars fanning out around him like the rays of a twisted sun.

"That cannot be comfortable," Theo said.

"It hurts me just to *look* at it," said Jaime.

Darnell Slant set aside the phone and folded his hands. On TV, the man looked youngish, younger than Jaime's dad, with thick dark hair buzzed close at the sides. In person, he looked older, paler, his pink mouth not much more than a slash. He didn't seem so scary, this man who had taken so much from them already. Jaime marveled at that. He'd thought facing down Darnell Slant in the flesh would be momentous, like David facing down Goliath. But Darnell Slant didn't look scary at all.

Which, now that he thought about it, was even scarier.

"Children," said Darnell Slant. "To what do we

owe the pleasure of your visit?"

"We're doing a school project," said Tess, though earlier she'd thought it was a silly excuse. But she was nervous. Only someone who knew her well could have guessed how nervous she was. Her face was relaxed, her expression open. But if you tried to unclench her fists, you'd need a pry bar to do it.

"A school project," said Darnell. "School hasn't started yet."

"It's due when school starts," Theo said.

"Sure, sure," said Darnell Slant. He swiveled in his throne, something that Jaime didn't know was possible. Who had a swiveling throne?

Slant said, "Did you search them?"

"Not yet," said Candi.

"Do it now."

Candi searched Tess, who had little on her but her phone. Candi took it and tossed it on Slant's desk. The two beefy men searched Theo.

Theo said, "Which one of you is Bruno?"

"Both," said the Brunos.

They found Theo's phone and threw that on Slant's desk, too.

"Hey!" said Jaime as the Brunos patted him down and started pulling things from his pockets—the sketchbook, pens, pencils, a stick of gum, a business card. "Watch it!"

"This one has little paper toys," said one of the Brunos. He put an origami bird, fish, snake, crab, and heart on the desk. Jaime held his breath as Darnell Slant pawed through the paper figures, popping them into 3D before flattening them again. But he seemed more interested in the phones. He tried Tess's, then Theo's, then Jaime's.

"You can't go through our stuff," said Tess.

"You're trespassing on private property," Candi said. "We can do anything we want."

"That's not the way laws work," said Theo.

"It's the way the world works," Darnell Slant said. "Listen, I know who you are. I know your mother is a detective. I hear she's pretty good at it, though she hasn't come through for me."

The locket. The one with Jaime's mother's picture in it. The one that Lora Yoshida said had been hidden in a book at the New York Public Library. Jaime's nerves flared with rage. He didn't know what any of this had to do with this mother, but it had *something* to do with her. His mother! Jaime wanted to slap the face right off of Darnell Slant's skull.

Through gritted teeth, Jaime said, "She did come through."

"What?" said Darnell. "Who? What are you talking about?"

"The thing you're looking for? The detective knows where it is."

"Jaime, what are you doing?" Tess said.

Darnell Slant's thin lips got even thinner. "You don't know anything."

"Do *you* know anything?" Jaime said. His fists were as tight as Tess's. He didn't know what he was doing, but he seemed to be doing it, and he didn't care.

"Someone should have taught you some manners," said Darnell Slant. "But I guess that's what happens when boys don't have a mother to raise them."

Jaime launched himself at Darnell Slant, thinking, just for a moment, that he would be able to hurt someone, really hurt someone, and that this someone deserved it. But the burly men grabbed him by the shirt collar and yanked him back. They shoved him to the floor. He rolled over, coughing, rubbing his throat.

"Stop it!" yelled Tess. She tried to run to him, but Candi grabbed her arm. Tess tried to kick her, but Candi swept her leg and Tess ended up on the floor, too.

Darnell Slant looked at Theo. "You going to try something?"

"I already did," said Theo.

"Huh?" said Slant.

The doors burst open, and a crowd of people marched into the office.

The twins' mother flashed her badge. "Mr. Slant, before I arrest you, do you want to explain why you've detained these children against their will?"

The ride back to the Tombs was quiet as a funeral. Detective Biedermann sat stiffly in the passenger seat. Detective Clarkson kept glancing from her to Jaime, Tess, and Theo, who were crowded in the back.

Jaime didn't know whether he was happy or furious that Theo had managed to contact his mom before their phones had been taken. Maybe both. Happy that they had been saved from whatever Slant had planned for them, furious that now their parents knew and they had to face whatever *they* had planned for them.

It was going to be ugly.

Seriously ugly.

When they got to the police station and Jaime saw Mima and his father, along with the twins' father and Aunt Esther, waiting for them, he wondered if dealing with Slant would have been easier.

"Jaime!" said Mima, his name rough in her throat. "Are you okay?"

"I'm fine, Mima."

"What were you doing there with that man?" said Mima.

"Did you really break into Morningstarr Tower?" his father said. "What were you thinking?"

"Mr. Cruz, Ms. Cruz, we'll get to that in a minute," said Detective Biedermann. "If the three of you will follow me." She brought Jaime and his grandmother and father to an interview room. Tess and Theo looked as confused and terrified as Jaime felt as Detective Clarkson and another detective led them to different rooms.

Inside the interview room, Jaime sat down at the table. This time, Detective Biedermann sat across from *him* with a folder and a notepad. She had a bag full of the things that the Brunos had taken from his pockets: the sketchbook, the origami figures, his phone, the heart. A wave of shame washed over him, followed by another wave of anger. He hadn't done anything wrong. Or at least, he hadn't done anything more wrong than Slant had done.

"Where's Slant?" he asked.

"Don't worry about him. He's being questioned, too. So are his people."

"Good," said Jaime. "Ask him . . . ask him . . ."

"What should I ask him, Jaime?"

If he told her about the locket, then he'd have to tell her how he knew about it. He could get Lora Yoshida in trouble. Or he could get in more trouble.

"Ask him where Ono is," Jaime said. "My robot. He's gone."

"I'll ask him," Detective Biedermann said, her voice low and gentle. "I need to ask you something as well. Would you tell me why you and Tess and Theo went to the Tower today?"

"We just wanted to look around. Before Slant changed everything."

"Are you sure that's the only reason you were there?"

Jaime didn't answer.

"Jaime, you're on video sneaking up the escalators and entering a closet on the second floor. Would you tell me what you were doing?"

"Like I said, we just wanted to look around a little bit."

"You wanted to look in a closet?"

"We just wanted to see if there was anything behind the doors, that's all."

"Did you find anything?"

"We found some toilet paper," Jaime said, which was not a lie.

"Anything else?"

"Did you know that the woman working for Slant is the same woman who accused Nine of biting her?"

"Yes, I did know that. And she'll answer for it." Detective Biedermann pushed the folder and the bag of his things aside. "Jaime, I'm trying to help you. I know that it might not feel like that, but I am. I'm worried for you. I'm worried for my own children. I'm afraid . . ." She paused, and in that pause, Jaime saw that she *was* afraid. "I'm afraid that you're mixed up in something that's nothing more than a lie."

Jaime frowned. "What do you mean? What lie?"

"The Morningstarr Cipher."

Detective Biedermann was looking at him so intently, and with so much concern, it was painful. Jaime rubbed the surface of the scarred table. "I don't think it's a lie."

"It is. A beautiful lie a whole city told itself because it was grieving a loss, a lie it still tells itself whenever things get bad or sad," she said. "I know about the Cipher. More than I want to know. It was my father's life's work. He believed in it with all his heart. But he was chasing ghosts. And now I'm worried that you three have been chasing the same ghosts. The problem is that over the years very dangerous people have also believed the lie and chased the ghosts. Very dangerous people who might want to hurt you if they think you've found something, or that you're getting in their way."

"We've already been hurt," Jaime said.

Detective Biedermann closed her eyes, opened them. "I know. Me too. And I'm sorry. I really am. Would you at least tell me what you were looking for today?"

What was he looking for? So many things. His mother. His home. His city. His past. He wanted to know if Tess and Theo Biedermann grew up to be Theresa and Theodore Morningstarr. He wanted to know whether the Morningstarrs could predict the future, or if they had lived it themselves. He wanted to follow the plans, build the machine and understand what it was and what it did.

I was looking for truth, he wanted to say.

I was looking for justice, he wanted to say.

Instead, he poked at the plastic bag that held all his things. A lone business card sat on top of the pile of pens and paper and origami.

SAMUEL DEERFOOT, ESQUIRE

Jaime said, "I think I'd like to talk to my lawyer."

CHAPTER TWENTY-EIGHT
September 6, 2025

Shakespeare wrote: *What is the city but the people?* And New Yorkers were a very particular type of people. When New Yorkers talked about "the city," they did not mean the old city of York in England. "England?" they might say. "Who's talking about *England*? I'm talking about the Capital of the World, the City of Dreams, the City That Never Sleeps, the Big Apple, capisce?" That the City That Never Slept dreamed anyway was no contradiction to them, but rather a kind of magic. And that the Big Apple was once the Big Orange never occurred to them at all.

This is how it went: The land belonged to the Lenape and other native peoples for thousands of years before the first Dutch ship crashed into lower Manhattan.

The Dutch insisted on naming it New Amsterdam. Forty years later, the British came and said the place was called New York, after the Duke of York. Then the Dutch brought a fleet of twenty-one ships back into the harbor and rechristened the colony New Orange, a name that lasted only a year before the Brits got control again and named the place New York, though it was no longer new to any of them. Of course, it wasn't new at all to the native people, who had their own names for this island and the rivers and the surrounding lands and themselves. Neither the Dutch nor the British bothered asking them for their opinions on the land or the water, or on anything else, for that matter.

They wouldn't have liked what they heard.

On a gray and gloomy morning in the fall of 2025, this was what Tess Biedermann heard: "Listen, are you going to buy any of those oranges, or are you just going to manhandle them all?" The grocer stood in the doorway of his shop, hands on his hips. He was a fire hydrant of a man, with tan skin, black-furred slashes for brows, and a stained white apron, a man whose barrel chest and hawkish expression intimidated most people.

Theresa was not most people. She continued her inspection of the rather sad-looking fruit on the stands outside the shop, thinking about the Big Orange but not finding it here. "I'm not manhandling them, I'm woman-handling them. *People*-handling."

"Yeah, well, stop all the handling, Handsy-Hands. Buy or go, capisce?"

She picked up the best of the worst and held them out to the grocer. "I'll take these two."

The grocer grunted, bagged up the fruit in wrinkled paper sacks by the register just inside the open door. Most of the oranges grown in Florida had been decimated by weeks of freezing temperatures that had killed vast groves of trees. What was left of the harvest were these dry, shriveled things, barely recognizable as the large, succulent oranges Tess had eaten as a child, juice running down her chin.

"How much?" she asked, and then winced at the answer. She winced again at the price of the two hot coffees she added to her bill. She and Theo could just take caffeine pills like so many people did, but she hated taking pills when the real thing was still available. Like the oranges, the smell of freshly brewing coffee in her parents' kitchen had marked her mornings when she was little, even though she hadn't drunk a drop of the stuff herself until she was sixteen, during her first year of college, seven years ago now. She didn't want to give it up until she had no other choice.

She sipped the drink as she walked home, savoring the bitter taste. The morning was growing warmer and more humid by the minute. At noon, the day would be almost as hot as the coffee in her cup. At least, it would feel like that. Air as heavy as a drenched comforter, comforting nothing.

"Stop being so glum," she muttered to herself.

A man passing by with a thin, nervous greyhound overheard her. "Hard not to be glum," he said. "It's supposed to rain again."

She knew that. Everyone in the city knew that. Listening to the hourly weather updates was a ritual that no one could escape, not if they wanted to know how to dress or which subway to take or which roads were blocked off or whose grandparents with a house on the bay might be underwater in a matter of hours. It wasn't always like this. But, after Adam, the citizens who prided themselves on their resilience were shaken, wary as the stray dogs and cats that roamed lower Manhattan still.

Adam was named Adam because he was the first of his kind. At least, he was the first that people had ever recorded. For years, the severity and frequency of hurricanes in the Atlantic had been increasing, creeping farther north, but nothing like Adam had been seen before: a Category 5 storm so fast and so powerful that he obliterated all wind and rainfall records as he smashed into the northeastern coast of the US, leveling everything in his path. And then he turned into the ocean and came back to do it again, just to be sure everyone understood his message, his unbelievable and unrelenting wrath. Subway tunnels flooded. Whole neighborhoods were swept into the sea. Boats and docks and boardwalks simply vanished as if they had never been there in the first place. Swaths of Long Island peeled away from the edges like old paint. Battery Park was submerged for weeks. Water lapped at the feet of skyscrapers. Manhattanites rode boats and canoes down Wall Street, looking for the trapped and desperate and hungry. Staten Island, well. A mere shadow of it was left, but the people weren't, not anymore, evacuated at the first signs that Adam was coming, most of them still bunking in the Bronx or Jersey. Now, a year after the storm, the earth and the water and the wildlife were reclaiming Staten Island for their own purposes, whatever those were.

Maybe it was to get away from all the people. Maybe it was to plan to overthrow them altogether.

Theresa didn't blame them.

She finished off her coffee and tossed the empty cup into an overflowing trash can on the street. The garbage already stank in the heat, but the garbage truck was blocks away and wouldn't pick up this particular can for hours. There had to be a better way, she thought. There had to be a better way to collect the garbage, there had to be a better way to predict the weather, there had to be a better way to establish a city, there had to be a better way to inhabit the planet, there had to be a better way, period.

"You can't fix everything," her brother, Theodore, would remind her every time she said it.

"I can't fix anything," she would reply.

"Yet," he would say. "We'll just have to keep working."

They were working on a small solar cell that would capture the energy of the sun and an even smaller battery capable of storing that energy for months, even years. They had finished their doctoral dissertations on this work this past spring, and both hoped to get funding to continue the project at a decent research university. When she was feeling glum, which was all too often, Theresa wondered what in the heck they were thinking. No one wanted to fund solar energy projects, now that the Arctic had been opened up for oil drilling. Just a few weeks ago, US and Russian and Chinese warships, all spearheaded by the world's largest energy companies, had squared off in the first clear channel through the once majestic icebergs, each threatening to destroy the others if they didn't give way. Everyone wanted to be the first to tunnel into the deep and bring up the stuff that powered the world, that burned it all so hot.

Too hot, thought Theresa, a trickle of sweat making its way down her back. Walking this morning felt like wading through soup. Just ten years ago, this kind of weather only made an appearance in the late summer, just before the heat broke and something like autumn, however brief, would set in. But even the seasons were addled now, all tumbling over one another, scrambling for other parts of the country that had not previously known them, and weren't exactly pleased to make their acquaintance.

"What's in the bag?" a small voice said.

She looked down to find two small, pale kids sitting in the doorway of a dingy building. A boy about six, a girl maybe eight or so. They were clean and well-fed, but they had a starved look in their gray eyes. Not for food, but for attention. Parents getting ready for work, or already there, the grandparent or babysitter perched in front of a screen, shooing them away with an absent hand.

"It's fruit," said Theresa.

"Oh," said the girl, disappointed.

"What kind of fruit?" said the boy, his hair shorn almost to his pink scalp.

"Oranges."

"Oranges!" the girl scoffed. "You don't have those. They cost a million dollars each."

"Not quite."

"My dad said they do," said the girl. She had long, silky light hair, the kind of hair that Theresa used to wish for.

"They're expensive," Tess said. "But they still exist."

"Can we see?" said the boy.

"Why not?" Theresa opened the bag.

The two peered down inside it. "Oooh!" they said, as if the fruit weren't so bruised and sorry looking, as if they were seeing something else entirely, something out of a fairy tale—a bag full of butterflies, a bag full of spells.

"Here," Theresa said. "You take them."

"What?" said the girl, wary now. "Why?"

"I just remembered that my brother doesn't like oranges anyway."

"Is he weird?" said the girl.

"Depends on who you ask," Theresa said.

The little boy wasn't as cautious as his sister. He took

the bag and cradled it in both hands. His sister elbowed him, and he bleated, "Thank you!"

"You're welcome!" Theresa said, feeling a little lighter as she continued the walk home. The feeling didn't last. She turned the corner and had to shield her eyes against the light beaming relentlessly from a billboard atop the nearest building. The city didn't have enough money to improve bus service, their corrupt mayor yammered, but it had enough money to build these LED billboards on every surface of the city, blinding everyone with ads. On this billboard, a forty-foot-tall laser-eyed blond woman in a slinky dress stood with her arms crossed next to a picture of her latest book: *LASHBACK: A Return to Traditional Values in Our Troubled Times*.

"*Traditional values* like women not being able to own property or get an education?" Theresa snapped before she realized she was speaking aloud. "*Traditional values* like polio and body lice and tuberculosis? Smallpox-infested blankets and manifest destiny? Those values?"

Some tourists, who were taking photos of the billboard, frowned at Theresa. One woman said, "I've read her books and she makes a lot of sense, you know."

"If she made sense," Theresa said, "then she wouldn't be writing books at all. She'd keep her mouth shut and stay home to bake pies like a 'traditional' lady should.

Or order her servants to do it."

"What are you talking about?" said the woman. "Who said anything about servants?"

"Forget it," Theresa said. It wasn't even nine a.m., and she was already exhausted. Think of the children, she told herself, think of how they were enchanted by two sorry pieces of fruit. Think about the sun that grew the fruit in spite of the killing frost.

She reached 354 W. 73rd Street and punched in the combination, pushed open the glass door with her shoulder. She stopped to fetch the mail from the bank of boxes along one side of the lobby. She didn't have to open the envelopes to tell that they hadn't received any good news about jobs or funding. These envelopes were too light for good news. But she tucked the whole bunch under her arm anyway, because you never knew what might surprise you. She headed for the stairs—elevator was broken again—and took them at a run, careful not to spill Theodore's coffee in the process. By the time she burst into the apartment she shared with her brother, she was winded, but just barely. She tossed the mail on the table.

"Took you long enough," Theodore said, his face bright in the light of his laptop.

"Got you coffee," she said, plunking it next to him.

He moved the coffee cup a safer distance from the precious computer. "You shouldn't have. Too expensive."

"I'll drink it, then," she said, reaching for the coffee.

"I didn't say I didn't want it," he said. He took a sip from the cup. "Did you hear about this?"

"About what?" she said, her gut twisting in alarm.

He turned the laptop so she could see the article he was reading. On the screen was a picture of a grinning black man seated at a drawing table, stylus in hand. The headline read: *Lionsgate Nabs Film Rights to Online Comic Series in Eight-Figure, Multipicture Deal.*

She let out a breath in relief that it wasn't news of another storm, another political nightmare. A good surprise this time.

"He looks familiar," she said. "Who is it?"

"Jaime Cruz."

"You're kidding," she said, leaning in farther to examine the man's face. "We haven't seen him since . . . when was it?"

"His dad got transferred to Houston when we were in fifth grade."

"Right," Theresa said. "I remember his drawings. He was hilarious, but in that laid-back way? You never really knew what he was thinking?"

"I remember that he carried that hedgehog in his pocket for weeks. He called it Thor, or maybe it was Loki."

"Until it escaped and crawled up Mr. Jenkins's pants and then left green poop all over the classroom."

Theresa laughed. "And all over Mr. Jenkins."

"He was a nice kid. I wonder if he wants to finance some poor PhDs from the old neighborhood," Theodore said. He stood and moved to the window, sipping his coffee. The view from their grandfather's old apartment was better than the one from their parents' apartment, a few floors below—or it would have been, if the sky weren't so gray. "Anything in the mail?"

"I don't think so," Theresa said. She flipped through the thin envelopes, wondering why they bothered to send paper responses instead of email when all they wanted to say was no. No and no and no and no and no. No, we don't have a teaching job for you, No, we don't care about your little projects. No, solar energy isn't of interest to us, haven't you heard about the Arctic drilling? No, we don't care about the penguins or the polar bears, or any other bear, for that matter. Bears, schmares. We'll turn them all into burgers. Everybody loves burgers.

"You forgot one," Theodore said, pointing to the

last envelope on the table.

She picked it up. Where the address should have been, someone had written *TRUST NO ONE*. She turned it around and showed it to Theodore.

"That's curious," Theodore said. "How could that have gotten into our box with no address on the envelope?"

"The mailman," Theresa said dryly. But she tore open the envelope and pulled out the pages inside. They were creased and crumpled, as if someone had crammed them in rather than folding them. On one of the pages was a hastily drawn but detailed schematic; on the other was a handwritten letter. Theresa read through the note once to herself, and then out loud to her brother:

I couldn't think of who else to turn to, who else to trust, and so it will have to be you. I'm sorry for that. Truly and deeply sorry for the choice you will have to make, both of you so young, as young as

I'm desperate. And someday, you will be, too.

I've enclosed the schematic. Once the machine is built, you will note the date on the meter, right before the Industrial Revolution. It's absurd, I know, to think you could reset everything, but you're all the hope I have left. Please believe that if I could have done it any other way, I would have. Please believe. Believe.

Oh God, they're coming.

I'm sorry. I'm sorry. I'm

"That sounds awfully dramatic," Theodore said, standing and taking the pages from Theresa's hands. He examined the drawing. "I wonder what this person wants us to build."

"I don't know," Theresa said.

He shrugged and laid the schematic on the table. He sipped his coffee and read the article about Jaime Cruz aloud to Theresa. It was a good story, a happy story. In a world with so much unhappiness, Theresa was glad for that.

After he was finished reading, however, Theodore again picked up the schematic.

"What?" Theresa said.

"I don't know. I'm curious. Aren't you?"

"I'm more curious about who wrote the letter."

"Maybe we can solve that mystery if we figure out this one." He shook the schematic at her. He pulled his laptop closer and started tapping the keys, eyes darting from the plans to the screen and back to the plans.

While he typed, Theresa entered all the recent rejections into the spreadsheet on her own laptop where they kept track of such things. She tossed the pile of empty envelopes into the trash with the other paper recycling. Which was an exercise in futility, because she'd read that the city simply dumped the paper and cans and glass and plastic that people had so carefully collected in with the rest of the garbage. But she couldn't bring herself not to do it.

"Huh," said Theodore.

"What?"

"Some of this math. It . . . works."

"Works how?" Theresa stood behind him and tried to make sense of what she saw on his screen. "Wait. Wait. Is this supposed to be a schematic for a . . . ?"

"No," said Theodore. "It couldn't be."

Together, they scoured the pages. "This must be some kind of joke," Theodore said.

"Doesn't sound like a joke."

"It has to be. Because this is impossible. Scientifically, physically, logically, and in every other way impossible. It's—"

"—absurd," Theresa finished. But even as she said it, she could feel the fear of the letter writer, whoever it was. She wished she could help, but . . .

Theodore made the decision for them, as if there were an actual decision to be made about an anonymous letter with an utterly ridiculous idea. Theodore folded the pages and stuffed them back into the envelope. He tossed the envelope into the trunk where they kept all their rejections and other junk. "Come on, we have some more grant proposals to write," he said. "And then we have to get back to the battery. Energy retainment is still dropping below seventy percent within twelve hours of initial charging."

"More juice," said Tess, thinking of the oranges. "More juice."

They sat down at the table—the iron-gray sky behind them, the city churning below—all too quickly forgetting about the envelope and the pages inside.

They thought they understood desperation, you see.

It would take years for them to realize how very desperate a person could become.

CHAPTER TWENTY-NINE
Tess

T ess had been in trouble before. When she and Theo were two and counted how many things they could flush down the toilet, which included several stuffed animals, seventy-nine cents in pennies, and their dad's underwear. When she and Theo were three and a half, got onto their dad's computer, and ordered more than six hundred dollars' worth of *Star Wars* Lego sets and a whole bunch of lightsabers. When she and Theo were five, woke up before their parents one Sunday morning, and took themselves out for brunch. In Brooklyn. (As it turned out, you couldn't pay for Belgian waffles with Monopoly money.)

But Tess had never been in this kind of trouble. The kind of trouble that makes your parents so upset that they can't even speak. The kind of trouble that means your parents have a hard time being in the same car or the same room or the same country as you without shaking their heads or even tearing up. The kind of trouble that means you could be spending the next few years of your life, maybe the rest of your life, trying not to disappoint them again, even though you're sad and angry and frustrated that they were so disappointed in the first place.

During an interview at the police station, they had been interrupted by the arrival of one Samuel Deerfoot, the Seneca lawyer they'd just met. Though Sam's specialty was treaties, Jaime had called him for help, and miraculously, he had agreed. After Sam spoke with the police, Jaime and the twins were released into their parents' custody with a warning not to break into places they didn't belong. Darnell Slant and company, who arrived at the station with a team of lawyers, also got a warning, and no punishment for anything he'd done. And neither did Candi. The Brunos were charged with assault but also released on bail. On top of that, the twins' mother had received official reprimands, first from her boss and then from the mayor himself—wildly overcompensating so he didn't look prejudiced against his political rival—as if the twins hadn't worked entirely on their own.

None of it was fair.

Which was what Tess said to Aunt Esther. They were sitting with Theo and Nine on the back porch after a dinner where everyone hadn't said much, and had eaten even less. Aunt Esther had made them some tea and put out a plate of Fig Newtons, but Tess wasn't remotely hungry.

"I know it's not fair," said Aunt Esther. "The world isn't fair."

"It should be," said Tess.

"I know," said Aunt Esther. "But the world is unfair because a lot of people prefer it that way. And your parents know that getting in the way of those particular people makes you a target."

"What if we don't care about being a target?" said Tess.

"Maybe you don't. But consider this: If you are a target, all of your family is also a target."

Tess didn't say anything. She didn't know what to say. Her mother had done a search of Tess's and Theo's phones—something that Sam said he could not prevent—and the sheer number of locations they had visited without her permission and the evidence of the lies they had told had horrified her. She wouldn't listen to Tess or Theo when they said they'd been following clues, real clues, and that they thought they were close to discovering something important, maybe even the solution to the Morningstarr Cipher. When Tess had tried to appeal to her father, hoping that he would understand, he told her that she was grounded, and Theo was grounded, too. They wouldn't be able to leave the house without supervision, they wouldn't have access to their computers except for schoolwork, their phone usage would be tracked. And since they had done all of this with Jaime, they had spoken with his father and grandmother and they had all agreed that the three of them needed a "cooling-off period." They weren't to have any communication for a month, which would give them all time to settle into school and focus on what was important— their futures.

"But that's what we're doing!" Tess had protested.

Her father had shaken his head and walked out of the room.

Now Tess picked at the Fig Newtons on the table between her and Aunt Esther. She didn't know whether to cry or scream or both. She wished she could call Grandpa Ben, talk to him about the Cipher that had been his life's work, but even if her parents allowed her to make a call, or visit him at the memory care home where he lived now, they wouldn't let her speak to him alone for fear that she'd pump him for information.

They weren't wrong.

Tess sighed one of those where-have-I-gone-wrong sighs you can only learn from your parents. Aunt Esther patted her hand. "They're afraid for you. Give them some time."

School was starting. Slant was running for mayor and soon would have enough power to buy every building in Manhattan if he wanted. Jaime's mother had something to do with the Cipher, but they didn't know what. The Morningstarr Machines were growing restless and unpredictable, and someone, somewhere, was creating hybrid monsters out of innocent animals. They didn't know how it was all connected, but they were so, so close. Tess could feel it all the way down to her toes.

And even if her gut wasn't telling her that they had reached the end of the line, Slant did. Not to her directly, but to a gaggle of reporters gathered on the steps of the Tombs: "I want to thank New York's finest for their hospitality. I have every belief that certain members of the force will keep a better eye on their children from now on. But let's also keep our eyes on the future. We're going to sweep out the old and make way for the new. In five days, you're going to wake up to a whole new city!"

"But what does that mean?" asked a reporter.

"It means that you're going to love it!"

Tess didn't know what Slant was intending to do in five days, but she knew it would be horrible.

They didn't have much time left.

Jaime had known this, too. As they were leaving the police station—the twins with their parents, Jaime with his father and grandmother—Jaime had dropped the origami heart. Tess had picked it up without anyone being the wiser, without anyone knowing that the heart held the plans for the mysterious Morningstarr Machine inside it.

Though it was still early, Tess and Theo said good night to Aunt Esther.

"Going to bed so soon?"

"No," said Tess. "We're off to feel sorry for ourselves."

"Go have yourselves a good sulk. I promise you will feel better in the morning."

Tess and Theo went upstairs to their room. Nine sprawled in front of the door, keeping watch for nosy adults. They unfolded the origami heart to reveal the plans that had gotten them into so much trouble, and might get them into more. Then they pulled out the various items they had gathered so far and set those out on the carpet—the chess pieces, the gear and puzzle box, the strange and creepy doll—all of it.

They studied the schematic. The device they were making appeared to be a small but complicated mechanism that fit inside a case about the size of a soda can, with some sort of lens on the front.

"It looks like a camera from the seventies," said Tess.

"A camera from the seventies would be a lot bigger than this," Theo said.

Tess ran a finger down the list of parts required to build the device, then sifted through the pile of random treasures and clues they'd gathered. "I think we're supposed to take all these things apart and use those parts to make this instead. What do you think?"

"I think you're right."

"I'll get my tools," said Tess. She went to her closet and rummaged in The Magix, pulled out a small tool kit Aunt Esther had given her for her eleventh birthday.

"Aunt Esther comes through again," said Theo.

For the next two days, they unscrewed and wrenched and disassembled, labeling the bits and pieces as they went, and quickly found, surprisingly and yet unsurprisingly, that those bits and pieces matched up with parts on the schematic—springs, screws, plates, brackets, gears, nuts, bolts. They took breaks only to shower, to skim the summer books and math packets that they hadn't bothered to read for school, and to make appearances at meals, looking as glum as possible to keep their parents and Aunt Esther from getting too suspicious.

"What's this?" Tess said on day three, showing Theo a bracket on which some characters had been etched.

תיבת אבשי החחסד הראשובים

"It's Hebrew," said Theo.

"I *know* it's Hebrew, you dork. I mean what does it say? Can you read it?"

"Not well," Theo said. "I think this means 'ark,' right? And this means 'first.' Or something.'"

"Mom would be so disappointed in us."

"If we had our phones, we could use a translation program."

"We don't have our phones."

"I know we don't have our phones," said Theo. "Let me get my Hebrew books. Wait. They're downstairs in the bookcase."

"Never mind. We'll figure it out later. Let's keep going."

They continued disassembling and labeling until

they had nothing left but the coins, the chess pieces, and one creepy doll's head.

Theo sat back on his heels. "We don't have enough parts."

Tess grabbed the schematic and checked the parts list, but of course he was right. Except. "We've got most of the parts," she pointed out. "All we're missing are a few at the end of the list. Let's build as much of it as we can."

"But we can't build something if we don't have all the parts! I mean, if this is a machine, where's the power source?"

Tess took a deep breath and put the creepy doll's head on her hand like a puppet. "Theo, we're going to build what we can, okay?"

That she finally got Theo to agree was proof that he was as anxious as she was. (Or scared of the doll's head.)

So they began the careful assemblage. This screw fitting into that bracket, that bracket attached to the next bracket, the brackets attached to the gear they'd found back at the Tredwell House. They had to sneak down to the basement to use Aunt Esther's vise—of course Aunt Esther had a vise—to bend some metal plates into rounded shapes, and then they used her mechanical punch press to put holes in each corner of the plates.

They nested the intricate innards of the machine inside the rounded metal plates to form a small canister.

Exhausted, they looked at what they had built. And though it didn't look much like a camera from the '70s, it also didn't appear to be anything special. Tess had been so sure that all they needed to do was build the machine and the rest would come clear. But now they were stuck. Really and truly stuck. They didn't even know what the machine *was*. And they couldn't talk to Jaime, they couldn't call Grandpa Ben, they couldn't go to the library or use the internet or contact anyone at the Old York Puzzler and Cipherist Society. School was going to start in a few days, and all they had managed to do was help level their own home and get their mother in trouble with the current mayor and the man who would probably be elected mayor. Did that mean their mother could be out of a job? And since their father worked for the public school system, did that mean *he* would be out of a job, too? How much more could they be punished?

Tears stung in Tess's eyes. Nine roused herself and rubbed her big stripy ears against Tess's arm, purring loudly. The black dye that had camouflaged her so well was fading, and her spots and stripes were more visible.

A knock on the door startled them all. Theo threw a

blanket over the parts and the plans and sat down on it with his schoolbooks.

Tess said, "Come in."

Their mother pushed open the door. The dark circles around her eyes told Tess how tired she was, how wrung out.

"Hi," she said.

"Hi," said Tess and Theo.

"I just wanted to check on you two. Make sure you're okay."

"We're fine," Theo said. "Reading some stuff for school."

"Oh! What are you reading?"

Theo showed her the book. *"Alexander Hamilton, Revolutionary,"* she read. "Do you like it?"

"It's really good," Theo said.

"Glad to hear it," said their mom. She leaned against the doorway. "Well. Don't stay up too late."

"We will," said Theo, a little joke.

Their mom smiled an exhausted but loving smile. "I know." She stood in the doorway a few moments, running a hand down the old wooden doorjamb. "Maybe this weekend, you two would like to visit Grandpa? We haven't been in a while. Too long. And I think he'd love to see you. What do you say?"

Tess buried her head in Nine's fur. Maybe their mom was checking up on them, maybe she was trying to keep them occupied so they couldn't do any more damage. But it didn't matter what her mother's motives were. The tears that had been threatening to fall for days finally did.

"I'm sorry, Mom," Tess said. "We didn't mean to make such a mess out of things."

"Oh, Tess," said their mother. She held out her arms, and Tess ran into them. She cried into her mother's shoulder because she had lied and stolen and destroyed her home and her family's trust, and because she knew that if it meant she could build the Morningstarr Machine, solve the Cipher, and finish what she and Theo and Jaime had started, she would do it all again.

Nightmares:

A scuttling monster in the shape of a hand chasing her down an empty street.

An Underway car as it hurtled through the city, a Guildman grinning skull-like as he urged the train to go faster.

The walls of 354 W. 73rd Street shivering, shuddering, and crumbling into a pile of rubble.

The giraffe-owary's beak snapping, vicious claws

tearing into her as she screamed.

A blond woman in a red dress pushing Jaime into dark and murky water.

Twenty Brunos at the door, saying, "You'll do what you're told if you know what's good for you."

Cops at the door, telling her that they were sorry, but they would have to take her mother and father away now, they had to investigate every complaint, they had to go by the book, sorry, they said, sorry.

Tess tossed in her sleep, clawed at her throat, struggling for air.

"Mrrow."

She woke up to find Nine sitting on her chest.

"Nine, what are you doing?" she mumbled.

Nine licked Tess's nose. Tess sneezed.

"Land of Kings."

Tess almost fell out of bed. Framed in the window screen was Ono, hovering like a hummingbird, if hummingbirds had propellers on their heads.

"Ono? How did you get here?"

"Land of Kings," Ono repeated, dipping low to display his propeller. Then he banged into the screen. "Oh no." Banged it again. "Oh no." Banged it.

"Okay, okay, I get it. I'll let you in." Tess opened the screen and Ono whirred into the room. Nine charged.

"Shhhhh! Quiet! Both of you!" Tess said. "You'll wake everybody up."

"You woke me up," Theo mumbled. He rubbed his eyes. "What's going on?"

"I don't know. Ono's here."

"Is Jaime with him?" Theo asked.

Ono landed in Theo's hair and spat out a piece of paper. Theo plucked the paper out of his hair and sat up. He read, "'I'm in the backyard, hiding by the bushes. Ono can be your ladder.'"

Tess and Theo flew out of bed and pulled on some clothes, some sneakers. They put the small unfinished canister in Tess's messenger bag, along with the plans for the machine and the tool kit from Aunt Esther. Just in case, they dumped the chess pieces, the coins, and the creepy doll's head in, too. Then Tess shouldered the messenger bag. Ono flew out the window again and latched onto the sill. Its limbs elongated, forming a narrow ladder all the way to the ground outside. Nine didn't bother with the ladder. She sprang out of the window and landed in a nearby tree. She jumped to the grass.

Tess hesitated. "Mom and Dad will worry."

Theo grabbed a piece of paper and a pen from the nightstand. He wrote:

Don't worry about us.

"That's convincing," said Tess.

"What do you want me to write?"

Tess took the pen:

We know you don't understand. And maybe we don't understand everything. But we've found more clues to the Cipher, so many more than you know. We've almost figured it out. So we have to follow this through to the end. We'll be back as soon as we can. We love you.

"I guess that's better," said Theo.

"You go first," Tess said. "I'm right behind you."

She waited until Theo was safely on the ground before she climbed out the window. With each rung, she took a step farther away from her parents. She did love them. So much. But she remembered watching a movie with her dad some months ago, before they'd left 354 W. 73rd, a movie about a guy who'd found out his whole life was a computer-generated reality. To keep living the way he'd been living, all he had to do was open a white box. To learn the truth, he had to open a black box. Her father had argued that the problem was that too many people thought they'd already opened the black box, that they were the only ones who could see the world for what it really was, the only people who could not be fooled. And Tess thought maybe children were their parents' black boxes, boxes that they didn't want to open for fear of the truths they'd find inside.

She landed on the grass with soft *thump*. If they left this yard, there was no turning back.

Jaime appeared out of the shadows. Ono snapped back into his regular form and flew down to where they stood.

Tess took one last look at Aunt Esther's house, still and quiet in the night air.

"Come on," she said. "Let's go."

CHAPTER THIRTY
Theo

Theo, Tess, and Jaime had snuck out before, but it had never felt like this.

"We're going to be grounded till the end of time," Theo whispered.

"Probably," said Jaime. "Keep your eye out for Brunos. And blond ladies. And wolf-spiders. And politicians."

They crept along the line of bushes, passing the empty fer-rabbit's cage in their neighbors' yard.

"Where's the bunny?" said Tess.

"Maybe it went off to seek its fortunes," Theo said.

Nobody said what they were all thinking: that it had been kidnapped the way Karl had. That someone, somewhere, was experimenting on it.

They crossed the street, avoiding the light from the solar lamps, and walked briskly to the nearest Underway station.

"Where are we going?" Theo asked as they walked down the steps.

Jaime stopped walking. "I thought you guys would know."

"We don't!" Tess said.

"You haven't figured out anything new?"

"Well, there was that bit of writing on the bracket," Theo said.

"Let's get into the station and I'll show you," Tess said.

Once they were downstairs, they loitered by the token machine. Tess searched her bag and came up with the machine. She flipped it over.

תיבת אבשי החסד הראשובים

"It's Hebrew," said Theo. "But I can't translate it. Not the whole thing, anyway."

Jaime pulled out his phone. "Maybe I can."

"How did you get your phone back from your father? Didn't he take it?"

"Yes," he said. "I'm not supposed to get it back until I retire. But Ono found it for me."

"How did you get out of your apartment without anyone seeing you?"

"It's a long story," Jaime said. "I don't even know how to key in these characters."

"Let me try," Theo said. He did a search and found a Hebrew-to-English translation program. Then he punched in the Hebrew letters.

"Anything?"

"Yes. This says it means 'The first box of grace people.'"

"Huh?" said Jaime. "What's that?"

"I'm not sure," said Theo. "These translation programs aren't very good."

"No kidding," Tess said.

"I wasn't kidding."

"Theo! Think!"

"I am!"

"We have to convert the Hebrew words into the English alphabet. But there's no real standard. It's why 'Hanukkah' is spelled so many different ways. People disagree. Jewish people are always up for a debate," said Tess. "Usually, it's fun."

"And after that, you can translate the Hebrew word

into an anglicized word," Theo said. "I think we have the right idea with 'original.' But I don't know about the rest."

"What's the anglicized word for 'person' or 'people'?" Jaime asked.

"You want I should take a look?"

All three of them whipped around to see a smallish old man standing there, deep lines in his olive skin. "Or not," he added.

Theo looked at Jaime and Jaime looked at Tess. Tess said, "Might as well."

Theo held the bracket out to the old man. The man put on a pair of glasses and held up the bracket. "This says, 'Teivat Anshei HaChesed HaRishonim,' which means, roughly, 'the ark of the first people of grace.'"

Theo blinked. He had no idea what to make of that. "Thank you."

"Or it could mean Ansche Chesed, the synagogue on the Upper West Side."

"Thank you!" said Tess.

"No problem. Now would you and your big kitty move aside so I can get my tokens?"

The three of them and Nine moved away from the machine. The man fed a ten-dollar bill into it and got a pile of tokens. "I hope your parents know where you are," he said.

"Sir—" Jaime began.

"Never mind! Just be careful. The city isn't always a place of grace."

"We know," Jaime said.

"I bet you do," said the man. "Good luck. I'll keep you in my prayers." He walked away, disappearing down another flight of steps.

Theo turned to Jaime. "Look up—"

"Already got you. That guy was right that Ansche Chesed is a synagogue uptown. But the original location was 172 Norfolk Street on the Lower East Side. It was built in 1849, the oldest Reform synagogue in the United States. It's now called the Angel Orensanz Center. They have weddings there."

"I guess we're going to a wedding," said Tess. They slipped the bracket back into Tess's messenger bag and ran for the N train that would take them into Manhattan. Like the other trains they had taken lately, the train car was uncharacteristically messy, with rolling bits of trash, windows streaked with grime. The caterpillar was nowhere to be found. And the Guildman in his glass enclosure wasn't texting anyone. He sat in his chair, face in his hands, as if he was mourning the death of a friend.

"I should be scared, but instead I just feel bad for the guy," Jaime said.

"Let's wait until we actually make it into Manhattan to feel bad for him," said Theo.

They did make it into Manhattan without the train derailing or exploding or any other disasters. And though the next train was as dirty as the first, and the Guildman just as mournful, there were no disasters on that one, either.

When they made it up to street level, Jaime said, "Do you think the Guildmen know about the obelisk? About the stuff we took?"

"Borrowed," said Tess.

"I don't think your mom would agree with that," Jaime said.

They walked the rest of the way to the Angel Orensanz Center, which turned out to be a beautiful building with a facade of redbrick and stucco. It had three narrow windows in the middle and square towers on either side, with grand steps leading up to three doorways. Though it was late, after eleven, faint music emanated from the doors and windows, and drumbeats vibrated in the sidewalk. They went to the middle door and cautiously opened it. Behind the doors was a lobby with two separate coat checks, both empty because it was still so warm outside. Music blared from the main space, carrying shrieks of laughter with it.

They peered into the huge room, where a party was in full blast. The building's former life as a synagogue was still visible in the architecture of the building, which looked like pictures Theo had seen of the Cathedral of Notre-Dame in Paris. Above them, ornate balconies rimmed the perimeter of the room. Strings of tiny white lights were wrapped around the railings of the balconies and the centerpieces on all the tables. The dance floor was packed with people, their smiles as bright as their clothes, and a band played. At least half the women wore colorful saris, while others wore fancy dresses in lace and satin. Many of the men wore yarmulkes. The people in the crowd were white and brown and black and everything in between; they could have been from anywhere and everywhere. The band struck up another song, and the crowd roared its approval, some of the guests holding up glasses or bottles or simply a fist or finger or phone to take a picture.

Theo stood on his tiptoes to see over the crowd. "It looks like the ark is behind the band."

"It is? I thought we were talking ark as in 'ship.'"

"Ark as in 'Ark of the Covenant.' It's a sort of chest or closet where you keep the Torah," Theo said. "I'm guessing we need to look in it."

"How do we get over there without anyone noticing us? We're not dressed for a wedding."

"We dance over," said Jaime.

"What? No. I don't dance."

"Tonight you do." Jaime danced into the crowd. In seconds, Theo and Tess and even Nine were surrounded.

"Excuse me!" said Theo to no one in particular. "Pardon me! I'm sorry, I don't dance, please let go."

An Indian girl not much older than he was, with a tumble of dark hair pinned with winking jewels and a pink sari trimmed with gold, yelled, "Watch me!" She put one arm up like she was hailing a cab and the other low in front of her as if she were about to shake someone's hand. She rocked back and forth to the heavy beat.

"Now you!" she said.

"Me?"

"Come on!"

Theo did his best to imitate her. Tess and Jaime did, too. And soon they were as caught up in the music as anyone in the place. So when the music changed to "Hava Nagila," Theo joined a circle to do the hora, Jaime's arms entwined with his. Rings within rings of people surrounded the bride and groom, who were lifted up on chairs in the middle. The bride wore a white dress that contrasted with her olive skin and dark, curling hair; her South Asian groom wore white pants and a white tunic with elaborate designs down the front. The dancers grapevined around them, moving faster and faster as the band got more frantic. Theo stopped focusing on the steps and lost himself in the dance, dizzy with the heat and the stamping of feet and the ecstatic smiles of the married couple and the happy cries of the crowd. Though this wasn't a synagogue anymore, it still felt like a holy place. They were here to find parts for a machine that could possibly tell the future, or change it, and he didn't know what would happen, if he was a Biedermann or Morningstarr or both, he didn't know if he'd ever be able to have a wedding or a family, or if Tess or Jaime would, so he danced and Jaime danced and Tess danced until they were breathless, as if this was the last chance they'd ever get.

The music changed again and the spell broke. Reluctantly, Theo, Tess, and Jaime started pushing through the churning mass of partiers to get to the stage.

"Did you bring a tiger? That's so cool!" said a beautiful brown girl in a green sari dancing by.

"Uhhh," said Theo, speechless.

"Yes!" said Tess. "She'll do tricks later."

"Mrrow?" Nine said.

"Awesome," said the girl, whirling away.

To Nine, Tess whispered, "You won't have to do tricks."

"Mrrow," said Nine. Not for the first time, Theo wondered how much English the cat understood, what kind of book she would write if she could.

The band dialed up the tempo, breaking into a furious klezmer tune, and the crowd went bananas. Theo, Tess, and Jaime danced around the stage to the back, where the ark stood against the wall. The cabinet was painted gold and gleamed like metal under the twinkling lights. Theo checked to make sure that both the musicians and the revelers were too wrapped up in their revelry to pay attention to the fuzzy-haired kid skulking behind the drummer. Then he tried to open the cabinet. It wouldn't budge. Was it painted shut? No, it was locked. Of course it was locked. Why wouldn't it be locked? Plus there were three separate keyholes in the plate on the door. Three keys? As far as he could remember, they didn't even have *one* key in the messenger bag they'd brought with them.

"What's wrong?" Tess said.

"We need keys!"

"Keys? More than one?" Jaime said.

"Three! And they're big keys, too."

"We don't even have *one* key," Tess said.

"I know!"

"We've had to use things that didn't look like keys as keys before," said Jaime.

"Yes, but we don't have anything that . . . wait. Where are those chess pieces?"

Tess dug around in the messenger bag and came up with the three pieces. Theo took them. He tried the king. Nope. Queen. No again. Knight. That fit. Tried the king in the second keyhole. Nope. The queen, then. It fit. And then the king in the last keyhole. In order from top to bottom, he turned the keys. The door still wouldn't open. Think, Theo, Think. Did it have something to do with the chess pieces? You lose a chess game when you lose the king, but it's vulnerable, and not much stronger than a knight. The knight isn't technically as powerful as a rook, but it's the only piece that can jump. The queen is the most powerful piece, though two rooks can be stronger sometimes.

He put one hand on the cabinet and turned the keys back to their starting positions. Then he tried turning the king, then the knight, then the queen.

Still nothing.

He tried another order: queen, knight, king.

Nope.

Knight, queen, king.

No and no and no.

He took a deep breath, tried to tamp down the panic crawling up his throat. The band still flailed. The people still danced and laughed and shrieked with joy, jumping up and down as one.

As one.

He crawled over to where Jaime and Tess and Nine crouched. "I think we have to do this together."

"Won't they see us?" said Tess.

"They don't care! Come on!"

Tess and Jaime climbed up on the stage.

Theo said, "One, two . . . three!"

CHAPTER THIRTY-ONE

Jaime

Just three days before, back at the police station, things had been going well, or as well as could be expected under the circumstances, until Jaime asked to talk to his lawyer.

Then everything went to heck.

His dad yelled in two languages, Mima yelled in five. Detective Biedermann asked them to settle down, but nobody was interested in settling down. Who was this lawyer Jaime wanted to call? How could he trust a virtual stranger over his own family? What, exactly, had he been up to? How much trouble was he in? What was he trying to *do*?

And Jaime, who was so smooth most of the time, could charm moms and dads and aunties and uncles and grandmothers and teachers, didn't have the words. Or didn't have enough words. Or enough time. How do you tell your dad that you believe that your friends—the twins with the knobby knees and messy hair and freckles—could be the Morningstarrs who had built the city and invented the Old York Cipher? How do you tell your grandmother that you believe that you are a part of the Cipher, too? How do you tell anybody that you drew a woman before you ever saw her, a woman who should have died in the nineteenth century? How do you tell everyone that the city, maybe the world, depends on solving this mystery, especially if you have no proof of this except a feeling in your gut and a picture of your mom?

So he didn't speak. He kept his mouth shut until his dad and his grandmother relented, and Detective Biedermann gave him a phone and some privacy. Even Jaime was stunned that this lawyer, who he had met for only a few moments, had agreed to come and help. It was Samuel Deerfoot who had calmed his grandmother and father, Samuel Deerfoot who had smoothed things over with the police department and gotten them all off with a warning.

But Samuel Deerfoot couldn't change how badly Jaime had hurt his father and Mima. And he *had* hurt them. Not because he had betrayed their trust so much as because he hadn't trusted them enough to tell them what he was doing, and still couldn't. The disappointment, the fear, the sadness on their faces that he'd been keeping so many secrets, sneaking around where he shouldn't be, would be burned into his brain into eternity and back. He didn't want to think about what they would look like in the morning if—when—they found his bed empty.

Now he focused on the wild music, the hammer of the drum in his ears and in his feet as he and his friends all turned their keys and the ark opened.

Theo fished around in the cabinet and pulled out . . . a doll.

"Not another doll," said Tess. "What is with the dolls?"

"There's nothing else in the ark," said Theo.

Tess took the doll and shoved it into the bag along with the chess pieces. "Were the Morningstarrs trying to creep us all out?"

"Hey! What are you guys doing back there?"

It was the drummer, who had finally noticed something going on behind him.

"We love this song!" Tess said.

"What?"

"Thank you, bye!" Tess jumped off the stage, Theo and Jaime with her. They danced back through the crowd. This time, though, some of the wedding guests gave them curious looks, and there was concerned murmuring as they passed.

"Who are those kids?"

"What are they wearing?"

"Herman, are those Lydia's kids? I bet they belong to Lydia. Lydia's children always look like ragamuffins."

They did not, in Jaime's opinion, look like ragamuffins, whatever those were, but it was clear they had to get out of there.

"Faster," he said in Tess's ear.

"I know," she said.

More murmuring. More faces turned in their direction. A wave of faces. Not angry, just confused.

Which was when Jaime nearly headbutted the bride. He looked up.

"Hi there," she said. "Do I know you?" She smiled at Nine, and then the smile died a slow death when she took in Tess's tattered cutoffs.

"We're Lydia's kids," Jaime said.

"Oh!" she said, nodding. "Right."

Ono, who had been chilling in Jaime's pocket most of the evening, picked that moment to pop its head out. "Land of Kings!" it buzzed.

"Yikes!" said the bride.

"Great wedding! You look beautiful!" Tess added, as Jaime dragged her and Theo out of the ballroom and out the door. They bounded down the steps and across the street before anyone decided to follow them, then ducked into a nearby alcove where the light from the solar lamps didn't reach to catch their breath.

"Now what?"

"Let's look at that doll," Jaime said.

"Do we have to?" said Theo. "Just kidding."

Tess pulled out the doll. Its face and limbs were cream-colored porcelain, but its body was metal, like the last one they'd found. Most of its hair was gone, but it had a few blond strands left. She handed it to Jaime. It was strangely heavy.

"I don't think this is a crawling doll like that other one. Maybe it walks?" Theo suggested.

"No," said Jaime. "Look right under her neck. That's a speaker. I think it talks." He flipped the doll over. On the back was a pull string.

"Wait! What if it's dangerous?" Theo said.

"What hasn't been dangerous?" Jaime said, and pulled.

In a wavering, crackling voice, the doll warbled:

> *"Twinkle, twinkle, little star,*
> *How I wonder what you are.*
> *Up above the world so high,*
> *Like a diamond in the sky,*
> *Twinkle, twinkle, little star,*
> *How I wonder what you are!"*

"That's the creepiest voice I ever heard outside of a horror movie," Theo said. "Correction: That's the creepiest voice I ever heard, period."

"It's still going," said Tess.

> *"When the blazing sun is gone,*
> *When he nothing shines upon,*
> *Then you show your little light,*
> *Twinkle, twinkle, all the night.*
> *Twinkle, twinkle, little star,*
> *How I wonder what you are!*
>
> *"Then the traveler in the dark*
> *Thanks you for your tiny spark.*

He could not see which way to go
If you did not twinkle so.
Twinkle, twinkle, little star,
Exquisite Engines take you far."

"Engines?" asked Jaime. "Is it talking about the device you built?"

"Maybe," Theo said.

"Little star, little light, tiny spark," said Tess, thinking. "Spark as in flame? Spark as in trigger? Spark as in power?"

"The power source!" said Theo. "Yes! That's what we're looking for."

"But maybe it's also talking about *where* we find this power source. Wasn't the original Morningstarr lab called Exquisite Engines?" Jaime said.

Theo hit himself in the forehead so hard he almost fell over. "Yes! Why didn't I think of that!"

"Shhh!" said Tess, lowering her voice to a whisper. "The building is still there in Red Hook, Brooklyn. But it's been abandoned for years. And it's probably surrounded by Slant's goons at this point."

"Brunos," said Theo.

"And Guildmen," Tess said.

"And monsters," Jaime said.

They went quiet. In that silence, they agreed. They wouldn't stop until they had the answers they wanted, the ones they needed, no matter who—or what—they had to face.

Tess took the doll and stuffed it back in her bag. "Who wants to chip in for a cab?"

The young cabdriver with the pale skin and the backward baseball cap was happy to take them to Brooklyn. He was also happy to ask a million questions and offer a million opinions:

"So, are you kids related?"

"What's your dad do for a living?"

"You ever take one of those DNA tests? I'm a mutt—twenty-three percent Irish, fourteen percent Swedish, thirty-two percent German, nine percent Italian, and three percent unknown. What do think the unknown part is?"

"Your mom is okay with you being out so late by yourselves?"

"How old are you?"

"Why's your cat so big?"

"I really can't stay hydrated unless I drink pickle juice."

"You shouldn't feed your cat so much."

"The government is always watching, always listening. They watch us through our phones and listen through our microwaves."

"I'm guessing I'm part alien, that's what it is."

"I hope you wear sunscreen when you're out in the sun. I don't care how brown your skin is, you can still burn."

"My nephew is five months old today. His head is gigantic. Like a pumpkin on a tadpole. I don't know why babies' heads are so big. It feels wrong."

Luckily, all they had to do was say "Huh," or "Hmmm," and the man kept chattering on. As he talked, Jaime watched the city go by—the cobbled streets, the buildings, the solar lamps—all a blur. What would this all look like if the Morningstarrs hadn't built it? What would someone else's vision be? He thought about Samuel Deerfoot and his people. What could they have dreamed up had this land not been taken from them?

Finally, they arrived in Red Hook. It was so late it was early, and so early it was late, an hour at which even the most determined night owls put their heads under their wings and went to sleep. Exquisite Engines, the ancient and rundown former Morningstarr lab, loomed in the strange gloom, reflecting eerily off the water of the Henry Street Basin.

At the corner of Clinton and Bryant, the cabbie said, "Are you sure this is where you want to be dropped off? Doesn't look like there's much around here."

Tess counted out the fare plus a tip. It was all the money they had. "Thank you!"

"Sure," said the cabbie. "Remember what I said about the microwaves." He drove off, leaving them in almost total darkness.

Jaime used the flashlight on his phone to light the way. They walked past some other buildings toward the sound of the water—*gulp, gulp, gulp.* Then they were standing on the edge of the shore, looking out over the Henry Street Basin to the lab on the other side. Though the building had a brand-new "Slant Properties" sign on it as well as "No Trespassing" and "Alarms Will Sound" and "Guard Patrols" and "Beware of Dog" signs, the building had seen better days. Better decades. The once-white exterior was blackened as if by a fire, and whole staircases sagged into the water.

"How are we going to get across?" Tess asked.

"We could walk all the way around," Theo suggested.

"That will take forever. We can borrow that," Jaime said, pointing to a rowboat tied up against a nearby dock.

The rowboat was in almost as bad shape as the

Morningstarr lab. Paint peeled off it, and it stank of fish.

"Seems real safe," said Theo. But he didn't argue. Nine jumped into the boat first. As carefully as they could, they got into the boat one at a time. Jaime untied the boat from the dock and Tess and Theo used the oars to push off.

"I hope there are no—" Tess began.

"If you are about to complain about sharks, do not complain about sharks," Theo said. "Just keep rowing."

"This is going to take forever, too," said Tess. "I wish we could have borrowed a boat with a motor."

Ono popped from Jaime's pocket. "Kings! Kings!"

"What is it?"

"Kiiiiiings," buzzed Ono. His propeller whirred.

"You want to be our motor?"

"KINGS."

"Are you sure?"

Ono beeped and buzzed, annoyed.

"Okay, okay, I was just asking." Jaime pulled Ono out of his pocket and leaned over the back of the boat. "Not too fast, though. I don't want to end up in the river again."

Ono burbled. Jaime gently lowered the robot into the water. Ono started up his propeller and the boat lurched forward. They zigged and zagged until they got the hang of it. They motored across the water, which went from midnight blue to black in the shadow of the lab.

They tied the boat to the only thing they could find: one of the warped and disintegrating staircases dangling off the building. Tess gave Theo the messenger bag and carefully pulled herself up the stairs and onto the ground. Theo tossed the bag back to her and she helped him out of the boat. Jaime got Ono out of the water.

"Thanks, dude," he said, drying Ono on his T-shirt. He slipped Ono back into his pocket and held out his hands so that Theo and Tess could haul him up. Once they were on solid ground, Jaime fired up his flashlight again and aimed it at the building. Ivy snaked over the walls. Windows and doors were missing, and plants had taken their places, draped across or sprouting up in the spaces. They stepped over a pricker bush that squatted in the biggest doorway and walked inside. Not much different in here. The vines crept along the ceilings, sticks and dried-up leaves crunched underfoot, echoing in the cavernous space. Maybe there had been walls here once, walls that had separated the space into lobbies and waiting rooms and offices and labs, but all that was left were odd patches of tile marking the floor, stalagmites of plaster and wood jutting upward like shark fins.

"Let's work fast," Jaime said. "I don't want to be here any longer than we have to be. This place freaks me out."

They set down Tess's messenger bag and pulled out the doll they'd found in the ark. Reluctantly, Tess pulled the string so that they could listen to its song again, made that much eerier because of their surroundings:

"Twinkle, twinkle, little star,
How I wonder what you are.
Up above the world so high,
Like a diamond in the sky,
Twinkle, twinkle, little star,
How I wonder what you are!

"When the blazing sun is gone,
When he nothing shines upon,
Then you show your little light,
Twinkle, twinkle, all the night.
Twinkle, twinkle, little star,
How I wonder what you are!

"Then the traveler in the dark

Thanks you for your tiny spark.

He could not see which way to go

If you did not twinkle so.

Twinkle, twinkle, little star,

Exquisite Engines take you far."

"If I were a power source, where would I be?" said Tess.

Jaime shone a dim light on the peeling walls, the empty shells of Rollers and other machines strewn around the wide expanse of floor like so much junk. He aimed the light at the ceiling, scouring the cobwebbed corners, then back down to the floor again.

"Wait!" Theo said. "Turn it off."

Jaime did as he asked.

"There," said Theo. Above them, in the very center of the huge room, was an old light fixture missing every bulb but one, which was now glowing a weak bluish purple. "Solar glass, I bet. It absorbed the light from your phone."

"Little star, little sun, little spark," said Jaime. "I bet that's the power source."

"How do we get up there?" Tess said. No sooner had she said it than Ono rocketed from Jaime's pocket, propeller whirring softly.

"Oh no, oh no," it murmured, as its tiny metal fingers worked at the screws. The whole fixture came away from the ceiling with a *thunk!* Ono lowered itself to the ground, laying its prize gently at Jaime's feet.

"Ono, you're amazing!" said Tess.

"Land of Kings," Ono burbled. Jaime scooped Ono up and slipped him back into his pocket. Then the three of them knelt on the floor to see the fixture better. A small box was attached on the underside of the fixture. When Jaime shone his light on the box, the etched figure of a lion was visible.

"A Lion battery. The power source. But we'll have to charge it," Theo said.

"But all we have to charge it is the phone," said Tess.

"In a few hours, we'll have the sun," said Jaime.

Tess put her bag on the floor and rummaged in it for the schematic and for her tool kit. Jaime unscrewed the box from the light fixture. Following the instructions on the plans, they inserted the battery into the canister. They connected the wires. Then they used the round metal piece covering the doll's voice box on the back end of the canister.

"We're done," said Tess.

It really wasn't anything to look at, Jaime thought.

It didn't look as if it had the power to change the city or the world. It didn't look like the key to the greatest treasure known to man, if that's what it was. It didn't even look like a Morningstarr Machine. No whimsical shapes, no giggling, no movement.

Nine growled.

Tess stopped. "What is it, girl?"

Nine sniffed, rotated her sensitive ears. Her mrrow was long and low.

"Do you think someone's in here?" said Theo.

Jaime shone the flashlight around the cavernous interior. "Maybe there are guards? Or dogs?"

"Oh no," buzzed Ono.

Tess jammed the plans and the tool kit back into her bag. "Let's get out of here," she said. She was reaching for the machine when a voice yelled:

"Stop! Do not touch that!"

CHAPTER THIRTY-TWO

His name was Lee, and he was the big one.

Bigger than Edouard, which had hit Cuba and then barreled up the Florida coast to level Tallahassee in 2026; bigger than Debby, which had erased Georgia's barrier islands in 2030; bigger than Odette, which hit Galveston in 2039 and killed too many people to count. But Lee wasn't just bigger. Lee was *different*. He was the product of not one, not two, but three separate storm systems that had converged in the Caribbean and were only gaining speed. There were no categories for Lee. He was unique.

And he was headed right for them.

Days before, the mayor and the governor had declared a state of emergency and pleaded for people to evacuate. And then they got in their helicopters and evacuated themselves, as did many of the people who could afford to do so. But still, Theresa Biedermann, now thirty-eight years old, stood in the window of their apartment, hammering boards over the window, watching the rain attempt to submerge the cars on the street below as she did. The cars had been abandoned there, their owners opting to hike to the mainland if they had to. The news showed pictures of highways and bridges that looked more like parking lots. The tunnels were already closed, as were the subways. The storm hadn't even hit yet, but the surge had already swamped FDR Drive, and the wind was already howling, clawing at anything not tied down. Uprooted trees, roof tiles, barbecue grills, umbrellas swirled around the abandoned cars. The sky was bruised green and purple. The rain seemed to be falling sideways. When the sun rose again—whenever that was—it would shine down on nothing.

Theresa should have been terrified. But she was numb.

Theodore sat at the kitchen table, their solar cell in front of him. Some years before, they had perfected it, as well as a battery that could store the power almost indefinitely, a battery they called the Lion. It was a triumph. Or should have been. If funding for universities hadn't been gutted. If the oligarchs hadn't seen dollar signs when the Arctic melted, if the US hadn't gone to war for the right to drill where the ice and the bears and the seals used to be. They were still fighting, a dozen countries shooting at one another's ships, exploding one another's submarines, setting fire to one another's drilling platforms. Meanwhile, a trillionaire had decided that this planet was done for and made himself a generation ship to take him and his friends to a new planet. In his last transmission, he talked about finding another place, a better place, for his children and grandchildren and their children, a green place with clean water and enough food for everybody. He said these things right before some of the passengers mutinied, stuffed him in a suit, and ejected him into space. Theresa imagined him bobbing along in the deafening silence, wondering what had gone wrong.

Everything had gone wrong.

She hammered the last board into place. Something thumped against the window and made her jump. Theodore said, "Hail. It will probably smash the windows soon."

"That's what the wood is for," she said. Still, she backed away, joined him at the table. The solar cell wasn't what he was looking at. He held an envelope with the words *TRUST NO ONE* on it.

"What are you doing?"

"Thinking," he said.

"About what?"

He tapped the envelope on the table.

"You're joking," Theresa said.

Theo glanced up. His hair was normally cropped close to his head to avoid its tendency toward bushiness, but now it looked big and knotted and unkempt. Dark circles were draped under his eyes. "Why not think about it?"

"Because . . ." She trailed off.

"Tess, we're going to die here."

"You don't know that."

"The probability is high. Maybe the storm won't smash all the windows, but it will take out the power. The sewers will back up in the storm surge, and disease will follow. Chaos. We have enough food and water to last a few weeks, but what then?"

"We evacuate like we should have!"

"But what if we could fix it?" He fumbled with the envelope in his hands.

"Fix what?"

"Everything that's wrong."

"Theodore, you can't be serious. You can't."

"I did some research. There was a physicist. Renée . . . something." He pawed through the other papers on the table. "She did experiments back in the beginning of the century. She was looking for proof of the mirror universe. I think she found it."

"What happened to her?"

He didn't answer.

"Theodore?"

"She died in an accident at her lab."

"Theodore!"

He pulled the handwritten letter and the schematic from the envelope. Tess knew the letter by heart:

I couldn't think of who else to turn to, who else to trust, and so it will have to be you. I'm sorry for that. Truly and deeply sorry for the choice you will have to make, both of you so young, ~~as young as—~~

I'm desperate. And someday, you will be, too.

"We're not that desperate," Theresa said.

"Aren't we?"

"Are you?" she asked. Theo was not a desperate person; he was determined and driven and logical. She was the desperate one.

Was.

"I already built it," he said.

"You *what*?"

"I had to. And our battery is ready—it can power it. All we have to do is try it."

Theresa sat there, stunned at this admission. "It won't work."

"Then it won't matter," Theodore said.

"We should work on our own research, we should—"

Theodore slammed a hand down on the table. "Nobody cares about our research. They know it works. They've known for years. But people don't know how to change. Or they don't want to. It's too hard. And it's too late."

"No, no, it's not too late."

"If *we* don't change, if *we* don't try anything different, it will be too late for us."

"You can't ask me to do this."

"I'm not asking. You don't have to do it. I'll do it alone."

She sat back in her chair. "You'd . . . leave me?"

"I don't want to, God knows I don't want to." His eyes shimmered with tears. "But . . ."

"You will."

The wind picked up. A flying piece of debris smacked into the window in the living room with a loud *CRACK*.

The building itself made a strange creaking sound, as if it, too, were crying.

"Everyone we had is gone now," Theodore said. "Maybe we can't do anything about that. But we can do something about *that*." He jabbed a finger at the green-ish sky peeking between the wooden slats.

"It's more likely that we'll die trying," Theresa said, almost laughing at the absurdity of it all.

"No, that's what we've been doing, dying slowly. I've packed what we need."

"Packed? Packed? Do you hear yourself?"

Theodore stood up. "I do. And I know how it sounds. But I don't care. Are you with me?"

Was she? She'd always been before. To the exclusion of almost everyone else. She had no partner or chil-dren. So many friends had moved inland. She had her city and she had her work and she had Theodore. And now she might not have any of them.

Another piece of debris hit the window, shattering it. The wind shrieked and a blast of humid air hit them both. Papers cycloned around the apartment. The com-puter screen, which had been blaring the news, cut out.

It was madness. But then, the whole world had gone mad. Maybe the only way you face madness is with more madness.

"If we do this, we might have a future," Theo said.

"In the past?"

"Maybe."

What had Carl Sagan said? *The cosmos is also within us. We're made of star-stuff. We are a way for the cosmos to know itself.*

"Okay, Theodore. Show me."

CHAPTER THIRTY-THREE

Tess

Jaime whipped his light around. Ava Oneal stood in the doorway in her long silvery coat, a Morningstarr moth flapping lazily on her shoulder.

"Ava!" Tess said.

"Ava!" Theo said.

Jaime didn't speak at all.

"Why shouldn't we touch the machine?" said Tess.

Ava stepped across the threshold and into the building. "It's dangerous."

"No, it isn't," Theo said. "Not yet, anyway. We haven't charged it."

"And you don't have to. You can simply walk away," Ava said.

"Walk away?" Tess said. "No! We need to see what it

does! We need to know who we are!"

"You already know," Ava said. "At least, you know one possibility. But that's not the only possibility. And if you leave now, you can discover new ones."

"What are you saying?" Theo said. "Why don't you just tell us what you know?"

"Please," Jaime said, so softly that Tess could barely hear him.

Ava approached. She reached up and touched Jaime's cheek with her fingertips the way a mother would. "You fix one thing, and so many other things are broken in the process."

"What does that *mean*?" Theo said.

"More than a hundred years ago, someone set a fire in an orphanage. It was a refuge for black children, one of the few in New York City. And they wanted to burn it down. So they did. I saved every one of those children but almost didn't survive myself. Almost all of my skin was gone. My heart gave out. My face . . ." She touched her cheek with her palm. "I asked for help, and the Morningstarrs helped me. I knew that it would cost something, but I didn't know how much. They saved me and they doomed me all at once. I have been wandering this ugly, vicious world ever since. At first, I saved who and what I could, and that was enough. But it never stops. Never. And I have watched every single creature I have ever loved die."

"But you're not a machine!" Tess said. "You're a . . . a . . . lady!"

Her smile was so sad that Tess's chest ached. "Yes, I am a lady. A person, a human, just like you. But not like you, too." She unbuttoned the jacket and slid it from her shoulders. Her brown skin shimmered and gleamed as if it were dusted with glitter.

Tess said, "Are those . . . ?"

"Solar cells!" Theo said. "Millions of solar cells!"

"Now you see," said Ava as she pulled the jacket closed. "And I have the heart of a Lion."

"A Lion battery," Theo breathed.

"So as long as the sun shines, here I am," Ava said.

"What about my mother?" Jaime said. "You . . . you look so much like her. You could be her sister. What does she have to do with this?"

Ava cocked her head. "Your mother?"

As soon as the words were out of Jaime's mouth, lights, previously hidden behind vines and grime, turned on. The lights were so bright that Tess, Theo, and Jaime had to hold up their hands and turn their faces away. Even Ava winced. More than a dozen men—including the Brunos, who leered and cracked their knuckles—poured into the building from all sides.

"You'll never get the machine, Slant!" Tess yelled into the air, holding on to Nine's collar so she wouldn't charge.

A pale, redheaded woman dressed in a white suit emerged from the blinding light, a woman Tess had never seen before. *"Slant,"* the woman said. "That's hilarious."

"Wait . . . who are you?" said Theo.

"That is a much bigger question than you think it is, Theodore," said the woman. She snapped her fingers and one of the Brunos ran out the door. He came back with a folding chair. He unfolded the chair, and the redheaded woman sat down. She said, "You can call me Miss Roberts."

"Where's Slant?" Tess said.

Miss Roberts waved a slim hand. "Sleeping, I suppose. It *is* the middle of the night."

"Isn't he in charge?"

"In charge of what?"

Tess didn't know how to answer this. Darnell Slant was the reason they'd started this whole thing. He was the reason they were here.

Wasn't he?

"You really don't have any idea what's going on, do

you?" Miss Roberts said. She crossed her legs. "But I can't blame you for that. You're just children. Resourceful children, I grant you—you thought to bring a bodyguard—but children nonetheless. All of you, back away from the machine. Slowly."

"I don't think so," said Ava.

"I thought you might react that way. Candi?"

Candi moved so fast that she was just a red flash. She had an arm around Jaime's neck and some sort of baton at his throat before they knew she was there. Candi grinned at Tess.

"Hello, Candi," said Ava Oneal. "Always the minion, never the boss, I see."

Candi's grin turned into a snarl.

Miss Roberts said, "If you'd like to keep this child in one piece, you'll take a few steps back. That weapon Candi has shoots a million volts."

Tess started toward Jaime and Candi, but Ava held her arm, shook her head. Tess had to stand there like a fool while one of the Brunos scooped up the small machine and carried it to where Miss Roberts sat.

"That's ours," said Jaime, struggling in Candi's arms.

"And now it's mine," Miss Roberts said. She looked at her fingernails.

"You can't do this," said Theo.

Miss Roberts rolled her eyes. Candi rolled her eyes. The Brunos rolled their eyes. So much eye rolling made Tess want to scream.

"Let me make this as clear as I can," said Miss Roberts. "This isn't a movie. You're not the heroes. And we can do whatever we want. And we will keep doing whatever we want until the end of time."

Tess said, "Do you work for Slant?"

Miss Roberts looked so offended that Tess thought she might slap the nearest person, whether it was Tess or not. "People like Darnell Slant are actors. They play their parts. If they do it well, they're rewarded. If not . . . well . . ." She trailed off, her meaning clear. "You can think of me as a director. *The* director. This is my show, my game. I call the shots, I direct the moves."

"Show? Game?" Tess said. "What game?"

"The game called New York City, the game called America," Miss Roberts said. "Someone has to run things. Someone has to push civilization in the right direction."

"Who elected you?" said Theo, red-faced.

"Oh my goodness," said Miss Roberts. "You are so sweet. The people don't *elect* other people to run things. They never have. You're pawns, that's all. You are all pawns."

"I thought we were actors," said Jaime.

"You're not actors, you're ants," Candi said over Jaime's shoulder. "Insects, like your precious Morning-starr Machines."

"I don't like all these mixed metaphors," said Theo.

"Aren't ya listening?" said one of the Brunos. "Nobody cares what you like or what you don't like, okay? Jeez." A moth fluttered past him toward the lights and he lunged at it, missed.

"All this time we thought Darnell Slant knew what he was doing," said Jaime. "But you're saying he was just doing what you wanted him to do?"

Miss Roberts said, "I'm shocked you thought otherwise. Then again, I prefer to operate behind the scenes, so to speak. Anyone with real power doesn't have to announce it." Another moth flitted by, or maybe it was the same one. The first Bruno jumped and clapped his hands, but it flitted out of his reach. The second Bruno slapped at the air. The little moth easily evaded him, wings glinting silver in the light.

Silver? A machine? Tess glanced at Ava, at Ava's shoulder. The moth that had been there moments ago was gone.

Miss Roberts's eyes narrowed. "Bruno, catch that thing!"

"Yes, Bruno, catch!" Ava said. Nine tore out of Tess's arms and jumped into Ava's. Ava launched Nine at the Bruno, knocking him to the ground. Ava jumped over both of them to land a running punch into the nose of the other Bruno. He stumbled over a stalagmite of half wall into Candi and Jaime. Jaime elbowed Candi in the gut and twisted away.

Candi ignored Jaime and kept her eyes on Ava, circling, keeping her hands low. She faked with her left and attacked with her right. Ava dodged and pushed the arm aside, spinning Candi around. Another kick to the backside sent Candi flailing. She got her feet under her and faced Ava again, her face twisted in fury.

"You seem angry," said Ava. "Are you angry, Candi?"

Candi replied with a roundhouse kick that missed Ava entirely. Ava swept Candi's standing leg and Candi fell to the ground. One of the Brunos came charging at Ava, but she used the bottom of her long coat like a cape, draping it over his head and then coming down on his back with a ferocious elbow. She rolled over him to deliver a knee to the face of the other Bruno, who toppled like a tree into a pile of rotting leaves and vines.

The other guards glanced at one another, uncertain. Tess couldn't help but grin.

Ava paused, took stock of the scene, and then relaxed. The silvery moth fluttered over to her and came to rest on her shoulder.

Miss Roberts, who had abandoned her chair and was standing there in shock, said, "Who are *you*?"

Ava smiled, lovely and dangerous. "I'm tired of playing games. I'm here to ruin your fun."

Behind Candi, an older white man, lean and gray haired, said, "And I'm here to ruin yours."

"Dad?" said Miss Roberts. "Dad! What are you doing here?"

"Checking up on you," said the man. He held something in his arms, some kind of fuzzy thing with a long tail. Or was it an arm? "Good thing I came."

The fuzzy thing's tail—or arm—waved lazily, and Miss Roberts's lip curled. "Dad, you need to go home. Let me call you a car."

"Sit down in your chair, Merry."

Merry?

Miss Roberts bristled and hissed, "Do not speak to me like that."

"Yes, yes, you're the big boss or the big bad or the director or something like that. I think your game nights went to your head," said her father.

"That's it," Miss Roberts said. She reached into her

jacket. "You've forced my hand, Father. I'm going to have to call the authorities and have you taken somewhere where you'll be safe. I hate to do it, but you've left me no choice."

"Call whoever you'd like," the man said. "It won't get you anywhere."

Miss Roberts dialed the phone. Her voice was softer, more soothing, when she said, "I know you don't understand, and that's all right. You spend time with your . . . pets."

The man's gray face went stony. "I said, *sit down*." Moving much more quickly than Tess would have thought possible, he tucked his pet under one arm and plucked the phone from her hand with the other. He threw it on the ground and smashed it with his foot. Then he pushed Miss Roberts down into her chair. Miss Roberts opened her mouth to protest, but the man held up a hand. "Before you say anything about your money or your power of attorney, I regret to inform you that you have neither."

"What? Yes I do."

"You silly girl. Those bankers, those lawyers work for me. They did what you told them to because I asked them to. You don't have anything I haven't given you."

Jaime said, "So who's the big bad? I'm confused."

"That would be me," said Merry's father. "My name is Hunter Roberts."

"I've never heard of you," Theo said.

"Because I didn't want you to have," said Hunter Roberts.

"What *do* you want?" Ava said.

"Everything that's due me," he said, still petting the creature in his arms. He kissed its head. "This is Ramona. Say hello to the children and the lady, Ramona." He held up the creature. It looked like a fuzzy . . . koala-crab? It clacked its one big claw and waved the small one. Nine growled.

Hunter Roberts sniffed. "Ramona doesn't like cats."

"I don't think cats like Ramona," Jaime said.

"What do you want *from us*?" Tess asked. "Why are you here?"

"I already have what I need," Hunter Roberts said to Ava. He nodded at the machine, and one of the guards scooped it up and handed it to him.

"You don't know what it does," Jaime said.

"I know exactly what it does," said Hunter Roberts. "Do you?"

"I cannot let you have it," Ava said.

"I already have it."

"Not for long," Ava said.

"And what are you going to do about it?"

Ava scanned the circle of guards who were closing in on them. "You're going to need more men."

Hunter Roberts sighed. He held out the koala-crab thing and a guard took it reluctantly. Hunter pulled out a device from the inside pocket of his jacket.

"Is that a flip phone?" said Theo.

With a flick of Hunter Roberts's wrist, the phone opened. He pressed a button and held the phone to his ear. "It's time." He listened for another few seconds. "Your experiments can wait."

The floor beneath them shuddered. A panel that had been hidden amid the debris on the floor gaped wide. Three cages rose up.

Each one housed a monster.

CHAPTER THIRTY-FOUR
Theo

"Oh no," said Theo.

"Oh no," buzzed Ono.

"Oh yes," said Hunter Roberts. "Aren't they beautiful?"

Nine growled. Jaime slowly backed away. "That's not the word I'd use."

All the cages were about fifteen by fifteen feet. In the first was a giraffe-owary, nearly as tall as its cage, biting at the bars with its vicious beak. In the second was a spider-wolf fat as a bull, bristling with a truly disturbing number of legs. In the third, a crocodile, its skin a strangely bright shade of green, smiled a crocodile smile, and then a barbed tail flipped up and curled over its back.

Theo, Tess, and Jaime were so absorbed with the monsters, they almost missed the man who had come up from the depths with them. He wore a lab coat and had large bulging eyes that reminded Theo of a salamander.

"This is Dr. Munsterberg," said Hunter Roberts.

"Oh, come on," Tess said.

"As you can see, he's been working on a few experiments." The spider-wolf thrust a dagger-like leg between the bars, but Dr. Munsterberg sidestepped it, his expression never changing. He was scrolling through his phone, as if this whole display was unnecessary, or even distasteful.

"You mixed a scorpion with a crocodile? Why would you do that?" Theo said. Even Merry Roberts seemed horrified. She practically fell out of her chair and scrambled behind Tess and Theo. Tess glared down at her.

Hunter Roberts blinked. "I didn't mix anything. Dr. Munsterberg did."

"Yes, but *why*?" Theo practically howled.

"Have you ever heard of a species of jellyfish called *Turritopsis dohrnii*?"

"Jellyfish?"

"It starts its life like other jellyfish, as a fertilized egg. It develops into a larva, which swims to the bottom of the ocean. There it changes into a bunch of polyps that in turn spawn a bunch of jellyfish. But that's not the interesting part. The interesting part is that when faced with a threat—starvation or predation, a big boat that goes by and slices off a few tentacles—the jellyfish can revert back to being a polyp, which then spawns more jellyfish identical to the adult. Because it can literally turn back time, some people call this jellyfish 'the Immortal Jellyfish.'"

"Okay?" said Theo, who had no idea why this weirdo was blathering on about jellyfish, even immortal ones.

But Ava knew. Of course she knew. "You want to live forever."

"What?" Merry Roberts said. "No!"

"Now you understand me," Hunter Roberts said. "These beautiful creatures were by-products of experiments designed to help me find a way to stop time, or even reverse it."

"Dad, you cannot be serious about this," Merry Roberts said. "You're eighty-one. You've had a good, long life." She added, "And you probably have two or three more years. Maybe two. Or one. Maybe one."

"It's not enough," Hunter Roberts said. "I want more. And why shouldn't I have it?"

"B-but," Merry Roberts stammered, probably

thinking about the inheritance that her father would never give her. "It's not natural."

Hunter Roberts stroked Ramona the koala-crab. "Nature is meant to be manipulated. Wouldn't you agree, Ms. Oneal?"

At the sound of Ava's name, Dr. Munsterberg glanced up. His eyes lingered on Ava.

Theo did not appreciate this. He did not appreciate this whole situation.

But Ava flicked the mechanical moth from her shoulder, and it flitted away. "You might be surprised to hear that I don't agree at all."

"He knows who you are? How?" Tess said.

From the doorway, Imogen Sparks said, "Because he's been listening."

"Well. I guess we have ourselves a party. I don't like parties," said Hunter Roberts.

"Imogen!" Tess said.

"That's how he made his fortune," the Cipherist said, walking into the room. "By collecting all the searches made on all the computers and all the phones and keeping track of them. By listening in on everything that everyone does."

"You mean the cabbie was right about our microwaves recording us?" Tess said.

"I thought he stole a letter from Mary, Queen of Scots, from the archives," Imogen said. "But you had one of your monsters plant a bug, didn't you?"

More figures appeared in the open doorways all around them. Priya Sharma. Ray Turnage. Delancey DeBrule. Gunter Deiderich. Gino Ventimiglia. Adrian Birch. Flo Harriman. Omar Khayyám. All of the Old York Puzzler and Cipherist Society, armed with weapons that would have been appropriate for fifteenth-century soldiers: shields, swords, clubs.

"Historians," said Hunter Roberts. "So self-important. You look like rejects from a Renaissance fair."

"Thank you," Imogen Sparks said. "Be a good boy and slide that machine over here."

"Come and take it," Hunter said.

Before anyone else thought to move, Ono did. Its arms racheted out from Jaime's pocket, snatched the machine, and snapped back, leaving the machine at Jaime's feet.

"Oops," said Jaime.

"Jaime Cruz," said Hunter Roberts. "Your mother was Renée Christophe Cruz. Dr. Renée Christophe Cruz."

"Yes," Jaime said, frowning. "What about her?"

"I funded the university where she worked. Studied

the mirror universe, your mother did. Before she disappeared."

"You mean before she died?"

"Maybe."

"What do you mean, maybe?"

"Maybe she's dead, or maybe she's just missing."

"Don't listen to him," Theo said. "He's lying."

But Jaime ignored Theo. "I don't understand," Jaime said to Hunter Roberts.

"What if I told you that that machine looks very much like the one your mother used in the test that allegedly killed her? The test that was designed to prove the existence of the mirror universe? What if she did, in fact, prove it existed?"

"What . . . I don't . . . ," Jaime said.

"It was covered up, of course. An accident that big, a discovery that important? People couldn't handle it."

"That's enough," said Ava Oneal.

"Why don't you turn it on and see?" said Hunter Roberts.

"No!" Ava said.

"The boy wants to know where his mother is, and he should find out, shouldn't he?"

"Stop it!" Tess said.

Dr. Munsterberg walked over to Hunter Roberts and

whispered something in his ear.

Hunter Roberts said, "We have a proposition. We'll let all your friends go, Ms. Oneal, if we can have that machine and the pleasure of your company. Dr. Munsterberg has many . . . questions for you. Things he's sure you can help with. Mysteries you can solve."

"Mysteries," said Dr. Munsterberg, drawing out the *s*.

"Ew," said Priya Sharma.

Theo and Tess and Jaime surrounded Ava, as if she were the one who needed protection.

Ava smiled another one of her lovely and ferocious smiles, "No thank you."

"It would easier if we worked together, Ms. Oneal," Hunter Roberts said. "Aren't you tired of fighting?"

"Yes," she said honestly. "But I think I might have one more fight left in me."

Hunter Roberts shrugged and held up one finger at Dr. Munsterberg. Dr. Munsterberg sighed and threw a lever on the side of one of the cages.

The cages opened and the monsters exploded out of them. The giraffe-owary charged and Theo, Tess, and Jaime scattered, trying to find a place to take cover, but there was nowhere to hide. Ava managed to duck right before its beak snapped where her head had been. Priya Sharma took her shield with both hands and brought it straight up, whacking the bird monster under the chin and sending it tumbling. Ray Turnage and Imogen Sparks took turns clubbing the spider-wolf. When the crocodile-scorpion raced toward Omar Khayyám, Theo yelled, "Look out!"

Omar adopted a fencer's stance, feet wide and sword up. The crocodile circled and Omar did the same. When the creature stabbed with its barbed tail, Omar sliced it off with one chop. The crocodile roared and charged again, knocking Omar to his back and clamping down on his leg. Omar screamed. Theo, Tess, and Jaime kicked the animal, but it wouldn't let go.

"Ava!" Tess shouted. "Help! Ava?"

But she was in the middle of the room, away from the melee, eyes closed. She was humming. Theo remembered back to North Brother Island, when they were trying to escape, that same humming sound that burrowed into his skin, seemed to set the air around him vibrating, the unidentifiable creatures in the water that seemed to obey her.

A moth swooped into the room. Then another, then another. In an instant, the enormous room was filled with the furious beating of hundreds of shining silvery wings—the wings of moths, of dragonflies, of eagles. The *click-clack* of Rollers joined the giggling of spiders as the lab was swarmed with machines of all shapes and sizes. The machines dive-bombed the monsters, attacking with metal claws and metal beaks, metal jaws and metal teeth. Guildmen ran in from every direction, wrestling with Hunter Roberts's guards. A portion of the floor exploded and a giant digging machine churned up from the depths. The giraffe-owary attacked, but the digging machine ran right over it, and then it chugged to where the spider-wolf had Ray pinned. It took the spider-wolf in its mandibles and threw the monster against the wall. Rollers converged on the crocodile. The Guildmen pried open its jaws, and Theo, Tess, and Jaime pulled Omar's leg free. As the three of them tried to stop Omar's bleeding, the Rollers rolled the crocodile right back into the pit from where it came.

Ava and the rest of the society ran to Omar. "Is he okay?"

Delancey DeBrule said, "He'll be okay, but we should get him to a hospital."

"Wait," said Theo. "Where's that Hunter guy?"

"And where's the machine?" said Tess.

"I just had it!" Jaime said.

"No, no, no," said Ava. "He can't use the machine!"

"Don't worry," Imogen Sparks said to Ava. "We'll find him. Everything will be all—"

The whole building lurched, and everyone slid into one another and then into the wall.

"What the heck?" said Ray Turnage.

The building lurched again. Dust rained from the ceiling. Cracks zigzagged along the floor. The rebar inside the concrete walls moaned.

Omar gritted his teeth and panted, "I'm not enjoying this turn of events."

The building lurched once more, so abruptly that Theo bit his tongue. Water poured into the room from the open windows, rising fast.

"Something is sucking this whole place into the river!" Jaime said.

"But what could do that?" Theo said, sure he both desperately wanted the answer and also didn't want to know, ever ever ever.

"Crawl that way!" Tess said. They tried climbing to the highest point of the floor but slid all the way back again when the building teetered and then tipped into the Henry Street Basin. Theo fought to hold on to Tess as they were plunged into the river, but a rush of water tore him away and blasted him out an open doorway. He dropped into the water like a stone. He thrashed and fought to get clear of the sinking building, hoping that Tess and Jaime were doing the same. He burst through the surface, coughing and gagging. All around him, the water was frothing, the waves taller than he was.

But what was making the waves?

He kicked his legs harder to keep his head above water. He looked up toward the sky, which was an eerie gray before the dawn. And standing in the middle of the Gowanus Canal, just beyond the Henry Street Basin, was the biggest monster of all, the precise monster that Theo should have expected but hadn't. He froze, and the water swallowed him down.

Somewhere behind him, Tess screamed for them both.

CHAPTER THIRTY-FIVE

Jaime

The first thing he thought when he found himself underwater was: Again?

The second thing was: Mima's going to be so mad about my hair.

The third thing was: Swim! Swim! Swim!

He kicked, tried to get his bearings, but it was so dark, and he didn't know which way was up. Something hit his leg and he swallowed water, choked, swallowed more. He kicked harder, but didn't know where he was going, where there was air.

A light appeared next to him—no, two lights: Ono's red eyes, pinking up the gloom. The propeller on the top of its head whirred. Its arms grew to many times their normal length and wrapped around Jaime. It rocketed Jaime up to the surface and dragged him to a nearby dock, then lifted him from the water and laid him down. Jaime turned over and coughed up lungfuls of river. Ono buzzed and beeped at him.

"I'm okay, I'm okay," he said. He sat up.

The river seethed and frothed. People—society members, Tess, Theo, everyone—bobbed in the waves that were too big, why so big? A dark shape was silhouetted against the brightening sky, a shape that was so large and impossible and awful that he couldn't put a name to it. It was as tall as a building—eighty feet? A hundred?—with the bulk of a whale. It had two enormous legs and a strangely smooth, bullet-shaped body that culminated in a head made mostly of rows and rows of teeth. Its two shorter arms ended in claws the length of the swords the society members had carried with them.

It was a shark.

The biggest shark Jaime had ever seen, a shark with two arms and two legs and teeth and claws and it was *standing* and it was *walking* and it was *roaring* and oh no oh no oh no oh no.

Someone screamed. He scanned the water. Theo's dark head bobbed in and out of the waves. Without thinking, Jaime jumped in, grabbing one of Theo's arms just as someone else grabbed the other.

Tess.

They pulled Theo to the surface, and Ono helped to tow them all back to the dock.

"It's a shark," Tess said, once Ono had gotten them on solid ground. "It's a shark."

"Megalodon," Theo said, and then nearly hacked up his esophagus. "Biggest shark that ever lived."

"Did it have legs and claws?" Jaime asked.

"No," said Theo. "Those came from some other animal. It's a hybrid."

"Yes, but a hybrid of what?" said Jaime.

"I don't know."

The monster roared and stomped its feet, sending waves that nearly swamped the dock. Jaime, Tess, and Theo fought the water, holding on to the wooden posts as tightly as they could to keep from being washed back into the monster's path.

And then they heard it: the singing.

Among the ruins of Exquisite Engines, Ava stood in her shimmering gray coat, arms aloft. In a clear and resonant voice that Jaime felt all the way inside his veins, inside his heart, Ava sang a wordless tune. The machines, those glorious Morningstarr Machines, whirled, Rollers and diggers and ants and Guildmen running around her, moths and dragonflies and eagles swirling overhead. The flying machines flew faster and faster, and the force of their movements lifted the earthbound machines until there was a tornado of them in the air. There was the screeching sound of metal on metal, and fiery sparks rained down on Ava, and still she sang and sang and sang. Above her, the machines flew so fast that Jaime couldn't tell one from another, until finally, they slowed, and in their place was a single machine, as vast as the monster in the water, but far more beautiful. Its flapping wings were made of thousands upon thousands of silver feathers, the curve of its enormous head and beak more majestic than any eagle's. It gleamed in the light of the dawn like some kind of avenging angel.

"The Zīz," Theo breathed.

"Renanin," Tess said. "King of the birds, the singer and the seer."

The bird threw back its head, but its cry wasn't a screech or a scream as much as the sound of a million violins. It launched itself into the air, right at the leviathan in the water. The shark took two huge, bone-rattling, tsunami-making steps to meet it. The Zīz flew right over the shark's head and jack-hammered it with its beak before flying past. The shark roared. The Zīz came back around for another attack. The shark jumped up and sliced its claws right through the Zīz. Tess clapped her hand over her mouth.

But instead of the Zīz falling into the Gowanus in pieces, it splintered into a cloud of tiny Zīzes before coming back together as one.

"That's not a machine, that's magic," said Jaime.

"Same thing," Tess said.

"Help!" said Theo. He was lying facedown on the ground, arms out over the water, reaching for Imogen Sparks and Priya Sharma, who were struggling with Omar Khayyám in tow. Tess held down Theo's legs to keep him steady and Jaime helped him haul all three of the society members to safety. As the Zīz and the shark battled, Jaime, Tess, and Theo got Ray Turnage, Delancey DeBrule, Gunter Deiderich, Gino Ventimiglia, Adrian Birch, and Flo Harriman out of the river. And then they all watched as Ono airlifted an angry, dripping Nine from the water to the land.

"What in the name of all that's good and holy is that thing in the water?" said Imogen Sparks.

"Shark monster," Omar said. His skin was gray and clammy. "Who's singing?"

"Shhh. Save your strength, you silly man," Priya said.

"I am not and have never been silly," Omar said. "Oh, that's a pretty bird."

"How are we going to get him out of here? Our airship's in the river," said Ray Turnage.

"Car?" said Priya Sharma.

Jaime looked around for a car just in time to see the creepy scientist with the creepier eyes sneaking up behind a still-singing Ava Oneal, a brick in his hands. She was so focused on the Zīz and its ferocious battle with the monster shark that she didn't seem to hear him.

"No!" Jaime yelled.

The man brought the brick down on Ava's head. She slumped to the ground. In the Gowanus, the Zīz broke into pieces, flapping haphazardly everywhere. The shark monster jumped up, biting at the silvery bits, crunching them in its teeth.

Jaime took off for Ava. He lowered his head as he charged and caught the scientist in the stomach, knocking him down. But Dr. Munsterberg was stronger than he looked, wiry and muscular under the lab coat. He shoved Jaime off and got to his feet. Jaime came at him again, but the doctor shoved him back easily.

"She was ruining everything," the man said, his creepy eyes burning with triumph. "Now she's going to help me. I have so much more work to do. So many more experiments. You should understand. Your mother was a scientist."

"What do you know about my mother?"

The man smiled for the first time. "I know she failed."

Jaime charged again, but the man caught him under his arm and punched him in the kidney so hard that Jaime's vision wavered.

"I have many more pets where these came from, but I can take care of you myself," the doctor said. He dropped Jaime.

Jaime rolled in the dirt and debris, gasping. "Why are you doing this? What do you want?"

"What everyone wants," said the doctor. "To leave something behind that will be talked of and written about for generations."

"Like the Morningstarrs?"

"Better, much, much better," said Dr. Munsterberg.

"I don't see how making monsters is better."

"Because you're a small-minded fool, and small-minded fools never see brilliance when it's staring them in the face."

What the doctor didn't see: a tentacle climbing from the surging water, and another, and another, and another. A creature slithering across the ground, its skin changing instantly from the blue of the water to the grayish-brownish of the stones and the dirt beneath it. Jaime would have thought it was an octopus if it hadn't had more than eight legs. Its three round eyes were focused on the doctor's back.

"You're working for that other guy," Jaime said, stalling. "That doesn't make you powerful."

"I'm using that other guy," the doctor said. "And you heard him. Nature is meant to be manipulated. So are men."

"Yes, they certainly are," Candi said. She kicked the doctor into the waiting arms of the octopus. Half of its tentacles wrapped around the man while the other half slithered across the ground as it headed for the water.

"Help me!" Dr. Munsterberg said. "Candi!"

"I never liked you," Candi said. "And I don't think your pet does, either."

The creature dragged the screaming doctor into the water with a wet *PLOP*.

"Hmmm," said Candi. "On second thought, maybe I'm wrong about that."

Jaime got to his knees. He braced himself for Candi to hit him, but all she said was "Idaho is better than this. Anywhere is better than this." She ran off and didn't look back.

Jaime crawled to Ava's side. In the Gowanus, the shark swung at the machines. It snatched one out of the air and crushed it.

"Ava!" Jaime said, shaking her. "Wake up!"

Ava moaned but didn't open her eyes.

"Please!" he said. "Please!" He wanted her to wake up and sing the Zīz whole again. He wanted her to wake up so that the Zīz could defeat the monster. He wanted her to wake up so that she could tell him the truth about the Morningstarrs. He wanted her to wake up and tell him who she was so that he could understand who *he* was. Was his mother alive? Could it be possible?

He hummed the tune she'd been singing, a tune that sounded so familiar but also so strange: *La la LA la la, la la la LA la la.*

Her eyes opened. "Jaime?"

"Yes!"

"Help me up."

He helped her get to her feet. In the canal, the monster had wiped out nearly half the machines.

"Oh no," she said.

In an instant, Ono was by her side. She sang and he buzzed in reply.

"Wait, what's going on?" Jaime said.

Ono moved over to Jaime and hovered at eye level

for a moment, its eyes flashing from red to green to blue. "Land of Kings," it said. It reached out and patted Jaime on the head. And then shot into the sky.

"No!" Jaime said. He grabbed Ava's arm. "You can't make it do this!"

Ava kept singing.

Ono grew bigger and bigger as it rocketed toward the remaining machines. It joined them in another silvery tornado, from which the Zīz was reborn. Tess and Theo and the others cheered, but tears streaked Jaime's cheeks as the Zīz swooped and took out one of the shark's eyes. The shark screamed loud enough to shake the earth. The Zīz swooped and took out the other. The shark monster reeled, wildly swinging its arms. The Zīz attacked again and again, driving the monster back from the shore and into deeper water, pulling chunks of flesh with its talons, tearing it with its beak, slicing it with sweeps of sharp metal wings, until the beast teetered and fell with a tremendous splash.

The Zīz soared over the water, where the beast had fallen. The morning sun turned the Zīz from silver to a fiery red-gold. When the shark beast did not arise, the Zīz called with the voice of a thousand violins.

Ava's song ended. "Thank you, my friends," she whispered.

The Zīz shimmered, burning so brightly that Jaime thought its form would be etched on his eyes and in his mind and in his dreams forever.

Then it burst like a star.

Jaime searched the sky for signs of Ono, but there were only streaks of silver and gold and blue.

Ava laid a hand on his shoulder. "I didn't force Ono to help, Jaime. I simply asked. It made its own choice."

"Will it come back?"

Ava hesitated. "I don't know," she said.

"What *do* you know?" Jaime said. The Exquisite Engines lab was missing its top half and two of its walls. Dr. Munsterberg's lab beneath the lab was temporarily blocked off by piles of stone and wood. Hunter Roberts's guards were strewn about the grounds or bobbing in the water, but where was Hunter Roberts himself?

There, behind the half-destroyed building, Hunter Roberts and his daughter were hurrying toward a waiting airship.

And he had the machine, Jaime's mother's machine, under his arm.

Jaime took off after them, running faster than he'd ever run in his whole life.

Merry Roberts glanced over her shoulder and saw

Jaime heading for them. She wrenched the machine from her father. Jaime wrenched it away from her. He fell backward, cradling the machine, and Tess and Theo, who must have been running behind him, caught him.

"Get on the ship, Merry," said Hunter Roberts.

"But—"

"Get on the ship!" To Jaime, he said, "Come with us, young man."

"Are you out of your mind? He doesn't want to go with you!" said Tess.

"Are you sure about that?" Hunter Roberts said. "Mr. Cruz, you have in your hands your mother's machine, a time machine. Why do you think that the Morningstarr Cipher asked you to build it?"

"I . . . I don't know."

"Yes, you do. Because the twins wanted you to use it."

"My mother was studying the mirror universe. She wasn't building time machines."

"Ah, but she was. The mirror universe is simply another timeline. But maybe she discovered much more than that. Not only a way into the shadow world, not only a way to jump to another timeline, but a way to rewind this one."

"Impossible!" Theo said.

"Which would mean," Hunter Roberts continued, "that your little friends need this machine at some time in the future to get back to the beginning of the Industrial Revolution."

"What? How do you know that?"

"I have eyes and ears everywhere," said Hunter Roberts. "Why do you think I let you solve the Cipher?"

"*Let* us?"

"Yes. You, too, were doing precisely what I wanted you to do. Now," said Hunter Roberts, "why would the twins need this machine to go back in time?"

Jaime's whole brain hurt. "Maybe they wanted to fix something."

"Maybe they did. But how do you know if they fixed anything? How do they know they haven't made things a thousand times worse? Don't you understand? If the Morningstarrs knew that 354 West 73rd was going to come down, then they had to have lived through it already. It had to have happened at least once. Maybe it's happened a thousand times. A million. FOREVER. So what did they change? Nothing! The building came down just as the Morningstarrs knew it would—as well as all the other clues operating as they did. You're stuck in a pointless and endless loop. Maybe every disaster that has ever befallen the people of New York City—of the world—is inevitable, no matter what the twins do. Maybe the breaking of your home, of the city, of the entire world, is *their fault*."

Tess got up in Hunter Roberts's face. "You shut up!"

But he kept talking to Jaime over Tess's head. "People have tried to make the world a better place. The twins, they've tried it. And still, here we are. Maybe someone else deserves a chance to design the city, don't you think? Why not not you? And don't you want to live in a place where your mother is alive?"

Jaime did. He did want this so badly. He thought now that the Cipher was less a set of clues placed in the streets and the artifacts and the monuments of New York City, and more that he and Tess and Theo and all the other people in the city were themselves the clue. That the Cipher—what they had thought was a grand puzzle made up of a lot of little puzzles—was just a whole bunch of people asking themselves questions, trying to find answers—a chain reaction.

"Come with us, bring the machine, and we can bring her back. Don't you want her back?"

Even though he knew that Hunter Roberts was lying, even though he knew that Hunter Roberts wanted nothing more than more of everything—more money, more power, more life lived in a world of his own making, no matter what or who was destroyed in the process, Jaime took a step toward Hunter Roberts,

That's when a solarcar crashed through the grass, sirens blaring. Detective Biedermann jumped out of the driver's seat and yelled, "Everybody freeze!"

CHAPTER THIRTY-SIX

Tess

Her mother had her weapon out. So did Detective Clarkson.

"Mom?"

"Officer," Merry Roberts said, turning away from the ship, "I'm glad you're here. My father is quite out of his mind and—"

"Be quiet, Merry," Hunter Roberts said. "Officer! Arrest these children!"

"Put that thing down, Jaime," said Detective Biedermann. She wasn't making eye contact with Tess at all.

"Mom?" Tess said.

Her mother ignored her. "Jaime?"

Jaime did what she asked and put the Morningstarr Machine on the ground.

"Mom," Theo began. "How did you find us?"

"The giant shark in the Gowanus gave me a clue. Plus I put a chip in Nine's collar," said Tess's mom, still not making eye contact. "Now step over this way. All of you."

"We really need to be going," Merry said.

"You're not going anywhere," Tess's mom said. "Nobody is going anywhere."

"What in the baked Alaska happened here?" said Detective Clarkson. He shook his head at the destruction all around them—a good chunk of Exquisite Engines sheared off and floating in the river; the Robertses' guards slumped on the ground like felled soldiers; the dripping Cipherists bent over with exhaustion and the one Cipherist on the ground, gray with pain; the Robertses themselves, frozen by their waiting airship.

"It's a long story," Theo said.

"You're going to have plenty of time to tell it, young man," said Tess's mom. "Because you're going to be grounded for the rest of your life and all the next ones."

Tess crossed her arms against the sudden chill of the wind against her soaked clothes and began to walk toward her mother. She bobbed and weaved around the rubble, around the slumped bodies. As she skirted around one of the Brunos snoring like a hibernating bear, and then around Ramona the koala-crab, motionless as moss next to the Bruno, Hunter Roberts lunged forward and grabbed her. Tess shrieked and struggled, but he got an arm around her neck and shoved something into her side. A knife? A stun gun? Something worse? Detective Biedermann raised her weapon, but Hunter Roberts squeezed tighter. His breath was hot and dry in her ear. Nine growled.

"Back off, Detective," he said. He didn't have to say what he would do to Tess if she didn't.

"Let's stay calm," Tess's mom said, lowering her weapon a fraction.

"I am calm," Hunter Roberts said. "Put that machine on the ship."

"Mom! Don't!" said Tess. She struggled against Hunter Roberts's grip, but he only pressed the weapon harder against her ribs.

"It's all right, Tess, everything will be all right," her mother said. "Don't worry."

"Mr. Cruz! The machine! Now!" barked Hunter Roberts.

Slowly, Jaime picked up the machine, but before he could take a step, Tess stamped on Hunter Roberts's foot. When the pressure on her ribs lessened, she snapped her head back as hard as she could. Her skull rang with pain, but Hunter's grip loosened. She slipped from his arms and fell to the ground. She looked up to see Ava grabbing Jaime's elbows from behind and whirling him out of the way of Hunter's weapon. Instead of shooting Jaime or Tess, Hunter shot Ava.

"No!" Jaime yelled, and the Morningstarr Machine tumbled to the ground.

A shriek tore itself from Tess's throat as a million volts of electricity coursed through Ava, momentarily stunning her, making her face and her hands glow like the Zīz had. Ava screamed, a sound that started low and got higher and louder.

Jaime reached for Ava, but Imogen Sparks held him back. Written on his face was everything Tess was thinking: Ava would not be able to survive this, no matter how strong she was, no matter how long she'd lived till now.

The stun gun began smoking in Roberts's hand, and he yelped and dropped it.

Ava stood there, glowing like the Zīz, otherworldly as an angel.

"You're not dead," Hunter Roberts said in wonder. "You should be dead."

"It only makes me stronger," Ava said sadly.

"Don't move!" said Tess's mom, aiming her weapon at Ava.

"Mom! She's our friend!" Tess screamed.

Detective Clarkson pointed his weapon at Hunter Roberts, then Ava, then Hunter again. "We're in the soup now."

Ava, still glowing, approached Tess's mom.

"Don't come any closer," her mom said. "Stop."

But Ava kept coming. She said, "I'm your friend, too, Miriam."

"Stop!"

"Benjamin Adler's little girl, his little song."

"What? What are you talking about?"

Ava pushed the weapon aside. *Far kinder tsereist men a velt.*

Tess's mom blinked, her arm sagging. "How do you . . . what do you . . . ?"

"You should visit him. He's still here."

Her mom's eyes filled with tears. The weapon wavered. "Not the way he was."

"No one is the way they were, and no one is the way they will be," Ava said. "Neither are you."

Despite herself, Tess thought about what Hunter Roberts had said. That even if she and Theo really were the Morningstarrs, and had used the machine to go back to the Industrial Revolution to fix something, they could just as easily have broken something else, or a whole bunch of things. Or maybe things were so broken that nothing they did worked, nothing they did mattered. Maybe they'd been here before. Maybe they'd been here a billion times, stuck in their own terrible immortality.

Out of the corner of her eye, Tess saw Ramona twitch. The koala-crab scurried across the debris, launching itself at Ava.

"Biedermann!" Detective Clarkson yelled. "Watch out!"

Tess's mom knocked Ava out of the way and pulled the trigger on her weapon. Ramona easily dodged the stream of sticky foam and sank a claw into Tess's mom's ankle. Howling, Nine jumped on top of Ramona. Ava pulled Nine off Ramona and then punted the koala-crab like a furry football.

Then Merry Roberts rushed forward, grabbed the machine, and ran back toward the ship.

Tess scrambled to her feet and ran after Merry. Rage made her fast. She shoved Merry from behind. Merry fumbled the machine, juggling it from one hand to the other.

"I'll take that," Tess said, and swiped the machine out of the air, away from Merry.

"Let go, you horrible little girl!" said Merry, her face screwed up like a toddler about to have a tantrum. "I earned it!"

"No, you didn't."

"Tess, give it here!" said Clarkson.

"Here!" said Imogen Sparks.

"Here!" said her mother.

"Here!" said Merry Roberts.

"Here!" said Hunter Roberts.

For the first time in her life, Tess thought: They should have left the Cipher alone. They should have left the treasure of the Morningstarr Cipher—the greatest treasure known to man—hidden forever. For every person who would use it to save the world, there was someone who would destroy it. And for every attempt to try to make a world where that didn't happen, there was someone, or something, that would be there to unmake it. Was that the point of everything Theresa Biedermann did? Of everything she would do?

Tess wanted to make a different choice, except how was she to know what that choice should be?

"Tess!" said her mother.

Her grandpa Ben always said that the Cipher was

about process, not about the end result. And he said that the Cipher studied you as much as you studied it.

Maybe they were all the Cipher, were all the treasure. Tess and Theo, Jaime and Grandpa Ben, Ava Oneal and the society and even Detective Clarkson. Maybe they were all the treasure they ever needed. Maybe the world wasn't perfect, and it wouldn't be, no matter how may times they tried.

But that didn't mean they *shouldn't* try.

"Ava!" Tess said. She tossed the machine into the air.

But she didn't count on how fast Jaime was, and how desperate he had become. As desperate as Tess had been and Theresa Biedermann would be in the future, as desperate as a person who has witnessed the world falling to decay and ruin and will do whatever it takes to fix it. When he met Tess's eyes, she knew what he was going to do before he did it, because it was exactly what she would do.

Still, still, she said, "Jaime, no!"

He pressed the button.

Nothing happened.

He pressed it again and again. "This can't be for nothing, this can't be for nothing, this can't be!"

Still glowing with her fire, Ava went to him. "Jaime."

"It can't be, it just can't," he said. Tears fell. "Please. Please."

Ava hesitated, then reached for the machine. She put her finger on top of Jaime's.

"Jaime," Tess said. Everything she felt was in that one word: her exhaustion, her rage, her relief, her sorrow, her love.

Jaime looked at her one last time, his expression so sad, but steely, too, as steely as any hero he'd ever drawn.

Together, he and Ava pressed the button.

The air around Ava and Jaime seemed to fold in on itself, and then they were gone.

CHAPTER THIRTY-SEVEN
Theo

The city had many nicknames: Gotham. Metropolis. The Big Apple. The City That Never Sleeps. These nicknames were not always accurate. For example, why would anyone refer to a city as an overlarge piece of fruit? Also, the city *did* sleep, but it slept the way a cat does, eyes half open, watchful, ready to spring at the first sign of fun, or danger.

That evening, a very different kind of cat was getting ready to spring. The cat in question lived in the Biedermann family's apartment at 354 W. 73rd Street and kept her sock collection underneath the Biedermanns' coffee table. This was not normally a problem for the Biedermann family, except when they had guests or when their feet were cold.

Tonight, they were having guests.

They were also having a problem.

The cat—a large, spotted animal that would have looked more at home in a South African savanna than in the living room on the Upper West Side—had the business end of a striped sock gripped firmly in her teeth. Tess, sitting on the floor gripping the other end of the sock, growled right back.

"Seriously, Tess?" said Mrs. Biedermann.

"This . . . is . . . my . . . favorite . . . sock . . . ," Tess said, her dark braid whipping like a tail. The cat's striped tail lashed in kind.

Theo, who was standing at the kitchen counter, counting plates and silverware, said, "The cat's winning."

"I shouldn't have to clean this up," Tess complained.

"I had to move my entire tower into my room!" Theo said. "Do you know how much space twenty-six hundred Legos take up?"

"Yes," said Mrs. Biedermann. "Since we've been tripping over your model for three months."

"Also, I helped you finish that tower, so technically, it's *our* model," Tess said.

"You helped me one afternoon!"

"But Jaime's seen all this anyway," Tess said, going

back to the socks. "He doesn't care."

"*I* care," said Mrs. Biedermann. "We can't have piles of socks *or* piles of Legos around with people coming for dinner."

"My model is not a *pile*," said Theo.

"*Our* model."

"In any case, we have to have room for everyone."

"We have plenty of room!" Tess protested. "This place is huge!"

"Not big enough for you two," said Mrs. Biedermann. They used to live in a smaller space on a lower floor, but when their grandfather got sick and had to move to a nursing home, they took over his old apartment on the top floor. Real estate agents might call the place a penthouse, but it was more like a museum with very big windows. Mr. and Mrs. Biedermann liked it because it had so much more space than their old apartment, which meant that Grandpa Ben could come and stay with them on weekends. Theo liked it because it came with Lance, a suit of armor who liked to whip up batches of cookies and pancakes, and because the enormous windows gave them a view of the whole city. Tess liked it because what could be more awesome than living in a museum?

"Why don't you stop playing with Nine and help your brother set the table?" said Mrs. Biedermann. "Your father will be home any minute."

"Sorry, Nine," Tess said, and let go of her end of the sock.

"Mrrow," said Nine, forlorn at the abrupt end to her favorite game.

Tess and Theo set the dining room table with plates and napkins, silverware and water glasses. They were filling the glasses with ice and water when the door to the apartment opened and Mr. Biedermann came in, Grandpa Ben in tow.

"Hello, Grandpa!" said Tess. She ran to him and gave him a hug.

"Good-bye," he said. "Did I miss anything?" He asked this every week when he visited.

"I made history, Grandpa," said Theo.

"Someone once said that history doesn't repeat itself," said Grandpa. "But it does rhyme."

"History is also a model of Morningstarr Tower," said Theo. "I finished it!"

"*We* finished it," said Tess.

"We'll show you the whole thing after dinner," Theo said.

"Speaking of dinner," Mr. Biedermann said, "I have to check on the brisket!"

The bell rang. Tess ran to answer it. Cricket Moran

was standing in the doorway wearing what looked like an old prom dress that her mother had hemmed and belted for her.

"We are here for the FESTIVITIES and the VICT-UALS," Cricket announced.

Mrs. Moran said, "You can use the word 'party,' Cricket."

"Why would I do that when there are better words?" Cricket stepped inside the apartment, Karl lumbering behind her on a pink glitter leash. Mr. Moran followed with Cricket's brother, Otto. Otto had one of his dad's ties wrapped around his head. He pretended to karate-chop Tess, and then Theo, and then everyone else in the room, including Nine. In response, Nine licked his face.

Soon, the apartment was full of neighbors and friends. Mr. and Mrs. Adeyemi huddled with Mr. and Mrs. Yang and Ms. and Ms. Gomez. The Hornshaws bragged to Mr. and Mrs. Moran about their first-row tickets to the brand-new musical *Penelope*. Mr. Perlmutter, who had lived approximately a thousand years so far and didn't seem too happy about it, brandished his walker at no one in particular. Aunt Esther came armed with her customary Fig Newtons, and told Cricket about the time she had worked on a cricket farm. Cricket told

Aunt Esther that Karl was an Instagram poet and had over a million followers (which was, of course, nonsense, no matter how many times Cricket insisted it was true). Mrs. Biedermann put on her favorite Mary J. Blige album and sang as she arranged appetizers on the counter: *la la LA la la, la la la LA la la.*

The bell rang again. This time, Theo went to answer it. "Jaime!"

"Hey, Theo," said Jaime.

"Well. Come in!"

But Jaime just stood there, his fingers tapping on the side of his cargo pants. His dad and grandmother, who were standing behind him, frowned.

"Is everything okay?" Theo asked.

"Sure!" Jaime said. But he didn't sound okay. His eyes darted every which way as if he couldn't quite believe what he was seeing. Theo had the strongest sense of déjà vu, as if he'd seen Jaime look exactly like that before. But he didn't believe in things like déjà vu.

Tess ran to the door. "Hey, Jaime!" She gave him a kiss on the cheek.

Jaime jumped as if Tess were electrified.

"What?" Tess said. "Did I shock you?"

"Yes?" said Jaime.

Theo's mom called, "Jaime, are you joining us, or

are you going to party by yourself in the hall?"

"Yeah, sorry," said Jaime. He gestured behind him. "You remember my dad and grandmother?"

Jaime's grandmother pushed past him and marched into the apartment. "Of course they remember us. What's gotten into you?"

"Teenagers," said Jaime's dad. "They're all spacey."

"I'm fine!" Jaime insisted.

Jaime's dad said, "We made salsa." He held up a big bowl.

"Oh, that's fabulous," said Theo's mom. "We have tortilla chips. You can put the bowl over there."

Tess took Jaime's hand. "You're acting all weird. You need something to eat. We have all kinds of food." She hauled him over to the counter where Jaime's dad was making room for the salsa.

"Here," said Tess. She spiked a piece of cheese with a toothpick and handed it to Jaime. Jaime took it. He eyed it as if he'd never seen cheese in this lifetime.

"It's just cheddar," said Tess.

Theo said, "You want to see my model of Morningstarr Tower?"

"*Our* model," Tess said.

"Morningstarr Tower," said Jaime.

"Yes," said Theo. "You know. The model I've been working on?"

"Uh-huh," Jaime said. He popped the cheese in his mouth, chewed, swallowed. "Okay, so this is probably a weird question."

Again, Theo felt that strange déjà vu. But he wouldn't say anything about that. Instead, he said, "Weird questions are my favorite. Shoot."

"What's the date? I mean, what's the year? No, what I mean is . . ." Jaime shook his head, as if he didn't know what he meant and didn't even know how to shape the right question about it.

This time, Theo's sense of déjà vu was sharp, almost painful.

Before Theo had a chance to answer Jaime's not-very-precise questions, the bell rang yet again. Tess ran to the door and opened it.

"Hi!" she said. "Come on in." She turned. "Jaime, your mom's here."

Jaime, who had just taken another cube of cheese, dropped it.

"Mi'jo, watch what you're doing," said his dad, who stooped to scoop it up.

"Sorry I'm late," said Dr. Cruz. She was tall, with

'locs piled high on top of her head. "The traffic coming from the airport was terrible. I should have taken
the Underway." She kissed Jaime's father, and then she
looked at Jaime. "No kiss for me, baby boy?"

Jaime stared, open-mouthed. And again, there was
Theo's déjà vu, more insistent now. Theo remembered
Cricket's mother talking about a story she'd read in a
magazine. The story was called "What Might Have Happened," and it was a story made up of a lot of smaller
stories about the same series of events that unfolded in
various ways. Sometimes the changes from one story
to the next were so slight, the reader could miss them,
but they had a huge effect on the outcome; sometimes
the changes were big and sweeping, but didn't seem to
affect the outcome at all. Theo had thought it sounded
supremely annoying, but Cricket's mom had loved it.
"It's going to be made into a movie. Well, as soon as
they can identify the author. The name she used was 'A
Lady.' Isn't that funny? Like something straight out of
Jane Austen."

"What's wrong, Jaime?" said Dr. Cruz. "Is it my
hair?" She reached up to tidy the swirl of braids.

"No," Jaime said. "You're perfect."

Dr. Cruz exchanged a glance with Mr. Cruz. "I'm
perfect? Did you hear that, honey? I'm perfect! Jaime,

I'll remind you that you said that the next time you're mad."

"I'll never be mad," Jaime said.

"Nobody gave my son wine, did they?" said Dr. Cruz.

"Maybe he has a fever," said Mr. Cruz.

Jaime did look a little pale, a little ashen. And he was shaking. Theo was as well. After Mrs. Moran told them about "What Might Have Happened," Tess wondered if time wasn't a line at all, if time was a helix instead, a series of helixes, perhaps, or an ocean you could dive into. That every event was happening in a million different ways all around, and people swam the best they could.

"Where . . . where is she?" Jaime said.

"Where's who, honey?" Dr. Cruz said.

"Ava," Jaime said.

"Ava?" said Theo. "Who's Ava?"

"Maybe I'll tell you one day," Jaime said. He ran to his mother and flung his arms around her, leaving the rest of them to puzzle things out for themselves.

New York City
December 3, 1855

It was early evening, but the night chill was already
biting. Theresa Morningstarr stoked the fire one last
time. She did like a good roaring fire, especially at her
advanced age. But there would be no fires where she was
going.

"Are you sure about this?" Ava asked. In the fire-
light, she looked so young, even though she wasn't. Still.
Theresa couldn't help feeling a bit maternal.

"Our work is done," Theresa said. "Whatever we
could do, we did. It's up to you now. It's up to the city."
She didn't have to say it, not to Ava, but she did anyway.
"There's always work to be done. Too much."

"But you don't have to go! You can retire. You can
rest, finally, after all these years." Ava's hands gripped

the armrests of the chair she sat in.

"We will rest, dear. We will. But we have one last place we wish to explore. You can understand that, can't you?"

Ava could not, it was easy to see. But she nodded.

Theresa said, "How is your new book coming?"

"I have been rather stalled, I'm afraid to say. As it turns out, writing about the last people on earth isn't the easiest thing to do."

"The most ambitious projects are the ones that take the most time. Be gentle with yourself," Theresa said.

"I will try," Ava said.

She would not be gentle with herself, because that wasn't her way. Ava was as stubborn as Theresa, perhaps more stubborn, more determined. These were her best qualities, and they were her worst. Theresa hoped they wouldn't cause her too much pain. Ava had already endured so much at the hands of others, including Theresa.

"Ava," Theresa began.

"Do not say it," said Ava.

The apology died on her lips. "All right." She held out her arms. Ava stood and Theresa took her hands. "I will not say it because you do not want me to. But I am thinking it."

"What's past is past," said Ava.

Theresa had to laugh at this. Ava always had a fine sense of humor.

"I will miss you," Theresa said.

"And I will miss you."

"Here," said Theresa, unclasping the locket she wore around her neck. "Take this."

"I can't take your locket!"

"I have no need of it anymore. Besides, it's more yours than mine."

"What do you mean?" Ava asked.

Theresa opened the locket and showed Ava the picture inside.

"She looks like me," Ava said. "Who is she?"

"Someone I never met but always hoped to," Theresa said. "Perhaps you will one day."

Theresa put the locket around Ava's neck. Ava clutched the locket. She said, "Good-bye," and ran from the room.

Theresa pressed her fingers to her lips and then held them in the air. But she did not cry, for she was not sad. It was her time.

She left the parlor and walked down the marble hallway to the elevator. As if it knew that she was feeling a little sentimental, it took her on a leisurely ride, left and right, zig and zag, until it chose to bring her down to where Theodore was waiting. The elevator opened into a cavernous space underneath the Tower, a space that smelled of the river that ran through it.

"What took you?" said Theodore. He was sitting in the submersible. The ship had the most charming shape, that of an octopus. Theresa felt a brief pang of regret. She should have built more machines in the shape of cephalopods, perhaps mammals, too.

Oh well. She would have to leave that work for some-one else.

She climbed into the submersible. Theodore closed the hatch and checked to make sure everything was air-tight.

"Ready?" he said.

"Ready."

He turned on the engines and the submersible began to move, its tentacles acting as oars. They traveled under the Tower, under the Underway, under the houses and the streets and the farms and the whole of the city that they had loved for so long. When Theo put them into a dive, Theresa kissed New York good-bye, too.

The lights from the submersible shone in the water. All kinds of fish darted past, silvery bright. Theresa clapped her hands together. They were headed for the one place they'd never been, the open ocean, and she was so looking forward to this last frontier.

"I hope we see some sharks," Theresa said.

"No, you don't," Theodore said. "Perhaps some dolphins."

"Or whales?"

"Those as well. Who knows what the future will bring?"

Tess patted his arm. "Especially since we haven't been born yet."

And then they went quiet, falling asleep to the soft heartbeat of the machine, the gentle lullaby of the kingdom by the sea.

New York City
May 10, 2114

In a coffee shop in the middle of Greenwich Village, she sits at a table outside, sipping a cup of coffee. It's the perfect place to people-watch, which is what she has been doing for nearly an hour already.

"Need anything?" the server, a young white man with a scruffy beard, asks her.

"I'm fine, thank you," she says.

"Nice day," he says.

"Beautiful," she says, and inhales. She loves the smell of the city. The strong scent of the coffee, the flowers from a nearby shop, pretzels and hot dogs from the carts parked on the corners. It's a strange juxtaposition with the hover cars speeding by.

"What are you working on?" the server asks, gesturing

to her notebook. He's bored. It's the middle of the day and he has only one other customer. "Most people don't use paper anymore."

"I'm a bit old-fashioned," she says.

"I can see that." She's wearing her long silver coat, as always. She also has her cane, which is resting against the side of the table, and a top hat, which is perched on an empty seat.

"Are you an actor?"

She considers this. She is. Sometimes. When she has to be.

"Of a sort," she says.

"So you're practicing your lines?"

"I'm thinking about directing my own pieces," she says.

"That's great! What's your piece about?"

"I'm not sure yet," she says. "I'm still—I mean, *it's* still a work in progress."

"I hear that," he says. "You don't want to lose the magic by talking about it too much."

"Something like that," she says. She thinks of all the stories she has told over the years. "This is a bit more hopeful than my usual. It's taking me a while."

"Hopeful, huh? I carry this one around with me." He shows her the worn paper book that he has stashed in his apron. *Empire of the Moon.*

Her lips twitch. She wrote that book in 1879. The reviews were terrible.

"I'm not sure I know that one," she says. "What's it about?"

"Talking machines, space travel. It's old. Kinda weird. Ahead of its time."

"Who wrote it?"

"A Lady," the server says. "That's her pseudonym. A Lady."

"You're a little old-fashioned, too, aren't you?" she says. "A paper book?"

He blushes a little. "I guess."

"I'm sure this lady would be very happy to know that you enjoy her story so much."

He slips the book back into his apron. "You from around here?"

"Yes and no," she says.

"Staying long?"

She promised Samuel that she wouldn't be away for more than a few days. And in truth, she can't stand to be away from him for more than a few days, ever since they met at the police station after the events at Red Hook.

Samuel Deerfoot thinks all this traveling is a bit

514 • LAURA RUBY

much. He prefers to keep both feet on the ground. Samuel Deerfoot likes to be surprised.

"This is only one stop among many," she tells the server.

"So what's your name? In case you get famous."

She thinks about it a moment. She is Ava Oneal. She will always be Ava Oneal. A lady for sure. But she is also someone else, someone new, broken free from time. What's the word for "traveler"? In Latin, *viator*.

"You can call me the Viatrix."

"The Viatrix? *The*?" He laughs. "What's that supposed to be? Some sort of superhero name?"

The Viatrix cocks her head, smiles. "Time will tell."

THE END

ACKNOWLEDGMENTS

Ursula Le Guin once wrote: "Love doesn't just sit there, like a stone; it has to be made, like bread, remade all the time, made new." And I believe that justice is like that, too: it has to be made and remade all the time, made new. The pursuit of justice never ends, and that pursuit is never made by one person alone. It takes all of us, all the time.

Another thing that's never made alone: a book. When I started the York books back in 2013, I couldn't have anticipated the various directions my life would take for good and for ill, let alone the direction this country and this world would take. I could not have finished this project without the support and encouragement of so many people: Tina Dubois, my extraordinary agent.

Jordan Brown, my equally extraordinary editor. Everyone at Walden Pond Press and HarperCollins, including Debbie Kovacs, Tiara Kittrell, Donna Bray, Renée Cafiero, Mark Rifkin, Josh Weiss, Patty Rosati, Vaishali Nayak, Mitch Thorpe, Amy Ryan, David DeWitt, Andrea Pappenheimer, Kerry Moynagh, Kathy Faber, Jennifer Wygand, Heather Doss, Suzanne Murphy, and so many more. My Hamline MFAC family, the ladies of the LSG, Harpies, the Shade, Hedgewitches—you know who you are. Gili Bar-Hillel and Meg Medina, who helped with some of the translations. Jenny Myerhoff, Sarah Aronson, Brenda Ferber, Carolyn Crimi, Miriam Busch, Annika Cioffi, Gretchen Moran Laskas, Melissa Ruby and all the other Rubys and Metros who have kept me going. Anne Ursu, who has been the first reader on every book I've written for over a decade and whose heart is bigger than a planet. Steve—you are everything and everything is you.

And thanks to all the readers of this book: the world is yours. Never stop trying to make it a more just and beautiful place.